RAVEN

NOCTURNAL TRINITY SERIES (BOOK TWO)

LEONARD D. HILLEY II

For Christal, as always, my love.

CHAPTER 1

ailey awakened with a start. Her eyes flicked open, quickly surveying the room. Her heart pounded in her chest. For some reason she sensed an intruder in the bedroom. Almost paralyzed by the sudden fear, she held her breath and remained still, listening for soft footsteps upon the plush carpet. She had heard something, a slightly disruptive sound, stern words perhaps, either in her dream or the intrusion had been what yanked her awake.

She stiffened.

She hated the feeling of being watched, and that sensation hovered over her. She didn't dare move. Feigning sleep wasn't the safest option should someone actually be approaching the bed with a weapon already drawn, but nothing stirred. But that didn't mean no one else was in the bedroom besides her and Brady. However, hearing anything else, other than the pulsing of her heartbeat ringing in her ears, was impossible. She could have sworn someone had spoken. Perhaps that was what had awakened her?

Sweat glistened on her nude body. Beneath the sheet Brady lay beside her with his arm draped around her, and his hand cupping one of her modest breasts. She moved his hand and arm and eased her back against the headboard, sitting up. A cold rush of air sent a chill across her goose-pimpled skin. She gasped and shook with fear, flipping on the bedside lamp.

When the light cut through the darkness, Kailey half expected someone to be standing nearby. To her relief, no one was. No one visible at least, and that made matters worse. She felt certain someone had passed by the edge of the bed, glaring and whispering at her the entire time. The heat of anger lingered in the air, mingled with another fragrance she recognized, a faint trace of perfume.

Raven's perfume.

Brady stirred and groaned. With his eyes shut tightly, he mumbled, "Why'd you turn on the light? Is something wrong?"

"Raven." Tears rolled down her cheeks as she gasped her former friend's name in a harsh whisper. The name flowed off her tongue without any thought.

"What about her?"

"Something's not right."

Brady propped himself on his elbow and placed his hand on her firm stomach. "You had another nightmare about her?"

Kailey shook her head. "No. This was more than just a dream. She spoke to me. She's going to kill me."

Brady rubbed his eyes and sat up. "Kailey, it was just a bad dream."

"No, I don't think so."

"Flora assured us that she'd keep tabs on Raven at all times since her brother had turned Raven into a vampire."

She took a deep breath and sighed. "I know that's what she said, but do you really trust *her*?"

"Don't you?" He wiped the tears from her cheeks.

Kailey gave him an incredulous stare. "Not really, no."

"Even though the power has shifted within Nocturnal Trinity?" he asked.

"Especially not after their council has changed."

"Why not? You don't think it will help having Micah, Jacob, and Ashley on the council?" Brady asked. "And Jaclyn has brought in two witches she trusts and neither of them have ever been associated with Nocturnal Trinity. So that's three witches who would side with you and the werewolves instead of the vampires or demons should another power struggle ever emerge."

"I believe these changes will make Flora and her siblings even more resentful. Don't you agree? They lost a lot of their strength after Nicodemus was killed."

"She led us to Nicodemus. She wanted him, *her own brother*, dead. That's not something anyone does on a whim."

Kailey sighed. "I understand, but considering she's had a lot of time to reevaluate what transpired on that night, she might well believe what she did was the ultimate betrayal to her family and seek to rectify her wrong to prove herself to her brothers and sisters. Flora resented me days *before* Forrest killed Nicodemus. I'm certain she despises me even more now and casts the blame for Nicodemus' death on me."

Brady shook his head. "All those bad things that happened, all the changes, her brother's death, she brought these things upon herself. Nocturnal Trinity was already headed in the direction that it has, even if you had never come into the picture. The core of their Unity was already fractured."

"Perhaps," Kailey said softly. "But I can't force the words from my mind that Cassie told me."

"Which words were those?"

"That Raven would kill me if ever she got the chance."

Brady gently rubbed Kailey's muscled stomach. "She doesn't know where I live. You're safe here."

Kailey shook her head. "She gets inside my head sometimes."

"What do you mean?"

"Like Flora did."

"No. As a vampire, Raven's too young. She's not powerful enough to do that."

Kailey put her hand on his. "I know what I feel. I know it's her voice I hear. I'm certain it was she who awakened me earlier. She's reaching out to me with her mind. She may not have the power to physically do anything to me from so far away, but she's tapping against my mind, trying to get inside. Perhaps she's trying to find out where I am."

Brady gave a tired smile. "Even if she discovers where we are, she cannot enter this apartment without one of us inviting her inside."

"You know she hates you, right?"

"I got that impression every time I had tried talking to her after you first introduced us," he replied.

"She hated you *before* she was turned by Nicodemus," Kailey said. "Which means that hatred has also magnified. To hurt me the most, she might try to kill you before she does me. But, then, she might turn me instead, just so she can punish me for what happened to her."

"Kailey, you worry too much."

She shrugged. "Maybe. Or maybe *you* don't worry enough."

"To be honest, I try not to."

Kailey wiped her eyes. "I'll always be a mess inside, I suppose. Always worried."

"Why?"

"Because my life has been filled with one tragedy after the other. I feel cursed."

"Misfortune comes to everyone, Kailey. And the more you focus on the bad rather than the good, you're always going to weigh the bad over the good and miss the blessings in life. Focus on the good things that happen, no matter how small they might be."

Kailey nodded. "You're right. I have you now."

He cocked a brow and glanced under the blanket at his nude body. "I hope you don't consider that *small*?"

She popped him with a pillow. "Heavens no. I have nearly as much pain as pleasure when you're inside me."

"I'm sorry."

She shook her head and gently poked his ribs with her elbow. "The pain's not a bad thing any more."

He frowned.

"It had become a pleasurable pain. Something I anticipate and crave the more we're together."

Brady laughed. "I've turned you into a kinky nympho?"

She slugged him with the pillow again. She giggled, blushed, and covered her face with the pillow. "*No.*"

"I love to hear your laugh."

Kailey lowered the pillow enough to peek at him.

"And you have a marvelous smile," he said.

"They've been rare lately," she replied.

"They don't have to be."

She swallowed hard and placed the pillow over her stomach, hugging it. "There's been far more sorrow than laughter in my life. The current threat I'm faced with is my own doing."

"Raven?"

She nodded.

"How do you figure?"

"Forrest wanted to slay her and Flora. Because of my persistent begging, he spared both of them. He had Flora several inches away from death, he could have easily staked her, but because of my selfishness, *my* stupidity, he released her."

"For the moment. But if you were listening, he told Flora he hadn't pardoned her, which was a subtle hint that she's traipsing on borrowed time."

Kailey shrugged. "But from now on, she will be guarded, expecting him. I ruined his best chance for him to slay Flora and Raven. The longer Raven is a vampire, the more powerful she'll become. She will use that to her advantage. She carries unrelenting bitterness and grudges to the grave. Without Skye in her life to keep her rational, Raven will unravel. I suppose she already has."

Brady nodded his agreement. "That's because she's still a feral vampire, but since she did resent the two of us before she was turned, nothing will ever lessen that. Magic couldn't reverse that, just like a love spell eventually sours, too. The good news is that Forrest is still in Seattle."

"He is?"

"Yes. With the vampire population what it is in our city, he plans to reduce their numbers."

"I didn't realize he had decided to stay. Are you suggesting that I ask him to slay Flora and Raven?"

"Kailey, that decision is yours."

"It's not an easy one for me to make."

Brady sighed. "I know. It isn't. But if you fear she's going to attempt to kill you or me, talk to Forrest. Raven will never be the friend or roommate you once knew. Never."

"Cassie said the same thing."

Brady chuckled.

"What?" she asked with a curious frown.

"I never imagined I'd be in agreement with a demon."

"Why not? She kisses great, doesn't she?" Kailey asked, remembering how Cassie had spellbound him into the most intimate kiss she'd ever witnessed.

Brady blushed, averted his eyes from hers, and shook his head. "I thought you were going to let that go?"

"I'm a little jealous."

"Of her?"

Kailey grinned and shook her head. "That you got to kiss her and I *didn't*."

He tickled her sides. She arched her back, squealing with laughter. "*You've* imagined kissing her?"

Still laughing, Kailey said, "Oh god, you have *no* idea what images she put into my mind the morning after Nicodemus was killed. The things she said that she and I could do as lovers."

"Oh, do tell!" He tickled her even more.

"Stop! I've got to pee."

He pulled back his hands, she slipped off the side of the bed, and then she walked to the bathroom, feeling less apprehensive than when she had awakened.

"You're not going to tell me?" he asked.

Her voice was lighter veiled beneath a sense of laughter as she spoke. "All I will say right now is that she can do numerous things with her succubus tail while love-making."

"Well now *I'm* jealous."

"You shouldn't be," Kailey replied.

"Why not?"

"She invited us to join her in a threesome."

"She didn't?"

"I swear she did." Kailey walked back to the edge of the bed and sat down.

Brady smiled.

"Does her offer excite you?"

"No, your gorgeous body excites me and having you in my life completes me. You weren't the only one who has felt alone in life. Now that you're a part of my life, I can look forward to a more positive future."

Kailey blushed. "You couldn't before?"

Brady shrugged. "Not really. Not because of what I am. But you know about my wolf and don't seem threatened by me. You're willing to love me in spite of the risks."

"I trust you and know you'd never hurt me whenever you change. I knew it when you came to me in the underground tunnel in your werewolf form. I didn't fear you. Your eyes revealed your devotion and love for me."

"Come closer," he said. "Let me hold you, and we'll go back to sleep."

She eased beneath the sheet with a sly grin and a throaty sultry voice. "I'd rather you pleasure me with a bit of pain first. Make love to me and don't hold back."

"I can do that."

Kailey bit her lower lip and looked into his eyes. She loved the warmth in those dark brown eyes. She felt safe with him. She slid down beside him and let him wrap his muscled arms around her.

During the heat of their passion, he brought her to the highest levels of ecstasy she'd never experienced in her life before. She couldn't get enough of him being inside of her. His powerful thrusts—driving himself deeper into her softness—made her shiver. She clung to the sheets, moaning, panting, and begging for more. Something in his sweat drew out her needful hunger, her lustful desires, and she ached for him in ways she could never explain with mere words. It was such an intense yearning that she didn't believe she could live without the pleasures *and* needful pains he brought to her.

There were times when she believed he had tapped into the stamina of his wolf because he seemed to last forever. She loved that he never rushed. The longer he went, the more intense and incredible her multiple climaxes became, and that seemed to drive him wilder, too.

Occasionally, his eyes shifted, showing his inner beast, but he had never changed like Ashley had warned he might. But she liked his forcefulness and his growls at the edge of her ear. For the better part of an hour, everything else in life faded from her thoughts. The rest of the world ... was gone.

With he finished, he collapsed beside her, panting. Sweat rolled off him. His face was snug against her breasts. Her body continued tingling, enraptured with euphoria. She ran her fingers through his hair as he eased back to sleep. While he found sleep easily, she knew she would not.

Since she had started her preternatural news blog, she had gained nearly thirty thousand subscribers, which was a better salary than she'd have ever gotten with a major newspaper. The beauty was that she remained anonymous as a reporter, which protected her from repercussions should she piss off any of the vampires and demons in the city. Her website was also location protected, always pinging from different cities around the world, and that made her feel safer. Nothing tied her reports back to her directly. But even so, it didn't guarantee that Raven wouldn't eventually find her. Contrary to what Brady insisted, Raven was reaching, searching.

Kailey understood that it wasn't because Raven had loved her. Raven had been obsessed with Kailey, and now Kailey understood the scariest part of that obsession. Just like the unstable spouses who kill their significant others, Raven held to the same philosophy: "If I cannot have you, no one else ever will."

The thought jolted Kailey. Her mind returned to the near-waking dream.

Her premonitions before had become true, so she took this warning to heart. Raven wanted her dead. Whether it was out of spite, obsession, or revenge, Raven wasn't going to shirk on her promise. She'd find a way to at least *attempt* it, if not outright succeed. However, what Kailey didn't foresee was that Raven was going to become the beginning of bigger problems.

CHAPTER 2

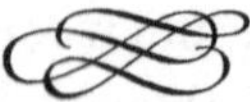

The alarm clock beeped at 6 a.m.

Kailey tapped the button to turn off the alarm. Brady snored softly and seemed undisturbed by the villainous clock. She smiled and slid her feet over the edge of the bed. Rubbing the sleep from her eyes, she stumbled to the bathroom and flipped on the light.

She glanced at the mirror and her hand covered her mouth for several moments. She was stunned, and she quaked inside. "Bra-a-dy! Come in here, quick!"

The bedsprings creaked as he rolled off the bed and ran to the bathroom door. "What's wrong?"

She pointed. "Read it."

Drawn across the mirror was a large witch's pentagram painted in fresh blood. 'R.I.P. Brady' was written in blood to the side of the pentagram, followed by, 'Rest in Pieces.' Someone had drawn it with a finger. It was signed, 'Raven.'

Kailey glanced nervously at Brady. "Still don't think she wants revenge?"

Visible chill bumps covered his arms. His eyes narrowed with the fierceness of his wolf. He rushed to the shower and slung back the curtain. The shower stall was empty. He sniffed the air and peered through the bathroom door.

"She was here, Brady. I know it. Do you smell her perfume?"

"I do, but it's not possible. She cannot enter without being invited."

"But she's also a witch."

Brady shook his head. "That still shouldn't matter. Vampires need an invitation into a household. No spell should bypass that."

She pointed to the mirror and shrugged. "Somehow she did."

"No. It has to be something else."

Brady's cellphone rang. He ran into the bedroom and took it off the nightstand. "It's Micah."

Kailey studied the drawing while Brady spoke to Micah. The shapes of the letters were identical to how Raven wrote. A little heart dotted the lowercase i's. The cursive R's were excessively looped and curled. If Kailey could find one of Raven's old notes, she could prove beyond a shadow of a doubt an identical handwriting analysis in a matter of seconds. Raven had been in the apartment while they were sleeping.

Chill bumps covered Kailey. She shook slightly, thinking about how vulnerable she had been.

Brady returned to the bathroom. He tucked his phone into his back pocket. He looked troubled.

"Not more bad news?" she asked.

"No. But Micah has asked us to come to Nocturnal Trinity later today."

"Why?"

"Memorial service."

Kailey frowned. "Seriously?"

He nodded. "Not for Nicodemus but for Debra, Rose, and Skye. Also for the members of our pack we lost as well."

"Will Raven be there?"

"No. I told Micah about … this." He pointed at the mirror.

"What did he say?"

"He's not happy about it. Said that he'd talk to Flora."

"She'll just lie."

"I assume Micah expects that as well. He told us that we need to keep our guard up."

She cocked a brow at him. "Really? He thinks we need to be *told* that? Like my guard hasn't been up since Raven *became* a vampire? I doubt I can sleep peacefully for a long time to come. Isn't Micah even worried about her siblings?"

"What do you mean?" Brady asked.

"Think about it. We entered Nocturnal Trinity and attacked them, killing Nicodemus. Not only is there going to be animosity, but I truly expect a major target is already on Micah's back. Forrest insists that no vampire can ever be trusted."

"Micah is naïve at times, Kailey."

"Are you certain he's the best choice to lead your pack?"

Brady's eyes narrowed slightly. "Don't overreact and jump to premature conclusions."

"Premature conclusions? Brady, I have no doubt this *is* Raven's handwriting. Perhaps Micah is trapped in his delusional mindset and too blind to notice the obvious."

"Kailey—"

She shook her head. "No. I can't ignore this threat. You can't either."

"I'm not."

"You *are*. You want to shrug this off, and your pack leader is, too. We need help and insight into what's going on, especially since Raven seems to be defying and bypassing what's supposed to be impossible for a vampire to do. If she can come into this apartment without an invitation, no place is safe from her. Maybe I should consult with Jaclyn and see what she thinks?"

"No. I want you near me until we get this resolved. Besides, Jaclyn will be at Nocturnal Trinity for the meeting."

"Okay, then I can talk with her there."

"I will bring up this threat before the council members this morning," he said. "It needs to be dealt with."

"I agree."

Brady stared at the bloody writing on the mirror. "I'm telling you there's no way she could have physically been inside our apartment."

"Perhaps she wasn't. Perhaps she was on a different plane altogether?"

He frowned. "Like a ghost?"

"I don't know if that's even possible. But I'm not a witch. I don't know how much power Raven had."

"If she was in such a ethereal plane, she still shouldn't be able to make such a drawing on the mirror. Ghosts can't do that. But, I think you're right. We need to talk to Jaclyn about this." He took out his cellphone and snapped a few pictures of the drawing.

"Are you going to write up a police report?" she asked.

Brady shook his head. "Are you serious? There's no reason to do that. Who would I report it too? This is something that stays within our pack and the witches."

"Do you think it's safe for us to stay here?" Kailey looked around nervously. "She could have killed me, us, while we were asleep."

Brady pulled her to him and wrapped his arms around her. "It's going to be okay."

"I want to believe you," Kailey whispered in his ear. "I truly do, but—"

Brady eased from their embrace and looked her in the eyes. "Honestly, I don't understand, if this is Raven, how did she even find out where we live?"

Kailey forced a tired smile. She liked how he referred to his apartment as their place, even though she hadn't been living with him more than a few days. "I can't see how this could have been done by anyone else. But it seems worrisome to go to sleep with the fear she might return. Like you said, a ghost shouldn't be able to physically draw on the mirror, but if she is capable of this, I imagine she can do far worse."

"Then why didn't she?"

"To mentally torture me?"

"That could be," he replied. "In case it is her, I'm opening all the blinds."

"Not a bad idea, but would the sunlight hurt her?"

"Not if she's in a different plane, but should she accidentally slip back into ours, I expect it would inflict some damage."

Kailey sighed. "I'm going to take a shower and head to the gym."

"The gym?"

"That's how I work through my stress."

"And what we did earlier … didn't?"

She grinned. "Oh, believe me, my mind doesn't dwell on the negatives when we're making love. But now that I'm awake and my mind is wandering, everything's coming at me all at once. Beating a punching bag and a kicking dummy for an hour or so helps. You could go spar with me or hold the bag. That is, if you're up to the challenge."

Brady laughed. "I can hold the bag, but I'm not exchanging punches with you."

"No?"

He shook his head.

"Afraid a girl might beat you up?"

"Kailey, I just got my ability to transform into my wolf back. None of the pack members have this under complete control yet since we can turn without the full moon."

"So you might get all wolfie on me?"

He swallowed hard. "I hope not. But a few solid punches from you might trigger the fight mode of my wolf."

Kailey crinkled her nose and nodded. "Yeah, you go with that excuse."

"It's not an excuse."

She stepped into the shower and turned on the water.

"Is there room in the shower for me?"

"That's why I left the curtain open."

"Ah, I thought you were trying to turn me on."

Kailey laughed and turned to face him. "Did it work?"

He wrapped his arms around her. "You didn't notice?"

"Oh, *my*," she replied as he pressed against her. "At this rate, we're never going to get anything else done."

He yanked the curtain closed, cupped his hands on her buttocks, and lifted her up. She wrapped her legs around his waist and slid him inside her and closed her eyes, groaning.

The bathroom door slammed shut. Glass shattered in the bedroom. Kailey slid off Brady and peered through the gap in the curtain.

"What the hell was that?" he asked.

In a whisper, she replied, "I don't know."

He pulled the shower curtain aside and headed to the closed door.

"Be careful," Kailey said.

Brady nodded as he slowly opened the door. The bedside lamp was shattered on the carpet. The top mattress had been flung off the bed. "Get dressed. We're getting out of here."

Kailey nodded. A lump rose in her throat, and in spite of the hot shower water, she was chilled to the core. She toweled off in a few seconds, rushed to the dresser and grabbed a sports bra. After squeezing into it, she took some black panties from a drawer, slipped them on, and pulled a pair of black yoga pants from another drawer.

Brady hurried and slipped into some gray sweats and a tight workout tank top.

CHAPTER 3

$\mathcal{K}$ailey sat in the passenger seat of Brady's squad car while he drove. Her eyes watched the blurred outlines of trees and pedestrians pass by, but none of those images registered. Her mind was a million miles away.

The more she thought about the situation, the more she regretted not allowing Forrest to stake Raven and Flora. She had clung to her feeble hope that somehow Raven could be rational, caring, and remembered who she was, even after Forrest had told her such beliefs were foolish. Raven was forever altered, both mentally and physically. What positive human traits she once held were gone now. Forever.

To think you were once my ... best friend ...

Raven had become vindictive and cold since she had been turned into a vampire. Deep down, Kailey realized Raven had probably been that way all along and after becoming a vampire, these attributes had escalated. She couldn't understand how Raven had held almost complete control over her true personality for the four years they had lived together as college roommates. She wondered if magic had helped hide her true nature. Once Raven's façade had begun exhibiting the inevitable cracks, it hadn't taken much longer for the outer shell of her disguise to shatter like a delicate wine glass dropped on concrete, revealing the true nature of the monster within.

For the past few weeks, Kailey had been weighted by guilt because of Raven's fate. It saddened her because Raven's future had seemed as bright as

Kailey believed her own career to be after graduation. But now, seeing how Raven had vowed to kill her and Brady, she believed Karma had struck properly. Raven's deceptions had been brought to light, which was a direct contradiction to the darkness that had crept in to replace her soul.

The final straw for Kailey had been when she had discovered Raven's proposed love spell to bind Kailey's heart to Raven's. No matter how much Kailey desired to be with someone, she'd never seek an underhanded way to force another person into loving her. Hell, if Brady decided to leave her tomorrow, she'd mourn and ache for months. She'd probably curl up on the sofa and pray to die, but eventually she'd get past it. There wasn't any reason to make a person stay in a relationship when his heart was elsewhere.

Kailey simply couldn't comprehend the degree of selfishness that had possessed Raven. Her obsessiveness had decomposed into sheer contempt, turning whom Kailey had once considered was her best friend into a mortal enemy. Kailey was now faced with a major decision. Either she sought Forrest and requested him to slay Raven, or eventually Raven was going to kill her and attempt to kill Brady. She believed Brady could handle and defend himself against the young vampiress. Even with all of Kailey's martial arts training, she did not see herself being a close match in a fight against Raven.

Raven was more than disgruntled. She was filled with rage and a lust to commit murder; true traits of a newly turned vampire. This alone boosted Raven's strength and determination, making her more deadly and calculated when their paths inevitably crossed. Kailey, on the other hand, was much more vulnerable due to her guilt and sympathy for Raven, and if Kailey wished to survive, her perspective about their former friendship and relationship needed to change. As much as she hated the idea, Kailey needed to view Raven for what she really was—an enemy—and never let her guard down.

Brady had called Raven a feral vampire. The word, when he had first used it to describe her former friend, seemed too harsh, but after the threat written in blood, she thought the word was probably *too* kind.

"Everything okay over there?" Brady asked.

Kailey jerked slightly.

"You're awfully quiet for someone who is often more chatty. My guess is you're thinking about Raven?"

"Of course. I hate knowing she's going to have to die."

"She's already dead."

"You know what I mean," Kailey said, turning toward him with slight agitation.

"Sorry," he replied. "I do. I know too well."

"I didn't mean to snap at you," Kailey said.

"It's been a … stressful morning."

"Some of it has been more than pleasant," she said with a teasing smile.

He grinned back.

"Can I ask you something? It might be too personal, and if you don't want to answer—"

"What is it?"

"Diana."

His hands tensed on the steering wheel. His jaw tightened and his voice deepened. "Okay?"

"When was the last time you checked on her?"

Brady's eyes focused on the road. He remained silent for a while. She could tell by how his eyes shifted back and forth that he was searching his thoughts. "A couple of years."

Kailey's mouth dropped open. "Years?"

He nodded. "I'm not proud of it, but opening her casket is like sticking your hand into a dark hole filled with rattlesnakes, only the risks are worse in lifting the coffin lid."

"Don't you think she's been tortured enough being locked away like that?"

"I plan to hire Forrest to slay her." Tears crested in his eyes.

"Really?"

"Yes. It's time she rests in peace and is no longer be tormented. But once it's over, I don't know if I'll ever have peace within myself once it's over."

"You see?" Kailey said, sliding closer to him in the seat. "That's how I feel about Raven. I know she needs to be slain, but when I stop to think about it, I feel so guilty. I can't forget about the past memories and some of the good times we had shared."

"Exactly. But with Diana, it's much harder than that for me."

"Why?"

Brady wiped away a tear, but still couldn't look toward her. "She was my partner—a damned good police officer—who was willing to put her life on the line at all costs. Those qualities cannot be ignored."

"They will never be erased," she said softly. "At least not in your mind."

"Probably not," Brady said. "But I feel like driving the stake into her heart is like saying all she had done on the force wasn't worthwhile. She deserves a better fate."

"I hate to say it, but she definitely deserves better than being locked inside that casket."

"I'm not arguing with that, but after what happened to Raven, I've done some soul searching of my own. I realize it's time Diana is permanently laid to rest."

Brady pulled the squad car into a parking spot across the street from Nocturnal Trinity. Titus stood at the main entrance with his huge muscled arms crossed. His white T-shirt was a direct contrast to his ebony skin.

"Why's he outside so early?" Kailey asked. "The nightclub never opens this early."

"Nocturnal Trinity is actually closed for the day."

"Closed?"

Brady nodded. "Yep. First time that it's been closed since its opening over a hundred years ago."

"Wow. For the memorial service?"

"Yes. Of course, once the sun has set, I imagine they will reopen. They won't want to lose a full day's income."

They crossed the street. Titus eyed them as they approached. His tight brow and narrowed eyes were intimidating. He offered no smile. His long curly braids were tied into a neat ponytail that hung halfway down his back. Thick ropelike veins stood out like snakes on his muscled ebony arms.

"Morning, Titus," Kailey said with a polite smile.

He cocked a brow as he stared at her.

"We're here for the service," Brady said.

Titus didn't glance toward him. He kept his attention on Kailey. "I see you're still together."

She nodded.

"Is he treating you properly, little lady? Cause if he isn't—" Titus straightened his posture, making himself look even bigger and more imposing as he turned and stared down at Brady with a harsh frown. Brady didn't show the slightest hint of fear. After about ten seconds of the intense stare down, a huge grin crossed Titus' face. He burst into deep laughter, shaking his head. "I'm just playing wit'cha, man."

"I was about to direct your attention to my squad car and show my badge," Brady said.

Titus laughed heartily, leaning forward in a bow, and clapping his hands. "Ah, man, you know that won't intimidate me. Besides you're out of uniform, too. But, you know, I have to have a bit of fun while standing out here, especially since I'd normally be in bed at this time of the day."

Brady smiled. "At least you can go back to bed later instead of working."

"Are you kidding? That'd mess up my sleep schedule for tomorrow. You know that I'll be out here tonight anyway, right? They're not going to keep the night owls from coming inside. In the end, it's always about the money." He turned and opened the door. "I'd say enjoy yourselves, but I know this is a grim situation today, which is why I tried to lighten the mood."

Kailey nodded. "Thanks, Titus."

"Don't mention it," he replied with a wide grin.

CHAPTER 4

*E*ntering the nightclub without all the blaring music and lights was almost like walking into a cemetery in the middle of the night. Dead silence rang in Kailey's ears before they took their first few steps across the hardwood floor. Breaking the silence, the aged walls creaked, as did the floorboards beneath their feet, which normally would have gone unnoticed on a regular active day. Without the life of the mingling crowds and dancers, the place was eerier, darker. For Kailey, the quiet place seemed more disturbing and sinister, making her uncomfortable as her eyes searched the shadows.

While Brady hadn't expected Raven to be in the nightclub, Kailey feared her ex-friend might still be and use this opportunity to carry out her threat. Kailey ran her fingers over the stake she had hidden in her back pocket to reassure herself it was still there. Nervously, she reached for Brady's hand and intertwined their fingers together.

Their soft-bottomed running shoes were even audible as they walked from the door, past a curtain wall that smelled like an old ashtray, and toward the first dance floor. Kailey understood why most restaurants and nightclubs had a 'No Smoking' policy. She wondered if a nonsmoker could succumb to lung cancer simply by standing near these curtains for long periods of time. She was thankful she didn't smoke and couldn't see how anyone else ever tolerated such an addiction. But, then, that was the problem, more so than one's enjoyment she guessed.

"Where is the gathering?" she asked.

Brady gave a slight shrug. "Micah told me that someone would meet us here."

She glanced around the perimeter of the dance floor, seeing no one. "We are quite early."

"That doesn't matter. Micah called me from the nightclub."

"Of course, behind the rows of curtains, who knows how many people might be hiding."

"Unlikely," he replied.

"How can you be so certain?" she asked.

"The nightclub is scoured nightly by the vampires and demons for possible skulking intruders. The last thing the vampires want is for someone to remain behind with a stake and attempt to kill one of the six. Well, five now."

"I thought they didn't sleep inside the nightclub?"

Brady shrugged. "I know that's what we've been told, but it's possible they do at times. Even if they don't, and an outsider discovered they didn't, that's not information the founding vampires could afford the public to know."

Kailey nodded. "That makes sense."

"Kailey!"

Startled, Kailey covered her mouth to prevent screaming and turned in the direction of the voice. "Cassie?"

Cassie's red hair was long and spiraled. The succubus was in her seductive human form without flaunting any of her demon appendages—tail, horns, claws, etc. She wore a light purple, deep V-cut top that also cut above her midriff, a short black skirt that barely covered the tight lower curves of her buttocks, and netted stockings that hugged her perfectly proportioned legs.

Seeing the demon dressed like this, Kailey wondered if anyone ever noticed the fiery red tint in the succubus' eyes. A rich aroma permeated the air, the closer Cassie came toward them. The pleasurable scent aroused hunger, but *not* for food. Kailey felt desire growing inside as she lusted after the demon's incredible figure. She forced herself to stare into Cassie's eyes, fearful of losing her sexual self-control.

The succubus rushed from the shadows and embraced Kailey with a fierce hug. Kailey grinned, squeezing Cassie tight and much longer than she had intended. Brady blushed, gave a slight smile, and turned his attention toward the empty bar.

"You told him, didn't you?" Cassie said with a sultry, teasing voice as she peered over Kailey's shoulder, giving Brady a sly grin.

"She kinda did," Brady said softly.

"See?" Cassie said to Kailey with a beaming smile. "I told you that you'd never forget. So, is he interested?"

"I am not," he replied in a quick stern breath. "Where is Micah?"

"Oh, you fantasy spoiler," Cassie said, scrunching her nose and winking at Kailey. She released a long sigh. "Micah excused himself to the restroom. He should be back at any time."

Brady stood at the edge of the bar and leaned, resting upon his elbows upon its polished surface. His face was still red, and Kailey laughed inside herself. She never thought a werewolf could get so embarrassed.

Kailey walked to the bar and climbed onto a tall padded stool and sat down. "Who all is here?"

"Right now?" Cassie's mouth twisted to one side as she thought. "Jaclyn's here with the two new witches. Micah, of course. Jacob came. I talked to Jinn earlier. He went to the demon lounge to grab something. Blaze and Luna are on their way."

"What about Flora?" Kailey asked with a nervous glance.

Cassie shook her head. "It's doubtful she or any of her siblings will attend this service."

Kailey sighed with relief.

"Why?" Cassie asked. "You're giving off nervous vibes. Your heartbeat just spiked. Has Flora threatened you again?"

Kailey shook her head. "No. *She* hasn't."

"Raven?"

"Yes."

"In what way?"

Kailey explained the incidents that had occurred at the apartment. "Show her the pictures, Brady."

Brady took his phone from his sweats pocket and handed the phone to Cassie.

Cassie glanced through the pictures and frowned. "Raven's never received an invitation into your home?"

"Never," Brady replied. "She doesn't even know where I live. Well, didn't and shouldn't know."

"Hmm."

Kailey said, "Can you think of anyway she could have done this?"

"If it is her," Cassie said.

"Oh, *it's* her," Micah said, walking behind the bar.

"How can you be certain?" Cassie asked.

"Because," Jaclyn said, emerging from the other side of the bar. Her black hair with gray streaks was pulled back into a ponytail. She wore a midnight blue robe. Her long fingernails were painted a glossy black. "She's a witch who's been turned into a vampire, making her a dangerous enemy."

"And how does that make a difference?" Brady asked.

"She's studied witchcraft for many years. According to Kailey's accounts, Raven was dedicated to the craft. Physically, because she's a vampire, she isn't able to enter your home without an invitation. But, a lot of witches practice astral projection, which is how I believe Raven might have done this."

"I thought for one to successfully use astral projection, they had to have at least been to the place where they wish to go?" Brady said.

Jaclyn nodded. "Usually, that is the case."

"And in this one?" Cassie asked.

"It's possible Flora or one of her siblings followed you home. Otherwise, I don't know. I will consult with other witches and see if we can interpret what spells Raven might have used. But generally, yes, a person needs to visualize the place they wish to project their spirit to, so it's essential they know the proper layout of the room where they want to emerge. Otherwise, one risks the grave possibility of becoming trapped inside a wall or another solid object."

"In that situation," Micah said, "she cannot return to her body."

"She's not trapped, Micah," Brady replied. "She trashed the bedroom while making her exit."

"And if it were her spirit that visited our home, how could she have physically drawn pictures on the mirror with blood?" Kailey asked. "And like Brady just mentioned, how could she destroy the lamp in our bedroom and toss the mattress completely off the bed?"

Jaclyn gave an even smile. "Rage is a remarkable source of energy, even by one's spirit. Do you understand why it's important for witches to 'Do no harm?' There are three forms of magic: White, Black, and Gray."

"Gray?" Kailey asked.

"Gray magic is using a caster's magic against her," Jaclyn replied. "While a pure witch should never do harm to another, by reflecting the dark magic of another witch's spell back onto the caster, the white witch has inadvertently used dark magic. But she was not the original caster, nor did she seek to cast a spell to inflict harm. She didn't originate the spell. She has merely reversed the evil hex back onto the person who had intended to wreak pain and havoc on someone else."

"So she's not guilty of harming another?"

Jaclyn shook her head. "Technically … no. She's simply defending herself. A white witch seeks peace. By walking such a solitary path, she refuses to harm another because, as most witches agree, threefold harm comes to those who use magic solely for revenge or personal gain. This is why Raven is so dangerous. She is filled with rage, and rage combined with dark magic is one of the deadliest combinations. As a vampire, she has little to fear in reaping harm for her disdain. She's undead. A normal death isn't possible. She has no fear of disease or disfiguration."

"But she does need to fear a stake through her heart," a deep voice thundered from across the room.

Everyone turned.

Forrest emerged from the dark shadowed area of the dance hall. He wore his old Hunter hat with silver bullets tucked around the hatband. The worn leather trench coat was dusty and hung to the top of his boots. As he made his way toward them, his huge boots thudded across the floor. He walked to where they stood and placed his heavy Hunter box on the table with a loud thud. She was surprised a man of his size could have hidden so well, even in the shadows. He eyed Kailey. "Did I not warn you about Raven?"

Kailey bit her lower lip, closed her eyes, and nodded. "You did."

She had taken to Forrest quite well when they had first met. She loved hearing his accent and oftentimes, the timbre of his voice reminded her of Sean Connery.

"She will never again be the person you had known," Forrest said, running a hand through his neatly trimmed beard. He shrugged. "Telling you that, giving you such a warning, I knew you wouldn't listen. No one ever does until he or she sees firsthand what a soulless person truly is. Now do you regret allowing her to escape?"

Kailey nodded. "I do. You were right. So you knew I'd change my mind?"

"Of course."

"Then why didn't you just stake her anyway?"

"And have you resent and hate me for the rest of your life?" Forrest shook his head, chuckling softly. "N-o-o. I've witnessed it so much in my past that I know it's best to not interfere when irrational emotions run high.

I don't need any more unnecessary enemies. I have enough with my profession. But for people to believe, often they must witness it for themselves. That's part of the reason for why I've not left Seattle yet."

"So you'll stake her?" Kailey asked.

"Don't you think that's the best solution?"

Kailey looked at Brady for a moment and then back at Forrest. After Raven's threatening intrusion into their apartment, she couldn't ask Forrest *not* to do his duty as a Hunter. Her pity for Raven had not impressed her former friend and roommate. Raven was ruthless, and the situation would only escalate, not lessen. From the bloody message left on the mirror, Raven intended to kill Brady first to make Kailey suffer more loss. There was no way to misinterpret Raven's intentions. "It is the best solution."

Forrest gave a solemn nod. "Then consider it done."

"You have other reasons for being here, Forrest?" Micah asked.

Forrest nodded. "My arrival in Seattle has been long overdue."

Micah frowned. "What reasons, other than Raven?"

"It's personal," Forrest replied.

"In personal, you mean, none of my business?" Micah asked with a slight smile.

"It's best not to divulge others with relevant information about secretive objections." Forrest crossed his huge arms. "Enemies have spies everywhere."

Micah glanced around the room. "Here? Now?"

"Not within our group," he replied. "But don't think we're the only ones gathered here."

Cassie nodded. "He's right."

Everyone gazed toward the darker shadowed areas in this section of Nocturnal Trinity. Chill bumps rose on Kailey's arms. Although no one had pricked to pry inside her mind, she sensed they weren't alone. If Raven had indeed been the one to enter their apartment, her spirit could very well be inside the hall now, watching and listening, and as Forrest had said, *spying*.

Kailey shook inside. She wondered if Raven had watched her and Brady during their heated passionate sex. So many questions flooded through her mind, but the one she wanted the answer to the most was how Raven had learned where Brady's apartment was? Was spying how she had discovered where they were? It was quite likely she was watching her now. Unlike the layout of Brady's apartment, Nocturnal Trinity was a place Raven knew. Kailey jerked from sudden coldness, realizing she had verbally told Forrest to kill Raven, which was perhaps the greatest threat Kailey could have made against the young vampire.

Nervousness twisted her stomach. The hinges of the main entrance door opened. Heavy sets of footsteps echoed from the main hallway, heading in their direction. She hoped these were allies and not more enemies. She didn't believe she could deal with any more bloodshed in this nightclub.

CHAPTER 5

Stepping into the light was Ashley. Her hair was pulled into a ponytail. She was dressed in all black. Her tight jeans hugged the curves of her butt and her well-shaped legs. Her defined muscular abs were visible through her thin satin blouse. She smiled the instant Kailey's eyes met hers.

Blaze and Luna followed behind Ashley. Luna's eyes were red and puffy from crying. Blaze had an arm wrapped around her as they walked. Luna leaned her head against his chest. Normally a chipper young woman, Luna was lost in her sorrows. If she had seen Kailey, Luna's eyes had not revealed it.

Barry was the last in their line. The eldest werewolf had tied his long silver hair back into a ponytail. His wiry beard was trimmed shorter than the last time she had seen him. All of them wore black clothes, for the service, she guessed. Even Luna, who normally liked more vibrant colors streaking through her hair, was solemn. Her clothes were modest and not her normal Goth-type apparel.

As they came closer, Kailey glanced toward Jaclyn and whispered, "Don't you practice darker magic?"

Jaclyn nodded.

"And you don't fear the repercussions of 'Do no harm?'"

"Kailey, there's a cost whenever you use magic, good or bad. Granted, there's no penalty for good spells. In fact, some give the caster blessings for sending good out into the world for others. Although I practice black magic, I never direct it against another except where emergencies demand it. I'm a necromancer. I can raise the dead, but I only do so to gain vital information that is useful for others to survive. But there's always a price. We can talk later in private, if you wish."

Kailey smiled. "Sure."

Micah looked around. "I believe this is all of us."

"Except Jinn," Cassie said.

"You expect he wants to attend?" Micah asked.

"I had thought so."

Forrest pulled a heavy chair from a table, slid it across the floor and sat down. "Are any of the vampires going to appear?"

Micah shook his head. "Highly doubtful."

"Pity," Forrest replied with a broad grin.

Micah ignored the jest, but Kailey wasn't so certain the Hunter was joking at all. He probably wasn't since he had brought his box of weapons, which was an open threat all its own.

"I know a lot of you have jobs, so I don't want to keep you from your work," Micah said.

Ashley walked behind the bar to stand next to Micah.

"Work doesn't matter," Jacob said with a firm brow. Anger tightened his face. "These were our family members."

Micah nodded. "They were, and due to the nature of things, we cannot exactly do a memorial service in public, nor can we risk the possibility of others learning about our true nature. Autopsies would have revealed the abnormalities."

"You cannot insist on not having an autopsy?" Kailey asked.

"No," Brady replied. "We have enemies within the police department and possibly the coroner's office as well. Such a request would gain their attention, and they'd perform one even without consent."

"Which is why most of our pack hasn't attended this function today," Micah said. "We cannot allow our enemies to discover the identities of our group. We're safer with them not knowing."

"Enemies?" Cassie asked. "What sort?"

Forrest cleared his throat. "Take a look around and see what factions aren't in attendance for the memorial. The vampires and the demons, other than you Cassie, have made it quite obvious. While the reorganization of Nocturnal Trinity might be a good thing from what it formerly was, the addition of werewolves and new witches to the alliance has not been a welcomed decision. They do not accept them as part of Nocturnal Trinity, nor do they accept the deaths of Debra and Rose as losses. Am I right, Micah?"

Micah sighed. "That's true. We've been trying to reconcile with the vampires but all our requests for meetings have been silently declined."

Forrest grinned and shook his head.

"I understand, Forrest," Micah said, "that you believe such attempts at this alliance are futile, but at least I've extended an offer. That's the cordial thing to do since we are now part of the Circle of Unity."

"An oxymoron larger than an elephant. To the vampires, all of you are imposters," Forrest replied. "We are their enemies, Micah. Don't ignore that key fact. Vampires and werewolves will never come to a real truce. *Never.* Forcing them into an alliance does not resolve the situation. It simply incites their spite. There isn't balance. There wasn't even balance *before* Nicodemus was killed. Don't be foolish enough to think they'll forgive us for his death. At least Flora accepted that her brother was evil and turned her back on him. She's fortunate they've not punished her for her hand in his death but since he had sought to rule over all of them, they've allowed her a pass, for now. Even so, there is still great resistance toward the rest of us."

"If it's a fight they want," Jacob said. A snarl formed on his face. Anger firmed his brow.

"It *is* a fight they want," Forrest said with a stern glare. "It gives them the excuse to kill more of your pack. The vampires have always wanted complete control. Since they are immortal, they view themselves the dominant race throughout the world. Don't think you can threaten them with another invasion. The biggest reason for Nicodemus' death was his vanity. He thought himself invincible, but the others have become more cautious, which is why they're not here this morning. Be forewarned, they welcome another attack."

Micah shook his head. "Starting another fight is not in my agenda. We've lost too many. We almost lost Barry."

Barry stared at Micah without any emotion showing on his face. "I don't die easily."

Micah acquiesced a slight smile. "And for that, I'm thankful. Since it appears Jinn is not returning, it's time we remember our departed pack members, and the two witches that stood against Nicodemus with us."

～

After the memorial service, Micah invited Kailey, Brady, Forrest, and Jaclyn to the Werewolf quarters of the nightclub, which was nothing more than a small, unfinished office with a desk and a couple of filing cabinets. Kailey asked Micah to include Cassie. He agreed. Jacob insisted he and Ashley were in the meeting as well. Micah didn't object.

Since Nocturnal Trinity previously only had three sections in the club, the VIP for the werewolves was still incomplete and currently under construction. But once it was completed, and a few of the lower walls were rearranged, the nightclub would expand to have four dance floors and bars. While Micah had originally thought this would increase the nightclub's activities, Kailey expected the opposite to occur. With the festering internal strife between the vampires and werewolves, this division could possibly sever what little unity remained after Nicodemus' death. Not to mention the possibility existed for rival vampire and werewolf patrons to resort to brawls on the dance floors. It almost sounded amusing for paranormal gangs to form except the possible dangers existed.

She didn't understand why Micah had insisted the werewolves become a part of the Circle of Unity in Nocturnal Trinity. Had he really thought his plans through? It was obvious the vampires and demons wanted no association with them. Micah's overall intentions were to better the club and Seattle, but he couldn't force his ambitions on the other factions. Forrest was right about the vampires' resistance, and she guessed the demons would side with the vampires, simply because the three new witches were not known to them. Those who had worked together the longest would, no doubt, continue to work together. Since they had no history with these witches, the vampires and demons didn't know their actual trustworthiness and openly kept their distance. There was no unity. Nocturnal Trinity had been split in half.

Kailey supposed that since Flora and her siblings knew Jaclyn had Eva permanently banished from the nightclub and Seattle, the vampires understood the impending threat the dark witch imposed to the rest of the group. In fact, their fear of Jaclyn might have been the only reason the founding vampires had even agreed to sign a new pact for the nightclub.

Forrest stood beside the door. He glanced at Micah. "When's the last time you've talked to Flora?"

"A few days ago. Why?"

"She knows why I am still here, which is probably why she's avoiding the nightclub."

Micah frowned. "She thinks you're going to kill her?"

"She knows I intend to. And now that Flora's probably protecting Raven, I need to find where their lair outside Nocturnal Trinity is."

Jaclyn grimaced. "My mother never knew that information, and she had been a part of the Circle of Unity for almost all of her life. I doubt that anyone outside of their vampires' immediate family even knows."

"Someone has to know," Brady said.

"What about their limo driver?" Kailey asked.

Forrest's brow rose with keen interest. "You might have found the answer I've been searching for. The driver might be … *persuaded* to give me the information."

"We'd be better off if we can put a tracker on the limo," Brady said.

Jacob nodded. "But you'd have to be able to find the limo first."

Brady grinned. "I know. The only way we can do that is to wait until they return to the nightclub, but from the looks of the situation, it's unlikely they plan to return anytime soon."

Micah shook his head. "Look, the whole reason I've called you into this private meeting is *because* of Raven's threat, not to take down all of the vampires. I cannot conspire to kill the remaining five founding vampires."

Forrest stood and glared at Micah. His jaw tightened and he spoke through gritted teeth. "You cannot be serious."

"I pledged my oath as the leader of the werewolf faction," Micah said.

"You of all people should understand the foolishness of such a union."

"Forrest," Micah said softly.

Forrest took his Hunter box by the handle and headed for the door. "You cannot conspire to take down mortal enemies? I cannot stomach listening to you come to their defense. Do you realize how disappointed Jacques would be to learn of your decision?"

"Don't bring my father into this," Micah replied with a frown.

"At least he had the backbone to fight and slay vampires. You cannot coddle a sworn enemy and expect them to not take the advantage to kill you while you try to hug them."

"That's not what I'm doing!"

"What do you call it then? Your wife died at Nicodemus' hand. Lest you've forgotten."

"I'll never forget what happened to her," Micah replied. His eyes grew dark from his inner rage. A glimpse of his wolf peeked through. Kailey expected him to turn. Forrest seemed to hope Micah did, as he hadn't backed down from his prodding challenge. He didn't flinch, nor did he break eye contact. Forrest's anger was too deep, edging close to resentment.

Forrest held a stern gaze at Micah, one that held no compassion. "Joining an alliance with them proves that you have. Downplaying vampires as something less vicious than what they really are is a route that will either cost you your life or the lives of your pack members. I'd think you have enough on your conscience without adding more bodies of loved ones to the list."

Rage contorted Micah's face. His eyes were no longer human. Froth formed at the sides of his mouth. His brow and cheekbones were contorting. He pointed a stern finger toward the door. "Get out!"

Forrest grinned. "The rage you're directing toward me should be cast toward the remaining five founding vampires. To the rest of you, *mark my words*. Should you continue with this nonsense of befriending the undead, you'll find your fate not so pleasant. Believe me, I know from my own experiences. It's why I refuse to see vampires in any other light than the blood-thirsty predators that they are. While I don't question Micah's leadership capabilities, his blindness will certainly lead all of you to early deaths."

Ashley glanced at Micah and then to Forrest. She looked torn, uncertain of her obligation to Micah's alliance because she was in love with him, but the startling revelations Forrest had made about the untrustworthiness of the vampires unsettled her. Jaclyn frowned, but not out of anger. Her mind seemed to be taking in the information, too.

Jacob walked over to Forrest and stood. "I agree with Forrest. We cannot align ourselves with these undead monsters."

Micah's snarled. His teeth altered. "See what you're doing, Forrest? You're causing contention within my pack. Now, go, before you make me do something I'll regret."

Forrest shook his head. "The contention was already there. The same as what stirs within Nocturnal Trinity's so called *unity*. Your pack deserves to know the truth, Micah, so they can make the proper decisions. And the only regret you'll have if you attack me is the beating I will give you in front of your pack members."

"Don't try me, cousin," Micah growled.

Everyone in the room gasped and looked on with wide eyes.

Cousin?

Micah stood behind the desk. His eyes and teeth had changed. His fingertips extended into longer claws.

Brady stepped to the edge of the desk, blocking Micah's view of Forrest, holding his hands up in a peaceful manner. Barry was showing early signs of transformation, as was Jacob. Perhaps it was the rising pheromones in the room or the growing rage causing their inner wolves to react. Without someone calming down the situation, a brawl was about to unfold. Invisible lines had been drawn. Jacob stood beside Forrest and his anger was directed toward Micah, not Forrest. Jacob didn't seem to have forgiven Micah for holding their wolves hostage for over two years under a powerful spell.

Forrest shook his head. "Micah, my fight's not with you, unless you make it so. You have neither age nor fighting experience on your side. And should we come to blows, I promise you that it will not end well for you."

"You dare threaten me in front of my pack?"

Forrest's jaw tightened. His upper lip curled. "I'm simply warning and reminding you of *who* I am. Your father and I have disagreed over the years about a number of different situations, but never have we resorted to fighting it out. We've never struck one another. You might be a man, but you're still a boy in my eyes. Your father would be disappointed to learn about your choices within Nocturnal Trinity."

Micah swallowed hard and took a few deep breaths to calm down. Tears brimmed at the sides of his eyes. "I have always sought peace."

"Really?" Forrest asked. "You have an interesting way of showing it. Trying to maintain peace with the very individuals who've killed members of your pack contradicts what you once stood for."

Regret came to Micah's face.

Forrest glanced toward Kailey. "I will find Raven, and when I do, she won't be a problem for you any more."

Kailey started to reply, but Forrest exited through the door with Jacob following him out.

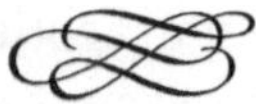

CHAPTER 6

Micah plopped down on the chair behind his desk and sighed. Ashley stood behind him, rubbing his shoulders. Everyone in the room focused their attention on him, waiting for some sort of explanation or instruction.

"My apologies," he said. "I shouldn't have allowed my temper to get the best of me."

Barry rubbed his bearded chin. His hardened face was unreadable. "I'm not trying to add any more animosity to what Forrest said, but he has made some valid points. Our goal had been to kill Nicodemus and shut down Nocturnal Trinity, and we did that. We killed him. Never did you tell us that you had intended to become a part of this Unity. Had I known that was your goal—Hell, I wouldn't have placed my life on the line … for *this*. It contradicts everything I stand for."

Micah gazed at Barry with cold eyes. "It wasn't a part of my plan until afterwards."

"Then it should have been a matter for us to vote on. Don't you think? Forrest is right, though," Barry said. "Vampires are our sworn enemies. They have always been and in my mind, they always will be. By softening your stance, you've placed targets on our backs."

"You're free to go, if that's what you wish."

"That's not what I was implying. But, understand that what Forrest has said is the truth. Vampires are not only bloodthirsty beasts, but they hold no compassion for mortals or shifters of any kind. Hell, a lot of them hate their own kind. The thing is, Flora and the others have not returned since you set up the new Unity. It's a strong possibility that they are preparing to avenge Nicodemus' death and kill all of us."

Micah ran his hands through his hair. He gazed from one person to the next. "Okay, who else? I've never had my authority questioned as much as I have during the past few months. More so within the past half hour. For a long time, you argued about me releasing you from the spell that prevented your metamorphoses. Now, you think my hope for peace with the vampires and demons is a bad decision? Brady? What's your take on this?"

"Right now? The best argument is Raven. She's threatened my life and Kailey's. With the symbol she painted in blood, she's not simply taunting. She intends to act upon her threat. So, either Flora is unable to keep her in check, or Flora is helping Raven. If Flora is, that's the clearest indication we're still enemies. They don't accept your forced alliance. There is no unity, and I'm inclined to believe, no such pact between us and them can ever be successful."

Micah flicked his gaze to Jaclyn. "Do you agree?"

"I can't believe you'd even need to ask. You're the leader of a pack of werewolves, and yet, you need *our* input? My reason for becoming a part of the alliance is far different than your own."

"Oh?" Micah said. "In what way?"

"I refuse to say within the walls of Nocturnal Trinity. As Forrest said earlier, we aren't the only ones here," Jaclyn replied.

"So everyone agrees with Forrest?" Micah looked perplexed.

Everyone crossed their arms and stared at Micah without saying a word. They didn't need to say anything. The expressions on their faces indicated they agreed with the Hunter.

"I see." Micah looked away and sighed.

Kailey said, "I believe the Circle of Unity should have been completely abolished after Nicodemus was slain."

"Why?" Micah asked.

Everyone's interest turned toward her.

"By allowing the vampires to remain, you're encouraging and supporting their ability to sire new vampires. This nightclub is a breeding ground with even more hopefuls coming each night, wanting to be turned into vampires. The atmosphere in this club has always been deceptive, and the crowds are naïve to believe becoming an undead is a blessing rather than the curse it actually is."

"You're implying that I'm responsible for more people getting turned into vampires?" he asked.

"Aren't you?" Kailey asked, unflinching.

Micah's jaw tightened. "The reason I need this club to remain open is so that we can find out which city officials are vampires. Should the nightclub be closed prematurely, we might never know who our true enemies in Seattle are."

"So you're wanting to monitor their behavior?" Brady asked.

"I believe Flora might have some higher up city officials protecting her as well as her brothers and sisters."

"I know there's been some prominent members in Nocturnal Trinity, but do you really think it goes that deep?" Brady asked.

"I don't know. Some well-known people in Seattle frequent this club without any fear of repercussions," Micah replied. "Favors have been exchanged."

"Like Mr. Langston? The attorney my brother had worked for?" Kailey asked.

"Yes."

Cassie frowned. "While your intentions might seem good, Micah, your actions show loyalty to the very people who killed my husband, Vincent. I'm not even going to pretend that I'm not offended by your decision to seek peace with Flora and the others. All six of them worked together to bind those shadow demons to me, forcing me to unknowingly cause a lot of harm to others. Shit, they had even planned to kill me to prevent the truth of their involvement from being known. Nicodemus isn't the only one who was guilty. They worked in unison. Each one of them takes a share of the blame."

"I understand that, Cassie," Micah said.

"And yet, *you've* decided to ignore it," Kailey said. "Vincent was my brother. He's dead because of them. Hell, Raven is a vampire because of these cruel vampires. She shouldn't be. Flora had promised not to turn her. I should have listened to Forrest then. Vampires cannot be trusted to keep their word. Now the only way I can have peace is for Forrest to kill the person who was once my best friend. At least Forrest has proven where his loyalties lie. Where are yours? To say that I'm disappointed in where you stand is an understatement. I'm sorry, but I can't listen to any more excuses. Brady, you can do whatever you choose, but I'm out of here."

"Me, too, sister," Cassie said, sashaying to the door.

~

Outside the door, Kailey leaned her back against the door and broke down in tears.

"Oh, Kailey," Cassie said, pulling her into a close hug and gently shushing in her ear.

Kailey sobbed. "I miss Vincent so badly, Cassie."

"I know. I do too."

"How can Micah be so blind?"

"I believe his heart is in the right place. I didn't detect anything deceptive about his want to maintain a level of peace with the others in the Circle of Unity. He sincerely believes he can achieve this."

Kailey pulled back from Cassie and looked into the succubus' eyes. For a moment she was lost in her gaze, seeing the unique crimson flecks that blended in with Cassie's hazel eyes. A year ago she would have been alarmed to see such color in a person's eyes, but she found the combination frighteningly beautiful and seductive. Of course she had never thought she'd be embracing a demon she considered to be a close friend, either.

Kailey wiped her eyes. "But you know as well as the rest of us. These vampires cannot be trusted."

"You have no argument from me. Had it not been for your stubbornness to investigate Vincent's death, I'd be dead, too. Trust me when I say that I'll do whatever's necessary to stop Raven and Flora."

"I appreciate that."

"Honey, I owe you my life. But you need to know something else."

"What's that?" Kailey asked.

Cassie pulled Kailey close and whispered in her ear. "The vampires aren't the only ones you cannot trust. There are demons that frequent Nocturnal Trinity who hate humans worse than the vampires."

"Like Jinn?" Kailey asked, leaning back and looking into Cassie's eyes.

Cassie shook her head. "No, Jinn's a playboy. He loves to fulfill his lusts with women. In many ways, he's harmless. But there are imps who disguise themselves like humans. They're more tricksters than anything else, but some of them can be quite dangerous. And then there are stronger types of demons that make me tremble inside. You've never seen power like theirs. And frankly, I'm not certain if a human could kill them. They are pure evil. They benefit from being aligned with the vampires."

"Why?"

"Blood. Like the vampires, they need blood to survive. Lots of it. That's why I know what you just told Micah is correct. The Circle of Unity should have been dissolved."

"Why didn't you tell this to Micah?" Kailey asked.

Cassie took Kailey's hand and turned, leading her down the narrow corridor toward the wide dance floor. "He'll discover them on his own the longer he insists in keeping the Circle of Unity together. Besides, at the moment, he doesn't have a unified pack, and when he learns the darker secrets of the nightclub, I know he'll become more determined to shut it down. These demons and vampires will kill him to prevent such an action."

"Shouldn't he at least be informed?"

"Not yet."

"Why not?"

Cassie sighed. "Because once Micah realizes how these demons help protect the vampires, he might issue a truce out of sympathy with them or he will foolishly attempt to kill them. Right now, his ignorance keeps him safer. Hopefully he can unify his pack before he learns about these behemoth demons. He's not a match for them. None of us are."

The information sent chills through Kailey. She had witnessed Cassie's power magnified by the shadow demons that had been attached to her. And if Cassie's enhanced strength paled in comparison to these behemoth demons, what exactly were they up against?

CHAPTER 7

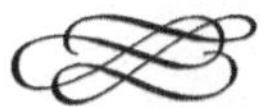

$\mathcal{K}$ailey and Cassie were halfway across the dance floor when Kailey said, "I sure could use a strong drink. It's a damn shame the bar isn't open yet."

Cassie grinned. "Does that matter?"

Kailey gave her a curious side-glance.

Cassie shrugged. "Tell me what you want. I can get it. I worked the bar quite often before I met your brother."

"Just anything to take the edge off."

"Sure."

Blaze sat at one of the barstools, trying to comfort Luna who was leaning her head facedown on the bar, sobbing.

Cassie walked behind the bar while Kailey climbed onto the stool beside Luna. She rubbed Luna's back.

Luna gazed up. Her tear-streaked cheeks were red and puffy.

Kailey hugged her. "It's going to be okay. I know how much it hurts to lose someone you love."

"That's not why I'm crying," Luna said in a sob-broken voice.

"What's wrong then?"

"Raven's going to … kill me."

The statement jolted Kailey. She looked toward Blaze. He confirmed Luna's statement with a simple nod. His brow was firm with anger.

"What makes you think that?" Kailey asked.

Luna pulled a crumbled piece of paper from her pocket and handed it to Kailey. Kailey uncrumpled it and froze. Scrolled on the paper was the same symbol that had been drawn on the mirror, only instead of Brady's name it had Luna's. The blood used for the symbols had already turned a rusty brown.

"When did you get this?"

"This morning," Luna replied.

"Did you show Micah?"

Luna shook her head.

"Why not?"

"I didn't want to ruin the memorial service."

Cassie took the paper and studied it for a few seconds before setting it on the bar. "Seems Raven has a series of vendettas."

Kailey hugged Luna. "You should still tell Micah."

Blaze nodded. "That's what I told her, too."

"I will," Luna said softly. "I wanted a better time, rather than earlier when we were gathered to remember our loved ones."

"When someone's threatening to kill you," Kailey said, "it's something you need to take seriously. You don't put it off, or you might end up as one of the casualties."

Luna's face contorted with sorrow and confusion. "I don't understand *why* she'd want to kill me. What did I ever do to her? I was friendly to her. I let her borrow my clothes. Remember? I thought she was so cool. Since she had been your friend, I had hoped she could be mine, too, you know?"

"I know. Not that it helps matters much, but she wants to kill Brady, too."

"What?" Blaze said, rising on his barstool.

Kailey nodded. "And me, of course."

Luna wiped her eyes and snorted a deep breath through her stuffy nose. Cassie tossed a box of Kleenex onto the bar. Luna took several and wiped her eyes and then beneath her nose. "Was she always this demented?"

"I'm afraid so."

"Then why would you be her friend?" Luna asked.

Kailey placed her hand atop Luna's on the bar. "I didn't know that she *was* so twisted inside. I was just discovering it myself when I first met you and Blaze."

"Really?"

Kailey nodded. "She hid it quite well for four years."

"That's scary," Blaze said.

"Yes, it is," Kailey replied.

"But why does she want to kill me?" Luna asked.

"Out of jealousy."

"Why would she be jealous of me?"

"She's jealous of anyone who took any of my attention away from her."

Cassie slid a heavy glass of brown liquid across the bar to Kailey. Cassie glanced toward Blaze and Luna. "You two want anything? Bar's open."

Blaze shook his head. So did Luna.

"No charge," Cassie said, beaming a sly grin and a quick wink.

"Thanks anyway, but no," Blaze said with a polite smile.

"Suit yourself." Cassie put the bottle to her lips and tilted it back, taking a long drink.

"I had thought Raven and I were getting along the night she came to Micah's magic shop," Luna said.

Kailey sipped the drink Cassie had made for her. The liquid hit the back of her throat with a slightly pleasant burn. "Sorry, but no. Raven was making fun of you behind your back with all sorts of mean insults. I scolded her for it, and her actions opened my eyes to how possessive she was about me. Even Skye warned me. Raven seemed to think she owned me. I realized then that by being with her, I was in a dangerous relationship. I should have told Micah to postpone our coming to the nightclub that night. It would have prevented a lot of what's going on now."

"Like her becoming a vampire?"

Kailey nodded. "Yes. That has enhanced her anger and resentment even more. Not to mention, she's now much more powerful."

Luna blew her nose. "Raven wants to kill you and Brady?"

"Yes."

"Aren't you … afraid?"

"In some ways, I'm absolutely terrified."

Luna shook her head. "You don't look like your frightened at all."

Kailey smiled. "It always helps to hold a stern confident appearance. It keeps your enemy guessing."

"I don't see how you do it," Luna said.

"It was something I was trained to do in martial arts." She shifted on her seat and pulled the stake from her back pocket.

"You brought *that* into the nightclub?" Luna asked.

Cassie's eyes widened slightly. "That's a direct violation."

"No worse than Flora helping Raven harass and threaten us," Kailey replied. "I should have the right to protect myself, right?"

Blaze frowned. "So, are you planning to stake Raven?"

The question took Kailey by surprise. Her stomach twisted from the thought of what that required. "Forrest said that he was going to find and slay her. I thought he'd be out here."

"He and Jacob left before you joined us," Luna replied.

"Odd," Kailey said.

"Why?" Blaze asked.

"It's no secret that Jacob resents Micah. Some of us believed he'd have challenged Micah for leadership before the old Circle of Unity was broken."

"That was fairly obvious," Blaze said, nodding.

Kailey said, "Which is why I found it interesting that Forrest would leave with Jacob. Forrest was pretty outspoken about his opinions in what should have happened with the vampires. He certainly knew how to push Micah's buttons and didn't let up, either. Micah nearly lost control of his wolf, and Forrest showed no fear."

"Why would Forrest do that?" Luna asked.

Kailey shrugged. "He's somehow related to Micah."

Blaze frowned. "Really?"

She nodded. "That's what he said. Forrest certainly knew Micah's father. I wanted to talk to him about Raven before he left the bar."

"And what if Raven confronts you when Forrest is nowhere around?" Blaze asked. "Are you capable of slaying her?"

Kailey downed the rest of her drink. She was trying hard not to show how much she was quaking inside and hoped the liquor helped settle her nerves. Every time she pictured staking Raven, conflicting thoughts battled inside her mind. She tried to work up her courage so that when she was faced with such a confrontation that she could plunge the stake through Raven's heart without any hesitation. Should she pause, she'd be dead. Raven would kill her. She swallowed hard. "I'll have to be, won't I?"

"I hope so," Blaze replied. "I imagine such a decision wouldn't be easy to carry out; killing a vampire that was once a close friend."

Tears burned Kailey's eyes. "You're right. It won't be."

"Of course it helps having a boyfriend who's a werewolf to protect you. Luna and I aren't that fortunate. Since Micah established the new Unity, he spends more time here than he does at his magic shop."

"Blaze, we're all in this together," Kailey said.

"Are we?" he asked.

"Yes. And if you need a place to stay where you feel safer—"

He shook his head. "No, we're safe inside the shop. Raven has full access to anything she needs for her magic spells. But it's once we need to leave to get food or other necessities that we become vulnerable. We have no idea if Raven has a human servant to do her bidding during the daylight hours or not. Flora has many servants, as do her brothers and sisters. We're easier targets for them to kill."

"You really think it's that bad?" Kailey asked.

"Do you even need to ask?" Blaze said. "It's much worse."

"Sorry. With Raven just recently turned, I never considered that she might have others working for her."

"I don't believe Flora will lack in teaching Raven all the necessities vampires need to know in order to survive," Blaze replied.

Luna blew her nose and snuffed. "And since she has magical strengths, more than I do … she has an even greater advantage. I've placed warding spells around the magic shop, but she probably knows ways of how to break through them."

"Have you talked to Jaclyn?"

"Not yet," Luna said.

Blaze shook his head. "That's a last resort."

"Why?" Kailey asked with a frown.

"Her magic scares me," Luna said.

"She's on our side," Kailey replied.

"She practices dark magic, which is something that contradicts my beliefs."

Kailey nodded. "I understand, but sometimes having an ally like her can be beneficial, even if you have to suspend your integrity."

Luna frowned. "Like shaking hands with the devil to get inside the Pearly Gates?"

Kailey laughed. "No, nothing that severe. But Jaclyn has powers you cannot tap into."

"I never want to tap into such magic," Luna replied. "There's a heavy price for using black magic."

"She said that there's a price for using *any* magic."

"Maybe so, but the magic she uses slowly eats away at your soul, taking control and consuming your essence. Eventually that magic controls you. You don't control it. That's why I fear Jaclyn. I don't know if she's gone beyond the point of where she is controlling the magic or it has taken control of her."

Kailey found the information interesting. "Have either of you met the two new witches that have become a part of the Unity?"

They nodded.

"Micah introduced us," Blaze said. "Raine and Gillian."

"And what was your impression of them?" Kailey asked.

Luna gave a quick glance toward Blaze. Both shrugged.

"You don't know?"

"We only met them in passing. We didn't get to talk to them. But since they were handpicked by Jaclyn, I imagine they practice darker magic, too," Luna said. "I believe they're the reason for why Micah has changed."

"You think they've cast a spell on him?"

Blaze shook his head. "No, but they are greatly influencing him and his decisions. However, unlike Micah, I think the witches like the idea of combining their magic to make them even more powerful."

Kailey said, "So do you think maybe he needs them for better protection?"

"Provided they are actually using their powers for good."

"You think they wouldn't?"

Blaze sighed. "They might have an ulterior motive that Micah doesn't know about."

Kailey thought about how Jaclyn had practically mentioned the same thing.

"Well," Blaze said. "The original 'Trinity' was supposed to be the three groups coming together for equal representation, but as we know, that didn't happen. Four factions joining forces has caused more division than before, and the witches can use this more to their advantage."

"How?"

"If these three witches are of the same mind," Luna said, "they are definitely a force to contend against the vampires and demons. Micah's safer being in their proximity."

"So Flora and her siblings might actually fear them? Is that why they're choosing not to come to Nocturnal Trinity as often?"

Blaze shrugged. "It's always possible, but that's only our speculation. Their real reasons could be something completely different."

"Then why don't you ask Micah to allow you to stay here with him? If he's safer with these witches, wouldn't you be, too?"

Luna forced a smile. At least her tears had subsided, but she could not hide her inner fears. She grabbed Blaze's hand. "I've ... we've discussed it."

"I still think we're safer at the magic shop," Blaze said.

"I understand," Kailey replied. "You need to be where you feel best protected."

"Not only that," Luna said, "but I have the freedom to practice my magic without outside interference or negativity."

Cassie leaned against the bar and with a teasing grin she whispered, "Your wolf is coming."

Kailey glanced over her shoulder. Brady was fuming. He formed fists and his jaw tightened as he stormed across the dance floor toward the bar.

"He doesn't look too happy, either," Cassie said.

"Not at all," Luna added.

CHAPTER 8

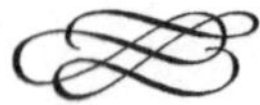

Brady stopped at the bar and sat on the stool beside Kailey.

"What's wrong?" she asked.

Brady shook his head, grinding his teeth. "Micah's absolutely lost his mind."

Blaze leaned on his stool so he could see Brady. "What do you mean? What did he say?"

Brady gripped the edge of the bar and squeezed so tightly every vein in his hands and forearms swelled. "He's adamant about keeping the Circle of Unity together. His decision has caused our pack to become torn. At this point our pack has no unity and much less with Nocturnal Trinity. Our group is like a large pie with several of the slices missing. Total disarray, but you cannot convince him otherwise. He's placing himself into direct danger by refusing to leave Nocturnal Trinity's circle. We've all heard of a lone wolf, but he's taking this to a whole new level."

"What do you intend to do?" Cassie asked.

He shrugged. "What can we do that we haven't already tried? Ashley's the only wolf who has chosen to stand beside him, but her reasons are not for the betterment of the pack. She's loyal and loves him, so she won't go against him. I don't blame her though."

Kailey agreed. Ashley had wanted Micah to choose her as his female alpha, and she had been a damned good choice. She was a fierce fighter, and for Micah, perhaps the most loyal companion he could ever ask for. But the two of them were far too outnumbered without the rest of the pack's support gathered behind them.

"So you told Micah that you opposed preserving the Circle of Unity?" Cassie asked.

"Yes. All of us have told him that except for Ashley," he replied.

Kailey shook her head. "And he still insists in keeping it together?"

"Unfortunately, yes." Brady glanced around the bar. "Where's Forrest?"

"He left before Cassie and I got here," Kailey said.

"Really?" Brady shook his head.

She nodded. "Why?"

"I have some personal things I need to discuss with him."

Kailey gave a curious stare. "Like what exactly? Raven?"

"Yes, but I can't divulge anything more," he replied.

"Luna, show him the paper."

Luna handed the crumpled paper to Brady. He opened it.

"So she has you in her sights, too?" he said.

Fresh tears came to her eyes. She nodded but couldn't speak.

Brady said, "Try not to worry. We're going to keep you safe."

Luna looked into his eyes for a long while before she replied in a tear-strained voice, "Thanks."

"Are you two still staying at Micah's magic shop?" he asked.

They nodded.

"Look, we have room at our apartment, if you two want to stay with us," Brady said.

Blaze smiled. "Thanks. Kailey has already offered. But since Raven somehow was able to get inside your apartment, I don't think we'd be any safer there."

Brady sighed. "Yes, I suppose not. We've not figured out how she was able to do that."

"But she's not appeared inside the magic shop. Luna has protection spells set. I believe we're safer there than where you are since she's already been inside your apartment," Blaze said.

Brady held up the paper. "Then where did you get this?"

"It was on the windshield of my car."

"So Raven came to the shop last night?" Kailey asked.

He shrugged. "My car was parked near the dumpsters at the edge of the alley. That's at least fifty feet away from the building, so I'm assuming she wasn't able to get any closer. Luna's magic has grown stronger."

Luna beamed a wide smile. "Thanks."

Blaze returned her smile and placed his hand atop hers, gently squeezing.

"But Raven's is still much stronger," Kailey said.

Luna's eyes widened.

"I'm sorry. I'm not trying to frighten you or belittle your abilities, but Raven has practiced magic since she was eight or nine years old. I want you to be safe. Don't become overconfident. That's the only reason why I bring it up."

Blaze leveled a frown at Kailey. Before he could speak, Cassie said, "Kailey's right.

Brady turned toward Kailey. "Look, I need to see if I can find Forrest before I report to police headquarters. Do you mind staying with Cassie?"

Kailey smiled. "You don't think I can take care of myself?"

"I know you can, but when someone is bent on killing you, it never hurts to have some extra protection."

"Especially from a demon, hon," Cassie said, winking at Kailey.

"Why don't you want to include me in this conversation with Forrest?" Kailey asked.

"It's a matter I'd rather talk to him about alone," Brady said. "Besides, it will only be a brief conversation provided I can even find him, but then I need to get to the police department ASAP."

"That's fine. Cassie and I can go to the gym and workout. I need to relieve some stress," Kailey said. She stood on tiptoes and kissed Brady.

In a sultry voice, Cassie asked, "Exactly what kind of workout did you have in mind? So many different things relieve stress."

Kailey's face flushed bright red. "Not *that* kind of workout. I need to hit a punching bag for a while."

Brady laughed and headed for the exit.

Cassie grinned. "After you work up a sweat, we always have the sauna afterwards."

"Luna," Kailey said, deliberately looking away from Cassie. Her face burned from embarrassment. "Would you like to tag along? Maybe some exercise can take you mind off of Raven."

"Thanks, but no," Luna replied. "I need to work on some new spells. Perhaps something stronger than the protective ones I have in place would relieve some of my tension."

"I understand. But you can't hide in the shop all the time."

"I'm … we're *not* hiding," Luna said with a tinge of anger in her voice.

"I'm not trying to offend you. I promise I'm not. But Flora and Raven are bullies. They not only instigate fear, they prey upon it. While I know you're working hard on perfecting your spells, Luna, your fear is evident. Just know that we're safer in larger groups."

"As I recall," Blaze said, slipping off his barstool and standing, "you were running for your life when we first met. Your fear was quite evident that night."

"Yes, it was, Blaze. I won't argue the facts. But I was running from creatures I didn't even know existed, which also backs my reasoning that we need one another. Without meeting the two of you, I would have been dead. No question about that. You saved my life. Both of you have taught me so much about these monsters I now detest. Without you, I wouldn't have met Micah—"

Cassie leaned over the bar and propped herself upon her elbows. "It's called destiny, Blaze. Had she not met you and everyone hadn't worked together, I'd have died as well. So Kailey is right. We need each other. If you wish to stay at the shop, then by all means, do so. But should danger arise, realize that a lot of us are a phone call away. However, that doesn't guarantee we won't be facing perils of our own, which might prevent us from getting to you quickly."

"Brady mentioned the lone wolf thing about Micah, right?" Kailey asked.

Luna and Blaze nodded.

"Well, there's a reason why werewolves tend to stay in packs. Power in numbers."

"I agree," Luna said. "I know you have our best interests at heart, too, but all my magical stuff is at the shop."

Kailey smiled, seeing the pure innocence in Luna's eyes. She was glad that Raven wasn't here to criticize Luna for her simple ways of thinking. "No one's forcing you to leave, but it's something you can think about, okay?"

Luna nodded.

"Cassie and I are going to the gym."

CHAPTER 9

Brady looked for Forrest outside the nightclub but didn't see the massive man. "Dammit!"

Titus noticed his frustration. "Is something wrong?"

"Looking for Forrest. The really big man with the strange clothes and large box."

Titus chuckled and grinned. "Yeah, even if he wasn't bigger than me, which is a rarity in itself, he'd still stand out in those clothes. Looks like he stepped out of an old western movie or something."

"Did you see which way he went?"

Titus pointed. "He headed up the sidewalk with one of your group."

"Jacob," Brady said in a near whisper.

"Ah, hell, man, I don't know all the names. I've just seen him come in with you or Micah from time to time, but yeah, the guy was with him."

"Thanks."

"No problem."

Brady crossed the street to his patrol car and got inside. He hoped Forrest and Jacob were still traveling along the sidewalk and hadn't gone into any side alleys or a coffee shop. He really didn't have time to waste because he needed to get to the police station and see if there had been any other odd occurrences during the previous night.

Chill bumps rose on his arms as he thought about how Raven had gotten inside the apartment. Too many puzzles about her somehow materializing inside their bathroom needed to be solved. What bothered him the most, and he wasn't completely sure that it wasn't even possible, was how she had managed to draw on the mirror if she had entered the apartment as a spirit. And if she was able to do that, did it also mean that she was able to use a physical weapon to kill him or Kailey while they slept?

Although he had offered Blaze and Luna the opportunity to stay at his apartment, he considered talking to Micah about using his estate on Bainbridge Island until after Raven was slain. But residing at Micah's house didn't change the situation much since Raven had actually visited the house as a guest before she had been turned, which meant Flora probably knew that location by now.

Before Brady pulled away from the curb, he thought about how Micah had come to the defense of Flora and the other founding vampires at Nocturnal Trinity. For a man who had lost the love of his life to Nicodemus, Brady couldn't comprehend why Micah would even consider defending *any* vampire at all. If something ever happened to Kailey because of Flora and Raven, Brady would declare open season on all vampires, regardless of where they resided. He'd spare none of them. He didn't doubt that he'd become cold and hardened like Forrest.

Then it suddenly dawned upon Brady. Forrest held an undying need to kill vampires. He thrived on slaying them. Forrest's crusade to kill every vampire he encountered stemmed from great losses of his own. For Forrest to call himself a Vampire Hunter made perfect sense now. Forrest apparently had lost others to the vampires and thus, he lived only to kill them all. It explained his unwavering MO.

Brady drove several blocks before finally noticing Forrest walking along the sidewalk with Jacob. They didn't seem to be talking. They walked with determination, probably both deep in thought.

Brady slowed the car, pulled into a parking spot, and lowered the passenger side window. "Forrest!"

Forrest slowed his pace and turned. He frowned for a moment and then looked left and right down the sidewalk. He feigned sudden surprise and worry. "Brady? Was I speeding?"

"No." Brady couldn't help but grin. He'd never seen a person who could joke without showing the slightest bit of humor in his eyes or a smile tugging at his lips, but Forrest could. Even causal conversation with Forrest was intimidating because he seldom smiled. It was impossible to read the giant Vampire Hunter's demeanor, so one never quite knew if he was a second away from getting struck by Forrest's giant fists.

Jacob walked up to the patrol car and clamped both hands over the door panel. "What was your decision?"

Brady's brow rose. "You mean with Micah?"

"Yeah. The whole Circle of Unity bullshit."

"I told him I'm against it, too."

Jacob gave a firm nod and a broad smile. "But, I'm guessing he's not going to budge from his decision?"

Brady shook his head. "No. Not any time soon."

Forrest laughed. "Micah's too stubborn for reasoning."

"I agree with that," Jacob said. He glanced at Brady. "I'll contact you later this evening, in case you hear anything new."

Brady nodded. "Good."

Jacob walked away.

Forrest said, "Micah's the opposite of his father. Not sure how that happened, as his father sought to calculate the risks before making any critical decisions."

Brady shook his head. "For as long as I've known Micah, his visions have been somewhat obscured."

Forrest changed the subject. "Since you yelled at me, Brady, what do you need?"

"A favor actually. A huge one."

"What kind of favor?"

"I need you to kill someone for me," Brady said.

Forrest offered a curious frown. "Who?"

"A friend of mine," Brady replied.

～

Kailey got into Cassie's sports vehicle. Misting rain covered the windshield after they closed the doors. "You ever feel gloomy, Cassie? From all this rainy weather?"

Cassie sped out of the parking spot into traffic. "Some demons get depressed, too. I occasionally get down, but not from the weather. The weather in Seattle is actually quite soothing to me. Rain hides the tears whenever you're outside. I grieve about Vincent every day. Some days are better than others, but I will always miss the warmth of his heart and his smile."

Kailey felt sadness for the loss of her brother but not on the same level as Cassie. "You loved him a lot, didn't you?"

Cassie drove. Her hands tightened on the steering wheel. She was silent. "I never knew—"

"That a demon could express love for a human?" Cassie asked without glancing toward Kailey.

"With all the things I've heard the strict religious people say about demons," Kailey said, "I was led to believe that demons couldn't exhibit love at all. That they were evil and spent their existence wreaking torment on humans."

"It's true some demons are pure evil and could never express love or affection toward a human or anything else. Those hope only to cause destruction due to their resentment and inner rage. But some demons are attracted to humans, hoping to receive love. Demons like myself ... we're capable of loving others. What I felt from Vincent was genuine, and from the heightened feelings inside of me, I know I loved him deeply. I still do, but my pain overshadows it."

"Anger overshadows mine," Kailey said. "Revenge does too since I know the other vampires held a role in Vincent's murder."

"None of them are innocent." Cassie turned into a parking lot of the gym, trying to find an open parking spot. She cocked a brow, giving Kailey an odd side-glance. "This is the right gym? Fists & Cuffs?"

Kailey nodded.

"Sounds more kinky than like a place to workout. Maybe it's both?" Cassie grinned and winked.

Kailey laughed. "It's owned by a former police officer. He gives great discounts to police officers, firemen, and military."

Cassie fanned her face and exhaled through puckered lips. "So this is where all the male calendar models hang out?"

Kailey gave her an odd side-glance. "Um, I'm not exactly sure *how* I should answer that question."

Cassie cackled, leaning her head back against the headrest. "Pardon the pun. That didn't come out like I meant for it to."

"Come on," Kailey said. "I'll introduce you to my trainer, if she's here."

Kailey closed the car door and crossed the parking lot toward the front door. Cassie followed close by her side.

"I can't believe this place is so crowded this early in the day," Cassie said, walking through the door as Kailey held it open.

"You'll find the people here are quite dedicated to their fitness and training. They're more passionate than the folks in the Boston gym where I used to train."

Kailey walked to the front counter. A television was on overhead. A thin brunette stood behind the counter and smiled at Kailey. Another young lady was at the other corner, preparing a smoothie for a waiting customer. The attendants wore tight Yoga pants and sports bras without shirts of tank to display their narrow muscular abs.

Cassie whispered, "Forget the male calendar models. If a demon could reach Heaven, I think I'm there."

Kailey grinned and shook her head. "Behave."

"Sorry, but I can't blind myself to such temptations. It's like …" She sighed heavily. "It's like they're luring me to them instead of the other way around. Usually *I'm* the seductress."

"Except that's not what they're doing, Cassie. It takes lots of training to get the body proportions they have, and well, they simply want to flaunt it. Unlike you."

"Oh, I flaunt it," Cassie said, placing her hands on her curvy hips.

"Yes, but you don't have to work to achieve it. You simply present yourself ever how you wish for others to see you."

"That's true, I suppose."

Kailey laughed. "No, it is true. Not to mention you can eat whatever you want whenever you want without the worry of gaining weight."

The brunette behind the counter smiled at them. "What can I do for you?"

Kailey swiped her badge through the scanner. It beeped, signifying her membership. "I need a day pass for my friend, Cassie."

"Sure," the woman replied. She reached beneath the counter and took a small card from a box. "Fill this out."

Cassie quickly filled in the blanks and then promptly showed her identification to the woman behind the counter.

The woman read the card and then her eyes widened as she fixated on Cassie's body. "I can give you a quick tour if you'd like, Cassie, or since your friend probably already knows her way around, she can show you."

"Kailey can show me."

The woman bit her lower lip for several seconds before finally beaming a smile in spite of her obvious disappointment. "Sure. If you have any questions about anything, let me know."

Kailey turned away from the desk. "Let's go to the locker room. I might have extra clothes in there if you want to change."

Cassie gave a sly grin. "I see. Already trying to undress me? Want to shower first and workout after?"

Kailey's face reddened. "Would you stop that? You're always trying to embarrass me."

"I would stop except you make it too easy."

"And you get a kick out of that?"

Cassie shrugged. "Amusement comes in all shapes and sizes. But you have a different cuteness about you when you're red-faced."

"And how's that?"

"Embarrassment shows innocence, depending upon the situation. You get flustered at any verbal sexual suggestion I make."

"So?"

"So, it means you have buried thoughts you don't wish to reveal to me."

"You can tell that by my blushing?"

Cassie nodded. "It indicates I've tapped into a part of your fantasies you didn't expect me to discover."

"You're being silly."

"Am I? Or have you never fantasized about us in the manner I showed you?"

Kailey's face darkened even more.

"You have, haven't you?"

"I'd rather not discuss it, thank you." She avoided making a slight glance in Cassie's direction.

Cassie laughed.

They entered the locker room. Several frosted glass shower doors were closed. Steam flowed through the narrow gaps near the tops of the doors where several women were showering. A faint outline of their nude bodies was visible.

"My locker's over here," Kailey said. She turned the combination knob back and forth until she had unlocked the door. "I … I don't see anything extra."

"This should do?" Cassie asked.

Kailey turned and noticed Cassie was now dressed in tight black Yoga shorts and a thin white sports bra that left nothing to the imagination. Her beautifully spiraled hair was pulled back in ponytail.

"How'd you do that?"

Cassie smiled. "I'm a succubus. I cannot only change my appearance, but I can also dress ever how I want, within reason. So, what do you think?"

"Clearly makes me wish I could change my clothes that easily."

"Well? Is this okay?"

Kailey cleared her throat. "Perhaps a darker top? Or one made from thicker material? You're a bit too ... prominent."

Cassie glanced down and placed her index fingers against her perked nipples. "Is that so? And that presents a problem?"

"Not for me, but management tends to frown on it."

"The women at the counter weren't dressed too much differently."

Kailey made a slight frown. "Um, actually their bras were padded and compared to you, they are definitely lacking."

Cassie sighed. "The world is filled with too many prudent people."

"I'm not complaining. I'm simply informing you of the rules. Of course the brunette probably wouldn't call you out for it."

Cassie closed her eyes and frowned. "How's this?"

Her bra was thicker and black instead of white, but not overly snug.

"Better."

Cassie rolled her eyes. "You'd think people had never seen nipples before. Will there be men working out without shirts?"

"Most likely, yes."

"See? Such sexist double standards."

"I agree, but I don't make the rules," Kailey said, closing the locker door.

They left the locker room and walked past a long row of treadmills and elliptical machines and entered a large room with several boxing rings, punching bags, and sparring mats.

Some people jumped rope in different corners. Large men pressed their weight against the heavy punching bags while boxers and MMA fighters practiced their kicks and punches. Sweat and an over abundance of testosterone filled the room. The aggressiveness of their training slacked as Cassie smiled and walked past several of the men. Without even trying, her seductiveness drew the men toward her. Their stares revealed how much they were drooling inside over her.

Cassie shook her head, watching the men ahead of her, and not noticing the ones behind her that had stopped jabbing the bags. "You weren't kidding. These people take their training seriously."

An older man wearing a white T-shirt shrieked his silver whistle at his trainees. "Hit the bags or hit the showers! You can't win any fight watching the seats!"

Cassie glanced back to see the fighters return to punching and kicking but not as enthusiastically. Their eyes were still focused on the succubus.

Kailey smiled at her. "Remember when I told you that I've been wanting to become this dedicated for some time now."

"Then why haven't you?"

"Raven."

"How was she holding you back?"

"It's a long story, but she knew this was something I wanted to do and a dream of mine. All she could do was insult the sport while insisting I not do it and she mocked me."

Cassie nodded. "Well, you don't have to worry about her doing that any more."

"I know, but it's odd, too."

"What is?"

"The person who wanted to hold me back is now the main reason I want to train even harder. Should the occasion ever arise, I want to have my fighting skills honed to defend myself."

"A stake works better against a vampire, dear," Cassie replied.

"I know, but now she's threatened my friends and my life. She needs to feel some pain before getting slain."

"I thought Forrest was going to take care of that for you?"

Kailey nodded. "He will. *Provided* he finds Raven first. I'm under the impression she'll be seeking some way to steer clear of him. Flora will probably help her every chance she can."

"Remember a few things," Cassie said.

"What?"

"Physically, vampires are much stronger than humans."

"I know that."

"She's filled with rage and spite, so she might use any chance to turn you into a vampire as well. She might not be seeking to kill you, and that for you would be a worse fate."

Kailey nodded. Kailey expected Raven to at least try that once, but she hoped that didn't happen.

"Plus, you can never look her in the eyes again. She'll glamour you so she can get you to do whatever she wishes. While you might eventually become an expert with your fighting skills, she will always have some advantages that require no fighting skills at all."

Kailey bit her lower lip. Chill bumps covered her arms.

"But," Cassie said, "not to worry. You have some strong allies who will stand beside you and help defend you. The greatest advice I have for you right now is that you never find yourself alone. Have one of us with you at all times. Do you understand why that's important?"

Kailey nodded. "I do. There's my trainer. Let me introduce the two of

you."
"Sure, as long as what I just said is perfectly clear."
"It is, Cassie, and thank you. Thank you for being such a close friend."
"Right back at you."

CHAPTER 10

Forrest frowned at Brady through the lowered passenger-side window. The hardened expression on his face became even more difficult for Brady to read. The dead look gave no indication of friendliness or growing rage. Brady had seen criminals with similar expressions but none quite this severe. Forrest had killed hundreds of vampires. Was that why the Hunter always had such a death stare in his eyes?

Forrest studied Brady. "You want me to kill your friend?"

Brady nodded.

"Why?"

"She's a vampire," Brady replied.

"I see."

"Diana was my partner on the force before she was turned."

"Where is she now?"

Brady took a deep breath and crossed his arms. "In a storage unit. She's inside a casket wrapped with heavy silver chains."

"How long have you kept her bound like this?"

"A couple of years."

"Why haven't you staked her, rather than torment her if she was your friend?"

Sadness softened Brady's face. "I just couldn't kill her. Believe me, I hate having kept her locked up, but I couldn't bring myself to stake her."

"Even though she's a monster?"

"She's tried to kill me once so you have no reason to convince me of what she has become. I know what she is, and that she's no longer the person I knew. There's nothing civilized about her, either. She's like a rabid animal."

"That should have been incentive enough for you to stake her," Forrest said with little emotion.

"Are you heartless? Physically, Diana looks the same. That's why I hesitate driving a stake through her heart. And all she needs to kill me is that slightest bit of hesitation on my part."

"Don't you realize how difficult a time she'd have killing you since you're a werewolf? Depending upon how long she's been locked away, she should be much weaker. When did you last open the casket?"

"A couple of years ago, but I wasn't a werewolf at the time. After she hadn't reported to work for several days, I entered her apartment and that's when I discovered the casket. Foolishly I looked inside. She almost had me before I got to the door. I came back later with the silver chain and wrapped the casket, securing it with a heavy lock. But I have never looked inside again. I have enough sense not to do that."

Forrest ran a hand through his beard while he thought. "If she's been bound for a couple of years, she won't look the same. Without feeding on blood for that amount of time, her skin will be shriveled, and her fingernails will be longer. She will look like the corpse she is, and not the woman you knew."

Brady sighed. "Look, can you slay her or not?"

"I can. But I still don't understand why *you* won't. Sympathy?"

"No. Sheesh. You seem completely void of compassion. Have you never loved anyone?"

"You were in love with her?"

Brady frowned. "No. I was asking if *you* had ever been in love."

Forrest's jaw tightened. He remained silent for several minutes. He spoke in a low gruff tone, but his lips never seemed to move. "A long time ago."

"I'm guessing it ended badly?"

Forrest shrugged. "It's a long story."

"It must not have ended well since you lack compassion."

"When you kill vampires for as long as I have, you find little to have compassion about. It leads to a lonely life."

"I imagine so."

Forrest scratched at his bearded chin. "When do you want me to end her misery?"

"When can you?"

"Right now."

Brady looked away for several seconds. "I need to report in to work right now."

"You look like your dressed to go jogging, not to go to work."

"I'm working undercover, and I keep a uniform in my locker at the station."

Forrest chuckled. "You and your girlfriend are suited for one another, but at least she has the sense to understand the truth."

"What are you implying?"

"Neither of you want to kill vampires you once knew as friends, but after last night, Kailey views the situation with new eyes. You requested for me to help you, and after I have agreed to help you, you decide that you want to delay the slaying. Denying the truth doesn't negate it."

"Get in," Brady said, reaching across the seat and opening the car door.

Forrest grinned, lowering himself into the seat. He placed his Hunter box on his lap. "This day is getting better already."

"Is it? You ever kill a vampire who was your friend?"

"I've never had a vampire for a friend."

Brady drove into traffic. Rain sluiced the windshield, so he turned on the wipers. "You know what I mean. Have you ever had a friend turned into a vampire and you had to slay him or her?"

Forrest nodded. "A long, long time ago."

"How did you cope with it?"

"I didn't actually kill him. The master vampire who had turned him was slain, which ended my friend's life as well."

Brady gave Forrest a side-glance. "And you were content with that?"

"Yes. He wasn't the friend I had known. He even tortured my father for a while until my father managed to escape. Why is it that I have to keep explaining that a vampire only *looks* like the person it was before? While it might have some strong characteristics of the person, it is forever controlled by darkness. Mercy and compassion are gone. Its main goal is to kill and feast on human blood."

Brady checked his mirrors and changed lanes. "So what becomes of the vampire after it's turned to ash?"

Forrest shrugged. "That's it."

"No afterlife?"

"A vampire has no soul. How can it possibly have an afterlife?"

"Where does the soul go when a person is turned into a vampire?"

"I have no idea," Forrest replied.

"None?"

Forrest shook his head.

"What do you believe?"

Forrest frowned at him. "About what?"

"Their souls?"

"I don't know. I don't really consider it. I don't even consider my own soul."

Brady gave a perplexed stare. "What? How could you not take yourself into consideration?"

Forrest laughed softly. "With all the deeds I've done in my life, my mistakes, and the cold callousness that has numbed me to the core, I honestly have no idea what awaits me after death."

"Seriously?"

Forrest nodded. His massive hands gripped the sides of his Hunter box.

"What about you? Are you catholic or protestant? What?"

"Religion isn't something I like to discuss. To me, it's personal, and since my beliefs are rather unconventional, it takes too long to explain," Forrest said. "I'm content with you believing however you wish to believe, and I ask that you respect the same for me."

"I get that, but with the numbers of vampires you've slain, I'd think you'd become more devoted to your faith."

"I wasn't called into the ministry, Brady. I was Chosen to be a Vampire Hunter. Some might even consider me the judge, jury, and executioner for these soulless undead creatures. I don't seek to have them repent because repentance isn't for them. It does them no good. They have no hope other than their final death. I'm happy to oblige that. Of course they vigorously fight to remain undead, which makes perfect sense as well."

"I suppose it beats becoming a pile of ashes," Brady said with a wide grin.

"Exactly," Forrest replied.

"So you believe Micah's goals aren't in the best interest of the Circle of Unity?"

"It's not in anyone's best interest. The whole reason the former Unity was dissolving was because of the foolishness in believing vampires could be trusted. They can't."

Brady turned the defroster on to remove the condensation forming on the inside of the windshield. "From the information you gave in the meeting earlier, you seem to have some sort of past with Flora? Am I misreading that, or not?"

Forrest grunted and adjusted slightly in the seat. "We do have a history. Not a good one. She escaped execution years ago, but she won't this time."

"So this is personal?"

"In ways you cannot possibly imagine."

Brady's hands tightened on the steering wheel. "You could have killed her when you killed Nicodemus, but you didn't."

"I spared her only because I had given my word that I'd do so then."

"And now she's taken Raven to mentor," Brady said.

"Since Kailey had insisted Raven not be slain, someone had to mentor her. Otherwise, Raven would have become a worse terror in Seattle. She'd have slaughtered dozens of people by now. But, to be honest, I don't know which fate is worse."

"What do you mean?"

Forrest sighed. "Flora has always had a thirst for blood. She lusts also to torture. I must say that the Circle of Unity and her being in the public eye probably suppressed a lot of those desires. She and Nicodemus were close."

"But didn't she hand him over to you?" Brady asked.

"Yes. That's why I stayed her execution. But, don't you see? If she's willing to sacrifice her dearest brother, there's no end to what she'd do to satiate her hidden bloodlusts. With Raven under her wing, you cannot possibly fathom the carnage that will come to Seattle, and trust me, if they're not stopped soon, you will discover exactly how dark Flora's true nature is."

"I believe you," Brady replied. "I occasionally have found drained victims in alleys, left behind like animals without remorse."

"Expect to find many more, but these will be aggressively slaughtered as a warning. She was the spoiled child of a wealthy aristocrat and for years she tortured peasants in the cruelest ways. She likes to taunt and display her power. She thrives on it."

"Not trying to change the subject, but since our meeting, you got my curiosity up. Are you and Micah really cousins?"

Forrest nodded. "We are. His father helped train me, along with my father, when I first learned I was a Vampire Hunter."

"Where is his father?"

"I don't rightly know. I lost touch with him years ago when we parted ways. I've not had a chance to talk to Micah, so I don't know if Jacques is still alive or not."

Brady said, "Then how did you find Micah?"

"Purely by accident. Micah contacted me by post some years back, requesting my aid to kill some vampires in Vancouver. I never replied to his letter, but I took his tips and hunted down the master, killing him and vanquishing his hold on the small village."

"I see. Why is there strife between the two of you?"

Forrest chuckled. "We don't have any bad blood between us."

"Really? He looked like he wanted to attack you."

"He probably thought he wanted to, but the truth is he has to act aggressive and dominant since he leads the pack. I smelled his fear, despite the little performance he offered. Even if he turned into a werewolf, he's no match for me. You actually aided him by stepping between us."

"How?"

"You gave him an excuse not to turn, which was something he needed, if only to save face."

"But you can take him in his wolf form?"

Forrest laughed. "Where were you in the tunnels beneath Nocturnal Trinity when we attacked?"

"Trying to protect Kailey, Skye, and Jaclyn. Why?"

"Ah, you didn't see the bear?"

A stunned expression hung on Brady's face. "Vaguely. That was you?"

Forrest nodded.

"So you're a shifter, too?"

"I am, and have you ever known a wolf to successfully fight against a grizzly and win?"

Brady swallowed hard. "No."

"Neither has Micah."

"This is more complex than I ever imagined."

"Very."

Brady ran a hand through his hair and shook his head, taking in the information. "Wow. So much that we've not been told."

"And a lot of things you'll never know."

"Okay. So how do you plan to find Raven?"

"Her aspirations are few. She has Kailey in mind most of all, and since you're with Kailey, you're an obstacle she intends to kill or at the very least, she'll make you suffer. I merely need to stay near the two of you. Eventually, she'll make her move."

"It's a bit more complex than that now."

"How's that?"

"Luna was left a note with the same threat."

Forrest cocked a brow and faced Brady. "Really?"

Brady nodded.

"Since Kailey isn't that close to Luna, biggest threat Raven has to offer is killing Kailey or you. I have my doubts she'll go for the kill with you right away."

"Why?"

"She knows you're a werewolf. That will make her second guess her approach. Although she has strength as a vampire, she's probably wondering how much strength a werewolf has in comparison. I could have easily killed Raven that night we invaded Nocturnal Trinity. Raven was still struggling with the realization of becoming a vampire. From what I understand about her, she was probably resentful and would have rather died than become an undead. She was her most vulnerable but now, it seems, she has embraced what she is and seeks revenge against all the people she considers traitors."

"That would be me since Kailey and I have moved in together," Brady said.

Forrest nodded. "That's why I plan to keep a closer eye on the two of you."

Brady turned onto a narrow alleyway and followed it out to the next street and turned right. He then turned left into a parking lot on the outside of a fenced set of storage units. The gate was open, so he drove the squad car through until they passed two long buildings of storage units. He turned into the narrow path between the third and fourth buildings, stopping the car at #369.

"This is the one," Brady said, opening his car door and stepping out into the steady rain.

"Good."

"At least it's daylight."

Forrest slammed the passenger door and stared up at the dark cloudy sky. He shook his head. "No sun. No direct sunlight."

"That makes a difference?" Brady asked, fumbling through his keys.

"Sometimes, depending upon the vampire. But not for your former friend."

"Vampires can't walk outdoors before sunset, can they?"

"Some can."

Brady frowned. "I thought vampires couldn't travel outside during the day."

"Not in direct sunlight. But an old vampire or an ancient one can move about when the sky's this overcast. The first vampire I ever encountered approached me during a blizzard. The clouds were so thick it seemed nearly dusk. But he was close to a century old. Vampires attain greater strength the older and the longer they survive."

"I had no idea. Good to know."

Brady unlocked the circular lock and slid the latch aside. Forrest reached down, grabbed the door handle at the bottom of the door, and slid the door all the way to the top. The dark wood casket was slightly visible in the back corner of the storage unit.

"Let's make this quick," Forrest said. "There aren't too many people out and about, but any witnesses at all will no doubt draw unwarranted questions, which is something we *don't* need."

"I agree."

"You didn't bring a stake?" Forrest asked.

Brady shook his head. "I'll watch."

Forrest's jaw tightened. He shook his head. "I don't know how Micah's pack has survived this long. You should always carry a stake, especially since you know about the vampires."

"I don't have the experience that you do."

"You never know what might happen," Forrest said. He pulled a stake out of his jacket pocket and handed it to Brady. "You might need this, and if you don't, consider yourself a lucky man. But slaying vampires isn't a game or a hobby. It's a life or death situation. You need to keep that in mind since Kailey is human."

"You're right. I'll definitely be more cautious and attentive in the future."

"Good. Now, before we open this casket, let me ask you something," Forrest said, holding a stake tightly in his hand.

"Sure."

"Do you know who turned your friend?"

Brady shook his head. "No."

"I suppose that's information we need to know before I stake her."

"How do you plan to do that?"

"You'll see."

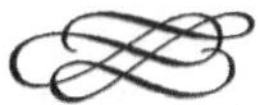

ailey walked to the short muscular blonde who was showing a teenage girl some defensive moves. The woman wore a tight dark blue bodysuit. Her hair was pulled back in a crude ponytail, which looked like it could unravel at any moment. She turned and saw Kailey and smiled. Although Kailey smiled back, her eyes focused on her trainer's cauliflower ears. She cringed inside, thinking immediately of Raven's constant warnings about one of the side effects of MMA fighting.

"Hey, girl," the woman said. "You're in early today."

"So are you, Eddy."

Eddy shrugged. "It really is a full-time job. Who's your friend?"

"Oh, Eddy, this is my sister-in-law, Cassie. Cassie, Eddy."

Cassie offered her hand and smiled. Eddy firmly shook Cassie's hand and her eyes wandered down Cassie's physique without any discretion or apology, which Kailey found strange since her trainer was straight and had never expressed any interest in other females. *None. Zilch. Nada.* Cassie seemed to emit pheromones capable of seducing anyone around her. *Could she not turn it off?*

"So are you thinking about MMA training, Cassie?" Eddy asked.

Cassie shook her head and smiled. She winked and spoke in her throaty voice. "I'm a lover, not a fighter."

Eddy stared into Cassie's eyes for several long moments. "If you could fight with as much passion as I imagine you probably exhibit as a lover, you'd be an undefeated champion."

Kailey's eyes widened and she turned away. *Dammit, Cassie!*

Cassie smiled. A slight purr came from her throat. "I appreciate that, but I'm rather fond of my face and don't like the idea of someone else trying to ram their fist through it … but when it comes to ramming something—"

A strange smile crossed Eddy's face.

"Cassie!" Kailey grabbed Cassie's arm and jerked her, walking with her several feet away. In a firm whisper, she said, "Would you *stop* it? Since you've walked through the gym, all the men and women have been swooning over you."

"Really?" she looked around with a flattered smile, suddenly noticing a lot of lustful stares from men and women. "I'm … sorry. I hadn't noticed."

"Can you not tone it down?"

Cassie frowned. "Tone *what* down?"

Kailey continued her stern whispering tone. "Whatever it is that draws others toward you."

"I can try."

"Please. You're disrupting everyone around us."

"Kailey?" Eddy said. "Are you up for some training matches this evening?"

Kailey turned and offered a curious frown. "What kind of matches exactly?"

"Another gym in Seattle wants our best to spar against their best. It helps to fight against people we're not familiar with. It better prepares us mentally when we actually fight in the real cage. Are you up for it?"

Kailey shrugged. "Sure. What time?"

"Around six o'clock this evening."

Kailey glanced to Cassie. Cassie nodded, and Kailey looked back at Eddy. "Sure. We can be here."

"Great!" Eddy said. "I've seen you spar with some of the others here, but I'd like to see what you have to offer against outside opponents. I'm certain you won't let me down."

"You know I'll give my all," Kailey replied.

"Yep, you always do," Eddy said.

Cassie offered her hand to Eddy again. "It's been a pleasure meeting you."

Eddy grinned. Her face was tinted red and she looked flustered. She almost panted her reply. "The pleasure's been all mine."

Cassie followed Kailey back to the treadmills.

"I can't believe how people fawn all over you," Kailey said. "You're like some sort of aphrodisiac for men *and* women. If you could bottle that, you'd become filthy rich."

Cassie stepped up on the treadmill and then placed her feet to each side of the belt. "I doubt the recipients would survive."

"They were like rutting animals."

"Kailey, I really did nothing except walk along beside you. Sure, I can willingly lay the charm onto someone if I chose, but I didn't. I could have done that to you when I made my indecent proposal, but you know I didn't."

Kailey set the speed for her jog, glanced at Cassie, and swallowed hard. Cassie hadn't done anything more than show Kailey a fantasy of what pleasures she could enjoy while lovemaking with Cassie's succubus form. Even now, Kailey's heart beat faster, her palms moistened, and she felt excited being wrapped inside Cassie's arms while being driven to vigorous ecstasy and heightened orgasms. The things Cassie had shown her in less than a few seconds had weakened Kailey then and was doing so now. She yearned to let Cassie explore her body, every inch and every crevice, taking full delight in the demon's embrace.

She had seen how Cassie's kiss had encapsulated Brady and nearly enslaved him to do whatever the succubus suggested when he had tried to fight the demon. The power of her seduction reduced his rage and aggression until all he could do was fall beneath her spell.

Kailey enjoyed making love to Brady, and he made her content, even when she begged him to be rough. Yet, she couldn't forget what Cassie had shown her. Often, while Brady thrust himself deep inside her, Kailey's mind ventured to Cassie. She had never had a threesome. She had never even entertained the idea, but she found herself wanting to be caressed by Brady and Cassie at the same time. She wanted to surrender herself to their lusts for her, and more than anything else—she craved it with endless hunger.

A finger tapped her shoulder. She opened her eyes and jerked her head in response. It was Cassie, frowning with grave concern.

"Are you okay, Kailey?"

"Uh, yeah, why?"

"You looked like you'd fallen asleep standing up," Cassie said.

Kailey took a deep breath and exhaled through her mouth. She then faked a yawn. "Sorry. I didn't sleep too well with all that happened last night."

"That's understandable."

"Not for you," Kailey said.

"I have fears, too."

Kailey started a slow sprint. "Really? Like what?"

"The abyss. Losing you. Amongst other things."

"I need to run three miles and then if you don't mind, could you hold one of those punching bags for me?" Kailey asked.

"Sure."

"Great. I need to kick the shit out of something."

"As long as it isn't me," Cassie said.

Without glancing in the succubus' direction, Kailey replied, "Believe me, harming you will never ever come to mind again. I … love you too much to ever seek to hurt you."

Cassie sniffled.

Kailey glanced out of the corner of her eye and watched Cassie wipe tears from her eyes.

"That's sweet of you, Kailey."

"It's the truth," Kailey replied. *In more ways than you'll ever know.*

CHAPTER 12

*B*rady stared out of the storage unit into the cold pouring rain. The thick overcast sky showed no signs of letting up. The sun certainly wasn't welcome and an invitation to appear wasn't in the next few days' forecasts. "I suppose the weather suits the mood today."

"Death comes regardless of the weather, Brady."

"I know, but it's kind of fitting."

"Are you ready?" Forrest asked, unraveling the silver chains from around the coffin.

Brady slipped thick officer gloves onto his hands to prevent directly touching the silver. "I've stalled enough, I suppose."

"Two years too long."

Brady ignored the snide comment, basically because Forrest was right. *Why couldn't I do this before now? Because you still have a heart. You still have compassion. Kailey's allowed you to move on, to live life, and to love.* He grimaced with his internal struggle, but all the points were valid. His life had changed for the better since Kailey, and it was time to let go of his past. It was time to forgive himself for something he had not been responsible for. Diana's fate was *not* his fault.

Forrest placed his hand on the lid of the coffin. "When I lift the top, carefully drop the chain upon her chest."

"Why?"

"We need some answers."

"You think she can give them to us?"

Forrest nodded. "Unless she's already turned to ash she can."

Brady frowned. "Why would she be ash?"

"If Nicodemus was the one who turned her, she's gone for good."

"I never considered that."

"But if he didn't, that's the information we need right now."

Brady held the thick silver chain in both hands and kept it at arm's length so the silver didn't touch him. He gave a nod to Forrest. "I'm ready."

Forrest lifted the lid in one swift movement. Brady dropped the chain inside the coffin quickly. A near hoarse feminine voice attempted to scream. Brady turned on a flashlight and pointed the light at Diana's face.

Diana squinted, flashing fangs. Her skin was gray and shriveled. Her eyes were sunken. Her frantic hands tugged at the heavy chain. Smoke rose off her blistering flesh and fingers. She writhed, trying to squirm from beneath the chain.

"Why, Brady?" she hissed through tight lips. "Why did you do this to me? Why are you torturing me?"

Brady opened his mouth to reply, but Forrest took a silver cross and held it near Diana's face.

Her pathetic squeal was barely audible.

"Silence!" Forrest said. "Speak quickly and your end will be fast and merciful. Who turned you?"

Diana hissed, shaking her head, and closing her eyes. "Get it away! You're hurting me!"

"Tell me," Forrest said, placing the cross against her forehead. Her flesh smoldered. She gurgled a weak growl. His face tightened and his eyes narrowed. "Tell me!"

"Irina," Diana replied.

Brady leaned closer to the coffin. "One of Flora's sisters?"

Forrest nodded, lowering the cross and tightening his grip around the sharpened stake.

"Wait," Brady said.

"What? She told us, so I intend to keep my promise to her."

"I understand, but I need to ask something else."

Forrest shrugged, but he didn't step back from the coffin.

"Diana, how did you encounter Irina?"

She spat at him but no spittle flew from her shrunken mouth. She was too dehydrated.

"When? Please tell me that? I promise she'll pay for turning you," Brady said.

"She gave me a gift, Brady. Eternal life."

"You call *this* a gift?" Brady asked.

"No, *you're* my tormentor, not her. She didn't lock me away. You placed me here. You've done this to me. I hope you rot in Hell!" Her face twisted, and she gnashed her teeth pathetically. In the places where the chain weighed upon her chest, her skin burned, blistered, and peeled. Smoke rose. She thrashed but couldn't get the heavy chains off.

"You know me better than that," Brady said. "I never wanted any harm to come to you. I kept you … here, hoping some way to reverse what was done."

"Irina never forced this upon me. I chose for her to make me a vampire. My choice. Not yours. There was nothing for you to save me from. I *wanted* to be a vampire."

"But why?"

"To live," she replied. "To never suffer or age. She delivered on her promise and you took it away from me. You've come to torture me even more. Get this chain off of me."

"She lied to you," Brady said.

Forrest nodded. "Anything else you need to ask her?"

Brady shook his head.

"There was a time when I loved you, Brady," Diana said. "Really loved you. Wanted you to make love to me."

"I could have never been with you because of this."

"I had no choice," she replied.

Forrest pulled the stake up into the air.

"Wait!"

Forrest stopped before plunging it through her chest.

"What do you mean you had no choice?" Brady asked.

"Cancer," she said softly. "I was eaten up with cancer."

Tears came to Brady's eyes.

Forrest plunged the stake through Diana's heart. Her body crumbled into a narrow pile of ash.

"What the hell!" Brady said with a fierce frown. "She wasn't finished talking to me. Why'd you do that?"

Forrest shook his head. "She was lying to you to gain your sympathy."

"You don't know that."

"Actually, yes I do. She knew I was going to stake her. She didn't want that. She wanted you to draw upon your past feelings in the hope that you'd set her free."

Brady fumed. He paced the floor of the storage unit. "I never knew she had cancer. She never even hinted that she had been sick. It makes perfect sense why she'd seek a vampire to turn her."

"And you believed her?"

"She has no reason to lie about that."

"She has *every* reason to lie to you, if it means she'd be spared. Let me ask you something. Did she ever flirt with you or insinuate she'd wanted to have sex with you?"

Brady stopped walking. "Actually, no. Never."

"See?"

Brady tilted his head back and sighed. "Why would she lie to me?"

"She was a vampire. A desperate one. She'd have said anything she possibly could to earn your sympathy. That's what I've been trying to explain to you. Vampires are soulless. They don't possess a conscience. Learn the lesson from her."

"What's that?"

"When it comes time for Raven to be staked, she's going to plead with Kailey with every fiber of her being. Therein lies the greatest challenge, fighting the voice inside your heads that long for compassion and forgiveness. If guilt weighs heavily, Kailey will be dead. Like you mentioned about Diana, remember? A slight hesitation."

Brady ran his hands through his hair. "How does anyone get to the point where you are, Forrest? You see through their guises. You hold no compassion for the undead."

"Trust me. Being cold inside like I am isn't a pleasant way to live. I've had no other choice due to my calling. I was robbed of my childhood, and I've never led a normal life. Treasure what you have and hope you are never forced to travel the path I do."

Brady nodded, walked to the casket, and rested his hands on the casket wall while looking down at the ashes.

"If it's any consolation, Brady, she died a long time ago. This wasn't Diana."

"I know, but the guilt remains heavy."

Forrest's huge hand wrapped over Brady's shoulder. He squeezed. "You have no reason to hold any guilt. This wasn't your fault."

"I'm realizing that more and more. I think I'll shake that soon enough."

"Good."

"And thanks … for doing this. More than that, for showing me how to accept the truth."

"Don't mention it," Forrest replied.

"Had you not been here, she'd have persuaded me to keep her alive."

"I know."

Brady stepped outside the storage unit and waited until Forrest joined him. Brady pulled the door down and locked it. "Where can I drop you off?"

"Nocturnal Trinity."

Brady studied Forrest for a few moments. "You sure that's a good idea?"

"Yeah. It's time for me to take care of other matters. What about you?"

"I'll give Kailey a call and see if she's still at the gym. Come on. I'll drive you back to the nightclub."

CHAPTER 13

Forrest Wollinsky sat at the bar inside Nocturnal Trinity, sipping whiskey. He wore his tattered trench coat and had his hat tilted down to hide his eyes. His Hunter box rested at his feet.

Jinn stood behind the bar, polishing a glass before placing it on a shelf above the bar. He stared at Forrest. "Starting a bit early, eh? The club hasn't even opened."

Forrest raised his head enough for Jinn to see his grim stare. "I'm not a fan of crowds or loud music."

"Then you're in the wrong place. How'd you get in here anyway?"

"Invitation."

"Ah, I see. Hey, you're the Hunter who killed Nicodemus, aren't you?"

Forrest downed the rest of his whiskey and nodded. "Yeah."

Jinn glared at him. The demon's eyes blazed like orange coals. "Either you're awfully ballsy or flat out stupid to show yourself in here."

Forrest's jaw tightened and his eyes narrowed. "Oh? Why's that?"

"You killed the vampire leader."

"I'm aware of that. The day's still young. I plan to slay the other five."

Jinn chuckled. His laughter rumbled like faint thunder. "There's a better chance they'll flay you open right here tonight."

"I highly doubt any of them will make an appearance tonight. Besides, that'd be bad for business, wouldn't you say?"

Jinn stood in silence for a few moments. "You'd be surprised how well these young people would cheer such a slaughter."

"Unfortunately, the younger generation has lost all reason and accountability."

Jinn nodded. "I may be a demon, but I agree with you there. They certainly have their priorities tainted. You, on the other hand …You don't have any fear of being poisoned or stabbed or turned into something immortal?"

"No. Should I?"

"You're not seated amongst friends, Hunter."

"But I have a relative on Nocturnal Trinity's council."

Jinn frowned. "Who?"

"Micah."

"Seriously? You're related to a werewolf?"

"He's my cousin's son."

"No shit?"

"Give me a bourbon," Forrest said, ignoring further conversation.

Jinn poured bourbon in the glass. "So why are you planning to kill the rest of Nicodemus' brothers and sisters?"

"Because they're vampires. I'm a Hunter. It's what I do."

"So, no gray area for you? It's kill them all?"

Forrest drank the bourbon, set the glass down, and nodded. "Yep."

"Really?" Jinn asked without hiding the sudden surprise on his face. "And what about those vampires who care about the welfare of mankind?"

Forrest replied with an annoyed hardened expression. "I've yet to meet one."

"You don't believe they exist?"

The Hunter shook his head. "Vampires have no souls and therefore answer to no deities. That's why Hunters like myself are called—to exact justice. How could anyone without a soul have compassion toward those who do? If nothing else, they glower with sheer resentment, using humans as prey and to torment."

"You think that happens at Nocturnal Trinity? Right out in the open?"

"Not in the open. But in the shadows, in your private VIP rooms, perhaps even under Seattle's streets or in the alleys after dark, but it happens. Vampires are self-serving. They always have been. They always will be."

Jinn frowned. His eyes changed from slightly golden, to a shimmering orange-yellow. "You've seen the lines outside the club, right?"

Forrest nodded. "A tragedy."

"These kids come from miles around and stand in lines for hours just *hoping* to be one of the chosen picked by the council. Some plead and beg, not just to get in, but that a vampire will have enough compassion to turn them into vampires, too. No one is ever forced to become a vampire here."

"*Compassion?*" Forrest chuckled. "The young people nowadays *are* delusional. Television and movies have glamorized the bloodthirsty vampires as noble and friendly. It's one of the biggest deceptions these kids have been served. They're naïve and gullible, and only realize it soon after they're turned. By then, it's too late. People should be fearful of what living a life as an undead is really all about. That's why I'm here. To protect them by eliminating the vampires."

"So how many vampires have you killed?"

Forrest's eyes narrowed. "I lost count after a thousand."

Jinn looked partially impressed and a bit horrified. "How many years did it take you to do that?"

"Hard to say. Time seems to fleet by at a rapid pace."

"Damn. How old are you?"

"I've almost lost count of that, too. But I'm a lot older than I look. I qualify for senior discounts many times over, but I've never been able to convince a server of that."

"Da-a-m-mn." He laughed. "That old? I suppose that could account for some of the memory loss."

"Well, there are a lot of memories I wouldn't mind losing," Forrest replied. "But those are the ones that tend to take root like weeds, refusing to die even if you pull them out."

Jinn nodded. "I get that."

Forrest stared absently at the shot glass.

"And how do you feel about us demons?" Jinn asked, placing his tattooed arms on the bar and leaning toward Forrest. "You have a vendetta toward us, too?"

"I've killed a few demons during my lifetime, but I'm not a Demon-hunter. Just don't get in my way, and you'll be fine."

Jinn's eyebrows rose. "You're one cocky sonofa—"

Forrest stood, placed his hand into his coat pocket, and towered over Jinn. "Careful. Just because I don't hunt demons, doesn't mean I don't know how to kill them."

Jinn glanced toward Forrest's hidden hand and waved his hands. "Chill,

Hunter, damn. Maybe you should look into Tai chi or some old school meditation. Hell, yoga even."

"Like I said, I'm not here for you."

Jinn grabbed a towel and started wiping down the bar. "You know by killing Nicodemus and now that Micah is on the club's council committee, you've offset the balance this club once held sacred, right?"

Forrest flicked an unamused gaze toward the demon. "Nocturnal Trinity was unbalanced from the very beginning, or were you too blind to realize that."

"What makes you think that?"

"Wasn't it obvious when Nicodemus was alive? I suppose he held you spellbound with his compulsion like all the rest, even his siblings. The vampires never considered themselves equals with you, regardless of your symbol over the door and plastered throughout the nightclub. They held the power, and they gave the orders to the demons and witches. They are mind parasites and everyone else was their mindless slave. The vampires presided over everything. Why do you think they never slept in this building after hours?"

Jinn wiped the bar. His brow furrowed while he thought. "You know, Hunter, you have a valid point. I think … I think you're right about that."

Forrest narrowed his gaze. "Let me ask you something."

Jinn shrugged. "Sure, that's what bartenders do with customers. Shoot the shit and all that."

"Were you one of the original demons that came through the portal when Seattle burned to the ground?"

The question took Jinn aback. "No, I came to Seattle much later."

"But you're one of the council?"

"Yeah. After a major mishap one of the original six demons died, and I was chosen to take his place."

"What sort of mishap?" Forrest asked.

Jinn shrugged. "From what I was told some crazy female Demon-hunter arrived and killed him as well as several dozen lesser demons."

Forrest sat upright on the stool. His jaw tightened. "How did that story end for her?"

"I don't know. I wasn't there and I've never asked. I count being a part of Nocturnal Trinity's council as a great privilege. So I don't ask too many questions and I don't stick my horns where they don't belong."

"So the other five demons on the council are the originals?"

Jinn nodded.

"Any way you could arrange for me to talk to one of them?"

The demon chuckled. "Hunter, you don't seem to have fear of anything. I wouldn't want to talk to any of them and *I'm* a demon. These demons are pure evil, unlike myself, of course."

Forrest frowned with a mocking nod and shrug. "Oh, of course."

"They never make an appearance here. At least not up here where our regulars drink, dance, and talk. Those demons are ancients and quite deadly."

Forrest stared at Jinn but didn't speak. He kept a hardened, intimidating stare. His silence spoke volumes.

Jinn put the towel under the bar. "I might be able to arrange a meeting for you, but why do you want to talk to them?"

"I want to know what happened to that Demon-hunter," Forrest replied in a low tone.

"Why?"

"She was a friend of mine."

Jinn looked surprised. "Hunter, that was over a hundred years ago."

"Closer to a hundred and thirty."

The demon frowned. "I know you said that you were old, but come on, you can't be that old."

Forrest gave a sly half grin.

"For real?"

"Yeah."

"And you knew her? This Demon-hunter?"

Forrest nodded.

"How old are you?"

"Not much older than when the *mishap* occurred."

"You don't look much older than thirty years by my guess."

Forrest shrugged. "That's why it's so hard to claim those senior discounts."

Jinn chuckled. "I imagine so. Damn. How do you stay so young?"

"It's complicated."

Jinn studied Forrest for a minute or so before realizing the Hunter wasn't adding any further information. "Look, I know you want to know what happened to her, but if I present this information to them, you're as good as dead. I have no doubt bringing up the subject of what she did will rile up harsh memories for them. They're not the forgiving type and they've never let bygones be."

"Then don't tell them."

"You don't realize the power these demons wield. I pale in comparison to them."

Forrest frowned. "Then why did they choose you to become a part of the council?"

Jinn beamed a pleasant smile. "Nocturnal Trinity needs an active attractive demon representative on the floor since it's part of our persona. Patrons expect it. Since I'm handsome, charismatic, and outgoing, they chose me."

"Is arrogance another quality?"

The demon paused momentarily, as if he started to refute the snide comment, but instead he shook his head and continued his explanation. "Basically, I'm the front-demon. The other five demons aren't friends of mine, not really even my acquaintances. I've met them only a few times, and trust me, I'm *content* with that. In their eyes, I will never measure up. I'm the only incubus on the council. If any one of them was the demon on the floor, business would tank. They are more than frightening and menacing. Kind of like you except they are the true definition of what monsters are."

"I need to talk to one of them."

Jinn looked concerned. "Hunter, I really wish you'd reconsider. Perhaps find another way to get the information? Maybe Cassie?"

"The succubus?"

Jinn nodded.

"She won't know any more than you do. Probably even less since the council had planned to sacrifice her to further their goals. Either you set up a meeting for me, or I'll find out where these demons are and talk to them anyway."

"No, trust me, you *don't* want to do that."

Forrest noticed the demon continued asking for him to trust it, which was humorous on so many levels. Few demons ever spoke the full truth, often giving a slight version of the truth, and when one kept trying to persuade his honesty, Forrest became even more suspicious. "It looks like it might be the only way I can talk to them."

Jinn sighed. "Look. Give me at least two days. Like I said, they seldom ever make an appearance. They have a lounge upstairs but I'm the only demon who uses it. Only *member* demon, that is. Demon guests of mine are in and out all the time. I will have to figure out where one of the five is. How can I get in touch with you?"

"I'll be around." Forrest took out his wallet and thumbed through the bills.

"It's on the house," Jinn said.

"I appreciate that."

"Consider it your first senior discount." Jinn gave a devious smile.

Forrest tipped back his hat, laughed heartily, and headed toward the exit.

CHAPTER 14

*L*ater in the evening Kailey returned to Fists & Cuffs with Brady and Cassie. The parking lot was full, forcing Brady to park about two blocks up the street. Dozens of people were making their way toward the gym.

Kailey wore tight purple Spandex shorts and a snug black sports bra. Cassie had braided Kailey's hair into a tight, spiraled bun to lessen the chance of having an opponent yank her hair.

In spite of the cold mists of rain, Cassie wore baby blue shorts that hugged her well-toned butt perfectly. Her heels were black and against Kailey's advice, Cassie wore fishnet stockings. She wore a vinyl halter-top, which under normal circumstances even Luna would have insisted it was tacky, but the rain-resistant material was perfect to prevent her from getting soaked by the endless mists of rain.

Brady had decided to wear his uniform in case people in the crowd got out of hand. Sometimes just the presence of a uniform was enough to deter some people from starting trouble. Not always. For some it was the entire reason why they initiated problems. But since the owner of the gym was a former cop, Brady was certain a lot of plain clothes officers were mixed within the crowd.

"There's no way all these people are going to fit inside the gym," Kailey said.

"I agree," Brady replied.

"As far as I know, no tickets were sold for this. It's not even a major event, so how would so many people know about it?" Kailey asked.

Brady shrugged.

Cassie grinned and swung her hip into Kailey, bumping her as they walked. She was looking at her iPhone screen. "Social media outlets have it as a hashtag must-see attraction."

Kailey sighed. "Why? This was for training against another gym's top competing fighters. It makes no sense shooting off a flare to let the whole city know about it."

"You don't like fighting in front of crowds?" Cassie asked.

"I've fought in small gyms in the suburbs of Boston, but nothing like this."

"Why let it bother you?"

"I don't know," Kailey said with a slight shrug. "In some ways it doesn't, but should I make a lot of mistakes and lose, I guess I don't want to embarrass myself."

"How long have you trained?" Cassie asked.

"Nearly eleven years."

"Then don't worry about it. You'll do fine." She placed her arm across Kailey's shoulders and squeezed her tightly. "I've fought with you before, and I don't want a rematch."

"I always get uptight like this before any fight," Kailey said. "Once I'm on the mat, the nervousness vanishes. I get zoned in, I guess."

"You won't be fighting indoors tonight," Brady said as they turned onto the side street. The large fighting cage was set up in the far corner of the parking lot near the gym and under a pavilion roof to shield the mat from the rain. Portable spotlights had been positioned on flatbed trucks to light up the fighting arena. Two large television screens were visible through the gym windows to allow the crowd to watch the sparring matches.

People stood in droves around the cage. If they weren't wearing raincoats, they held large umbrellas. The anticipation was already building. Conversations amongst the spectators grew to a steady hum. Television reporters with cameramen were unloading from several vans.

It doesn't seem to matter how bad the weather is. If there's a chance to see blood spilled, you people wouldn't care if a hurricane was coming ashore. You'd stand out here anyway. Kailey shook her head and grabbed Brady's hand, hoping to calm the growing nervousness inside her. "How am I supposed to get anywhere near the cage?"

"My guess is we enter through the gym. You should be able to register," Brady said. "Isn't that what's required?"

"Eddy never said, did she?" Kailey said, looking at Cassie.

Cassie shook her head.

"There's Eddy," Cassie said, pointing.

"Come on," Brady said.

They walked along the sidewalk that led to the front of the gym. Brady kept telling onlookers to 'step aside.' Most did without question. Others had to be more firmly coaxed with Brady raising his voice and demanding people clear the walkway. Though average height, he could be quite intimidating whenever he chose to be or when the need rose.

"This is worse than the lines outside Nocturnal Trinity," Kailey said.

Brady nodded. "On most nights, yes."

"Eddy!" Kailey shouted, waving her hand over her head.

Eddy turned at the mention of her name. She motioned them toward her table. "Kailey!"

The three of them hurried to the table beneath a large outdoor umbrella.

"What's going on? I thought this was a simple sparring match?" Kailey said, glancing around at the pressing crowd.

"That's what it was supposed to be," Eddy replied. "None of us expected this. The owner of the other gym swears he had nothing to do with it, either. So we haven't a clue who pressed to get the word out, but the owner will use it to his advantage by handing out Free Day Passes and brochures about our gym memberships. It's a win-win for him."

Kailey shook her head and rubbed her hands together.

"Nervous?" Eddy asked.

"A little. I didn't expect this to be so crowded *or* outside."

"You have nothing to lose, record-wise at least," Eddy said. "This is strictly practice, and having a crowd like this—well, that's a bonus for you, too. Makes you less nervous when your fight record allows you to compete in the bigger arenas."

Kailey forced a nervous smile. "That's true."

Eddy stared into Kailey's eyes. "I've fought in coliseums with over ten thousand onlookers. Believe me, once that bell rings, your focus is on the opponent. You totally forget about the crowd. It's almost like it doesn't exist because you've zoned in. Just don't lose your confidence, okay?"

Kailey nodded.

"Okay," Eddy said. She handed Kailey a square stick-on. "Here's your number. Stick it on before you enter the cage. Not out here in the mist, as it might not stay fastened on. And … you're in the second bout. Each person is only in one fight. We're not using a tier chart to eliminate down to one ultimate winner. Have fun."

Kailey laughed softly. "Easy for you to say."

"You're going to do fine," Cassie said.

Eddy smiled. "You will, Kailey. Keep your cool. I've seen your techniques. You're more qualified than most of the fighters here."

Brady took Kailey's hand. "Let's get out of this weather until your fight begins. You don't want overly chilled."

Kailey blew air through her mouth, puffing her cheeks. She formed fists and closed her eyes, trying to calm herself.

They went inside where it was warmer. A couple of men grunted and unapologetically stared at Cassie and Kailey as they walked past. Kailey paced a few steps back and forth, trying to gather her nerves. The narrow hall was filled with mingling people. Some were dressed in gym attire, covered in sweat, while others were causally dressed and had come indoors to watch the fights through the windows.

Kailey noticed other fighters wearing their numbers. A few she recognized from training in this gym. The ones she didn't recognize, she assumed were from the other gym. "I think I'm supposed to be where they are in the adjacent hall. That door opens to the cage."

Brady nodded, placed his arms around her waist, and pulled her close. He leaned down and kissed her. "You're going to do just fine."

"Thanks," she replied.

He backed away and smiled. "We'll be here watching you, okay?"

Cassie smiled. "If you'll pardon the expression, 'Give them Hell.'"

Kailey grinned, nodded, and turned to walk to where the other fighters were lined up. Once she found her place in line, more people gathered around, forming a tight wall where running or getting through the crowd was next to impossible. If anything, she figured this was a direct fire code violation. Too many people crammed together like sardines. If an emergency occurred, some of these people might get trampled to death.

Glancing around, she wondered which fighter was her opponent. The voices of trainers with fighters, coaches, and news reporters made concentrating difficult. She expected Eddy to be at her side since she was her trainer. Of course, with all the commotion and the pressing crowd, Eddy might never get to her before her fight began.

The MC entered the cage with a microphone and welcomed the crowd. With a few choice sentences, he brought the people to a chanting roar, making the anticipation more intense. Then he announced the first two competitors as they stepped into the cage. The referee was a massive man, probably bigger than any of the fighters, which often was necessary in MMA bouts. Some people didn't know when to stop, even after the other fighter had tapped out or fallen unconscious. Referees were like lifeguards once a fight became nasty.

Kailey stared through the window, watching the two fighters face off. Eddy came out of nowhere and began helping Kailey get her gloves on. Kailey had barely noticed her. Her mind was already preparing for her bout. Then something pricked the back of her head. Chills ran through her. She took a sharp breath from the horrifying sensation.

Flora!

Kailey knew the vampire was nearby, but in this crowd there was hardly any chance she could find Flora's exact whereabouts. She looked toward the area where Cassie and Brady had been standing, but too many people stood in between for her to see them.

It's been a while, Kailey.

Kailey hated when Flora spoke directly into her mind.

Now it shall be most interesting to see how you survive tonight. I suppose no one told you this was a death match, did they? Your blood shall spill tonight in front of all these people. I shall take delight in seeing your final fight. I will dance to the fading beat of your heart. Nothing else could delight me more.

CHAPTER 15

Kailey glanced back and forth in desperation, trying to get a glimpse of Flora. Her heart raced, thudding hard against her ribcage.

Where are you?

Eddy checked Kailey's gloves one last time. She gazed up, seeing the panic in Kailey's eyes. She grabbed Kailey by the chin and peered directly into her eyes. "Kailey, are you okay?"

Kailey was breathing hard through her mouth and tried to maintain eye contact. "Yeah, I'm fine."

"You don't look fine. You're not focused. Are you sure you want to do this? I mean, you don't have to and you have nothing to lose by not fighting."

"I'll be okay."

"Do you have a fear of crowds?"

"Here lately, they do make me a bit uncomfortable," Kailey replied, thinking about the time Flora took mass mind control of an entire dance floor to pin Kailey, preventing her from trying to escape from Nocturnal Trinity. That had been a gag, but tonight's threat was not.

Eddy wrapped her arm around Kailey's right biceps. "I'll walk with you. Close your eyes and regain your focus. Looks like the first bout is already over."

"So soon?"

"Choke out."

Eddy led Kailey through the crowded hallway.

Always trying to have someone else fight your battles for you, Kailey?

Kailey gritted her teeth. Inside her mind she thrust her thoughts toward Flora. *Get out of my head, you crazy bitch!*

I'm going to miss our little affable conversations. Pity, you have been a good contender. It's a shame you couldn't be more like Raven. She's such an obedient child, willing to learn and accept the power she now possesses.

Kailey formed fists. *Forrest is going to kill you and Raven. At one point I'd have never found any pleasure in either of your demises, but I look forward to seeing you as nothing more than a pile of ash! I'll do a cemetery dance around your powdery remains.*

Flora's taunting laughter rang inside Kailey's ears.

"Kailey," Eddy said, squeezing her forearm. "Get ready."

Kailey opened her eyes. The side door opened and the winner of the first bout came through with a broad grin. His dizzy opponent was propped between two bodybuilders. They were carrying the guy more than he was walking on his own. The dazed fighter blinked and shook his head, trying to get his bearings. His eyes indicated he didn't have any idea where he was.

Eddy looked Kailey in the eyes. "You can do this."

Kailey nodded with a serious frown. Flora's bullying threats had triggered a response of anger inside. But, while her anger might have been effective against a regular fighter, Kailey knew fighting someone under Flora's mind control would be nearly impossible to defeat. For one, the person could be compelled not to feel pain, or Flora could enhance the fighter's strength. Either way, Kailey was about to face an opponent unlike any previous one.

The MC placed the microphone near his mouth and halfway chuckled. "Okay, folks. Let's hope this next fight lasts longer than a few minutes!"

The outside crowd cheered. A few booed their disdain.

The MC smiled and looked toward the door where Kailey stood. He read from a small card held in his hand. "We have next Kailey Yates, five-foot three inches tall and one hundred twenty-five pounds."

Kailey rushed through the door onto the mat and stepped from foot to foot with her gloves held over her head. Although she faced the audience as she made her way around the cage, she really didn't see them. Everything was a blur around her. Her mind, while trying to focus on the fight, was preoccupied, wondering where Flora was and what the vampire planned to do. That was quickly answered when the MC announced her competitor.

"Her opponent is Raven Hawkins—"

Kailey stopped and stood completely still, holding her hands to her side. All movement and sound surrounding her vanished as though she was inside a vacuum. She gazed across the cage and met Raven's cold dark stare. She had never seen pure hatred or someone fully mean-spirited until that moment. Raven was not a fighter, but she was something far worse. Being a vampire, her speed, agility, and strength were something Kailey could not match. She now understood the full intent of Flora's threat and how she intended to kill Kailey. With Raven's boiling anger and hatred, Kailey could ask for no mercy. No sympathy. Raven intended to kill her, and she probably planned to inflict as much pain as possible before delivering the deathblow.

Reunions … it's been a while, huh, Kailey? Raven though, doesn't seem overjoyed to see you at all. Wonder why that is? You two have some catching up to do.

Tears of anger and regret burned the edges of Kailey's eyes but she fought to prevent them from spilling over. She forced herself to think about the threat written in blood on the bathroom mirror. The tears subsided. Determination set in Kailey's eyes.

The referee stepped to the middle of the cage mat, but for several seconds, Kailey didn't even move. He motioned for her to step to the center of the mat where he and Raven already stood. Her steps were slow, almost like the hands of time were stalling, and she couldn't take her eyes off Raven.

No white showed in Raven's eyes. They were black and glossy like obsidian. Kailey realized she stood facing a living nightmare, an unrelenting enemy. Other than the loss of her brother and parents, Kailey couldn't recall anything that felt worse than facing a competitor who had once been a dear friend and now planned to kill her.

After the ref briefly explained the rules, he started the fight with a quick hand motion and stepped back. Raven smiled. Her bulging mouthpiece hid her teeth, but Kailey pictured the sharp fangs behind the plastic barrier.

"Guard yourself, Kailey!" Eddy shouted from outside the cage.

Kailey brought her hands up and shuffled her feet while contemplating how Raven might attempt to attack. As roommates, Kailey often requested Raven to spar with her, but it always ended up more playful wrestling because Raven didn't like the idea of Kailey becoming an MMA fighter. Raven would have done anything to shatter Kailey's hope of reaching her dream, even now.

Raven rushed forward, swung and missed. Kailey ducked, and Raven left herself wide open. Kailey didn't hesitate to deliver a quick left jab, striking Raven's cheek hard. Raven spiraled from the blow and staggered. Kailey stepped back into a boxing formation, immediately regretting that she hadn't capitalized upon Raven's faulty imbalance when she had the opportunity to tackle her.

Kailey could have easily taken advantage of the fight by grappling but her cautious nervousness caused her to miss the moment. Although Raven was a vampire, she was not a seasoned fighter.

Raven turned with anger darkening her eyes. She growled and sprinted toward Kailey like an enraged animal. Raven moved swiftly, but Kailey managed to step to the side with a high kick that caught Raven's chin. The impact slung Raven backwards. Raven hit the mat hard. She rolled and sat back on her knees. She slammed her fists down on the mat and rose.

She snarled. Instead of making another hasty attack, Raven kept her distance and bobbed left to right, mimicking Kailey's fighting stance. Kailey took a step toward Raven and jabbed, but Raven moved before the punch reached her.

They circled one another. Raven seemed to have learned that Kailey could exploit any poor advance that Raven made within Kailey's reach, so she kept her distance.

"Come on, Kailey!" Eddy said. "You've got this."

Raven rubbed her swelling cheek where Kailey had jabbed. A bruise was forming. The intensity of Raven's glare had not lessened. In fact, she looked angrier, hungrier, but she had also been hurt.

People in the crowd started booing due to the lack of either woman attempting to strike the other. The jeers turned to angry shouts.

Kailey took a quick step in, bobbed her head forward with a fake right punch. Raven flinched and moved to dodge the strike only to be hit hard with a solid left. She grunted and winced from the pain, which only made her even madder.

Raven growled, lowered herself, and rushed forward at Kailey. Before Kailey could move, Raven wrapped her arms around Kailey's thighs, lifted her into the air, and slammed Kailey onto the mat.

The world spun and dimmed for several moments as Kailey attempted to maintain consciousness. Pain rattled throughout her body. Raven straddled Kailey, grabbed her wrists, and pinned her arms over Kailey's head.

Raven leaned close to Kailey's ear and whispered, "Hey, sweetie. Almost like old times, isn't it? Except I'm not *playing* this time. I'm going to hurt you real bad, then I'm going to kill you."

~

Perplexed, Brady looked at Cassie. "Is that Raven?"

Cassie nodded. "I didn't know she was a fighter, too."

"No. She's not. Which means—"

"She's here to kill Kailey," Cassie said.

"Dammit!" Brady glanced to find a quick way to get to the cage but the hall was jammed full of people in both directions. "We've got to get out there."

Cassie pressed her hands against the glass. Her eyes looked on in desperation.

~

Kailey struggled to free her wrists from Raven's grip, but she couldn't loosen Raven's hold. Raven pressed her knees firmly against Kailey's sides.

Kailey winced.

"I thought you liked pain," Raven said. "Wasn't that what you told Brady this morning?"

Kailey gasped and her eyes widened.

Raven nodded. "Yes, I watched the entire sickening display."

"I never took you for voyeurism. You must have enjoyed it if you watched that long." Kailey tightened her jaw and rolled slightly to the left, trying to dislodge Raven.

"When I'm done killing you, Brady's next."

Kailey brought up her right leg and placed her ankle against Raven's throat. A second later her left leg came up and she locked her ankle atop the other. She flexed her legs and then shoved with everything she had, prying Raven off. Kailey's muscled legs were her greatest strength. Once she got Raven off of her, she thrust downward, slamming Raven's back onto the mat.

Raven turned to roll, but Kailey grabbed Raven's right foot and twisted.

"Bitch!" Raven muffled through the mouthpiece.

Kailey thought for a moment that she might actually get the upper hand. She held fast to Raven's foot, twisting the ankle at a painful angle. Raven turned and pivoted her body in the direction her ankle was bent, relieving the pressure. As she rolled, she swung her left foot and struck Kailey in the face. Kailey immediately let go of Raven and rolled around to stand.

A second later both women faced one another. Anger and resentment possessed their facial features like bitter ex-lovers, which they had almost been. Kailey lost her fear of Raven, and even though Raven was stronger, Kailey understood that her years of martial arts training favored her better.

Kailey stood, staring at Raven, and her mind attempted to recall the good times she had had with her former friend, but no good memories surfaced. All of Raven's facial features she had once found attractive now repulsed her. The ugliness that had dwelt deep inside of Raven had tarnished her exterior. No amount of makeup could ever make Raven appear beautiful to Kailey again. The monster had broken free of its cage and once revealed, it had no hope of ever concealing itself. It was exposed for the entire world to see.

Kailey moved side to side, took a quick step in, and connected a sharp left, followed by a right, both striking Raven in the face. Raven brought up her hands to shield her face, so Kailey rapidly jabbed a dozen solid hits into Raven's gut.

"That's it, Kailey!" Eddy said. "Work the body!"

Kailey struck another hard right below Raven's ribcage. Something snapped. Her ribs? Raven gasped. Kailey hit a left, right, left. Raven backed away, but Kailey pursued, not letting up, hoping to keep striking until she weakened Raven's resolve. Getting an opponent to retreat was generally a favorable sign, so the best option then was to keep hitting until Raven tapped out or lost consciousness.

Pain creased Raven's face. Her anger seemed to be lessening. Raven backed into a corner of the cage, and Kailey lowered her stance and continued striking punches to the gut. Raven groaned from each jab but was unable to block the punches or return jabs.

Kailey grinned. *I've got you now, Raven.*

She expected Raven to drop to her knees any second. But what she had hoped to occur didn't.

Once the pain continued to escalate, Raven desperately thrust both fists straightforward and struck Kailey in the forehead. The impact staggered her. Kailey stumbled backwards, waving her arms and spiraling, trying to maintain balance.

Raven didn't hesitate. She swung a solid right to Kailey's jaw. Kailey stepped backwards and zigzagged, her feet attempting to steady her. Raven struck another punch to the face, sending Kailey facedown to the mat. She caught herself with her elbows. Again the world spun. She blinked and shook her head. Before she could move or attempt to push herself to her feet, Raven grabbed her left shoulder and flung Kailey over onto her back.

Through blurred vision, Kailey tried to pinpoint exactly where Raven was. Raven swung another vicious blow to the top of Kailey's head. Kailey let the back of her head fall against the mat. She placed both hands up in a pleading waving gesture, trying to get Raven to stop. Like Kailey had expected before the fight began, Raven held no compassion, no mercy. Neither resided inside the vampire.

Raven straddled Kailey.

Kailey could hardly open her eyes. Through narrowed slits she watched a blurred image of Raven beaming an evil smile.

"It's time," came Flora's whisper. *Time for you to die.*

Raven growled and struck Kailey in the face, again and again. Kailey's arms fell to her sides. Her fight was over. She didn't have enough strength to defend against any of the blows.

"Enough," the referee said.

Kailey barely felt the massive man trying to shove Raven off. Raven turned to face him with a wicked expression.

"What the f—"

Raven tossed the massive referee with the simple fling of her right hand. He crashed against the cage wall.

"Please, Raven," Kailey whispered, seeing Raven pull back a tight right fist to prepare for a hammer punch. She knew once Raven struck this time, she was dead. The rage that controlled Raven indicated death was coming. Raven's tongue pushed out her mouthpiece, and she bared fangs.

Before she could strike, Raven was suddenly lifted into the air and slammed to the mat with such force the entire cage swayed back and forth. The floor buckled. Some members of the audience shrieked. Others cheered.

A second before Kailey lost consciousness, she noticed the long succubus tail wrap around Raven's neck and squeeze.

"Let's play fair, shall we?" Cassie said in a low growl, bearing her sharp demon teeth.

~

Cassie reached down and wrapped her demon hand around Raven's throat. The long fingernails pressed into the vampire's flesh. She lifted Raven off the mat and held her at least one foot in the air.

Raven gnashed her teeth, revealing her fangs to the audience. People cheered and applauded, shouting, 'Good show!' and apparently too naïve to realize these weren't actors but actual monsters.

Cassie glanced over her shoulder at the cheering mob and shook her head. "Seriously?"

Raven used both hands and attempted to break Cassie's hold, but she couldn't. Cassie tightened her grip, causing Raven to choke. Her face reddened, quickly turning purple. Regardless of myths and legends, vampires needed to breathe, too. Total lack of oxygen might not kill them, but it could weaken them enough to make them vulnerable to an enemy.

Cassie looped her long tail and using the flat end, she smacked Raven's face repeatedly, which was more irritating than inflicting actual harm.

"How's it feel to pick on someone with similar strength? I like to even up the odds." Cassie hurled Raven across the cage against one of the metal pole supports. The pole bent slightly.

Raven dropped to the floor on her knees. Her hands formed tight fists. Her face contorted. Her eyes went fully black. She came at Cassie with everything she had and in full rage.

"Really?" Cassie said, vanishing.

Raven ran headlong into another metal pole and slumped to the floor. Cassie reappeared behind Raven, grabbed the vampire by the back of the hair, and yanked her to her feet.

The audience was going wild, hooting and whistling.

"It's a shame I don't have a stake," Cassie said in a whisper. Her left hand formed long six-inch razored claws. "But decapitation works just as well."

Cassie drew back her hand but before she severed Raven's head from her shoulders, the side of the cage buckled. The chain linked fence split in half and a second later, Raven was gone in a blur. The harsh echo of laughter could have only come from one person.

Flora.

Cassie hurried to Kailey's limp body, hefted her into her arms, and carefully squeezed through the opened cage wall. People clapped. A few asked for Cassie's autograph but she ignored them. She worried that Kailey needed to get to a medic soon or Kailey could possibly die.

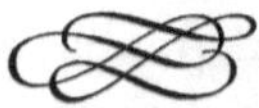

$\mathcal{B}$rady met Cassie outside the cage.

"Clear a path, people," Brady said. "She needs medical attention."

"There's an ambulance," Cassie said, nodding her head.

"With this crowd, the paramedics will have a hell of a time getting out of this parking lot. I can get her to the hospital faster in my car. I can carry her if you'd like?"

Cassie shook her head. "No, she's light. You open up a path so I can get her to the car."

Kailey's face was swelling. Bruises were forming around her eyes. Blood caked around her nostrils and a slight trickle of crimson flowed from the side of her mouth. Cassie held Kailey close but ensured her head was kept upright. Kailey was so limp that had she not been breathing, Cassie would have thought her dead.

People in the crowd were still applauding. "Incredible. Who'd have thought Nocturnal Trinity would play a role in this cage fight?"

"Those costumes look so real," another remarked. "How'd they get her to vanish and reappear like that?"

"Hidden trap doors?"

"The way the vampire disappeared at the end. That *wasn't* a trap door."

"Damn that demon is hot. Did you see her incredible body? She could wrap that tail around me anytime."

"The vampire teeth were a nice touch. Never expected that."

"Yeah, but that demon's body. Damn … Look at her ass. I'd really like to—"

Cassie hurried behind Brady. "Look, I'm sorry."

"For what?"

"Going full demon."

"You had no choice. A second later and Kailey would have been dead."

"I know, but this is going to hit the papers in the morning."

Brady looked over his shoulder and grinned. "Listen to the crowd. They believe this was all staged with props and illusions, so you're good. If anything, Nocturnal Trinity will gain free publicity from this, as well as the gym."

Eddy caught up to them after they had reached the sidewalk that ran along the street. "Is Kailey okay? Where are you taking her?"

Brady said, "She's banged up pretty badly. We're going to get her to the hospital."

Eddy stepped around Cassie and looked at Kailey. "I feel so horrible about this."

"It's not your fault," Brady replied.

"In a way, maybe it is."

Cassie frowned. "Why do you say that?"

Eddy sighed. "Kailey was shaken up before she entered the cage. Something was bothering her. I could tell that her mind wasn't into the fight. I tried to talk her out of going into the cage, but she said that she could handle it."

"Against a normal fighter, she could have," Cassie said, looking at Brady.

His eyes darkened in anger.

"What do you mean?" Eddy said.

Cassie shook her head. "Nothing. I think maybe the other girl should be tested for steroids or something."

"Really?" Eddy looked stunned. "You think—"

Brady increased his pace and Cassie kept up. "Look, we really need to get her to the hospital."

"I know," Eddy said. She looked at Cassie. "Nice costume, by the way."

Cassie forced a smile. "Thanks."

"You work at Nocturnal Trinity? Are you one of the dancers?"

Brady opened the rear door of his patrol car.

"I work there," Cassie replied. "On occasion."

"Jim, the owner of the gym, never told me that he had arranged a show with the nightclub."

Cassie lowered Kailey onto the backseat. "Last minute thing."

Eddy looked confused. "If that's so, why'd this other girl try to kill Kailey because I can see that Kailey's injuries are severe? These contusions are bad. She's not faking."

Cassie shut the car door and rested her hands on her hips. "That's a question you need to ask the little bitch Kailey was fighting."

Eddy raised her hands to her temples. Her brow furrowed from intense remorse. In contrast to her muscled physique, she was near tears. "It was just supposed to be sparring matches. No one was supposed to fight full force."

Brady opened the driver side door and got in. Cassie opened the passenger side. She faced Eddy. "In the future, if you plan another one of these *events*, I'd demand drug tests so something like this doesn't happen."

"You really think that girl was doped?"

"She never stopped fighting even after I intervened."

Eddy nodded. "Yeah, you threw her against those poles pretty hard. But steroids don't prevent pain. She still should have been knocked unconscious."

"PCP," Brady said, starting the car. "Sorry, gotta go."

Eddy's mouth dropped open.

Cassie shut the door.

Brady flipped on the flashing lights and siren and sped away from the curb. "Too many questions..."

Cassie nodded. "Told you."

"Not anything we can do about it now. But the press will most likely attribute it to stage acting, if Flora has anything to do with it."

Cassie shed her demon form and wore a tight red skirt with a zipper that ran down the right side. Her top was a lighter shade of red with a deep V-neck. "Are you going to call Forrest?"

"Can't," Brady replied.

"Why not?"

Brady chuckled. "The man doesn't own a cellphone, nor does ever he intend to."

"How are people supposed to get in touch with him?"

Brady shrugged. "No idea. I don't know how old he is, but he dresses like someone from the Old West. The only new things that interest him are the latest weapon innovations but only those he can use to kill vampires."

"It's all he lives for, isn't it?"

"I suppose so."

"I wish he'd have been at the gym."

"So do I, Cassie. So do I. But then, there'd be a lot more questions people would have."

Cassie gave a side nod toward the backseat. "Do you think this will convince Micah to withdraw from the Circle of Unity at Nocturnal Trinity?"

"I hope it opens his eyes. Had Raven simply acted on her own, it would be a completely different situation, but Flora had both of her hands in this. It was a blatant public attack, and since she was bold enough to do this, she has no fear of Micah or the other new members within the Circle of Unity."

Brady turned off the siren and pulled the car beneath the Emergency Room awning with the lights still flashing. Nurses and EMTs rushed to the car, carefully taking Kailey from the backseat and placing her upon a gurney.

Cassie glanced at Brady. "I'll stay with her while you park the car."

He nodded. "It shouldn't take me but a few minutes, and I'll be back."

Brady pulled away from the Emergency Room doors and found a spot in the adjacent parking lot. He put the car into park and gripped the steering wheel tightly. He fumed. A quick glance into the rearview mirror caused him to take a deep breath, trying to calm down. His eyes were dark encircled with gold. His anger was seeking to bring his wolf to the surface. As much as he wanted to release his inner rage, he couldn't. Not here. Not now.

He took his cellphone and scrolled through his contact list until he found Micah's number. He tapped it twice and the phone rang.

"Brady?" Micah said upon answering. "I thought you were on duty tonight."

"I am," Brady replied in a stern voice.

"Something's wrong. I sense it in your voice. What happened?"

"Flora and Raven." Brady explained a quick rundown of what had happened at the gym and that Kailey was in the ER.

"Damn," Micah said, softly. His voice was filled with remorse. "They acted a lot quicker than I had expected."

"I know. I didn't expect an attack so soon, and definitely not in public."

"I had hoped to talk to Flora before Raven did anything else, but she still hasn't come to the nightclub. I honestly didn't think Flora had anything to do with Raven's threat."

Brady's jaw tightened. "I guess now you know differently."

"Yeah, I'm sorry."

"Micah, I'll be honest and upfront with you. I don't think she or her siblings have any desire to return to Nocturnal Trinity. Not until they have buried you and the new witches."

"That's an extreme assumption."

"Are you so blind that you cannot see the obvious?"

Micah became quiet.

"Only one member of our pack honors your decision to stay in the Circle of Unity and that's Ashley. I'll always respect you as our leader, but this isn't a battle you can win by yourself. You cannot force change upon those who don't want it. Flora's public display tonight proves that she is willing to do whatever it takes to destroy us."

"I understand the point you're trying to make—"

"Do you?"

"Brady, I know this is personal for you."

"No, it's more than that, Micah. Flora might have gone for the weakest person first, or perhaps she did it to initiate Raven by introducing the power a new vampire has. I don't know. But what I do know is that your life is in grave danger if you continue to reside at Nocturnal Trinity. You were never a guest as all the previous council members were. You invaded, helped kill Nicodemus, and then forced them to bring you into their alliance. There's *no* unity in the council."

"They killed my wife, Brady. Don't forget that."

"All the more reason you should get out."

"I had hoped by joining them we could all let go of the past."

"With normal people, that's a noble gesture. But not with heartless vampires."

Micah sighed into the phone. "You've listened to Forrest for too long."

"I happen to believe he's right."

"You're one among many. But that's your choice. I harbor no grudges toward you or any of the others who have walked away."

"Have you seen Forrest?"

"Not since our meeting when he stormed out with Jacob. Why?"

"After Raven's attack, I'd like to speak to him ASAP."

"If I see him, I'll give him the message."

"Thanks. But consider something, okay?" Brady said.

"What?"

"Flora is now willing to attempt murder out in the open. We had news reporters and cameras, not to mention all of the audience were using their cellphones to record the fight. She's not worried about revealing her presence."

"You're right," Micah replied. His voice echoed inner defeat and loneliness, not the confidence of a leader heading into battle. "That's not good. I'd have never expected her to let others see her. That's not her typical behavior."

"As fast as she ran, no one actually physically saw her."

"That's good."

"You don't understand. She's on digital film, which means someone can slow down the footage and discover who she is. Right now, most of the onlookers thought it was a great staged act, but people who are more curious, like reporters, will slow it down to find the truth. And like a lot of things in social media, it will go viral, bringing us even more unwanted attention."

"If she's exposed herself as to what she is, her siblings will reign her back in."

"I don't think they will."

"Why not?"

"Because they are like her, and I believe they want a bloodbath."

"It contradicts everything they've accomplished with Nocturnal Trinity."

"Perhaps, Micah, but they might have decided to break their ties from the Circle of Unity. They've run the establishment for what? Over a century?"

"At least."

"None of us outside their original circle even know what city officials are vampires under their control or those who are sympathizers for the undead."

"We should call the pack together to discuss this," Micah said.

"It's doubtful you'll get any wolves to enter Nocturnal Trinity."

"It doesn't need to be here. Perhaps at my estate?"

"That's not a bad idea, and about your estate … I wanted to ask a favor."

"What is it, Brady? You need to stay there for a while?"

"I hate to ask but since Raven entered our apartment—"

Micah's voice was soft and solemn. "Say no more. My home is always your home and to the others who are loyal to the pack. Key's under the heavy flowerpot at the back door. Only someone with the strength of a werewolf or an immortal could move the pot. But you're welcome to stay there. But as you know, Raven has been to my estate. She knows where I live."

"I realize that, Micah, but I'm hoping the large body of water will be a deterrent. She and Skye had mentioned how the bay was a magic buffer, so if Raven used magic to get into my apartment, then maybe the water will make it more difficult for her to get there."

"One can hope. Make yourselves at home and stay safe."

"I appreciate it. Stay alert, Micah. You have no real safety residing in the nightclub. I have an uneasy feeling about what Flora and Raven might attempt next."

"I'll inform Jaclyn and keep a watchful eye."

"Take care," Brady said, ending the call.

Brady got out of the car and for the first time in a long while he felt fear. Not for himself, but for Kailey. Because until her, he had never known true love and couldn't stand the thought of losing her. He sprinted to the hospital. He needed to see Kailey. He needed to know she was okay.

CHAPTER 17

Brady entered through the ER sliding glass doors and walked to the reception desk. Cassie stood near the cushioned chairs with her arms crossed. She wasn't crying, but she looked like she might burst into tears at any moment. Brady crossed the room to stand beside her.

"They won't let me go back there," Cassie said. "I even told them I was family."

"Probably won't let any of us go since she's not conscious."

"From a legal standpoint, I'm the only family she has left, just not blood related, of course." She offered a wry smile. "And I can't … handle it, if something happens to her, too."

Brady placed his hand on Cassie's shoulder. "It's going to be okay."

Cassie looked into his eyes with a sad helplessness. Her captivating eyes were the most beautiful he'd ever seen. He'd never peered directly into them. At least he didn't remember doing so. The depth of the colors, especially the specks of crimson, mesmerized him. For a few moments, he lost the ability to speak. He became lightheaded. His eyes left hers and ventured to the cute curves of her narrow lips. The memory of when she had seduced him into one of the most passionate kisses he'd ever had flooded into his mind. He found himself wanting to jerk her body hard against his and kiss her deeply while his hands explored the contours of her perfect body.

A sweet fragrance permeated around her, irresistible, and like an essential longing need, he suddenly wanted her. No, he craved her like an addict needed a fix. His eyes roamed to the deep V-cut of her shirt. With her arms crossed beneath her breasts, slightly pushing them up, they looked even larger. Her ample breasts rose firmly as she took a breath … He became instantly hard.

Brady yanked his hand off her shoulder and quickly turned away. He placed a hand over his eyes, took in a deep gulp of air, and shook his head. *Oh God, what the hell just came over me?*

"You okay?" Cassie asked, stepping closer.

He took a deep breath and then cleared his throat. He shoved his fists into his loose pockets to make his erection less noticeable. "I'm fine."

"I hope they tell us something about Kailey soon."

"If it seems like we're going to get the runaround, I'll insist that I see her or her doctor. I won't tell them I'm her boyfriend. I'll tell them I need to get more information about what happened for my report. I shouldn't get any arguments about that."

"It's a shame you can't arrest them," Cassie said.

"Oh, I have grounds to arrest them but it would be hard to get the charges to stick."

"For what?"

"Attempted murder. Had you not knocked Raven off of Kailey, that last punch would have killed her."

Cassie nodded. "I know."

"Of course, taking two vampires into custody would be impossible should they decide to resist, and I'm quite certain they would."

"No doubts about that," Cassie said. She plopped down onto the corner cushioned chair, leaned forward, which caused her top to droop and exposed her breasts even more. Brady took a sharp breath and looked away. "But it'd be best to have Forrest stake both of them. Less hassle and little if any evidence left behind."

Brady nodded. "I called Micah. He's not seen Forrest since our meeting. But after the meeting, Forrest accompanied me to slay a vampire."

"Really?" Cassie asked.

Brady nodded. "I took him back to the nightclub."

"And Micah hasn't seen him?"

"That's what he said. Of course, with Micah trying to get everything set up for the werewolf faction, he might not be leaving his office too often."

A nurse stepped into the waiting room. "Anyone here with Kailey Yates?"

Cassie stood. "We are."

"She's awake and has asked for the two of you to come back."

Cassie glanced at Brady. "Thank goodness."

The nurse yanked the thin curtain around to form a wall for privacy, if such a thin cloth could actually succeed in doing so. It definitely blocked others from seeing the individuals inside, but it did nothing to stop voices from being heard on the other side. Not even whispers remained private should someone seek to eavesdrop. Of course, with Flora and Raven's telepathic abilities, solid brick walls offered little hindrance, either.

Kailey winced, adjusting the pillow behind her back to sit upright. "How long was I out?"

"I'd say a half hour at the most," Brady replied.

"It seemed longer," Cassie said, sitting on the edge of the bed. She placed a tender hand to Kailey's cheek. "I was so worried about you. She did a number on you. You'll have some nasty bruises."

"I'm surprised I'm still alive," Kailey said.

"Oh, she intended to kill you," Brady said. "Had Cassie not transported into the cage and attacked Raven, she'd have killed you."

"I know," Kailey replied. "Flora was there."

Brady frowned. "You saw her?"

"No. She whispered her death threat before I entered the cage. She told me I was going to die."

"She almost succeeded," Brady said.

Cassie smiled at Kailey with relief. "Raven's going to have some nasty marks on her, too."

"Really?"

Cassie nodded. "Oh, I kicked her ass. I was a second from cutting off her head except Flora pulled Raven to safety and fled."

"Thanks," Kailey said. She placed her hands to her temples and closed her eyes tightly. "My head is splitting."

"Have they not given you anything for pain?"

"Not yet. They're going to do a CT scan to check for bleeding since they insist I have a concussion."

Brady took Kailey's hand into his. "I'm trying to find Forrest. The sooner we get him to slay them, the safer we're all going to be."

"I wish I had listened to him to start with," Kailey said. "About Raven and Flora."

Brady sighed. "Sometimes it takes seeing for oneself before you can accept the advice from others. I believe Micah is eventually going to feel the same way about the Circle of Unity, provided he doesn't die before realizing the truth."

The nurse on the other side of the curtain said, "You can't come back here."

"Brady! Where are you?" a deep voice bellowed.

Brady walked to the curtain and slid it aside. "In here, Jacob."

"I must insist he waits in the waiting room," the nurse said. "It's already crowded enough."

"We'll be fine, ma'am," Brady said, allowing Jacob to step inside while Brady slid the curtain closed.

Brady and Jacob clutched right hands together and leaned in for a fierce bro-hug. "I came as soon as I heard, Brady. How you doing, Kailey?"

"It hurts worse than it looks, I'm afraid," she replied.

"Damn. It must be pretty severe then. We're going to get that little bitch," Jacob said. "And Flora, too."

"The bigger bitch?" Kailey asked with a wide smile.

"I suppose Micah called and informed you of the situation?" Brady asked.

Jacob nodded. His grim expression tightened. "Yeah. I almost didn't answer when I noticed it was his number. I'm still quite pissed at him, but I'm glad I answered."

"Me, too," Brady said.

"And me." Kailey forced a smile.

"You come alone?" Brady asked.

"No, Barry's in the waiting room." Jacob scratched the thick bristly evening shade covering his cheeks. He studied Kailey for several moments. His anger was obvious in his gestures and eyes, almost like it never faded. He seemed to have a score that he wanted settled, but she didn't think he'd ever get the satisfaction he longed for. Since vampires had killed his brother, she doubted Jacob would ever find peace. "These damned vampires … there's no way we can ever peacefully coexist with them. Micah has to realize that. Hell, it's part of the reason he cast the spell on us to prevent our wolf transformation, remember? Because he wanted us to work together as a pack and not have one of us attempt to strike solo."

Brady nodded. "I just can't figure Micah out. I get wanting to live peaceably, but there's no possible way to achieve such a goal when the people you're seeking peace with want you dead."

"He seems blinded to the dangers."

Cassie stood and placed her hands on her hips. "Before Nicodemus' death, there were few who could be trusted within that alliance. Their so-called Unity always seemed forced."

"When they played their prank on me," Kailey said, "they were at one another's throat. They couldn't even pretend to be cordial. The division was obvious."

Brady sighed. "It all fell apart in the end. Flora turned on her brother. One of the reasons two of the witches died and Eva was banished was because of their secret participations in human sacrifices."

Jacob's head jerked as he looked at Brady with a frown. "They really performed human sacrifices?"

Cassie nodded. "Yes. They did deplorable things."

"And Micah still wants to keep the Unity together?" He shook his head and his jaw tightened.

"But Jaclyn didn't," Kailey said. "She wanted it dissembled forever."

"Then why would she agree to Micah's decision?" Jacob asked.

Brady shrugged. "It's something we need to sit down and discuss with him as a pack."

"He's not going listen," Jacob said. "Hell, he wouldn't listen to our arguments this morning. At the most, he'll pretend to take our suggestions to heart, but you know he's not changing his mind."

"Eventually he will need to," Brady replied. "He wants the pack to meet with him."

"Does he?" Jacob said with a near snarl.

"I think this evening's situation might have given him better insight to understand what Forrest had tried to explain earlier today. The vampires have their own self-interest at heart."

Cassie said, "I agree. Once Flora is slain, the remaining four vampires will seek revenge, perhaps even go to war against all the humans in Seattle."

"Flora's death won't be taken easily," Brady said. "Even if they resent her right now, her brothers and sisters will seek to avenge her death."

"Then we kill all of them," Jacob said in a low growl.

"I imagine that's what Forrest plans to do."

"I think he came to Seattle for more than assisting Micah's revenge," Kailey said.

Brady nodded. "I had that feeling myself."

"Well, he hasn't left the city yet," Kailey said. "And if he slays the original founders, the Circle of Unity is gone forever."

"I won't weep over it," Jacob said with a crude smile.

"None of us will," Cassie said.

"Something I just thought of," Brady said, looking at Cassie. "None of the demons aided Micah in killing Nicodemus. Why is that?"

Kailey frowned. "You're right. That is odd. Jinn has been the only founding demon I've ever met."

Cassie became visibly uncomfortable. "Jinn's not one of the original founders."

"He isn't?" Brady asked.

Cassie shook her head. "No. And humans who frequent the club have never gotten to see the other five demons. It's rare they make their presence known or even come to the nightclub."

"Why?" Kailey asked.

Cassie licked her lips. "You've heard the saying about people being 'scared to death?'"

"Sure," Brady said.

"Few humans could actually survive seeing them. Lesser demons like myself, we hide or vanish whenever we sense their presences. They're hideous monstrosities. If they chose, they could exterminate the remaining five founding vampires without a second thought. The vampires actually do fear them."

"Then why don't these demons kill the vampires?" Kailey asked.

Cassie sat down on the edge of the bed again. Her nervousness hadn't faded. "Out of loyalty."

"To whom?" Brady asked.

"The vampires and witches who brought them out of the abyss and through the portal. Contrary to what a lot of religious people would have you believe, most demons keep their word. When they swear an oath, they stand behind it. Not all do, but most. Especially in this case, since they had been liberated from the abyss. Breaking the oath meant returning to the abyss where no demon ever wishes to be sent."

"But the portal was destroyed," Kailey said, rubbing her temples.

"Yes, it was."

"Then what do they have left to fear?" Brady asked.

"Not much," Cassie said. "I suppose they're content with whatever rewards they receive from Nocturnal Trinity."

"Invisible partners," Jacob said.

Cassie smiled. "You could say that. Demons can be as greedy as humans. Greedier in some situations. Even if they have no need to spend their earnings, they revel in knowing how great their wealth is."

Jacob turned and pulled the curtain slightly aside. He looked restless. "Brady, before I go, I need to know what our plans are?"

Brady crossed his arms. "Micah has given me permission to use his house on Bainbridge Island until Raven and Flora are slain since Raven has already intruded at the apartment. So, that means all of us could stay there. We're stronger as a pack than we are scattered across the city. Besides, it would be a good location where we can defend ourselves. It will also make it easier to meet with Micah whenever he—"

"Pulls his head out of his ass?" Jacob said with a stern brow.

"I wasn't going to be so poetic," Brady replied, trying to hold back his slight grin.

Kailey straightened on the bed and groaned. "The water of the bay should act like a good buffer to protect us from Raven's spells. But someone needs to check on Luna and Blaze. They insist on staying at Micah's magic shop, but I worry that they're not safe there."

"I can go get them," Jacob said.

"I wish Micah would open his eyes to what's going on," Brady said. "This isn't a good time for our pack to be divided."

"We aren't divided," Jacob replied. "He's the one who has chosen to remain apart from us."

"He's still our leader."

Jacob frowned and shook his head. His jaw tightened and he showed his teeth. The veins in his thick arms swelled. "No. Micah made a major decision without consulting us, which was a decision we should have held a vote on. Each of us should have been allowed to choose."

"We have chosen," Brady said.

"Yeah, *afterwards*. A true leader doesn't dictate such a radical decision over everyone else. When he chose to become a part of the Circle of Unity is the day he no longer led our pack."

Brady nodded. "Actually, you're right. I have to agree. We should have been included in that decision. Sadly, I fear Micah has set himself up for a quick assassination."

"Maybe so, but it was his choice. It's hard for us to defend him when we're not near him. I think it's time we pick ourselves a new pack leader," Jacob said.

"Let's take care of our current problems, first. Perhaps once we're all safe on the island, we can discuss it, okay?"

"Sure. Thanks for keeping it on the table. Micah has always shot down any idea he didn't agree on without given any consideration."

"I'm not Micah."

Jacob laughed in a deep growl and grinned. "That's already to your advantage."

"Jacob, if you can go alert Luna and Blaze, Cassie and I will remain here with Kailey. After her CT scan, we'll know if we need to cross to the island."

"You got it, brother," Jacob said.

"Be careful," Brady said. "We don't know who all is on their kill list."

"I will."

CHAPTER 18

Forrest sat on an old metal bench in the underground tunnel near the corroded railroad tracks long buried by time. Complete darkness surrounded him. He held an old pair of goggles in his hand and ran his thumbs along the frames. The brass rims that surrounded the lenses were scuffed with little dents from the many times he had used them while combating vampires in dark lairs or caves. He was surprised that the night-vision goggles were still usable after a hundred and twenty years.

Two sets of glowing eyes moved toward him, bobbing slightly to the left and right as his company approached. He held one lens over his right eye, which lit up the tunnel where these two walked. Ian and Gunner. At Forrest's request, they had been scouring the long tunnel and any side shafts that joined it for most of the day.

Forrest turned his attention toward them. "Any luck, Ian?"

"No, like I told you, she's not down here," Ian said, shaking his head. "No signs of any recent activity either."

"Gunner?"

"No, Forrest. Sorry. What Ian said. She's not here."

"No vamps?" Forrest asked.

"No," the brothers replied in unison.

"Damn," Forrest said through gritted teeth.

"Did you really expect after all these years to find her?" Ian asked.

"I had hoped," Forrest said in a slight whisper.

Ian sat on the bench beside Forrest. "She wasn't here a hundred years ago when we scoured the area. Why do you think she'd be here now?"

"I should've never left then until we found her," Forrest said softly.

"Then we'd have wandered for no telling how long, just wasting our time."

"Ian!" Gunner said. "No way to think."

"It's *always* the way I think."

"Then think inside your stupid head and bite your cynical tongue," Gunner said.

"Hope is a waste of time," Ian replied.

"I warn you no more, brother. Be nice. Can't you see how this troubles Forrest? Or do you not care about that either?"

Ian grumbled beneath his breath.

"Settle down you two," Forrest said. "Inside I've always felt there was more I should have done. I should have never let her leave without me."

"We know why *you're* an immortal, Forrest," Ian said. "But what makes you believe that she might be one?"

"She killed one of the main demons. A behemoth. Surely, she gained something in return."

"An early death," Ian said.

"Ian!" Gunner slugged him. "You don't know that!"

Ian growled and turned with his hands balled into fists. "Don't do that again."

"Sadly, Gunner, your brother is probably right." Forrest sighed, forming a soft fist around the goggles and pressing them against his chest. The goggles had been her gift to him before she departed. "I failed her. Penelope is dead because of me, and so is my father."

Gunner placed his hand upon Forrest's shoulder. "Don't think that way."

"How can I not? It's the truth. I made the wrong decision. Had I gone with Penelope to Seattle right after she had gotten the news of the Great Fire, I could have helped her. I should have stayed at her side. She might still be alive and my father would have lived a longer life."

"Or you'd have all died," Ian said.

"That's also a possibility," Forrest replied, nodding. "But a fate I might have accepted more readily."

"Forrest, you don't mean that, do you?" Gunner asked in a strained voice.

Forrest knew his friend was in tears, as the brothers had grown to depend upon him as the cornerstone of their *family*. Forrest wasn't blood related to them, but the trio had traveled the world together for so long, they regarded themselves as kin.

Forrest sighed. "I've carried this burden for a long time."

"As have we," Gunner replied. "Your pain is my pain. You're like the brother I never had."

"Hey!" Ian said. "I *am* your real brother."

Gunner turned toward Ian with a scrunched face, half showing his crooked teeth. "Yes, but *you* always dwell on negative thoughts and are filled with spite and meanness."

"I've protected you far longer than Forrest has. I looked out for you when the others picked on you. Remember?"

"I know. But Forrest … he's … well he's more like the *father* I never had."

"*We've* never had," Ian whispered, more to himself than into their conversation.

Gunner's words touched Forrest deeply. For the otter-shifter to view him as a father figure stirred emotions he'd never experienced before. It was nice for someone to look up to him in the manner that Gunner did. Gunner was a slow thinker. Even after knowing one another for over a century, Gunner still thought and acted like a child in many ways. Mentally, he had never matured any further. Throughout it all, Forrest was like Ian, and they had both kept watchful eyes over Gunner to keep him safe from the harshness of most societies and from making poor judgment decisions. "You're a good friend, Gunner. You saved my life right after my father was killed, and I've never forgotten it. That day changed my life."

"It changed us all," Ian said softly. He sniffled.

"Are you crying?" Gunner asked.

"No!" Ian walked away from them and a few yards down the abandoned tracks.

"He is, isn't he?" Gunner whispered to Forrest.

"Shhh!" Forrest shook his head. "Don't embarrass him."

Ian was bitter about a lot of things. Forrest had learned that long ago. Ian and Gunner's parents had abandoned them, leaving them as orphans before they had even become teenagers. The brothers had been left behind after their first transformation from human to shifter. How they had become what they were remained a mystery. Ian never knew, and he didn't know if their parents were shifters of a different species or not. Probably not. Otherwise, why would parents abandon two young boys during one of the harshest times in history?

During all the time the trio had traveled together, Ian had never shed a single tear, at least none in their presence. He hid behind his pessimistic nature. It was his defense system to prevent himself from suffering any more pain or ridicule. Although shapeshifters, in human form they were cursed with the prominent anatomy features of their beasts. Their teeth were overly large, twisted, and dark yellow. Regardless of what they had tried to remedy the deformity, nothing had worked. They had gone to dental surgeons who removed their teeth and replaced them with veneered implants to give them perfect smiles. But after the next time they transformed and returned to human form, the twisted yellow teeth had somehow replaced the veneers.

Needless to say, the brothers spent little time in public during the daylight hours. Ian despised his handicap far worse than Gunner, and that was another reason for Ian's bitter hostility and dim outlook on his prolonged life. He couldn't have the freedom to explore cities during the daylight hours.

While Forrest had often thought himself an outcast, he knew his existence was much easier than Ian and Gunner's. At least Forrest blended in with other humans. True, his massive size caught people's attention and perhaps made most wary, but Forrest didn't have any disfigurations that alarmed others or caused them to immediately shun him based upon his visage. He often felt guilty for causing the brothers to live longer lives because they had always hid in the shadows or came out during the dead of night when most people couldn't see them. And yet, at the same time, he couldn't imagine how lonely his life would become without their companionship. They had never begrudged their longevity, and were family.

Most shape-shifters possessed greater longevity than mortals and some were actually immortal. Others, like Ian and Gunner, lived normal lifespans but for some reason, the brothers had stopped aging physically after they chose to journey alongside Forrest. In fact, they had regenerated, looking younger than when they had nursed found Forrest near death and nursed him back to health.

Forrest couldn't explain why they had undergone such a transition. His best estimation was that they had become recipients of his rejuvenation. In appearance, Forrest had never looked older than his thirties, and he had discovered each time he slayed a vampire, years had been somehow added to his life, preventing him from physically aging. He had few wrinkles except those around the edges of his eyes, as a result of traveling during the daylight when the sun was harsh and overbearing. Because he favored the darkness, his eyes were overly sensitive to sunlight, causing him to squint whenever he ventured outdoors during the day.

Forrest often struggled about whether his added longevity was a blessing or a curse, but a gypsy witch had once explained the phenomenon to him and she deemed it a great blessing. Forrest never pictured it as such. With his mind forced to dwell upon the misfortunes of times past, nothing was closer to being a curse than the continued agony that gripped his soul. His heart ached for Penelope and despite all the evidence pointing to her demise, he held to the slightest sliver of hope that she might still be alive.

Forrest opened his Hunter box.

"What's that smell?" Ian said, sniffing the air.

"I brought you some food," Forrest said.

"What did you bring?" Gunner asked, sitting down beside Forrest on the bench.

"Philly steak sandwiches," he replied.

"We're in Seattle," Ian said in a wry tone.

Forrest laughed. "If you don't want one, it means more for me."

Ian snatched the wrapped sandwich from Forrest's hand and pulled it close to his chest, sniffing the top of the moist wrapping paper. "I never said that."

Forrest handed the other one to Gunner.

Gunner shyly and graciously accepted it. "Thank you."

"You're welcome."

While chewing a mouthful, Ian asked, "So we've searched this entire passageway from end to end twice. Now, what do you want us to do?"

"You're certain there was no trace of—"

"No trace of anything. It appears that *we're* the only ones who've explored this tunnel during the past one hundred years," Ian said.

"That's why I thought this would be the best place to search. Just in case they've imprisoned her here."

"We didn't find anything," Ian said before taking another big bite. "Did we, Gunner?"

"No, sorry."

"So Penelope's not here. No vamps. What about demons?" Forrest asked.

"If there's anything down here, Forrest, it never made its presence known. Best I can report, no vamps, no Penelope, no demons, no ghosts, and no ghouls. Certainly no zombies, gargoyles—"

"Okay, Ian," Forrest said. "I get the point. I apologize for my continued line of questions. I greatly appreciate both of you doing this."

"So back to my question," Ian said. "What's next?"

"Finding Flora and Raven."

Gunner hungrily devoured his sandwich.

"And then we leave Seattle?" Ian asked with a hopeful tone.

"Not until all of them are dead," Forrest replied.

"You mean Flora and her brothers and sisters?"

"Every single one of them."

"But you slew their father, Lorcan, for his deceit. Surely his children didn't play a role in your betrayal."

"Flora did. I'm certain Nicodemus aided her and their father. I assume the others did, too, but they're not brave enough to openly do so."

Gunner swallowed his mouthful of food. "But what if they had no hand in it at all?"

"Guilty by blood. Because of them I lost my father and two friends. There's no boundary to vengeance. Lorcan's bloodline will cease to exist. Besides, they're vampires. My duty is to slay them."

Ian sighed. "Won't that be dangerous since Flora already knows you intend to stake her?"

"They've all known it was coming for a long time. And since I'm here, they're in hiding. But they cannot hide from their fate. I will find them."

CHAPTER 19

As the CT table pulled Kailey inside the cylindrical machine, she tried to ignore the thought of being encased inside the large doughnut-shaped contraption while the doctors searched for possible brain hemorrhages and skull fractures. Instead her mind returned to the cage fight with Raven.

She had been apprehensive about the *training* bout, but the last thing she had ever expected was that Raven would be her opponent. Raven had never been more filled with rage than when they had faced one another earlier in the evening.

I can't believe I once loved you, Raven, and that we were almost ... lovers. I doubt that you ever really loved me. You couldn't have. Otherwise, you wouldn't have tried to kill me. No, I know you didn't love me. You wanted to possess me. To own me. You have no idea what true love is. You're a sick, twisted little bitch. I'm so ashamed of myself for never having seen it before.

Tears heated her eyes. She sobbed and her body shook slightly. She rubbed her eyes.

"Please remain still," a doctor said softly through the intercom. "Movement distorts the readings."

"Sorry," she whispered.

She closed her eyes. *I'm sorry about a lot of things in my life, but I'm mostly sorry for having fallen for your lies and deceit. I felt guilty about you becoming a vampire, I truly did and I've blamed myself ... but ... you've been a vampire all along, haven't you? You fed off of my energy, my ambitions, and my life force by pretending to be what you were not. You constantly showered me with flattering words as long as I was what you wanted me to be. But any time I focused my attention toward one of my own goals, my dreams, the real you surfaced, trying to beat me back into your mold for me. Belittling me for not doing what you wanted me to do when you wanted me to do it or exactly the way you wanted it done. I don't think it was an accident that you became a vampire. It has always been your destiny.*

Perhaps that's why Flora took you because she read your mind and noticed your true qualities. You were already good at mind manipulation and twisting my will. Now that you're a vampire with the power to glamour or compel people, you're far too deadly to remain in this world. You certainly aren't welcome in my life.

Are you so jealous of Brady that you needed to invade our privacy as an invisible voyeur? Did you secretly enjoy watching him make love to me? Perhaps that's why you're jealous and filled with spite? You know he and I fit. We're really the ones who are meant for one another. You and I ... we never were.

"Almost done, Kailey," the doctor said. "Just a few more minutes."

The machine whirled strange noises.

For most of my life, I was raised to believe that demons were evil, vile creatures, and I imagine many of them are. And for those that are, Raven you're no better than them. In truth, you're much worse. You didn't give up your humanity. It was taken from you because you weren't worthy. I never would have thought my best female friend would be a demon. I see what Vincent saw in Cassie, and I'm thankful the truth surrounding her surfaced before she was sent back to the abyss. How did it feel when she kicked your ass?

'Demons cannot fight all your battles, Kailey.'

Kailey gasped and her body jolted with sudden fear.

Flora.

Shit.

"Please lie still," the doctor said.

Flora laughed. 'Yes, please lie still. In many ways, the CT machine greatly resembles a coffin, don't you think? But don't get *too* cozy. Raven has picked one out for you and set it right beside hers. She hasn't decided if she'll turn you or just let your body decay inside. A jilted heart ... it never heals. Raven never forgives, but I think you realize that from earlier.'

Get the hell out of my mind!

'You haven't missed me?'

I won't miss you after you're turned into a pile of ash.

'Cassie hurt Raven fairly badly.'

Good.

'Oh, don't forget though. Since she's a vampire, she heals quickly. Of course, that means she must feed. Blood. Do you wonder what she has on her menu for tonight? She has a choice selection, but for some odd reason she's insisted upon one particular person.'

Kailey's chest tightened. Her stomach turned. She held her breath.

'Pale like the moon on a cloudless night.'

No.

'Luna. Raven detests her almost as much as she does you. There's also the matter of Blaze. Simple … shall we say … *casualties* for being in the wrong place at the wrong time.'

Don't you dare!

'Or what, Kailey? What are you going to do? Seems you're a bit preoccupied, but with today's technology, we'll be certain to leave you a video of what she does to Luna before draining her dry.'

"Okay, we're done," the doctor said.

Kailey pressed her hands to her sides and pushed, sliding down the CT table instead of waiting for the doctor to push the table's activation button. Her bare feet touched the cold floor, and she looked to find the door.

"Kailey, is something wrong?" the doctor asked. "What's bothering you?"

When Kailey didn't reply, he said, "I have a nurse coming to assist you. Please, don't rush off. You really need to sit and rest."

Kailey wrapped her hospital gown behind her and held it together in one tight fist while trying to hurry toward the doors, but the throbbing pain in her head forced her to place her free hand against the wall. She winced and closed her eyes tightly. She managed a couple more steps before one of the swinging hospital doors opened.

"Kailey?" Brady said, rushing toward her. When he reached her, she fell against him. He wrapped his arms around her and held her up. She sobbed, trying to speak. "What's going on? What are you so upset about, Kailey?"

"It's Flora," she stammered.

"Here?"

"I don't know, but she was making her threats again."

"About what?"

"She and Raven are going to kill Blaze and Luna tonight."

"She's just trying to scare you."

"No," Kailey said, looking into his eyes. "She was serious, just like she was before the fight."

Brady kissed her forehead. "Jacob called a few minutes ago. Blaze and

Luna are with him and Barry. They're on their way here, and once the hospital releases you, we're going to boat across to the island since the ferries have stopped transporting for the evening."

"You sure? They're really with Jacob?"

"Yes. Flora's trying to torment you."

"No, she *is* tormenting me."

Brady hugged her. "It's going to be okay."

"I don't think so," Kailey said softly.

"Why not?"

"If Flora was speaking to me—"

"She's somewhere nearby," he said, finishing her sentence. "Dammit."

She nodded. "She has to be inside the hospital."

"Shit." Brady unsnapped a latch on his belt that held and secured a flashlight. Instead of removing a flashlight, he pulled out a sharpened stake. "We need to get you back to the ER where Cassie is waiting."

"You think Flora would make another attempt on me tonight?"

Brady wrapped his arm around her back and walked along beside her, supporting her as she walked. "We cannot rule it out, but knowing how she likes to prey more upon a person's mind rather than an actual physical attack, I honestly believe she wants to keep you shaken up and in fear."

"Well, it's working."

"Don't let it, Kailey. Fear is a greater opponent than any physical enemy. I do recall you telling me something similar some time back, right?"

"I know, but since I've been injured, I am more nervous. It's harder for me to defend myself." With the bruises swelling around her eyes, seeing was becoming more difficult, too.

"You have me and Cassie. Jacob and Barry should be here soon. In fact, once we get you back to your bed, I will call him and let him know what's going on."

"Okay. Thanks."

CHAPTER 20

The door to the CT room opened behind them.

Kailey and Brady turned.

"Here," an elderly nurse said, pushing a wheelchair up beside them. "She doesn't need to be walking until after the doctor reads the CT analysis and has a more detailed prognosis."

Brady smiled and nodded. "You're right. She doesn't."

Kailey glanced at the nurse and then read her badge. "Thanks, Haley."

"Don't mention it, honey. It's why we're here. Looks like you've had a rough day." Haley took the handles and pushed the wheelchair toward the elevator.

Kailey sighed. "A very rough day."

Brady slid the tip of the stake behind his wallet, but about three inches of it remained visible. He walked beside the wheelchair and kept looking around, hoping to catch a glimpse of Flora.

"You seem a bit nervous, officer," Haley said in a soft but worried tone. "We've not been notified of any threats. Is there something you know that we don't?"

Brady sighed and shook his head. "No ma'am. Just a bad habit of mine. It's best to be alert than to be taken by surprise."

"Don't I know it, young man," she replied. "We get all kinds in the hospital these days with all those mind-altering drugs out there on the streets. You wouldn't believe some of the folks we have to care for."

"Actually, ma'am, I would. I arrest a lot of them."

"Heroin addicts are some of the worst," she said, pointing. "Could you be a dear and hit the button for me?"

"Sure," Brady said. He pushed the down button on the panel beside the elevator.

"Thank you."

They watched the numbers descend from the seventh floor downward.

Brady made causal side-glances, apparently trying to locate Flora without making the elderly nurse more nervous.

"Officer," Haley said. "Is this young lady under protective custody? Is that why you keep looking around? An abusive spouse or something? Cause I can call security to give you additional assistance if you need it."

"No ma'am."

Haley's brow suddenly rose. "*She's* not the one under arrest now, is she?"

Kailey placed her hand to her forehead and gently shook her head.

"No ma'am, she's not."

"Well, she's obviously been beaten up. All those bruises and a few cuts on that pretty little face. Now, *that's* something I don't see every day." The nurse took a deep breath and sighed. "Drugs and violence. Seems to get worse every day, doesn't it?"

"Yes ma'am. Sometimes it does seem that way, but trust me, that's not the case with her."

"Then whatever did she do to get hurt?" the nurse asked.

Kailey turned her head slightly to the side and looked up at Haley. "I'm a fighter. I get into a cage and fight other women."

"Oh, my gracious," Haley said in a high voice. "That's so undignified and unladylike."

"It's a sport," Kailey replied.

"Well, it's not a good one, not for a young … woman."

Kailey assumed Haley had almost said 'lady,' but then couldn't because she had already clarified that Kailey's actions had been unladylike.

"Did you have an abusive mother or father?"

"No, they died when I was quite young."

"Perhaps that explains it then. My goodness, you poor thing."

The elevator dinged and the doors opened.

Thank God!

Brady waited for Haley to push Kailey inside and then stepped in beside them. The nurse pushed the button.

"It's good to have dedicated officers like yourself on duty to protect us,"

Haley said. "Heaven knows what sort of world we're coming to. Things aren't like they were when I was growing up."

The elevator doors closed and the elevator started down.

Brady chuckled. "I imagine not. Things have changed a lot since I was a kid, too."

"I think it's all those fancy electronic gadgets everyone uses. Always a distraction. Texting and driving. I guess you see that, too?"

"Yes, ma'am."

"See? That's what I'm getting at. Everyone's always preoccupied. People seldom talk to one another. When my grandchildren visit, I can't get them to look up from those blasted cellphones, iPads, or their computers. It's the most annoying thing."

I can think of something even more annoying. Kailey rolled her eyes and was thankful to be seated where the women didn't notice her reaction.

"I just don't get what all the fuss is over those gadgets, though. Do you?"

Brady's jaw tightened. Kailey could tell the woman had gone beyond his patience, but he was doing his best to act like a proper gentleman. He stared at the silver door, and he didn't glance toward the woman. Kailey figured he was hoping the nurse would stop talking.

But she didn't.

"I have one rule in my house at dinnertime. Well, two, if you count saying grace every time we eat, but the other is for no one to have their cellphones at the table. They might not talk, but at least they can hear what I have to say."

Kailey took a deep breath and slowly exhaled. What she wouldn't give to have *her* cellphone right then or a powerful sedative.

"I guess I'm just a rattling on. Looks like the both of you are ignoring me now," Haley said. "Just like my kids and my grandkids."

"Oh, no," Brady said, shaking his head, but he still refused to glance in her direction.

"You do realize it's bad manners not to maintain eye contact when someone is speaking to you? That's why you must die first!" The nurse hissed and moved in a flash. She struck Brady's head against the side of the elevator, dropping him to the floor. She slammed the emergency button and stopped the elevator in-between floors.

Kailey screamed, tried to scramble out of the wheelchair, but Haley turned toward her in a split second, snarling and suddenly flashing fangs.

No dentures there.

Kailey shoved her right hand around the woman's throat and squeezed.

The old woman's eyes shimmered like pools of black ink. The wrinkles on her face deepened from her fury. Haley flailed at Kailey with her long sharp claws, slicing through the thin fabric of the hospital gown.

Kailey held fast and tightened her grip while shoving herself from the wheelchair. The vampire grabbed both of Kailey's arms and clung to them. She was much stronger than an elderly woman should be.

Brady moaned in the corner of the elevator. He shook his head and was trying to push himself up.

The vampire growled and gnashed her teeth at Kailey before turning and kicking Brady in the head. He fell to his side, dazed.

Kailey screamed, not in fear but from sudden anger. Her fight to survive kicked in, and she thrust the woman against the wall right above where Brady lay. Although the vampire was incredibly strong, she was also extremely light. The nurse squeezed her hands tightly around Kailey's wrists. A few more seconds and Kailey knew her wrists were going to snap. In spite of her head injury she dropped to the floor and flung the woman overhead. The movement was enough to startle the vampire, and she released her hold on Kailey. The worst part was Kailey had let go of the vampire.

Sharp pain jabbed Kailey's temples like needles.

The elderly woman struck the wall but didn't appear injured. Had she not been a vampire, the nurse would have been killed or horribly wounded. But Haley turned around, grabbed the wheelchair, and threw it.

Kailey ducked.

The wheelchair buckled as the vampire slung it against the wall. The impact sent it bouncing back, striking Haley. She promptly kicked it aside with little effort.

Kailey crawled to Brady, yanked the stake from his back pocket, and turned.

Haley growled. Her anger overwhelmed her and her voice deepened as she spoke. She no longer sounded like a sweet innocent old woman. Her voice became deep and raspy, sending chills down Kailey's back and arms. "Flora insisted you'd be difficult, but I swore to her that you'd not live to see tomorrow."

The vampire rushed across the elevator full force, apparently oblivious of the stake, and as she dove, Kailey used both hands to drive the stake through the woman's chest and straight into her heart. She shrieked, her eyes widened, and she dissolved into ash.

"Never make promises you can't keep," Kailey said, panting.

CHAPTER 21

Forrest placed the night vision goggles over his eyes, stood, and walked to the edge of the old metal tracks. He peered to his right and stared for a long while. For some reason, he had thought this underground passageway held the answers for what happened to Penelope over a century before.

The lack of evidence and the empty corridor matched the emptiness he felt inside his mind and soul from losing her. All he needed was one shred of proof that she had been here, and his fading hope could be rekindled instead of remaining thoroughly snubbed out. He sighed.

Gunner stepped beside Forrest. "Why did you think you'd find evidence here?"

Forrest was silent for several long moments. "It was a feeling I had, but I was wrong."

"But something prompted you to this tunnel," Gunner said softly. "Can you explain what you felt?"

"I studied the old Seattle maps for a long time, Gunner. This area had been used a lot before the fire. After the fire, everything was rerouted. My guess is the demons had something to do with these particular tracks being abandoned and eventually forgotten by the townspeople. One doesn't simply forget about a project of this size within his or her lifetime."

"I suppose that's true," Gunner said.

"And yet, everyone did, which leads me to believe the remaining five demons had something to do with the memory loss. Or the witches might have cast a spell to make people forget. Whichever is the actual case, it doesn't matter. What matters is why, and what they didn't want others to discover. So, that's why I thought this was the most obvious place. I still do."

Gunner glanced up at Forrest. "We did look everywhere, Forrest. But I will be happy to spend another day looking if you want. Just in case I missed what I was supposed to find."

"That's okay, Gunner. What I need is to find a witch who can discern whether a concealment spell has been cast over this place or not. If it has, none of us would ever find it, even if we spent a year searching."

Ian said, "As I recall, wasn't that the case in finding the underground entrance into Nocturnal Trinity? A spell had been cast to hide it."

"Yes, that had dawned upon me, too. That's why I plan to talk to Jaclyn about it. No sense wasting any more of our time."

"Too bad it didn't *dawn* upon you this morning, which would have been perfect timing," Ian said.

"Ian!" Gunner turned toward his brother with a glare and made a fist.

"What?"

"Mean."

"No-o-o, it was a joke. Dawn. Morning. Perfect *timing*. You don't understand … never mind."

"More a play on words, Gunner. It wasn't meant as an insult," Forrest said with a soft laugh. "But Ian, I'd have never put you through all this had I even considered that."

"I'm not mad about it, Forrest," Ian replied. "You've thought about this far longer than any of us, and I believe you might have stumbled onto the solution to prove your theory. Get Jaclyn down here and let's find out. If the former witches hid something in this tunnel, I want to know what it was, too."

"Thanks, Ian," Forrest said.

"You really think it might link to what happened to her, don't you?" Ian asked.

Forrest nodded. "Jinn mentioned a Demon-hunter who had killed one of the original demons. It had to be her."

"You're certain?" Gunner asked.

"I feel it deep inside. The coincidence is too much for me to ignore. I'm not saying there weren't other women Demon-hunters, but for that time period? Penelope would have been in Seattle when that occurred. I believe something is hidden in this tunnel, perhaps even distorted by magic."

Ian smiled. "Then let's find the truth. We've been a great team slaying vampires, but I'm not so certain about how to kill demons."

"Me, either. What I do know is each type of demon is different. Most cannot be killed, but they can be sent back to the abyss, which is a far worse fate than death in many ways."

"Why is that?" Gunner asked.

Forrest shrugged his huge shoulders. "I don't really know except that while they are in our world, they are apparently free from whatever persecution they endure in the abyss."

Gunner glanced toward Ian. "I wonder what that might be?"

Ian shook his head. "I don't know. Maybe it's the fire and brimstone you hear about or it could be total isolation in a completely dark place. Either would be worse than death to me."

"Y-e-e-ah," Gunner replied. "Me, too."

"It could be reliving the worst tragedies in one's life over and over," Forrest said, rubbing the goggles.

"That would be horrible, too," Gunner said. "But what tragedies would a demon fear reliving?"

Forrest turned and started walking toward the narrow passageway that led up to the surface. "If what has been taught for centuries is true, demons are fallen angels that fought against God and were forever cast out. Wouldn't that be Hell enough?"

"You believing that?" Ian asked in a high-pitched voice.

"I'm speculating," Forrest replied.

The trio came to a narrow spiral set of stairs carved from stone.

"Well, we've known you more than a century, and you've never been keen on any religion," Ian said.

"Do recall that I started the sentence with 'if.'"

"He did, Ian," Gunner said. "And you, brother? You've never held faith in much of anything."

Forrest laughed.

"It's true," Gunner said.

"I know it, but you won't get him to admit it," Forrest replied.

"I won't deny such," Ian said. "But even we need to admit at some point a higher power is watching over us. Don't we?"

"I agree," Forrest said. "Something higher did call me, but whatever power sought to place me amongst its Chosen isn't tied to any of the organized religions in the world."

"And how can you be certain?" Ian asked.

Forrest pushed aside the heavy sheet of metal used to conceal the entrance to the old tracks beneath the surface. They stepped outside the dark doorway and into the stormy night. Lightning flickered for several moments. About a hundred yards away was a sodium streetlight that brightened the end of a sidewalk.

Forrest glanced at Ian. "For one, the power has never demanded me to kneel before it or be cursed for eternity. It's never demanded gold or money from me."

"But it has demanded your obedience," Ian replied. "Your blood and your time have been required."

Forrest snorted. "Indeed, Ian, that's true. But no manual came with being Chosen. And for every vampire I've slain, my youth has been kept intact. To be honest, I don't know if that's a blessing or a curse within itself."

"What about your moments of intuition? When you discover something you otherwise would have never seen?" Ian asked, helping Forrest set the heavy metal door back into place. Gunner piled old boards and crossties against it in an attempt to make it appear that no one had disturbed the area.

"Those are given to me by Hunters who have died in the past. It's their instinct, their warnings. I learned a long time ago to heed such cautions because the consequences are too high."

"You mean Penelope and your father?" Gunner said.

Forrest's jaw tightened. His eyes moistened. "Yes. I didn't heed the warnings because in my gut I believed I was doing the right thing. Apparently I didn't, and they both paid a price for it. You see, that's my Hell. I carry the burden of loss every single day."

"We're all broken a little bit inside," Ian said. "Some more than others."

"Agreed," Gunner said.

Forrest nodded. "We are. I've dwelt on my memories for too long today. It's time for us to find Jaclyn and see if she will accompany us to these underground tracks. Perhaps she can find what we cannot see."

CHAPTER 22

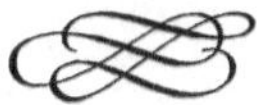

*K*ailey leaned her back against the wall. Her increased heartbeat caused her head to throb even worse. Sliding down the wall, she sat beside Brady. He was squinting in pain, slowly moving his head side to side. "Are you okay?"

Brady opened his eyes and frowned. "A little rattled. I take it that you staked her?"

Kailey nodded and immediately wished she hadn't. She rubbed her temples and leaned her head against his shoulder. "Yes. I grabbed the stake from your pocket."

"Good reflexes if you slew her that fast."

"Actually she did it to herself."

Brady chuckled. "How?"

"She wasn't paying attention and ran right into the stake."

Brady rose slowly and pressed the emergency stop button. The elevator began descending again.

"Are you okay?" Kailey asked.

"I'll be fine. She just caught me off-guard. If I was merely human, I'd probably be unconscious or in a coma. Because of her age, I didn't expect her to be a vampire."

"I didn't either, but she certainly was annoying."

Brady smiled and shook his head, trying hard not to reply. The glint in his eyes indicated he agreed, but he fought hard to keep his feelings inside. He didn't want to be rude. "Not any more."

Kailey smiled.

Brady offered his hand. She took it, and he helped her stand. "I hope this is the only vampire Flora has sent your direction tonight."

"Me, too." Kailey stared at the pile of ash on the elevator floor. "Can you tell me something?"

"What?"

"Why would someone at her age be turned into a vampire?"

He shrugged. "It depends upon a lot of things."

"Like what?"

"First, whether she was turned voluntarily or against her will. If she sought to become a vampire, she might have had a fear of death or maybe she was destined to die from a debilitating disease and she didn't want to suffer from the pain. Perhaps, she wanted to have more time to spend with her grandchildren, since she did mention them and she seemed sincere in her worries about how society was evolving for the worst. Any of those reasons are feasible. But I don't think she was turned into a vampire against her will."

Kailey frowned. "Why not?"

"Vampires are occasionally known to forcibly sire another, but generally it's for selfish reasons like lust or possessiveness. More often than not, a vampire would rather turn a willing soul. The reason for this is simple. Someone forced is usually resentful and makes it difficult to rein control over her. Those are considered feral vampires. And if you ever encounter the evidence of what's left behind after a rebellious vampire has exhausted a tantrum, it's carnage too hideous to report to the press."

"Have you seen that?" she asked.

Brady took a deep breath and slowly released it through his mouth. "Once. Believe me, that's more than enough. Of course there are repercussions for the vampire who had turned the unwilling offspring from his or her master. Older vampires don't like having to clean up the messes their children leave. They still crave secrecy and shun publicity."

"Except for Flora and her siblings?"

Brady shrugged. "She's pushing her agenda, but it might be that what she's doing doesn't have their approval. You see, part of why I supported Micah in the beginning was so we could shut down Nocturnal Trinity. The vampire population is growing in waves in Seattle. At the rate it's escalating and if left unchecked, the entire city will suffer a hefty price."

"You think the whole city will become vampires?"

"No. But once there are equal numbers of vampires to mortals, you can expect laws to become greatly altered in favor of the vampires."

Kailey caught her reflection off the silver elevators door. Although it wasn't as clear as looking in a mirror, she could see the purplish-black bruises around her eyes and her right cheek was swollen. She peered closer and gently touched the bruises. *No wonder I can barely see.*

The elevator door slid open, causing her to jerk back. Brady and Kailey stepped out cautiously. Seeing no one, they allowed the doors to close behind them and left the battered wheelchair inside the elevator.

She whispered, "Most people don't even believe in vampires. Well, they believe they're fictional, so there aren't *any* laws right now."

"I know. That's why we need to reduce the numbers of vampires quickly, starting with the vampire founders at Nocturnal Trinity. The worst thing Micah did was join the Circle of Unity instead of insisting that it be closed forever. He should have shattered the Unity completely. We had the perfect opportunity and he let it slip from our grasp."

"But the Unity is still in shambles."

"For now, but as long as the club remains open, it will continue attracting other wannabes."

"I agree that the nightclub should have been shut down, but I still can't see the vampires gaining enough of an edge to manipulate the laws," Kailey said.

They returned to the emergency room bed where she had been assigned. Brady pulled the curtain around the small partition. He pulled the chair to the edge of her bed so they could talk quietly and not to be overheard. "Look at it this way, Kailey. The worldwide vampire population is small. I'd say probably less than ten percent, but it could be more. So they are a minority and too small a group to emerge demanding rights and power. Should they make a lot of noise to draw attention to themselves, mortals will become alarmed and seek to find ways to eradicate them. Some might hire people to kill them. So, it's too risky for vampires to be prominent. But once they increase their number to fifty percent or more in the city's population, they will have enough power to insist protection and make it a capital offense to slay a vampire."

"But Nocturnal Trinity is drawing attention to the vampires, witches, and demons," Kailey said. "It's a beacon for the wannabes."

"Yes, but not to those who don't believe."

"So?"

"Right now, the ones who shout the loudest about the atrocities committed inside the nightclub aren't the ones being turned. It's the religious people. But more than announcing the iniquities of the younger people seeking to enter the club, these religious groups still don't believe vampires are real. They simply insist the hopefuls are doomed to Hell and everything about Nocturnal Trinity is of the devil."

"They're so far off the mark."

Brady nodded. "Exactly, but the devil—so to speak—is only one of the factions. They are all separate authorities and not spawned from the devil, like these churches would have everyone believe. You cannot defeat an enemy without fully understanding your enemy. Of course, they can't destroy vampires or other immortals when they don't even believe they exist."

"So without knowing it, the churches are aiding the vampires?"

"Every step of the way," Brady replied.

Cassie walked into their curtain enclosure with a steaming cup of vending machine coffee. She glanced toward Kailey and detected her uneasiness. The succubus' eyes narrowed. "Something's wrong. What happened?"

Kailey and Brady told her about the elderly vampire nurse and Flora.

Cassie set her cup on the floor beside the chair. "We have to end this, Brady, and fast. They're not going to stop."

He nodded. "I agree."

"Then what do you propose?" Cassie asked.

"As soon as Jacob gets back here, we'll head to Micah's place. During the night we keep watch and hopefully find Forrest in the morning. We can't succeed without his help," Brady replied.

"Why not?"

"He's a Hunter."

"So?" Cassie said. "We all know *how* to kill a vampire."

Brady sighed. "Yes, but none of us have the experience he has. Besides, we don't know how many vampires we're dealing with. We're also blind to our emotions. While I found the elderly nurse irritating, I never suspected her to be a vampire. Part of the reason for that is I couldn't help picturing her as someone's grandmother. Forrest has dealt with hundreds of vampires. He's more capable of seeing through their guises better than any of us."

"You're probably right," Cassie said. She picked up her hot coffee and downed it.

Kailey cringed. "Damn, didn't that hurt?"

Cassie laughed and shook her head. "Heat to a demon? Did you even have to ask?"

"Sorry. Wasn't thinking." Kailey removed the hospital gown and found her folded clothes beside the bed. She slipped into her shorts and pulled her top down, wincing the entire time. She grabbed her shoes, sat at the edge of the bed, and pulled them on. She placed her hand to her head, feeling dizzy, and then leaned back to keep from dropping headfirst to the floor.

"What are you doing?" Brady asked, holding her arm to balance her.

"You said that we're leaving."

"When they get here."

Cassie grinned. Jacob leaned his head through the curtain. "They are back."

Brady noticed Jacob. "Good. But Kailey still needs to know what they found out from her CT scan."

"I'll be fine."

"No, dear," Cassie said. "He's right. You took quite a beating."

"You don't have to remind me. My bruises have bruises, and they throb with every heartbeat."

Brady tenderly placed his hands to her cheeks and looked into her eyes. "You don't have to convince us that you're tough, Kailey. It's evident. It's part of what drew me to you. Even after your injuries, you've shown little pain. You're tougher than most of the men I work with on the force, but if you have a hemorrhage inside your brain, that's too deadly to risk or shrug off. Let the doctor clear you before we leave."

Kailey released a long sigh. "Okay. I just couldn't handle wearing the gown any more, especially with the possibility that I might find myself needing to run."

Jacob chuckled. "I think you'd have few complaints from onlookers."

Kailey glared at him.

Brady gave Jacob a stern frown.

"Sorry," Jacob said, waving his huge hands in surrender. "Just trying to lighten the mood."

"Right now," Brady said, "I don't think anything's capable of easing our tensions."

Jacob nodded. "Things are pretty grim with Blaze and Luna, too."

"Why?" Kailey asked. "Did something happen?"

"Nothing physical, but their apprehension made it nearly impossible to convince them to leave the magic shop. Luna was in tears and shaking as she came out the door. Blaze was trying to calm her, but he looks fearful, too."

Brady rested his hands on his gun belt. "I can't say I blame them. With Flora's vindictive mood, she's likely to target any one of us. I don't think she really has any preference for who she kills first."

"My sentiments exactly," Cassie said.

"Where are Luna and Blaze?" Kailey asked.

"In the waiting area," Jacob replied.

"Alone?"

"No. Barry's with them."

"Could you send Luna in to see me?" Kailey asked.

"Sure." Jacob nodded and exited through the narrow curtain opening.

The nurse pulled the curtain aside and approached the bed. She was thin with her silverish-blonde hair bunned. Her wrinkles indicated she frowned far more often than she ever smiled. "Why are you already dressed when the doctor has not released you yet?"

"I need to leave, but I am waiting to get his report," Kailey said.

"It takes time," the nurse replied.

Kailey crossed her arms. "I think time stands still inside hospitals. The waits are forever long."

"You should work the midnight shift here, if you think it's bad," the nurse said with no emotion.

"That painstakingly slow?" Kailey asked.

"Worse. When every thing is quiet, five minutes seems like an eternity, especially if you're working the station alone. And like this evening when a nurse up and leaves the hospital without informing any of us."

"One just left? Does that happen often?"

"Not too often, but the nurse who escorted you in the wheelchair cannot be found anywhere." The nurse shrugged. "But that's not your problem. The doctor should be by soon and give you the details of your report. I'd suggest you only have one person in here when he does."

"Why's that?" Brady asked.

"Unless you're married to her, none of you can be in here when he goes over the findings."

"How about engaged?" Brady said.

Kailey's eyes widened at the suggestion. She didn't believe they were anywhere near that stage in their relationship, but she didn't want to be left alone with a doctor she didn't know. The elderly nurse had turned out to be an unexpected living nightmare and had tried to kill her. She refused to place herself in another situation like that, which meant she'd argue for Brady to be with her when the doctor arrived.

Cassie gave Kailey an odd smile.

"That's up to the doctor and Kailey," the nurse replied. "But he should be here shortly."

The nurse pulled back the curtain to leave and was nearly knocked down by Luna.

"I'm sorry," Luna said, wiping tears from her eyes.

The nurse shook her head. "With as many people coming in to see you, we should charge admission." She flung the curtain closed again.

Luna hurried to Kailey and plopped down beside her. She wrapped her arms around Kailey and hugged her fiercely.

"Oh my God, Kailey. Raven did this to you?"

"Yes."

Luna squeezed Kailey and whispered, "Raven's going to kill me, isn't she?"

"No," Brady said. "We're going to keep you safe."

Luna's body shook.

"Is everything okay?" Kailey asked, returning the hug.

"I really don't like the idea of leaving the magic shop. I feel safer there," she replied.

"I understand," Brady said. "But right now, it's probably best if we put more distance between us and Nocturnal Trinity."

"You sure?"

Cassie and Kailey nodded.

The curtain slid open. "Whoa! Wasn't expecting a crowd. I'm Dr. Walden. If everyone would please exit, I need to talk to Kailey about her results."

CHAPTER 23

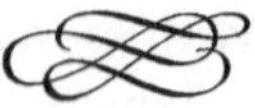

Forrest had walked about half a block when he noticed someone moving through the shadows and following them. The person possessed great skills at trying to remain hidden within the darkness, but Forrest's decades of hunting vampires and other paranormal creatures had gifted him the ability to notice the slightest movements from the corner of his vision. Often he sensed their aura, even when he had not seen them. Their curious follower was almost as good as a trained sniper, but had not gone unnoticed.

The swirling mists coated the trees, the sidewalks, and the few parked cars along the other side of the puddle-filled street.

"We have company," Forrest said in a low voice and without slowing his pace.

"Which direction?" Ian said without looking around.

"Along the trees on the other side of the fence."

"Vampire?" Gunner asked, placing his hand around his stake.

"I'm not certain. My guess, however, would be *no*. It's not a vampire but it's also not a human."

Ian grinned. "Parting ways, temporarily."

"Why?" Gunner whispered.

"You should do the same," Ian replied. "It makes an attack a harder decision for the stalker if we spread out."

Gunner nodded. "I suppose."

"And at the first sign of a threat," Ian whispered, "change and charge. It's doubtful this creature following us is capable of overpowering all three of us."

"I never said it was alone," Forrest said.

"You sense others?" Gunner asked.

"No, but I never expect a stalker to be alone. Each of you should understand that by now."

Ian shrugged, left the sidewalk, and crossed the street, stepping around a growing puddle to reach the other sidewalk.

Gunner turned and walked in the opposite direction, but not out of cowardice. Gunner would keep watch over his shoulder and act immediately if their shadower attempted to attack. He had never fled from any battle Forrest had entered. While mentally Gunner was a tad slower than other people, he was only that way in his human form. Once he shapeshifted into his otter form, his intellect sharpened, and he also lacked having any fear. It was the only time Gunner lost his gentleness and allowed his inner viciousness to emerge. In all the time Gunner had traveled with Forrest, Forrest had never witnessed Gunner's beast injure an innocent person. Gunner had, however, killed a lot of vampires and undead creatures.

Forrest pulled the rim of his Hunter hat downward, partially hiding his eyes, and continued walking. Although he felt no ill ambiences from the person following them, he had encountered numerous shifters over the decades who had concealed their intent quite well. Forrest wasn't taking any chances. His right hand gripped a stake inside his coat pocket, and in his left hand he held a globe-shaped bottle of holy water. If neither of these proved to be suitable weapons, he could easily pull his revolver from its holster. Silver bullets not only killed werewolves, but they damn near injured or killed most anything else.

The figure in the shadows leaned against the wide trunk of a tree and peered around. The whistling wind blew the mist in odd swirling sheets and helped conceal the sound of the person's footsteps, but Forrest could still see her from the corner of his eye. He continued walking with his hands in his pockets. With a causal glance, he looked for Ian on the other side of the street. Ian was gone.

It only took a few seconds for Forrest to locate him. Ian had already shifted into his otter form. He was on all fours, crouched in between two cars. His eyes glowed amber. If Ian had altered, then most likely Gunner had, too. They were less likely to take chances than Forrest often did, but he liked that they were ready to come to his aid when the situation proved necessary.

Forrest approached a bench near the fence. Due to the weather and this section on the outskirts of the city, no other people were walking along the sidewalks. The wooden bench dripped water from the layers of continuous mist. Forrest placed his Hunter box at the side of the bench and sat down with his back toward whoever had been following them.

"What do you want?" Forrest asked without looking over his shoulder. He had already released the stake inside his coat pocket and wrapped his fingers around the revolver. "I know you're there. If you wish to talk, say so, and I won't kill you."

The woman laughed softly as her wet footsteps tramped across the soggy sod. "I like aggressiveness, but if that's your pickup line, it needs some polishing. Besides, you know I can't die easily."

Forrest craned his neck and looked over his shoulder in surprise. "Lydia?"

"Yes. Let your mongrels know it's me. They have no need to be alarmed." She used her hand to wipe water off the bench before she sat down. Not that it mattered since the ensuing mists didn't seem likely to slack anytime soon.

Forrest waved his hands and shook his head at Gunner and Ian, informing them that she wasn't an enemy. Ian looked disappointed and retreated into the shadows.

"Calling off your watchdogs?" she asked.

"Letting them know you're no threat."

She replied with a short throaty chuckle.

Lydia wore tight black jeans, a black T-shirt, and a vinyl hoodie poncho. He was surprised that she had moved so stealthily through the trees on the soggy ground while wearing the heavy hiking boots. She pulled aside a long wet strand of blonde hair from her face. Coldness hardened her gaze. Even though he considered her an ally, she didn't greet him with a friendly smile. Her expressions were like his—difficult to read.

"What brings you to Seattle?" Forrest asked.

"I felt there was a need," she replied.

"In other words, you got bored."

Lydia replied with a firm nod. "Yeah, that too."

"How'd you know I was here?"

"Instinct, I suppose."

Forrest brought his huge hands out of his pockets and rested them on his knees. "I had the feeling after the last time we talked that you'd be laying low for a long while."

She shrugged. "When everyone thinks you're dead, I don't see the need. No one's looking for me any more."

"All it takes is for someone to recognize you."

"Nah, I never was one for social events."

"I seem to recall differently."

Lydia offered a sly grin. The iciness of her gaze melted ever so slightly. "That was years ago when I did motorcycle stunts and dirt bike races. My spotlight dimmed a long time ago, and well, now, it's completely out, thanks to you."

"I thought that was what you wanted?"

"It is. That's why I'm saying, 'thanks.'"

"Don't mention it."

"It's another reason for why I'm here."

Forrest turned and looked at her with a curious frown. "Why exactly?"

"To pay my debt."

"You don't owe me anything."

"Oh, but I do."

Forrest shook his head. "And what exactly did you have in mind to repay such a debt?"

"You told me before that you're a Hunter, and I'm an assassin. What are you and your … odd friends hunting? You never quite said, so I'm guessing bad seeds in society? If so, perhaps I can assist."

Forrest looked at her for a few moments and sighed. "If I told you, I don't think you'd even believe me. Besides, your world has been complicated enough."

"I lessened my complications, as you well know. So tell me *what* wouldn't I believe?" she asked.

Ian returned to his human form and walked across the street toward them. His voice was almost frantic, his gaze harsh. "Who is this, Forrest? What does she want?"

Lydia gave Ian an odd stare before a small grin curled on her lips. "I believe he's jealous."

"I am not!" Ian said, glancing toward her with fierce eyes. His crooked upper teeth formed into a snarl for several moments before he glanced at Forrest again. "She's not supernatural like you said. She's definitely not like my brother and I. She's human and you implied that she wasn't when she was following us."

Forrest hunched over, resting his elbows on his knees. "I never said that she was supernatural. I was speaking the truth. She's more than just a human."

Ian frowned at Lydia, studying her. "She's not a vampire, otherwise you wouldn't be talking to her."

Lydia frowned and glanced at Forrest in disbelief. "What the hell is he talking about? A vampire? What fairytale is he living in?"

"About that," Forrest said. "I was preparing to tell you what I ... *we* hunt."

Gunner joined them with a confused expression on his face. Forrest wasn't certain if Gunner had ever shifted into his otter form or not.

"Vampires?" she asked. "You're really serious about this?"

Forrest nodded.

"It's rare if Forrest ever jokes about anything," Ian said, crossing his arms.

Lydia gave him an even smile and cocked a brow. "He does appear to hold a serious countenance. Kind of like myself. I suppose that's why he and I get along."

"How could you ever tell that you get along?" Gunner asked. "Both of you are impossible to read."

Ian rolled his eyes and shook his head. "True, brother. But, Lydia, you should have seen Forrest back when we first met him."

"He was more rigid?" she asked.

"Oh, no, he was *much* worse," Ian replied.

"And how long ago was that?" Lydia asked, glancing toward Forrest.

Ian rubbed his scrubby chin and tapped his index finger to his cheek, pondering. "I'd say at the best estimate—"

Forrest cleared his throat and glared at Ian from beneath the rim of his hat. He gave a slight shaking of his head, enough that Ian knew not to give her any extra information. Forrest had never given Lydia much of his background information concerning his age and for now, at least, he had no intention of letting her know.

Ian visibly shook and lowered his arms to his sides. "Ah, sorry."

Lydia glanced between Forrest and Ian. Gunner stood nearby with his gaze toward the ground. "Is there a reason for the secrecy about that?"

"Actually there is," Ian said. "If you want more information, as you can see, you'll have to pry it out of Forrest. But ... let's discuss *you* for a moment, shall we?"

"Me? What do you want to know?" Although she remained calloused, a hint of amusement flowed in her voice.

"What are you, if not a normal human? I heard you tell Forrest that you're an assassin?"

"It's a long story," Lydia said.

"I've got the time," Ian said, swaying back and forth. His pessimistic nature had faded, he had *somehow* buried it, and his gaze at Lydia indicated he had been smitten by her presence, even though her rough exterior wasn't something that most men would be drawn to. She wore no makeup or perfume, and her calloused hands were more rugged than most men. Ian didn't mind and was trying to make a good impression unlike every other encounter he'd had with people. "Plenty of it, actually."

Forrest stood and leveled a frown at Ian. "Actually, we *don't*."

Lydia rose as well. Her poncho parted slightly, revealing her holstered Glock 9mm. Gunner gave a nervous glance to his brother but Ian was lost in her beauty and apparently hadn't noticed her weapon. It brought to Forrest's mind that some of the most beautiful things in the world were also the most deadly. This was the perfect example, but Forrest didn't have the heart to break it to Ian. Besides, no amount of flattery would endear Ian to her. Part of her reason for faking her death was to prevent her ex-husband from searching for her and for him to go on with his life.

Lydia stepped in front of Forrest. "Look, I've traveled a long distance to find you. You cannot interject vampires into a conversation and expect to not explain what you meant. Are you implying there are people who have risen from the dead and feed on human blood?"

"Yes."

Lydia cocked one eyebrow. "You're serious."

"I am."

"So it's not fictional?"

"No. Why should this news surprise you? From what I last heard, you're the one leading the pack of werewolves south of Seattle," Forrest said.

"You're Lydia?" Ian gasped, taking a step backwards.

Forrest sighed. "Sorry. Yes. I should have made the introductions. Lydia meet Ian and his twin brother, Gunner. Gunner and Ian, this is Lydia."

Lydia offered slight nods of recognition to each brother without offering her hand. "First, this *pack* I am with is not comprised of werewolves."

"That's the rumor going around."

She shook her head. "No. They're like me. They were created in a genetic laboratory. I was, too. Their genomes were tweaked with wolf DNA, and for some unexplained reason, they can turn into what the movies *call* werewolves at will. They don't need a full moon. But you and I both know werewolves don't exist."

Ian and Gunner exchanged glances and burst into laughter.

"What?" Lydia's glared at them. "What do you find so funny?"

Forrest cleared his throat. "Perhaps we should find a place indoors so we can get out of this nasty weather and talk privately."

"So you're saying other types of wolfmen exist?" she asked.

"I haven't said that, but let's go find somewhere to discuss it."

"Which basically means they do exist. Real werewolves that weren't made in a laboratory?"

"Yeah, if you find that unbelievable, wait until we tell you about the other creatures," Ian said.

"Come on," Forrest said, "if you want to know. But like I said before, you are not indebted to me. You're free to leave, but without me giving you the information."

"So if I stick around to find out these secrets, I'm obligated to help you?"

Forrest gave an even grin. "Seems so. The truth is we do need extra help, so it's your call."

"I guess you'd best fill me in on the information because it won't just be me helping you. A couple members of my ... *pack* ... as you call it, are already in Seattle."

CHAPTER 24

Kailey sat on the edge of the bed, waiting to hear the doctor's prognosis.

Dr. Walden placed an image of her skull onto an X-ray light box and leaned against the wall. "Well, the good news is you don't have any hemorrhaging in your brain. The bad news is you do have a concussion."

"I figured as much on the concussion," Kailey replied.

"From your file it says that you sustained these injuries due to *fighting?*"

She nodded.

Walden frowned. "On the street? Boxing or MMA style? How exactly?"

"I've been training for MMA for several years."

"Do you fight like this often?"

"No. It's been more training than fighting. This was the first time in a long while that I've entered the cage. And the first time I wasn't using cushioned headgear."

Dr. Walden offered a slight grin. He glanced at Brady for a moment and then back at her. "No offense, but I cannot see why a young lady as attractive as yourself would get into such a violent sport. But such a choice is yours. Tell me, do you have other hobbies that are less dangerous? Or a safer career choice?"

"I finished my college degree in investigative reporting."

"Then why not pursue that?"

Kailey sighed. "I am. The training and occasion bouts help relieve stress. To be honest, the training is far more attractive to me."

Walden nodded politely. "Don't get me wrong. I do like watching those fights, but to pursue that, you need to learn to be less on the receiving side and more on the giving side of the fights."

Kailey laughed softly.

"Look, I'd advise that you spend some time resting and not doing any rigorous activities. I've written you a prescription for the pain, but I don't suggest you go to sleep for a few more hours, okay? And if you do, have your boyfriend keep an eye on you for good measure."

"So I'm free to go?" Kailey asked.

"Yes. But take precautions. No more fighting or sparring for a few weeks. Think you can refrain from that?"

"I'll try," Kailey replied with a smile.

"You'd best," Walden replied. "To put it bluntly, any more head trauma could put you into a coma or worse, you could die. A concussion isn't something you should take lightly, and this is a reason you might want to reconsider getting involved with the MMA sport. You're lucky this isn't much worse, and you could suffer severe brain injuries from such head injuries. There are long-term consequences to what happens inside the fighting ring or cage. Most fighters shrug off such warnings, but I hope you have the common sense to understand what I'm trying to tell you. Too many solid shots to the head, and you can forget about journalism altogether. Please, while you're recovering, think about what I've said and take it to heart."

Kailey's smile faded. "I will."

"Good. I hate to see any young person risk memory loss or lifelong brain trauma. You have a full life ahead of you, but opportunities quickly diminish the further you proceed with such injuries." He turned off the X-ray box light, grabbed the X-ray, and handed it to Kailey. "A souvenir that I hope reminds you of the risks you've undertaken."

She stared at the X-ray and mumbled, "Thanks."

After Dr. Walden left the curtained cubicle, Brady looped his arm around Kailey's and let her lean against him as they walked out of the emergency room to the waiting room.

Jacob rose to his feet. "Is she okay?"

"I'm fine," Kailey replied, clinging to Brady's arm.

"You don't look fine," he said.

"Looks can be deceiving."

Jacob grinned. "How true that is, especially when you're talking to a undercover werewolf."

Blaze and Luna smiled at her. Barry stood near the exit with his arms folded and peered outside. He seemed to be on watch. His right hand was inside his jacket pocket, probably resting on his 9mm.

Kailey glanced around the waiting room. "Where's Cassie?"

"She said she needed to go to Nocturnal Trinity," Luna replied.

"Why?"

Luna shrugged. "She didn't say why, but she's going to meet us on the island later."

Jacob offered a slight smile. "So we're ready to go?"

Brady nodded.

"Good," he replied. "I suppose you'll drive to the dock with Kailey?"

"Yes."

"Everyone else, ride with me," Jacob said. He glanced at Brady. "I'll be waiting for you."

Brady clasped Jacob's shoulder. "We'll be right behind you."

Jacob and the others hurried to the parking lot. Brady slowly escorted Kailey outside, even though she could have moved faster.

"You don't have to baby me," Kailey said.

"You heard the doctor. It's not babying you to ensure that you get to the car safely."

Kailey huffed, but inside she held a warm smile, knowing how much Brady cared about her. And, essentially, he was right. Everything still seemed to spin around her, she had taken a severe beating, but she'd never openly admit her dizziness because she didn't want to seem weak. She hadn't mentioned it to the doctor or the nurses for fear she'd be forced to stay overnight in the hospital.

Since her parents' deaths, she had hated hospitals, though she vaguely remembered going to the hospital with her brother when her parents had been rushed to the emergency room. Perhaps she had blocked it from her memories, and at times, she was thankful she was too young to vividly recall the events that had occurred. The only real memory that clung to her was the dark dismal atmosphere that had hovered over her inside the waiting room while her brother talked to the doctor about their parents. When he had informed her of the unfortunate news later, she had been crushed inside and the shock prevented her from being able to express her emotions.

As Kailey walked alongside Brady, she realized that she had never really allowed those emotions to emerge. She had never truly dealt with the loss. Instead, she increased her martial arts training, spent hours deep in meditation, and struck practice dummies until she was drenched in sweat to alleviate the hollowness inside. Without knowing it, she had buried the pain and loss so deeply that she had never allowed it to surface where tears and sorrow might wash the hurt away. Even now, she was willing to keep those emotions locked away, basically because she had no other choice, given her current circumstances. She had enemies, vampires who wanted her dead, which left her little alternative except to fight or die.

With the news of a concussion, the last thing she needed was another confrontation with Raven or Flora where she might suffer more physical harm. This was another reason she felt safer outside the hospital and surrounded by part of Micah's pack. Flora had come close to killing her in the hospital by using one of her sired vampires. How many more vampires might be lurking inside the hospital or on their way to the docks? None of them had any idea of the number of potential lesser vampires they had as enemies. And with these vampires shrouded beneath innocent looking veneers, it was almost impossible to discern between those who were human and those who were not. The quicker they got to Micah's estate, the safer she expected to feel.

After Brady closed the passenger side door of his police cruiser, Kailey leaned her head against the headrest and closed her eyes. Even with her eyes closed she was overcome with dizziness. Her stomach twisted with nausea. She had to swallow hard to keep from dry heaving. Sweat beaded her brow, so she fanned her face.

Brady got into the driver's seat and glanced toward her before he started the engine. "Are you sure you're okay?"

Kailey nodded. She wanted to open her eyes to look at him, but doing so hurt too much. The puffiness around her eyes had reduced her visibility to the point it was a battle simply to open them. Any approaching headlights made her eyes burn and sting, even though she kept them closed.

"You look worse than you did earlier."

"Not exactly the type of compliment a woman likes to hear from her boyfriend," she said, trying to keep a slight edge of humor. "Looks aren't everything, you know?"

Brady sighed with frustration. "It wasn't meant as a compliment. I was implying how bad your injuries are."

"I know what you meant. I'll be fine."

"Look, if you need to stay the night here," he said.

Her jaw tightened at the suggestion. "No. That's the last thing I want to do."

"I know you don't *want* to, but if you need—"

"Brady, please," Kailey whispered. "I hate hospitals, okay? I always have. I want to go with you and the others. I know all of you can protect me."

"Kailey, from a physical outside attack, yes, we can protect you. But none of us have a medical background. If you get any worse, it will take too long to get you back here."

"I'll take my chances." She tilted her head in his direction and partially opened her left eye, seeing only an obscured image of him.

Brady nodded and turned the key. The engine roared. He gave her a solemn look before glancing over his shoulder to back the car from the parking spot.

She closed her eyes and leaned back. A long shallow sigh flowed past her lips. She whispered, "I'm sorry, Brady."

He didn't reply. Instead, he pressed down on the accelerator, making the engine grow louder. She didn't know if he had reacted out of anger, and she was afraid to chance another glance to know.

The sudden increase in the cruiser's speed caused her head to push against the headrest a bit harder. Small bursts of light appeared at the outer edges of each eye. Her nausea increased. She frowned and concentrated hard to keep from vomiting in the car. If she did, she knew Brady wouldn't hesitate to return to the hospital and have her admitted. She doubted he'd take any arguments, either.

"Could you turn the air on?" she asked weakly.

"Sure."

A few seconds later colder air came through the air vents, lessening the heat and stickiness of her perspiration. Inside she trembled, not from the cold air, but from the uncertainty of what might happen next with Raven. It wasn't exactly fear, but she had no words to describe the strange sensation that was attempting to freeze her from the inside outward.

"Is that better?"

Kailey nodded ever so slightly. "Do you think we'll have another encounter tonight?"

"With the vampires?"

"Yeah."

"Hard to say," he replied. "I've been watching the mirrors. No one followed us from the hospital parking lot. And the streets only have modest traffic, which is highly unusual at this hour. It's good in a way, though. We'll get there faster."

Kailey thought about Raven. The vicious glare her ex-friend had given her just moments before their fight had begun still chilled her. It was odd to see that level of hatred from the girl she had shared a dorm room with for four years. The worst part was discovering that her friend's mind had already been deeply unhinged the entire time they had lived together, and how easily Raven could have killed her during her sleep due to Raven's obsession.

She had often read about how people suddenly snap, but she believed Raven had run out of borrowed time. She had probably already been probing ways to eradicate Kailey soon after Kailey's next adamant rejection. The fact Raven had cast a love spell to draw Kailey to her was unnerving enough. Even Raven's mentor, Skye, had admonished Raven for selfishly using her magic for personal gain.

Kailey understood that love couldn't be bought. Real love didn't succumb to bribes, either. Love couldn't be forced. Love occurred naturally and at times ensnared one when the person least expected it.

Did she honestly believe in love at first sight? No. But she did believe attraction was the first major step. It kindled the very first spark. The following interactions determined whether that spark grew larger or was snuffed out immediately by the person's nature and attitude. She had met individuals that totally turned her off a few seconds into their conversation. She had also been smitten by a person's attractiveness and found them appalling rather than beautiful inside. Then she had seen men and women who were average and plain in every respect but had the kindest hearts, compassion, and weren't the least bit selfish. These were the people who appreciated and respected others' viewpoints, regardless of whether they agreed with them or not, and sadly, they were the rarest type of people to encounter.

How Raven had fooled her for four years, she still couldn't understand. Could she have masked herself with magic? *Probably.*

Because Raven had kept her in the dark so easily for so long, Kailey worried about her newfound relationship with Brady. Perhaps he was really dirt formed into the shape of a diamond? Deep down, she didn't think so. She certainly didn't want to believe that. But after being scorned by someone she had trusted, someone who had expressively said that she loved Kailey and Kailey had almost given her devotion in return; it was difficult for Kailey to fully lower the fortress walls that encased her tender heart.

Doing so exposed her to a critical fault. She didn't know if she could emotionally survive another bad relationship.

Kailey gritted her teeth. *Don't do this to yourself, Kailey. You have a concussion. Worry about all of this once your head clears.* For a moment she heard soft laughter and feared Flora was nearby. But she realized the laughter was her own because she had almost started arguing with herself. She could feel a split inside her mind as each side struggled to assert dominance over the other about Brady's romantic role in her life. *You really need to get some sleep.*

While Brady drove, the lull of the car teased her toward the edge of sleep, easing her dangerously closer to the dream realm, which could be the guise of the darker nightmares wishing to draw her in and capture her inside its inescapable web.

Brady remained quiet, and she assumed he had a lot more on his mind that he didn't want to share with her right yet. After all, his pack leader had essentially deserted them to better secure his role with Nocturnal Trinity. Even if this was what was plaguing his mind, she wished Brady would say something, *anything*. The verbal interaction helped her focus on staying awake, but she didn't want to interrupt his concentration should he be pondering what they must do as a pack once they reached Micah's estate.

It wasn't any secret that Jacob didn't want Micah to remain their leader. He was quite vocal about his opposition. Perhaps Brady's mind was drifting there as well. Without Micah leading their cause, it made sense for them to find a new Alpha. Jacob was strong and loyal, but his loyalty wasn't to Micah. She had seen them butt heads several times. He also had a short temper and acted out of haste. His kind of leadership might cause the pack more harm than good.

What she had seen of Brady thus far indicated that he was more than capable of steady, thoughtful leadership. Being a law enforcement officer he should have acquired the experience necessary to make logical decisions during the times of crisis. And while he and Jacob seemed to get along quite well, she wasn't certain how Jacob might react should Brady decide Jacob wasn't the best choice for a new Alpha. If Brady insisted Micah reside as the Alpha, Jacob's inner rage might surpass reasonable accountability, making him attack Brady or others in the pack to prove his dominance. Whether Jacob won or lost, the damage was done and probably could never be repaired.

"You still awake?" Brady asked.

"Barely."

"Hang on. We're almost there."

"Good. If I keep riding, I'm going to fall asleep."

"We can't have that," Brady replied.

The car slowed to a near stop. Brady turned to the left and downward into the parking lot near Elliott Bay. She opened her eyes as best she could. Through the watery film that coated them, she watched the boat dock come into focus beneath a yellow sodium streetlight. The police cruiser's headlights washed across several shadowy figures.

Blaze and Luna sat on the hood of Jacob's car with Barry and Jacob standing slightly in front of them. They held their guns to their sides.

"Is there a problem?" Brady asked, getting out of the car.

"We can't be too sure, yet," Jacob replied.

Brady frowned. "What do you mean?"

"Blaze and Luna saw the vampires' silver limo pass a few minutes ago while Barry and I were checking the boat's fuel level."

Kailey pressed her door closed. "You're sure?"

Luna nodded. "Yes, it stopped for only a few moments. By the time Jacob came over, it had pulled away."

Brady turned and looked toward the street, which was at a higher level than the parking lot. "It appears they had no intention to stick around. Just scare tactics."

Blaze shook his head. "No. The car door slammed on the other side of the limo. I think someone got out."

Brady's hand rested on his gun. "Why didn't you say that earlier? Jacob, is the boat ready?"

"Yep."

"Everyone, get on the boat, and let's get across the bay."

"You think someone's still up there?" Kailey asked.

"It's hard to say since the wind is blowing in that direction. I can't get a scent," Brady replied.

"I couldn't either," Jacob said, tossing the rope into the boat. He extended his hand to Kailey to help her into the boat.

Barry started the motor, adjusted the throttle, and said, "Let's go, Brady."

A gunshot echoed through the parking lot.

"Sonofa—" Brady clutched his left shoulder and dropped to his knees behind a large wooden tie post. He unsnapped his holster and drew his gun.

"Brady!" Kailey said. She tried to get back out of the boat, but Jacob wrapped his arms around her. "Let me go, dammit!"

"No. You need to get down," Jacob said.

Another shot echoed. The bullet struck the side of the boat, ripping through the fiberglass.

"Brady!" Kailey screamed, still struggling to break free of Jacob's stern grip.

"Stay down, Kailey," Brady said, anger stirring in his voice. "You're the target. Barry, get the boat out of here. Now!"

"Not without you," Barry replied.

Gunfire cracked again. This bullet struck the post, an inch above Brady's head.

Jacob fired several shots in the direction of where the gunshots were coming, but with the darkness beneath the lower end of the overpass, no one was visible. He was just shooting blind, but it was enough to give Brady cover to run to the boat, but he didn't.

"Get to the boat, Brady," Kailey said. "Please!"

Brady turned toward the boat. His eyes were golden brown. Long thick canine teeth lengthened in his mouth, making it difficult for him to speak. He hissed, "Get her to the island, Barry. Now!"

No further hesitation came from Barry. The front of the boat rose as he sent it into motion and increased the speed.

Brady, not fully a werewolf, charged from the protection of the large post and across the parking lot toward the street overpass. Another shot echoed. Brady's body jerked, and he dropped facedown on the pavement. His gun slid from his hand and spiraled a few feet from his reach. He wasn't moving, and with Kailey's blurred vision she couldn't tell much more. The boat was taking her farther into the bay. The last image was a shadowy figure approaching Brady's body and kicking Brady's gun farther out of his reach.

"Brady!" Kailey screamed. Her voice broke with desperate sobs. Tears burned her eyes. If Brady was dead, she might as well be, too. She couldn't handle any more loss or heartache. She'd rather die.

CHAPTER 25

"Vampires and werewolves?" Lydia said. "Do you realize how preposterous that sounds?"

"To you? Yes. But you have to understand that I learned of their existence when I was a child. And what about how you explain to others what you are?"

"I usually don't. I'm not too social, and I like my privacy."

"Then you and I have a lot more in common than I realized."

"You don't like people either?" Lydia asked.

"It's not really that. But humanity is filled with hateful cunning people and the longer I live, the more spite and evil I see veiled beneath human flesh. You'd think eventually people would wake up and attempt to find ways to work in harmony. But chaos is far greater and reigns supreme."

Lydia studied him for several moments. "You're not getting religious on me, are you?"

"Not at all. But, since you brought it up, do you believe in a Heaven and Hell?" Forrest asked.

"It's something I've struggled with for a long time. I don't even know if I have a soul since I was created inside a laboratory."

"You have a conscience, don't you?"

"I tend to ignore it, as much as I can."

"Just like seventy percent of mankind," Forrest replied. He frowned, thinking for a moment. "Might make that eighty-five percent."

"So what about you? Do you believe in these afterlife places?"

Forrest offered a slight smile. "For a long, long time, I did not."

"But now you do?"

Forrest shrugged. "I don't know that I completely do, but after encountering demons, several hundred of them, you tend to wonder what type of dark forces you're dealing with. It adds a sliver of credible to the evil we find in this world."

Her jaw slacked, and she cocked a brow. "Wait a minute. Vampires, werewolves, *and* demons? What are you smoking? I'd even venture to guess you are on peyote except we're too far north."

He laughed. "The demons I can prove exist quite readily, if you'll accompany me to Nocturnal Trinity. A lot of them work openly at the nightclub without bothering to disguise themselves."

"And the vampires and werewolves? Are they there, too?"

"Could be. But werewolves tend to keep lower profiles and not reveal what they are. At least not to normal humans and certainly *not* to the vampires who take sport in killing werewolves."

"What do you mean by normal?"

"Almost anyone else except for us."

"Is that so?" she said with a slightly amused smile. "I'd guess that your two companions are in our category?"

"You're catching on."

"So, if they're not normal, what are they?"

"They're a different kind of shapeshifter," Forrest said.

"I see. What do they turn into?"

"Otters."

Lydia sat in silence and leaned her back against the wall in the corner of her side of the booth, placing one of her legs across the cushioned bench.

"It's a bit much?" Forrest asked. "For you to take in?"

She shook her head. "No."

"Then what?"

"I just find it odd that you have these shapeshifters, which I'm guessing had somehow evolved in nature, and yet, I've seen similar creatures that have been genetically designed in the laboratories. How have these natural ones gone unnoticed by the scientific community?"

"Like you. They've gone into hiding. They are safer if they're not discovered. Doesn't that sound familiar to you?"

Lydia nodded. "It does. But I've had to hide simply because too many want me to do hit jobs for them."

"And you don't wish to kill these people?"

"Killing assignments don't bother me because most of the targets are ruthless people. What I want to avoid is being under the control of someone else. Most of these, I don't think *clients* is an appropriate term, are people who desire my assassin services and they are no better than the bad people they want me to kill. I mean, that's not always the case … because sometimes innocent people are on the run and need protection from an abusive spouse or they are like me and escaped from a lab. People like myself have never been considered human by the ones that created us. We're projects. Lab animals. Creatures they wish to study. Property. To escape their clutches … these labs go to no end trying to capture or kill those who were smart enough to break free."

Forrest gazed into her cold eyes. "Sounds like you've had personal experience with this."

Lydia nodded. "My creator tried to capture me several times. I was his prototype. I was never intended to roam the world free. Hell, I'd have remained inside an incubation chamber forever had …" Her voice broke. "Had someone not demanded my release—"

"At least you were rescued."

"His intentions were selfish, too, though he didn't intentional mean for them to be. But, the pursuit by different labs to obtain me never ended. So instead of running, I began hunting them. I sought to destroy their facilities and their data. They were dangerous people."

"And now you've chosen to hide?" Forrest asked.

"Faking my death doesn't mean I won't still pursue them. I can hunt them now without them being on guard. Besides, there are hundreds of underground labs. Our government has shadow agencies that perform the same type of genetic engineering. Whether people want to admit it or not, this world will soon be controlled by one large government, and unlike those who are eager to see that happen, it won't be what they have hoped for. All their glorious freedoms, at least in this country, will be gone forever. The type of government that's coming will be so rigid, any protestors will be killed immediately."

Forrest sighed. "You paint a grim picture."

"It's a grim world."

"Perhaps it is, but what you're predicting, and I have no doubt you're correct in your diagnosis, is what I'm trying to destroy as well. Not your labs or your greedy scientists or corrupt politicians, but the vampires. They are our greatest threat. And this one world government you're envisaging?"

She turned slightly in the corner to see his face. "Yes?"

"Humans … well, *mortals* won't be the ones ruling. Vampires will."

She frowned. "How do you figure?"

"Seattle is a prime example. Nocturnal Trinity has been a breeding ground for the vampire movement for decades, but the good news is, the founders of this nightclub are splitting into different directions. Once their Unity is dissolved, their power will begin to dwindle. It doesn't mean they won't seek a new place, but I intend to destroy the five remaining vampires who are part of the original founders."

"What makes you believe these vampires will take control of the government?"

"Because they have the power of mind control. These five vampires I am hunting … they are several centuries old. The older a vampire is, the more power he or she has. Trust me, one of these vampires has enough power to compel and control fifty or more people, hold them spellbound, and have them do whatever the vampire desires, which means, they can form an army in a matter of minutes should they be in a highly populated area. But what's worse. If powerful vampires start siring hundreds of devoted children, you're talking about a force far darker than your shadow government agencies. Hell hasn't seen such fury. And I speculate some of these agencies are already under the control of vampires. Vampires are already controlling some congressmen, mayors, governors, and military leaders. Some of them might even be vampires."

"Damn," she said in a low voice. "Most politicians are bloodsucking leeches anyway."

"No argument from me."

"To sire others, does that mean by force or does the recipient need to be willing?"

"Come to Nocturnal Trinity with me. I'll buy you a drink. And then you'll see firsthand how many naïve individuals are already begging to be turned."

"You're serious?"

"More than you can imagine."

"Will Ian and Gunner accompany us to this nightclub?" she asked.

"Not inside, but they will come close-by."

"Why won't they enter?"

A grim expression appeared on Forrest's face. He shook his head. "They both are ashamed of their appearances."

"So that's why they didn't come in here with us?"

"Exactly."

"That's terrible. You'd think they could have dental work done or something."

"They tried. It didn't last."

"Ah." She grimaced and shook her head sadly.

"So you didn't come to Seattle alone?" Forrest asked.

"No. Two of my group are here. They wanted to see if they could find some of the … well, we thought the werewolves here were more escaped lab experiments instead of what they really are. They'll be surprised to learn otherwise."

Forrest drank the last of his coffee and set down the cup. "How many are in your group?"

"A few dozen."

"They are all wolves?"

Lydia shook her head. "No. Over the years they have rescued other shifters from various laboratories. Some have large feline DNA spliced into theirs. Various large cats like panthers and lions."

"And everyone gets along?"

"As best they can. When you know your life is endangered by human scientists that give orders to mercenaries, it's best to stick with others similarly created."

"I can't argue with that. But what you have … these genetic differences, it's not contagious, is it?"

"No. We cannot pass this to others."

"We?" Forrest frowned.

Lydia nodded.

"Does that mean you can alter? I thought you were simply an enhanced human."

"I was."

"Then if it's not contagious like real werewolves, how is it that you have that capability?"

"Through an injection of wolf DNA."

"You did this intentionally?" Forrest asked.

She shook her head. "No. It was done to me by a scientist right before you and I first met."

"Why didn't you inform me when I was helping you?"

"At the time, I didn't know what the injection was. I found out after you helped fake my death."

"I see."

"So these werewolves you know can transmit their disease?" Lydia asked.

"Yes. Through bites or scratches. From what one of my cousins told me long ago, it's a virus that has bound to their blood cells, and often it's carried on their skin. He said that it lies dormant on the skin until it makes contact with human blood." Forrest glanced at the clock above the service counter. "Look, it's getting late, so we'd best hurry to Nocturnal Trinity."

"Do they close soon?"

Forrest released a deep hearty chuckle. "After midnight's when they're the most active. I just want to hurry before the waiting lines get too long."

"The club draws that big of a crowd?"

"Some people would fight or kill to become a member. My guess is that some have."

"Really?"

He nodded.

"What's the attraction?"

"Eternal life while on earth. That marketing slogan works pretty good, too."

"How?"

Forrest stood. "Their selection for members is slim. Over ninety-nine percent never get accepted."

"Then why do they keep coming?"

"Most people covet the items they're forbidden to have. For some reason, that seems instilled into most humans' minds."

"That seems counterintuitive."

"No, it's quite the opposite. Wait until we get there. You'll see. Eager people will be begging and pleading to get inside."

CHAPTER 26

Kailey fumed. "What the hell, Jacob? How could you leave Brady behind?"

She formed fists and wanted to stand, but the bouncing of the boat across the waves and her dizziness objected.

"We did what he told us to do," Jacob replied coldly.

"Is he dead?"

Jacob's jaw tightened, and he looked away without replying. Barry kept his eyes on the water ahead of them, careful that his gaze never met hers.

"We have to go back, Barry," Kailey said.

"That's not an option," Jacob said.

Luna wrapped her arms around Kailey and hugged her tightly. Although the sentiment half annoyed Kailey, she didn't push Luna away. An embrace was something she needed during such turmoil and not too often had she received one whenever her world was torn and falling apart.

Kailey closed her eyes and leaned back against the side of the boat. The cold night wind swept around her with beads of mist coating her. She sobbed and placed a hand over her face. Luna shushed softly in her ear.

Feeling the warmth of someone's approach, she lowered her hand and peered through the slits of her swollen eyes. Jacob had lowered himself into a crouch and was a few inches away from her.

He placed a gentle hand on her shoulder. "Brady will be okay, provided the bullets weren't silver."

"And if they were?" she asked through her tear-saturated voice.

"Then there wasn't anything that we could have done anyway. I'm sorry we had to leave him, but our priority is to keep you safe. That's what he wanted and what he insisted that we do, regardless of whatever else might happen."

She frowned and pain seared through her head. "When did he ever give such a command?"

Jacob's face tightened at her choice of words, but not from evident anger. "After you moved in with him, he insisted that the pack kept you safe, especially if anything ever happened to him. He loves you more than anything else in this world. More than life itself, but I don't need to tell you that, do I?"

He rose and sat at the front of the boat near Barry. He offered a grim expression to Barry, and both held a bit of sadness in their exchanged glances. Determined anger and revenge also stirred. If not for rushing her to safety, the two werewolves wouldn't have abandoned Brady, making her feel guilty, as the sole reason Brady might be dead.

Fresh tears burned Kailey's eyes. Jacob's reply indicated that his loyalty was to Brady more than it ever had been to Micah. If the pack needed a new leader, Brady was destined to become the one to take over. She didn't believe Jacob would even challenge Brady's authority.

He won't need to if you're dead, Brady. Please be alive. Don't leave me. She sent the wish across the water, hoping that somehow his spirit received the message.

Kailey shook with sudden chills, partially from slowly being drenched by the mist and splashing waves, but also from her growing fear. The only warmth she had was where Luna hugged her. With the knowledge that someone had gotten out of the silver limo, the person was associated with the remaining five founding vampires, so he ... or *she* ... knew silver bullets killed werewolves. There was a greater chance that Brady was dead than him still being alive. Unless ... they wanted to take him hostage or torture him.

Even though she didn't know if prayers could be answered, or if any god would bother hearing her after years of constant denial, she found herself actually praying to any higher power that might hear and grant her request for Brady to be alive. After several minutes, she realized it was a one-way conversation. She didn't know enough about prayer, nor had she any deep understanding or experience with the topic, to know if she was supposed to receive some type of verbal reply. Probably not, but she issued the request one more time.

Please be alive, Brady. I need you, more than I could ever say. I know ... for the first time in my life ... I know what true love is. Her heart ached. Her stomach twisted. *Cassie, where did you go? Why did you leave us? If ever I needed your help, it's now.*

She took a deep breath and released it slowly through her mouth. So much for her prayers to a higher power when it was followed by what some might have considered another prayer and one to a demon, nonetheless. But she was serious about needing Cassie's help. She truly hoped Cassie had heard her plea.

Where are you, Cassie?

~

Forrest and Lydia walked past the long line composed of impatient people. They booed and jeered at him, but he ignored them and kept walking until he faced Titus at the door.

"I need to see your membership badge," Titus said. His gaze peered past Forrest and gave Lydia a swift up and down glance, apparently trying to check her out in spite of the poncho. He gave a broad smile and a quick wink, which was ignored by Lydia. She crossed her arms and frowned in return. "Brought yourself a foxy lady tonight?"

"Yes, she's my guest."

"I need to see your badge. No badge. I can't let you inside. Sorry."

Forrest frowned and leveled a harsh stare. "I was here *this morning.*"

"That was this morning."

"I didn't need a badge then."

"You do now."

Forrest's right hand formed a tight fist. "And why's that?"

"Orders from higher ups," Titus said, taking a step back. Titus was a huge bouncer, but Forrest was a mountain of dread and muscle, towering over him.

"You're going to let me pass," Forrest said.

Titus cleared his throat, trying to maintain a strict composure. He whispered, "I can't. If I do, they will bring the hammer down on me."

"Not if I handle them for you," Forrest replied.

"Sorry, no." Titus shook his head.

Forrest's eyes narrowed. His jaw tightened. "You're worried about how they will punish you, but what about me and what I can do to you right now? Believe me, you don't want the humiliation of me pommeling you in front of all these people, do you? That would quickly diminish your toughness, not to mention lead others to believe they might be able to do the same. And when you go down, that leaves no one else to guard the door. I'll let all of them go inside. How does that rest with you?"

"Okay, but work with me now, all right?" Titus said.

Forrest cocked a brow.

Titus put out his hand to shake with Forrest. Forrest glanced at it and then gazed sternly into Titus' eyes. "Come on, go with it."

Forrest clasped his huge hand around the bouncer's.

Titus chuckled loudly and patted Forrest's arm with his left hand. "Just playing wit'cha, man. Welcome to the Nocturnal Trinity." Titus stepped aside and as Forrest and Lydia walked past, he whispered, "I hope you understand that you have officially signed my death warrant, Forrest."

"Don't be so melodramatic," Forrest said.

"What?" Titus said, turning sharply. "Hell, man, you have no idea what they're capable of at all."

"I know exactly what they're capable of. I've known it longer than you've been alive. What you need to understand is what I'm capable of doing. Trust me."

"Trust you? A dead man places no trust in anyone."

"You're not dead yet. I intend to keep it that way." Forrest pulled the door open and allowed Lydia to enter first.

After the door closed, Lydia said, "You have a charming way with words. You always this friendly?"

"I often have worse days," Forrest replied.

"Me, too."

"You saw the line?"

"Of course. Who could miss it?"

Loud music thundered from the speakers as they left the front and headed into the first dance hall. Strobe lights flashed while an assortment of various colored rays of light shot out in different directions. The smell of cigarette smoke, leather, and sweat permeated the air.

Forrest turned toward her and raised his voice. "That's what I was telling you. Most of them want inside this nightclub so badly, they'd eagerly offer their lives to become one of the undead vampires and *this* is a slow night."

"I see. Aren't you worried about the man at the door?"

"Titus?"

She nodded.

"Not particularly," he replied.

"So his—death warrant—as he called it, that's not real?"

"Oh, what he said is the truth. I'm certain he was told that I wasn't allowed to enter."

"They'd kill him for that?"

"Absolutely."

"And you don't care?"

Forrest looked into her eyes and chuckled. "There are two reasons why I'm not concerned about them hurting or killing him tonight. One, they've not been in the nightclub in several weeks. They've avoided this place altogether."

"Why?"

"Because of me. They know I'm here to slay them."

"Okay, so what's the second reason?" she asked.

"Unless he tells them that he's allowed me inside, they are not going to know right away. That gives him time, and if he needs help, I will assist in getting him somewhere safe and out of their reach."

Lydia leaned closer to Forrest and tiptoed to whisper in his ear. "You really believe there are vampires here tonight?"

"I have no doubts."

She glanced around at the dancers in the shifting crowd. Some wore capes, pale makeup, and streaks of fake blood dried at the edges of their mouths. Others had fangs protruded from their mouths. "How can you tell the real ones from the fake?"

"For starters," Forrest said, "those who look like cheap imitations at a Halloween party, are just that. True vampires won't be so flamboyant. It's not in their nature in a crowded room. They are covert, and use charm and seduction to lure potential victims."

"So you can't tell?"

"Not always, but there are ways of getting the proper reactions to cull them out. A silver cross or garlic is often enough to make them flinch. Then, it's slay or be killed."

"They don't flee?" she asked.

"Not readily. Understand though. They are incredible fast. Never make eye contact. And as I already told you, the older vampires are the most powerful. But I don't plan to cause a scene here tonight unless a certain two vampires happen to make an appearance."

"Then why are we here?"

Forrest smiled. "First, I'll buy you a drink, and then I'll introduce you to some people I need to talk to. While we drink, take that opportunity to scout out the area and study how these people interact. You'll learn a lot in fifteen minutes."

Lydia shrugged. "I've already seen enough to know you weren't exaggerating. If anything you were probably *under*selling the place."

Forrest set his Hunter box on the floor and sat on a stool at the bar. Lydia took the stool beside him. The female bartender stood with her back to them. She wore snug tether cloth pants that outlined her form perfectly. Her spiraled hair was pulled back into a ponytail. When she turned, she gave Forrest a warm smile and then turned her attention toward Lydia with a skeptical stare.

"Cassie?" Forrest said. "You're working here?"

Cassie grinned, coming closer to the bar, and placing her hand atop his. Her eyes narrowed at Lydia. "Who's your … new friend?"

"An old acquaintance," he said with his face tinting red. He tipped the rim of his hat forward to shadow his face a bit more. "This is Lydia. Lydia, meet Cassie."

Neither woman smiled or offered a warm greeting to the other.

Cassie tilted her head and studied the hardness of Lydia's brow, tightened jaw, and cold eyes. "She seems your type, I suppose. Icy stare and deep-seated anger. Ruthless Hunter like yourself?"

"Uh, no," Forrest replied softly. "Nothing like that."

"I'm not making a move on him, if that's what you're worried about," Lydia said in a low tone. "When he said, 'acquaintance,' that's exactly what he meant. We met only briefly before."

"I see," Cassie said with a smile. Her lips curled. A flicker of amusement danced merrily in her brilliant eyes.

"It's true," Forrest said, still slightly embarrassed and almost apologetic.

Cassie squinted, making her cute nose scrunch. She sweetened her voice in a mocking tone. "Well, if *that's* true, what brings her back into your life? Hmm?"

Lydia rose in her barstool and leaned partway across the bar. "Asking too many damn questions is dangerous."

"Careful, girl, sometimes you're entertaining demons unaware," Cassie replied, revealing her sharp demon teeth. Her eyes blazed crimson.

Lydia eased back. No fear showed on her face, but she had been caught by surprise. She glanced at Forrest with a question in her expression.

Forrest simply nodded. "She's a demon."

"She looks just like us, other than her teeth and eyes."

Cassie reared back her head, cackling with high-pitched laughter. Seconds later, her short horns protruded on her forehead, wings unfolded on her back, and her long tail whipped around, coming remarkably close to smacking Lydia in the face.

Lydia's hand went beneath her vinyl poncho. Before she drew her gun, Forrest placed his hand atop hers and shook his head.

"Don't," Forrest whispered.

"You saw that. She tried to strike me."

"If I intended to hit you," Cassie said, "I would have."

"Besides," Forrest added. "You're only going to piss her off if you shoot her. A bullet won't kill her."

Lydia placed her hands over her face and rubbed her eyes.

"Why is she here, Forrest?" Cassie asked.

"She insists she owes me a favor."

"I do."

"And," Forrest said, "she wants to help us."

"Ah," Cassie said with raised eyebrows. She offered her hand. Lydia regarded the offer for several long seconds before finally shaking hands. "Good. Why not say that during the introductions, Forrest? Why get all flustered over it?"

Forrest leveled an even stare at Cassie. "Give me two shots of whiskey."

Cassie laughed. "Coming right up. What about you, Lydia?"

"The same."

"Really?" Cassie asked.

Lydia shrugged. "Yeah, I think I'm going to need it."

Cassie took two thick glasses, set them on the bar, and poured two shots into each.

Forrest grabbed his drink and turned it straight up. He slammed the glass onto the bar. "Have you seen Micah tonight?"

Cassie shook her head. "No. I arrived about a half hour ago. Why?"

"I have some things I need to discuss with him."

"Flora and Raven?" Cassie asked.

"That would be part of it," Forrest replied.

Cassie frowned. Her crimson eyes blazed her inner anger. "They're the reason I am here tonight, too. I hope either one of them makes an entrance."

Forrest straightened in his seat. "What happened?"

"Raven tried to kill Kailey."

"When?"

Cassie did a quick run-through of the events that had occurred at the fight and afterwards.

Forrest stood and tossed a couple of twenties on the bar. "Let's go find Micah, Lydia."

"I'm coming with you," Cassie said. She tossed a towel to a shorter woman. "Watch the bar."

The woman took the towel and grumbled beneath her breath.

"If they show up tonight," Forrest said, "we can end all this nonsense forever."

"Nothing ever goes like you hope or plan," Lydia said.

"Amen to that, sister," Cassie said.

Lydia gave Cassie an odd side-glance. "Isn't such a statement coming from a demon somewhat contradictory and hypocritical?"

Cassie shrugged. "No worse than those pretending to be holy and living more riotous than me."

Lydia shook her head. "Seems you and I have met the same people."

CHAPTER 27

Forrest walked the narrow stairs that led to the werewolf quarters. Cassie and Lydia followed behind. When he reached the top of the stairs, he rapped his massive fist against the side of the open door.

Micah turned in his desk chair and faced the doorway. He smiled and motioned with his hand. "Forrest? Come in! I'm sorry for the harsh disagreement we had this morning. I was afraid you might never return."

Near the desk, Ashley was seated in another chair. Jaclyn stood across the desk with two more women. Forrest removed his hat and regarded them each with a polite smile and a nod. He returned his attention to his cousin and gave an even stare. "Micah, it's not that easy to rid yourself of family, no matter how often you clash in doctrine. I'm sure your father taught you that."

"Indeed, he did."

"I'm not interrupting anything, am I?" Forrest asked.

Micah rose to his feet. "Not at all. In fact, what we've been discussing is something we welcome you to offer your opinions as well." He acknowledged Cassie with a smile and looked to Lydia. "Hi, Cassie. Who is your guest?"

Forrest gave quick introductions, and then Micah introduced the other two women who were the new witches in the Circle of Unity.

Raine was slender—some people might have considered it an *unhealthy* slender—with auburn hair, pale blue eyes, an oval face, and a dimpled chin. Her smile was delightful and her eyes probed to read Forrest's aura. Gillian had a dark complexion and jet-black hair and eyes. She was plump, but not overly obese and she stood a little over five foot in height. She reminded Forrest of the Roma Gypsies he had met when he was young and lived in Bucharest. Power flowed from her and slithered its tendrils toward him. By his estimate, her power was equal if not greater than Jaclyn's, which made him wonder why Jaclyn had chosen her. Jaclyn had seemed more the type who wouldn't remain comfortable unless she held the most advantage when it came to the use of magic.

In some ways the comparison of power might not matter at all since Jaclyn was a necromancer. He didn't have any idea what kind of magic Gillian held an affinity for, but together, their power might have been more reason for the founding vampires to shy away from returning to a nightclub they had established.

Micah returned his attention to Lydia.

"So she's here to help?" Micah asked. Then his eyes widened. "Wait, is this the Lydia we've heard about?"

"The same," Forrest replied.

"Finally!" Micah said, crossing the room and offering his hand. "I was beginning to believe it was all pure conjecture. Something like the legend of Bigfoot, but of course, you're far too pretty for me to make such a comparison."

Ashley's eyes narrowed when Lydia shook Micah's hand.

Lydia frowned, glancing around at the others. "Thanks? I think."

Micah faced Forrest. "Did Cassie tell you about Kailey's encounter with Raven?"

Forrest nodded. "She did. We're hoping Raven or Flora stop by tonight."

"It's doubtful they will," Jaclyn said. Her long dark hair was pulled back and flowed down her rich blue robe like silken threads. She wore vivid emerald earrings and a matching broach. No makeup, but the radiance of her face detailed she had no need for it. Her face was almost as angelic as some of the statues Forrest had seen in cathedrals in Europe. But in the same manner vampires could glamour, some witches had mastered a similar art with spells.

"Jaclyn and I are preparing to perform a location spell to see if we can find their whereabouts," Micah said.

"How exactly do you plan to do that?" Forrest said. "I thought the undead were too difficult to pinpoint simply because you can't distinguish them from actual corpses."

"That's true," Jaclyn said. "But, we should be able to find their servant Andreas."

"And how will finding him help us find them?"

Micah smiled. "We don't know for absolute certainty, but there's a strong chance he's the driver of the limo. After they stopped coming to Nocturnal Trinity, he did, too."

"Not a bad idea, providing you can find him," Forrest said. He shifted his gaze to Jaclyn. "I need a favor, Jaclyn."

She regarded him with a curious stare. "What type of favor?"

"I need you to remove a concealment spell," he replied.

"What is this spell concealing?" Gillian asked.

Forrest flicked his gaze toward her. "I'm not exactly sure."

"Then how do you know something is hidden at all?" Jaclyn asked.

"It's a feeling I have. A strong hunch."

Raine shook her head. "For us to use magic it has to be something *more* than a hunch. So what is it that you're hoping to find?"

Forrest sighed and leaned his shoulder against the wall. "It's highly unlikely you'll believe what I tell you."

Jaclyn smiled. "You might be surprised. We're not narrow-minded people. How could we be with what we have devoted ourselves to?"

Forrest chewed on his lower lip as he slowly evaluated each of them. Their eyes and expressions revealed nothing sinister in their nature. "You remember removing the concealment spell in the tunnel beneath Nocturnal Trinity?"

Jaclyn nodded. "Of course. Why?"

"There's another tunnel farther away from here where I believe something quite useful to our cause has been hidden."

"Like what?" Gillian asked.

"I'll get to that in a moment. But first let me point out that the vampires are not the only enemies we have in the Circle of Unity."

"You'd be implying that the demons are our enemies, then?" Micah asked. He slowly sat down behind the desk and folded his hands on the desktop. He looked concerned by the accusation.

"Not all of them," Forrest replied. "Only the founding demons."

Micah glanced from Forrest to a worried Jaclyn and then to Forrest again. "Jinn? Has he given you problems? I don't consider him an enemy."

"I'm not talking about Jinn," Forrest said. "He's not one of the founding demons. I'm talking about the other five. When have any of you ever seen one of them?"

Micah and the others all exchanged bewildered glances as their minds raced.

"Come to think of it, never," Micah said.

All of the others shook their heads, too.

"But Jinn's here most of the time," Micah said.

Cassie placed her hands on her hips. "But Forrest is right, Jinn *isn't* one of the founding demons."

"He's not?" Jaclyn asked.

"No," Forrest replied. "I talked to him. He was given the status only because he has charisma and is able to get along with the patrons. The other five demons, however, are more horrific than anything you can fathom."

"That's what Jinn said?" Micah asked.

"Yes."

"He tends to … over embellish his stories," Micah said.

Forrest shook his head. "Not about this. I believe he was telling me the truth because his fear of them is genuine. I told him to set up a meeting with one of them for me. The terror on his face and in his voice was evident. He actually pleaded for me to reconsider."

"I think you should, too," Micah said. "If they're as bad as he indicates, why do you even want to be in the same room with one of them?"

"That's what I'm getting to. It's why I need Jaclyn's help in that abandoned tunnel."

Concern furrowed Jaclyn's brow. She folded her arms across her stomach and after several long moments, she offered a reassuring smile. "Your pain is deep. I sense it. Tell me why exactly."

Gillian smiled at Jaclyn and nodded. "I sense his pain, too. Please tell us."

"Jinn has become one of the founders because the original demon he replaced was killed many years ago by a Demon-hunter, who was a dear friend of mine." Forrest paused, trying not to cry as his mind focused on the pain of his loss again, and he became partially angered at himself for allowing his voice to break. "When the Great Fire of Seattle occurred, we received the news while we were in Germany. It was on the front page of a newspaper. She swore she saw demons in the picture of the flames. Because she was a Demon-hunter, she insisted she come here and eradicate them. I pleaded for her to wait until I was able to travel with her, but the urgency of an open portal to the abyss was too much for her to ignore. She left without me. I never heard from her again."

"Wait a minute," Raine said. "When the Great Fire occurred? Are you saying that you're more than a century old?"

Lydia gave Forrest an astounded look but said nothing.

"I'm close to one hundred and thirty years old," he replied.

The witches' eyes widened.

"We can discuss my age at another time."

Jaclyn nodded. "Okay, so what do you think we need to reveal that's in that tunnel? The Demon-hunter? Do you think she's somehow still alive, after all this time?"

Forrest shrugged. "Honestly, I don't know. I hope she is, but I truly believe that there's something in that tunnel that will answer a lot of questions for me and might be important enough to save all our lives."

Micah took a deep breath and released a long, slow sigh. "Forrest, until you brought this up, I never really thought about the actual demon founders. To the best of my knowledge, none of them came to help Nicodemus at all."

"No," Forrest said, "they didn't."

"Odd."

"What?" Forrest asked.

Micah leaned back in his chair. "Why would they sacrifice the strongest vampire? Surely, they could have come to protect him."

"They could have, if they had wanted to," Forrest replied.

"But they didn't," Micah said in a soft confused tone.

Jaclyn laughed quietly.

"What?" Micah asked.

"Don't you see?" Jaclyn said. "They gave you Nicodemus to appease you and probably Forrest because they knew they had five more vampire masters."

"So?" Micah said.

"My mother could have explained this better," Jaclyn said. "But Nicodemus' death was a warning to the others that the demons didn't actually need them. His death might have been a punishment, too. The division between the factions has been around almost from the time they consecrated the pact. Forrest is right. The demons have the greatest power in the Unity."

Micah nodded. "I never looked at it like that, but you're right. But ... I've seen a lot of demons in their VIP lounge and on the dance floor. A lot of them are employed here, too. I assumed the founders were simply blending in with the rest of the crowd."

Forrest shook his head. "No. Jinn allows demon guests to go into the VIP lounge. Very seldom, he said, do any of the founders ever make an appearance. Most humans cannot handle viewing them."

Jaclyn said, "And you want to meet one of them?"

"I'm not like most humans," he replied.

"Nor am I," Lydia said.

"You deem them a threat to us?" Micah asked.

"Yes. And here's why. We've been led to believe that the vampires are the controlling factor in the Unity circle, but that's what they wanted us to believe. These five demons, according to Jinn, could annihilate the founding vampires without hardly any effort, but they don't because they'd rather be in the background since their hideous forms would repel their client base. So, they need the vampires as the front, the appeal factor, but they're also obligated to protect the vampires in return for rescuing them from the abyss."

Cassie shook her head. "The abyss is not a pleasant place to abide. It's actually the cruelest form of punishment for any demon."

Forrest patted the side of his Hunter box. "Since Flora and her siblings know I'm not leaving Seattle until I've slain them, the demons also know. I expect some type of reaction from them soon."

"Then why do you want to meet one?"

"To find out what happened to Penelope," Forrest replied softly.

"She's the Demon-hunter?" Gillian asked.

"Yes."

Jaclyn glanced at Gillian and Raine. "Sisters, I say we aid the Hunter in his cause."

"I agree," Raine said.

Gillian nodded her agreement.

"Tomorrow at dawn," Jaclyn said. "Meet us here, and then take us to the underground tunnel. If there's anything hidden by magic, the three of us will find it."

Forrest's eyes moistened with tears, but they never spilled over. "Thank you, ladies."

CHAPTER 28

By the time Jacob docked the boat at the shoreline of Micah's estate, Kailey was shivering uncontrollably. Due to the rough crossing of the bay and because the mist had turned into light rain, she was drenched. Inside, she felt like her inner core was one big chunk of ice. Fear and uncertainty about Brady's welfare also chilled her. The only good thing was that she had not fallen asleep.

Luna and Blaze stood to each side of her and helped her step out of the boat onto the wave-polished rocks in the shallow water. They walked from the water and stepped upon the grassy bank.

"Don't go any farther," Jacob said. "Stay put."

Luna glanced at Blaze. He shrugged.

"She's freezing," Luna said.

Jacob grabbed the front of the boat and pulled it farther onto the rocky shore. "We need to check the perimeter before any of you go near the house."

Kailey tried to open her eyes wider, but the puffiness and swelling prevented her from doing so. She hated not being able to see more than a narrow sliver of the landscape ahead of them. In spite of her being numb and shaking, Jacob was right. None of them could risk assuming any place was safe at the moment. Raven had been to Micah's place, and since Raven knew where it was, Flora did, too. The last thing they had expected was to be fired on at the docks where Brady had been shot twice. Apparently the vampires had anticipated Brady might seek to head across the bay. And since someone had been waiting on the docks, Jacob was taking the proper precautions.

Jacob and Barry tied the boat, pulled their guns, and headed toward Micah's dark house shrouded by the drifting fog coming off the bay. Jacob headed to the left side of the house along the driveway while Barry took the right, disappearing into the thick shadowed row of evergreen trees.

Nausea swirled inside Kailey's stomach. She took a deep breath and held it, hoping to abate the urge to vomit. It didn't help. After exhaling, she jerked free of Blaze and Luna's hold, dropping to her knees. "Sorry."

She retched but nothing came up. Doing so hurt, and after several more empty attempts, Kailey groaned. Luna knelt beside her and gently rubbed her back.

"You okay?" Luna asked in her sweet tone.

"Peachy." Kailey wiped her mouth with the back of her hand. "I think it would've been better if something *had* come up."

Blaze dropped to one knee beside her. "When you're ready, we'll help you up."

Kailey offered a weak nod and reached for his hand and Luna's. They eased her into a standing position.

The two minutes it took for Barry and Jacob to return from the other side of the house seemed like an hour. They holstered their weapons and motioned Kailey, Luna, and Blaze toward the house.

"All clear," Jacob said. He lifted a heavy flowerpot near the backdoor, allowing Barry to grab the key that had been hidden beneath it.

Barry unlocked the door and entered with his hand on his holstered gun. It dawned on her that he'd have to be searching for someone or something that wasn't a vampire. A vampire needed an invitation to enter the sanctity of a house. While Raven had been here, that was *before* she had been turned. Did that matter? Could she still enter? Or did she need a new invitation after becoming one of the undead?

Of course Raven had somehow gotten inside Brady's apartment without an invitation, and the mystery of how she had accomplished it was beyond her understanding. A vampire capable of using magic might be a more difficult foe than Jacob and Barry had ever faced before. But if Raven was somehow capable of transcending between the physical and ethereal realms, bullets and stakes were useless. She would be as difficult to destroy as a ghost, provided one could cause a ghost any harm at all.

Lights on the lower floor of the house shone brightly.

Jacob held the door open and motioned with a nod for them to enter. The warmth of the house embraced her, but inside she continued to quake. It would take a while for her insides to thaw.

"Are you going back to check on Brady?" she asked.

Jacob pushed the door shut. A grim expressed settled on his face. He took his cellphone from his pocket. "He hasn't called or left me any texts. You?"

She frowned, looking toward the door. "Shit, I left my purse in Brady's police car."

"Sorry," he said.

Luna walked to the closed door and extended both of her hands over her head while mouthing a silent chant.

"What are you doing, kid?" Jacob asked.

"Casting a protective spell," Luna replied.

Jacob smiled slightly and turned to face Kailey's battered face. He cringed. Kailey feared what she might look like. From the burning and aches, her bruises had to be severely swollen.

"Aren't you going back for him?" she asked.

"If he calls and needs my assistance, yes."

"And if not?"

Jacob scratched the stubble on his cheeks. "Then there's no need."

"Why not?"

"Either they used silver bullets and he's dead, or he survived and has things under his control."

"Call him, dammit!" Kailey said.

"He's a police officer, Kailey. He's in the line of fire. That's his job. As a cop, his first priority is to call for backup from the force. Not us. Imagine what it would do for all of us if we were assisting him as the wolves we are and more police arrived at the scene? You can't explain that away. No, we cannot allow that."

"He could be dead!" She attempted a frown but the pain was too bad to hold it.

Jacob sighed. "You don't know Brady as well as you think."

"What do you mean by that?"

"You're picturing him as a helpless individual. He was an officer before he met you, when you met him, and he still is. He's more than capable of taking care of himself."

"I'm not denying that, but he was shot. *Twice!*"

"He's also *not* human. I know you two are living together, but you need to understand some things. He's a cop first. Wolf second. He honors his badge and his obligation to Seattle as the officer he is. He's not a weakling, Kailey. He has told all of his fellow pack members not to interfere unless he specifically calls us for help. As his friend and a pack brother, I will honor his request."

Kailey visibly shook. Tears burned her eyes, and blurred what little vision she had left.

Footsteps thudded down the stairs. It was Barry. "The upstairs is clear."

Jacob nodded. "Good. Luna, help Kailey upstairs so she can shower and change into some warmer clothes."

Luna nodded.

"Please, Jacob?" Kailey said. "At least call Brady to see if he answers."

Jacob frowned. "He won't. I'm sorry. Now please go take a hot shower and clean yourself up. You'll feel better afterwards and maybe I will have heard from him by the time you're finished, okay?"

Kailey ground her teeth, but didn't reply, even though the volcanic anger inside her wanted to erupt. She hated being filled with rage, but she hated feeling helpless even more. Anger kept her going and hopefully, ridded her of her temporary feebleness.

Besides, she could tell by the look in Jacob's eyes that no amount of demand or pleading was going to make him cave and call Brady's number. In a lot of ways she understood his decision and brotherly loyalty, but she wanted to hear Brady's voice. She needed to know he was okay.

After the battering she had endured, she was physically unable to help or do much of anything. Except cry, and she refused to do that. For the moment, she had to surrender to humility and remain out of the action. She could do nothing else. The exhaustion weighing upon her was almost more than she could handle. She was surprised that she was still standing.

Reluctantly, she took Luna's hand and followed her to the carpeted stairwell. Halfway up the stairs, Kailey whispered, "Can I use your phone?"

Luna's hand tightened around Kailey's. "To call Brady?"

Kailey nodded.

"You heard what Jacob said."

"I know, but this is important."

Luna remained quiet until they reached the top of the stairs and headed down the hallway. "Kailey, more than anything, you know I'd do whatever I could to help you. But … not this. I'm so sorry. I can't. You need to trust Jacob and you need to have faith in Brady."

"I do have faith in him."

"It doesn't sound like you do. You're his girlfriend. *Not* his protector."

"What if it were Blaze who was in trouble? What if you couldn't reach him and thought he might be dead?"

Luna released Kailey's hand and opened the bedroom door. "I'd be torn up inside, too. I'd be sprawled out on the floor somewhere screaming and crying."

"See?"

Luna shook her head, walking ahead of Kailey to the bathroom. "But you're forgetting something."

"What?"

"Blaze isn't a werewolf. Brady is."

Luna faced Kailey and placed her hands on Kailey's shoulders. "I can't truly know what you're feeling right now, but I can imagine how I'd feel if it were Blaze. Let me help you to the shower."

"Thanks," Kailey said softly. For a long time she had thought Luna was a pushover, but she had actually stood her ground.

"Jacob's right though."

"About what?"

"You'll feel better once you've stood under hot water and cleaned your-self up."

"I'm not so certain."

"Why?" Luna opened the closet, took a towel off the second shelf, and handed it to Kailey.

"Every place on my face aches at the slightest touch. Wind, mists, or if I barely touch my skin, the pain shoots through me. The water from the shower is going to hurt horribly."

"Did the doctor not give you something for the pain?" Luna asked.

"They called a prescription into the pharmacy, but we didn't take the time to pick it up."

"You shower. I'll go make you some tea to soothe your aches and pains. With your permission, I'll recite a healing blessing over you."

Kailey smiled and gave a slight nod. "Thanks."

Luna beamed a smile and hurried out of the bathroom.

Kailey set the towel on the sink counter and leaned closer to the large mirror. Beneath the soft lights, her bruises were various shades of purple, black, and blue. The outer edges were light maroon, and almost unnotice-able was the pale yellow tinge outlining everything else.

Her top lip was split and swollen. How she had never noticed any pain in her lip until after she had seen it was beyond her. With all the hits to her head, she couldn't understand how her nose hadn't been broken. She wondered how she had ever gained consciousness again. But all accounts, she figured she should have died.

Raven had meant to inflict pain, a lot of pain, before she killed Kailey. She definitely had succeeded in achieving the brutal pain. Luckily, Raven had not killed her.

"Raven, I hate you." She let the statement hang on the air for a moment.

She had never said that she hated anyone, not even the ones responsible for her parents' deaths. Yet, the bitter words rang true. As she considered her words, she realized her true feelings toward Raven were more than just hate. It was deeper, more hostile.

She seethed, "I've never despised anyone more than you, Raven. I don't know that you can hear me, but I hope you can. You will suffer for what you did to me. I assure you."

Kailey glanced at her reflection one last time before allowing her gaze to lower. On the other end of the sink counter was where she and Brady had had sex for the first time. Normally, she'd have been enthralled by the heated memory, but instead a harsh lump thickened inside her throat.

What if he's dead?

Her thoughts focused primarily on seeing Brady going down to the ground after the second bullet struck him. Even if he had survived, that event was brutal to witness, and it continued playing over and over inside her mind. She couldn't shake it until she knew for certain that Brady was okay.

Glancing at herself in the mirror, she placed two fingers softly against her cheek and then around her eyes. Her skin was hot and painful to the touch. She walked to the shower and turned on the water. After adjusting the temperature to the hottest she could handle standing in, she tilted her head slightly downward, allowing the hot water to penetrate through her hair onto her scalp and sluice off her forehead. Gradually, she eased her face upward, letting the water trickle across the dark bruises. The sting of the water faded after several minutes, and as the heat radiated into her, she no longer shivered.

Kailey took a small bottle of shampoo from the shower caddy, opened it, and squeezed a thick glob of green shampoo onto her palm. Afterwards, she worked it gently into her hair. While she worked the lather into frothy white bubbles, she thought of Brady.

The crack of the bullets echoing across the parking lot remained fresh in her mind, almost as if she heard it each time she saw Brady's body jerk in the nightmarish memory. When he had fallen she had wanted to get to him, but she couldn't break free of Jacob's hold.

She stuck her head back under the water and rinsed the shampoo from her hair. Once her hair was free of the suds, she pressed her forehead against the shower wall. The water rushed off her head and cascaded down her back and off her shoulders. Her body shook as she sobbed.

Anger rose inside her.

Everyone she loved and cared about ... died. Everyone.

Am I such a poison that kills anyone who gets close to me? Am I cursed?

She balled her hands into tight fists until her knuckles hurt. She couldn't fight against whatever power kept inflicting constant pain on her. There was no way to get the advantage, never an opportunity to win.

Her instinctual knowledge suddenly kicked in when she needed it the most. She didn't want to think Brady was dead, but after what she had witnessed, she had to accept the possibility. And while it was her duty to grieve, there was no point in doing so before she had all the facts. Instead, she needed to find a way to gather the information. If—Heaven forbid—the attacker had used silver bullets and Brady was dead, she couldn't rest until she found his killer. That was the justice Brady would deserve. Feeling sorry for herself and for her loss prevented her from doing her job as an investigative reporter. And, by God, she understood what the mindset of a great reporter was: Never stop the quest for the truth, never let someone stand in her way, and lastly, sink her teeth into them like a bulldog until they finally revealed the truth.

Kailey turned off the water, slid the glass door aside, and stared at her battered face in the mirror.

You might have physically beaten me within the last moments of my life, Raven, but you made one huge mistake. I'm still alive, and once I've healed, I'm coming after you. You best pray to the goddess that Forrest finds you first because at least he will swiftly slay you, offering you the only mercy you'll get. You're alive now, only because I pleaded for Forrest to spare you, something you've made me fully regret. Skye ...

Kailey grabbed a towel and began drying off. Her mind raced. Skye had offered what was left of her life to keep Raven from disintegrating to ash. Otherwise, when Nicodemus had been killed, Raven would have ceased to remain since he had sired her into the life of an undead. What exactly did that entail? Only a true witch would know the answer to that, but Kailey believed it might have something to do with how Raven had been able to enter their apartment and leave a message scrolled in blood on the bathroom mirror. Raven might actually be harder to kill than they had thought.

She hoped not, but she needed to get dressed and talk to Jacob.

CHAPTER 29

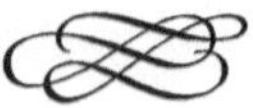

*B*rady clutched his shoulder as the first bullet struck him and passed through his flesh. Being a cop, the fear had always been in the back of his mind that one day the inevitable would occur. Some unstable person with a gun would either fire the weapon at him or worse succeed in shooting and killing him. After he had become a werewolf, though, his fears had lessened because his immortal metabolism was capable of healing and repairing itself from severe injuries that killed ordinary people.

But this attacker wasn't an *ordinary* assailant. He, or *she*, had apparently barreled out of the silver limo that belonged to the powerful founding vampires of Nocturnal Trinity. They knew what it took to kill a werewolf. Silver. And if the ammunition his unexpected enemy had used was cast or even plated with silver, Brady had only moments of life yet.

During the past few years hostile—often, misinformed—people had paraded and ranted with open threats to kill the police. In some major cities it was safer being a gang member thug than it was wearing a badge and blue. Never during his lifetime had he seen such utter disrespect toward his fellow brethren who donned the mantra *to serve and protect*. It saddened him to see parts of society view the very people who were hired to defend them as the enemy.

Were there bad law enforcement officers? Of course. Bad elements existed in every profession, regardless of race or sex, but the percentage of evil people walking the streets were far greater than the number of officers who were the bad seed.

Brady thought it odd that known criminals with miniscule consciences ran for high public offices in legislature and were excused by a large number of the general population for their crimes simply because they delivered lofty empty promises, which were nothing more than sugar-coated lies. Yet, these politicians were almost always given a pass, and those who had the backbone to verbally point out the evilness of the politicians were considered viler for exposing the truth and trashed as stupid idiots. He feared what society was becoming. The rising turmoil was leading to what one day might become a different kind of civil war. Civility had long passed and thanks to the vast reach of social media, people had a platform to which they could find thousands of others with the same distorted and dangerous views. They could hide behind the amenity of fake names and incite the masses to riots.

Police were now considered the enemy. By some groups all of the police were the same. Brady knew differently. He wondered what would happen, if for one day all police officers decided to turn their backs on society, leaving their guns and badges at home, and left mankind to defend themselves. Would it change the minds of those who insisted all guns should be banned? Would they wish they owned guns when the armed criminals decided to take whatever they wanted?

Brady had never been in favor of unarming America simply because the police couldn't be everywhere at the same time. Husbands and wives needed to be able to defend their households from danger because depending upon where someone lived, the police might arrive far too late to help.

Blood soaked into Brady's shirt. The fiery pain throbbed where the bullet had passed through, but he didn't feel weakened by the injury. He didn't think the bullet was made or laced with silver.

However, the pain aroused and angered the wolf inside of him. Rage seethed through him. He felt the change coming, rising, and his inner beast sought to be released. His jaw popped, lengthened, and larger teeth pushed their way to the surface. The first few times his body had undergone such metamorphosis, the pain had been excruciating, but now he welcomed it, especially since his life, and those in the boat behind him, were in danger.

His vision altered, colors fading, almost a grainy black and white, but through the eyes of the wolf, he could see what was in the shadows. He pulled his gun and glanced over his shoulder, shouting for Jacob to leave, barely understanding the words coming from his changing mouth. His command rang in a hollow echo in his ears. The boat motor revved, leaving the dock. A sense of relief washed over him, knowing Kailey was being taken to safety.

The next bullet struck him in the chest. The shock from the intense pain rattled him. Without thinking about it, the gun dropped from his hand as he fell forward on the pavement. With his transformation in process, he'd have lost the gun anyway. A werewolf had no need of such a weapon.

His eyes closed for a few moments.

Pain coursed through his body. The warmth of blood leaked from two bullet holes. No fear inhibited him. Instead, anger surfaced. To the one who had inflicted the painful injuries, Brady's sudden resentment quickened his transformation. His need for vengeance overcame all of his human rationality. His wolf despised anyone who threatened to kill or cause him pain.

Sharp nails thickened around his human fingernails. Thick hair covered his flesh. He shoved himself to his feet, snarling like a mad animal. His neck bones and all down his spine popped as his body yielded to his wolf.

The whine of the boat motor faded into the darkness of the bay. The sound annoyed his sensitive ears like a humming mosquito on a hot summer night, but at least it was fleeting. In seconds the sound was gone.

Beneath the shadows of the street overpass stood a figure that Brady's wolf eyes could see. The ominous bald man was tall and thin, wearing leather pants and a long leather trench coat. Death darkened the man's gaze. His arm rose as he took aim with the gun again.

Brady dropped to all fours and charged before the man squeezed the trigger. Fear widened the man's eyes on his otherwise hardened face. He stared in disbelief at his gun for several moments. He fired but Brady rolled and without hesitation, Brady continued charging as the bullet flicked off the pavement, a foot or more away. The man fired another round, but Brady moved safely out of its path. Although the gun held several more bullets in its clip, the would-be assassin turned and retreated in a sprint, possibly realizing at this point the gun was useless.

The path beneath the other side of the overpass was a narrow alley and the man darted into it without any hesitation. The one advantage Brady held was that this man had been dropped off on the overpass and probably wasn't even familiar with these streets or alleyways. Of course, Brady knew the dock area but had never ventured into the alley, not that it really mattered. He was pursuing a panicked man. Regardless of where the man ran, Brady's wolf senses allowed him to track his new enemy.

A fleeing person filled with fear was bound to hesitate and make foolish mistakes. This man proved to be no exception. His feet splashed through shallow puddles as he ran, never considering the noise he made was a direct trail in the darkness, amplified in Brady's altered ears.

Although the man was a swift runner, Brady was faster. His hardened claws clicked on the cracked pavement as he pursued. Halfway down the alley, the man turned while running, fired the gun, missed, and kept sprinting. Brady smelled the man's fear. Fear produced an odd odor in sweat. A pungent stink that carried on the air and for a predator such a scent was impossible to ignore. In fact, the odor excited most predators with a frenzied need to capture their prey and thrash it until blood spilled.

As Brady shortened the distance between him and his attacker, the man panted and wheezed with strange whines and cries blending with his labored breathing. The confidence the gunman had held earlier crumbled beneath his avalanche of fear. He pleaded with intangible words, desperate to get away from the wolfman, but his staggering footsteps faltered. He twisted his ankle on an uneven groove of the cracked asphalt hidden in a deep pool of water.

Groaning in agony, he hobbled forward, favoring his right ankle and trying to keep ahead of Brady, but he was unable to do so. In spite of his attempt to escape, his last splinter of hope vanished. The alley turned out to be a dead end. He stopped running and his shoulders drooped in defeat as he stared at the ten-foot brick wall. Gathering rain dripped from the rooftops and splattered in uneven streams onto the edges of the alley.

The man turned slowly to face Brady. Still on all fours, Brady stalked slow steps, baring his teeth, and his golden-brown eyes narrowed with an eerie glow. The gun shook in his adversary's hand. As a gesture of surrender, the man tossed the gun aside, perhaps to appease Brady and hope for undeserved mercy.

Brady's mouth widened. A guttural growl reverberated deep inside Brady's throat. Step by step, he approached the man, forcing him backwards until his back finally pressed against the wall. He had nowhere left to run.

The man shook. His breath was hampered, and his face became ashen white. Death was coming and nothing he did prevented it. Brady snarled and growled, slowly tilting his head back and revealing his large sharp teeth.

The smell of urine lofted on the air as a stream trickled down the man's right pants leg, forming a puddle around the man's shoe. The man shook with dread.

"Don't kill him, wolf! You need him alive as much as I do."

The intrusion of the unexpected voice caused Brady to turn slightly and take several steps back so he could view the person and still keep his prey from fleeing. He crouched back on his haunches, resting his clawed hands on his knees. In seconds he could kill either one that presented any new threat.

He snarled at the approaching stranger.

It was a woman wearing a long robe. The symbol on her necklace was a witch's pendant. She held her right hand in a 'stay' command like a dog trainer might to a Doberman. "Be calm. I mean no harm to you. But we need him alive. *Please.*"

Her scent was a familiar one. The wolf flinched from sudden recognition. He detected the familiarity of this witch from Brady's memories. The softness and sincerity of her voice caused him to yield to his desire to shred through the man's flesh like tissue paper. He acquiesced her request, only because he knew her.

It was Eva, Jaclyn's mother.

CHAPTER 30

$\mathcal{A}$ half hour passed before Brady's nausea ended from the abrupt shift back into his human form. Still leaning against the brick wall with a sheen of sweat coating his face, he glanced over to see the tall man he had been pursuing handcuffed to a metal dumpster and sitting in a puddle of water. The prisoner held a scowl on his face that displayed his obvious contempt.

"Here," Eva said, handing two handguns to him.

Brady shoved his gun into its holster and held the other one loosely in his hand.

"I took your handcuffs and secured him for you," she said. "I didn't want him to escape. I hope you don't mind."

"I appreciate that, Eva," Brady said with a curious frown. "Wait, I know him."

Brady walked toward the man.

"Leave him be for now," she said.

"But I know him. He's—"

"Andreas, yes, the vampires' human servant."

"I need to ask him some questions."

"It can wait. Besides, he can only see us. He cannot hear or speak since I have cast a mute and deaf spell on him to keep our conversation between us."

Brady gave her an inquisitive stare. "You can do that?"

She nodded. With a mischievous smile, she said, "And much worse whenever it's necessary."

He offered a slight grin. "Why are you here, Eva? I thought Jaclyn had banished you."

Eva rolled her eyes and laughed softly. "From the nightclub, yes, but not from Seattle."

"I pretty certain she had insisted upon that, too."

"She has power, but not at magnitude she likes others to believe. You think I'm going to listen to that haughty little ..." She cleared her throat. "Daughter of mine? She has some nerve, thinking she can dictate to me which city I can live in."

Brady nodded. "Okay, so *why* are you here?"

"Sleep has been rare for me since Nicodemus was slain. I've had bad premonitions. Lots of them. An uneasiness has overshadowed my spirit." Eva clutched the emerald pendant at her throat.

"Like what exactly? Jaclyn hasn't given us any forewarnings," Brady replied.

"Don't expect her to. She's a necromancer, but limited in powers outside of that. She has never exhibited any ability in foreseeing the future. She's in the now. Today. She'll worry about tomorrow when it arrives, but not before, which is sheer foolishness, especially for a witch."

"Have you attempted to get in touch with her about what you're sensing?"

"It would do no good. She's too thick skulled to listen to reason or to entertain my suggestions. Hell, she thinks she has it all figured out. She has allowed her strength in magic to go to her head. She thinks she's indestructible, now that she has stolen my Grimoire."

"Do you want me to relay a message to her?"

"It won't matter."

"I could at least try."

Eva shook her head. "Evil is coming to Seattle, Officer Brady, and your pack leader is the one to blame."

"How exactly?"

"He reneged on his promise to destroy the Circle of Unity that controls Nocturnal Trinity."

Brady nodded. "I know. We've been trying to convince him to leave, but he's too determined to make it work."

"That's the problem. It never worked before. Why does he think it will now? There wasn't any real unity. The scales were always unfavorably balanced. We witches were at the bottom in authority. The vampires dictated to us. They never solicited our input, but they always wanted to use our magic whenever it benefited them."

"Then why didn't you simply leave?" Brady asked.

Eva chuckled. "Leave? We'd have been killed before we got outside the club doors."

"Why?"

"The vampires would have killed us, and had we tried to defend ourselves by staking them, the demons protect the vampires and would have killed us before we came near the vampires. Essentially, we were enslaved to do their bidding. Besides all of that, we were bound to the symbol beneath the nightclub. Our magic fortified the symbol and because of our bond to it, our aging process slowed. Didn't you notice how much I've aged since you last saw me?"

Brady had noticed that she looked at least twenty years older than she had when he met her only months before, but he didn't mention it because doing so was considered bad manners. Men should always issue compliments to women, but the issues of weight and age were two topics to never discuss with a woman. At least that was what his father had taught him. It didn't take him long to realize politeness given was often kindness received.

"I'm sorry," Brady replied. "I wasn't aware of that."

A glum expression formed on her face as she nodded. "Yes. Even had we discovered a way to break free of their control, our vitality would have been sapped. That's why we held out hope when Micah had plotted to kill Nicodemus and the Vampire Hunter had succeeded. His success could have allowed our complete freedom without the consequences. Two of my dearest friends died because of what Micah initiated. They died in vain because we had willingly offered to help tear the circle apart."

"So killing Nicodemus wasn't enough to destroy the circle?"

"Unfortunately, no. His death caused a rift, which would have allowed us to break free by performing a ritual, but it would have taken all three of us combining our magic to fully succeed. But Rose and Debra died. I couldn't have performed the task alone. Jaclyn certainly wouldn't have aided me. She wanted to banish me and take her place in the Circle of Unity. Her resentment toward me has deep roots."

"Three members of the circle died that night. Why didn't that fracture a larger rift?" Brady asked.

"Jaclyn. She used the Grimoire to partially mend the tear, which is easier to perform than using opposing magic. Has she replaced Debra and Rose?"

Brady nodded. "She has."

"With whom?" Eva asked.

"Gillian and Raine."

Eva frowned, deep in thought. Her emerald eyes raced for several long moments, but finally she gave him a blank stare. "I've not ever heard of them. They must be friends of Jaclyn."

"Can I ask you something?"

"Sure."

"Each of the Nocturnal Trinity's former factions had six members. Three female and three male. I've never seen or heard anything about male witches having been a part of the Circle of Unity. Don't you have male witches?"

Her eyes moistened. She swallowed hard. "We do."

"Why haven't we ever seen them? Micah has never mentioned them. Why haven't you ever brought them up?"

"They are true prisoners of the demons, held as hostages to ensure we did cast whatever spells Nicodemus demanded. If we refused, they were tortured, and we were forced to hear their anguished cries."

"Are they still alive?"

"Yes."

Brady tucked the extra gun behind his belt. "Where are they being kept?"

"We never knew. I still have no idea. I have given up my hope of ever finding them so I could attempt to free them. Most likely, they are guarded by the behemoth demons. Those demons are the ones Micah had best worry about. Not just the vampires. His intrusion into the Circle of Unity has captured their attention. I can't believe he actually had the audacity to wedge his group into a unity that's more than a century old and assert himself as the overseer. Is he so pretentious and blind to think the others would bow down and accept his coup? He's dealing with enemies far older and more powerful than he is. Make no mistake, they will seek to kill him so they can return the circle back to their control."

"We've attempted to talk and reason with him about his irrational decision to no avail. But Nocturnal Trinity is no longer your concern, Eva. Even with your premonitions, you had no reason to bother yourself by returning to warn us. Don't get me wrong, I'm glad you have, but most people would allow spite to rule their actions and simply let whatever imminent destruction take its course. The animosity between you and Jaclyn was evident to me, so I wouldn't have blamed you if you had chosen to never warned us."

Eva offered a tired smile. Her wrinkles creased deeper. "Because I was one of the original founders and have been unbound from the circle, I don't have too much longer to live. I want to ensure the safety of others. It's the nature of a true witch."

Brady studied her for a few moments. The sincerity was in her voice, but he knew the evils she had committed. "What about the human sacrifices you participated in?"

Shame caused her to look away. "We were forced to do that. If we refused they would have sacrificed us."

"So your life was more important than the one sacrificed?"

"Not just my life or Debra's or Rose's. The threat on our lives wasn't enough. The vampires were also going to kill the three male witches, too."

Brady frowned. "That was an empty threat."

"Why would you say that?"

"Had they killed all of you, the unity would have been dissolved. They needed you for the circle to remain complete, right?"

Eva pursed her lips. Dimples puckered at the sides of her mouth and indented her wrinkled cheeks. What he had said almost seemed like a revelation to her that she had never thought of before. "I … I suppose it could have, but when you're faced with such intimidation and dread—because we had witnessed the fury of the demons—you don't think clearly about possible alternatives. You're more frightened about the potential pain and torture you will suffer."

Brady thought about some youth offenders he had arrested over the years. Kids that had turned to crime because, in their minds at least, they didn't have any other choice. It was common in gangs where the older tougher members forced the younger children to commit crimes they'd never otherwise commit or endure group beat downs for not doing exactly what they were told. The leaders capitalized upon those fears. Such threats were magnified inside the weaker kids' minds to the point they'd rather obey than face the possible consequences. "I understand somewhat of why you might have thought you had to do what you did."

Eva shook her head. Tears welled in her eyes. "It's not just that. I wasn't really thinking about losing *my* own life. I was more concerned about my daughter's. You see, I was pregnant with Jaclyn at the time. I can't say that I didn't have any other choice, I did, but I had Jaclyn's best interests in mind. Of course, I had no way of knowing what she'd become or what path of life she'd choose."

He nodded. "I can't imagine having to make such a decision. I'd hate to be put into that position."

"Even though it's not a legitimate justification for what we did, the person used in the ritual wanted to become a vampire. He was ready to yield his life to them, but my witch sisters and I convinced him that what we were doing was something necessary beforehand. It wasn't like we had chosen an innocent mortal to sacrifice. We took one who no longer wanted to live. I know it doesn't make it right. Not at all. Nothing I ever do with the remainder of my life can compensate for my evil deed."

Brady thought about what she had said. She was right. Even though the man wanted to be turned into a vampire, deceiving him into becoming a human sacrifice was wrong on too many other levels. He simply didn't know how he should reply. He didn't have the right to condemn her, and there wasn't any evidence of the crime to bring charges against her. She seemed to have endured years of mental anguish over what she had done. In the eyes of the court—perhaps her internal struggle wasn't an *exact* judgment—the judges never considered the personal Hell some people went through by berating themselves for transgressions they wished they'd never committed. A pure conscience could effectively hold more persistent condemnation over a tender soul than years behind bars ever could; because the weight of knowing what should have been done got heavier with each passing day, especially when a person chose not to forgive themselves in the depths of her sorrows. It was easier to berate oneself than to forgive.

Eva took Brady's long silence as an opportunity to continue talking. She unexpectedly diverted the conversation. "By no means am I trying to justify the misdeeds I've done, but what Micah did by reunifying the circle was pure evil."

Brady frowned at the accusation and opened his mouth to reply, but she held up her hand and cut him off.

"Before you offer argument, I'm not saying it was intentional on his part. But he did a disservice to your pack, Nocturnal Trinity, and the entire city of Seattle. He cannot preside over two different communities effectively. Don't you agree?"

"You're correct. He's pretty much abandoned us to concentrate on unifying the circle."

"It's all wasted effort."

"I agree. You insisted that we keep Andreas alive. How might that benefit us?"

"He can lead us to the remaining vampire founders."

Brady smiled. "That would be useful since we haven't been able to find them."

"I wasn't certain, but I suspected their absences after Micah forced his werewolf faction to become a part of the Circle of Unity. Andreas knows where they're hiding."

"Right now, we're having a greater problem with Raven. She made threats on Kailey's life and mine. Then she attempted to kill Kailey earlier today and almost succeeded."

Eva's brow furrowed. "Is this the young lady Nicodemus turned and her witch mentor sacrificed her soul to keep Raven living after Nicodemus had been slain?"

Brady nodded.

"Then perhaps Andreas can shed some light on that as well," she said in a menacing tone. "Provided he's willing to talk."

"We'll make him talk, but I won't interrogate him here. It needs to be a little better secluded where there's less of a chance anyone will hear."

"You know of such a place?"

Brady smiled. "Actually, I have the perfect place."

"Where's that?"

"You'll see."

"So you're inviting me?"

"Yes," he replied. "That is, if you'd like to be there."

Eva laughed. "I wouldn't miss it for the return of my youth."

CHAPTER 31

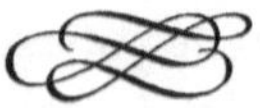

After Eva removed the deafness spell on Andreas, Brady took the key to the handcuffs and unlocked them. Throughout the entire process, Andreas glared menacingly at Brady. Rubbing his freed wrists, he rose to his feet slowly. He kept a hardened stare that could freeze fear into the minds and hearts of the ruthless serial killers. The unflinching intimidation that set deep inside his dark eyes hinted a greater threat than his thin frame ever imposed, but strength wasn't necessarily based on one's size or muscle.

A snarl formed on Andreas' thin blue-tinted lips and with his extremely pale skin, he looked similar to a corpse. By intent, Andreas appeared to be seconds away from attacking Brady. His eyes did a quick up and down as he sized Brady up.

Brady shook his head. He allowed his inner wolf to darken his eyes. "Turn around and place your hands against the wall, Andreas. I'm not releasing you. If you try anything, I can become what chased you down this alley, and this time I will tear you to shreds. Your death will be slow and painful. Eva won't stop me twice. Do you understand?"

Andreas opened his mouth to speak, but no words or sounds were uttered. He was able to hear, but remained silenced.

"He still cannot speak?" Brady asked.

"I thought it best to wait, unless you *want* to risk attracting attention should he decide to start yelling."

Brady patted Andreas down. "Good idea, but he can hear us, right?"

Eva nodded.

From Andreas' right jacket pocket, Brady removed a switchblade knife. In the left, he found a sharpened straight razor and a cellphone. Brady kicked Andreas' right heel twice to get him to widen his stance. He patted his thin legs and checked each pocket but found no other weapons.

Brady tossed the knife and razor into the dumpster. He slid the cellphone into his front pocket, so he could check the call records later. Often officers found necessary information from phone logs and text messages that proved more beneficial when the perpetrator refused to answer questions. Of course, one needed a warrant to search for information, but most judges readily issued them without question. But where Brady intended to question Andreas, he had no need to seek a warrant. No paperwork would be filed on this capture.

"Looks like he came ready for a fight," Eva said.

"And got more than he bargained for," Brady replied. "I don't think he expected to anger a werewolf."

Brady took Andreas by the right wrist and pulled his arm behind his back, and then brought the left around and cuffed his narrow wrists tightly. He never offered any resistance, even though his eyes showed absolutely no fear as they had during Brady's wolf-form pursuit.

Brady studied Andreas for a moment before yanking him around and facing him in the direction that led out of the alley. "Come on."

Lightning flickered through the thick clouds, shimmering like short strobe-light bursts as the sparks of blue tendrils spread across the sky. Low thunder rumbled softly. Cold raindrops suddenly fell in sheets, peleting off the roofs, awnings, dumpsters, and plinking odd melodies upon the small puddles scattered along the alleyway.

Brady looked at the sky and shook his head in frustration, as though he blamed God for the sudden downpour. He placed one hand against Andreas' cuffed hands and the other hand grasped the man's shoulder as he proceeded down the alley.

"Where are you taking us?" Eva asked, trying to keep stride with Brady.

"The dock first."

"The ferries have already closed for the night."

"I realize that, but that's where Andreas shot me."

Surprise rose in her voice. "He shot you?"

"Twice."

"I didn't realize—"

Brady shrugged. "At least he wasn't smart enough to use silver bullets."

Apparently offended by the remark, Andreas turned and looked at Brady with a harsh narrow stare. A wide condescending grin stretched his thin blue lips, revealing his large yellow teeth. The briefest flicker of contempt gleamed in his eyes. The smile seemed to indicate that he could have used silver bullets had he chosen to, but why hadn't he?

"Do you have any way to detect if Flora or any of the other vampires are nearby?" Brady asked.

"No. Do you think we might encounter them?"

"I hope we don't, but since they dropped Andreas off, it's possible that they will return for him."

Eva grabbed Brady's right elbow and tugged.

Brady stopped and faced her.

"How do you know that's not their intention right now?" she asked. "Maybe they are using Andreas as bait?"

Andreas shoved against Brady with the side of his body and bolted down the alley through the rain. A pale wall of fog drifted into the alley entranceway, slowly working its way toward them.

"Dammit!" Brady said, running after Andreas.

Running was difficult for Andreas with his hands cuffed behind his back. Brady caught him within a few seconds, but instead of nabbing him by the arm, Brady shoved Andreas forward, making him stagger and lose balance. Andreas crashed facedown into a shallow puddle. He rocked back and forth but was unable to roll over enough to right himself.

Brady pressed his foot atop the center of Andreas' back. Andreas craned his neck back to hold his face above the water.

Brady took the cellphone he had confiscated out of his pocket and pressed the lock button to gain access to the phone. He found no contacts, messages, or active apps. Basically, it looked like a throwaway phone, but Brady's suspicions led him to believe the phone was being tracked. Without any stored information, the phone was useless to Brady. He dropped it into the puddle of water, took his foot off Andreas' back, and stomped the phone several times. If the water didn't short it out, he was certain he had destroyed whatever tracking reception it had been giving off.

Car tires screeched to a stop at the entrance of the alley. Even though the car wasn't visible, Brady was certain the limo had returned for Andreas. If not, they had sent someone else.

Brady reached down, grabbed Andreas by his jacket on both shoulders, and heaved the thin man to his feet. By the expression Andreas had given earlier, he had known about using silver bullets, so Brady had not been the intended target. Apparently, Kailey had been.

Since they had failed to kill her in the cage fight and at the hospital, they had dropped Andreas off to finish the job. They wanted Kailey dead and quickly, it seemed. He wondered why they were bent on killing her. She really wasn't a threat to any member of the Nocturnal Trinity council at all. This pact to murder Kailey at all costs couldn't have been coming from the founding vampires. She wasn't worth their time and effort.

Raven had to be behind the attempts, but why was Flora so willing to satiate Raven's desire? Raven was acting like a spoiled brat throwing an overblown tantrum because Kailey had discarded her. No one could be pettier. And yet, Flora held an endearing affection toward Raven much like a mother would. It didn't make any sense.

Car doors slammed on the other side of the fog. Two doors. That didn't necessarily mean only two people had gotten out of the vehicle.

Since Andreas had not been successful in killing Kailey, if that had in fact been their original plan, and he had never used the phone to report in, Flora and the others might have suspected he had run into some difficulties or was dead. So these individuals who had returned were most likely armed with guns because they weren't going to take any unnecessary chances. But, if Brady guessed correctly, he figured these guns were loaded with silver bullets.

Brady pulled his gun from its holster, peering around the dark alley.

"What's wrong?" Eva asked.

"I'm trying to find somewhere to hide you," he replied.

"Why?"

"We have some unwanted company beyond the alley."

"Follow me," Eva said.

Brady frowned as she walked into the narrow space between two dumpsters and faced the graffiti covered wall.

"Hurry," she said.

Brady nudged Andreas by shoving the barrel of his handgun into the small of his back. Andreas took rapid steps toward the dumpsters.

Eva lifted her hands.

"What are you doing?"

"Opening a door," she replied.

"What door?"

Eva pressed an index finger to her lips. He nodded. She raised both arms and faced the wall. After she chanted softly, a crude wooden door slowly materialized. She pulled the level down, popping the door ajar. "Hurry, before they see us."

She pulled the door open wider. With the gun to his back, Andreas didn't fight or hesitate. He hurried inside. Brady followed.

After Eva closed the door, she flipped a light switch. An overhead fluorescent shop light buzzed to life. The room was small and filled with janitorial supplies: a mop bucket, cleaners, towels. These items had all been tucked into a corner of the room. A couple of old metal foldout chairs leaned against the wall while another one was unfolded and situated under the doorknob of another door to prevent anyone from coming inside.

Brady placed a hand on Andreas' shoulder and encouraged the man to seat himself on a foldout metal chair. He turned and faced her. "How'd you do that? How'd you make the doorway?"

"I didn't *make* it," she replied with a slight smile. "It was always there."

"You had it hidden?"

She nodded. "When someone has banished you from a city but you intend to stay, you learn a lot about how to remain concealed. After all, hiding the underground entrance to Nocturnal Trinity had been done by my magic, which had been enhanced by Debra and Rose's. That's how we prevented outsiders from sneaking into the nightclub for decades. We'd best hurry. Bring him along."

"So you've been living in a custodian closet?"

"No." She shook her head. "That door opens into an old room the owner rents as a one bedroom apartment, which is hardly enough for a person to live in, but in my case, it's sufficient. I don't desire much luxury. I never have."

"So, what do we do now?" Brady asked.

"We wait."

"What about Andreas?"

She smiled. "These walls are soundproof. If you'd like to interrogate him here, I can allow him to speak again. No outsiders will hear. I can assure you of that."

Brady leveled a stare at Andreas. The man's eyes flinched for a moment from fear. Brady grinned, feeding on the man's apprehension. "I think that's the perfect way for us to pass the time."

CHAPTER 32

When Kailey had toweled off outside the shower, she smelled the sweet scent of incense. Nag Champa. She wrapped and tied the towel around her, stepped to the edge of the bathroom, and peered into the bedroom. Lit candles flickered softly on the two nightstands and along the shelf of the headboard. A porcelain tea decanter and teacup set on the shelf as well.

Luna sat on the bed with her legs in a Lotus pose and regarded Kailey with a gentle smile. Luna had shed her clothes and wore a thin nightshirt with nothing underneath.

The alarm she had seen in Luna's face earlier had faded, perhaps because Luna felt safer being at the estate with other pack members who could readily protect them from the coming threat. But, Luna's change might have also occurred because she had time to draw upon her magic and fortify a better circle of protection.

Kailey glanced around the room nervously. "Blaze isn't in here, is he?"

"No. I insisted he give us some girl time. He's okay with it."

"What is all of this?" Kailey asked.

Luna patted the mattress. "Come. Sit down."

"Let me put on some clothes."

"Magic works best while we're skyclad," Luna said softly.

A nervous smile curled on Kailey's lips. She felt heat rise in her cheeks.

"While that may be, I'd feel more comfortable wearing clothes. Besides, *you're* the witch, not me."

"Didn't Raven ever do her rituals in the nude?"

"Whatever rituals Raven performed, she did in the privacy of her own room. Alone. So, I don't know if she was nude or not."

"I understand," Luna said. "It's not meant to be sexual. It's more … natural."

"Luna, I've had a rough day. Whatever reason behind it isn't the issue. Seriously, it's not. But right now, I want to be covered." Kailey pulled open a dresser drawer and found a pair of Brady's sweatpants. She slipped into those and then grabbed one of his T-shirts. She pulled it over her head as she walked to the bed. "What exactly are you doing anyway?"

"Sit across from me," she replied in her sweet voice. "I'll explain before we begin."

Kailey eased onto the bed and crawled to the center, where she sat on her knees across from Luna. The candlelight caused odd shadows across Luna's face, but with her pale complexion, the shadows didn't obscure her beauty.

Luna looked into Kailey's eyes, almost tearful. "Raven … she really hurt you."

"I'm okay," Kailey said, forcing a smile, which stung instantly.

Luna brought her hands slowly toward Kailey's cheeks. Kailey flinched and stiffened, but Luna didn't touch her. "With your permission, I'd like to perform a healing ritual."

Kailey shrugged and then gave a simple nod. "Sure."

Anything to stop the throbbing pain.

It wasn't a matter of faith or doubt because she knew Luna's elemental powers were increasing. She had witnessed her maturity, and Kailey was thankful that Luna didn't possess the same insane jealousy Raven had. Luna seemed pure at heart and wanted to use her magic to help others any way she could. She was a gentle spirit filled with love and generosity.

Luna took a small glass vial of oil and uncorked it. She placed her forefinger to the opening and tipped the bottle to the side, allowing a thick drop of oil to bead on her finger. She dabbed the oil near the center of Kailey's forehead. "Close your eyes."

The oil heated suddenly, almost like it pierced into her flesh and began permeating through her skin. Luna spoke softly, offering a prayer to the Goddess in a gentle tone, quietly whispering. Warmth spread throughout Kailey's body. Her body jerked. An invisible force enveloped her. Thousands of tiny unseen sensations prickled her skin. These felt like gentle caressing kisses, causing goose bumps to rise on her arms.

Her heartbeat increased. Excitement rushed through her. The warmth cascaded through her in such peaceful waves. White light shone around her, but she held no fear. She was in great comfort, indescribable bliss, and felt lightness as though she were floating. She wanted to open her eyes but feared doing so might cause these pleasurable sensations to vanish and the pain to return.

The words Luna spoke grew fainter and fainter until no sound from the young witch came at all. An extreme calm encapsulated Kailey. For several moments she wondered if she had died and was passing into another realm or dimension or whatever else might await one after death, but strangely she didn't have any sense of dread. She had never known such tranquility. There wasn't even a hint of her pain. No anxiety at all.

Lazily, she allowed herself to be consumed by the heated light, lost inside its shelter, and nothing else existed while she succumbed to the energy. She was adrift, submissive to the force tugging her spirit, her mind, and her soul. She had never yielded herself to any deity, struggled to even consider doing so, and for the first time in her life, she released her apprehensions and lack of trust. At this point, nothing else mattered. If this was dying and passing through into an afterlife, she was content knowing she was free from all the worries, pains, and heartaches she had already endured during her short life. If what existed beyond her world felt this wonderful, she'd never hope to turn back as long as Brady was where she was headed.

The thought of Brady reeled her back, made her hesitant to keep drifting within the delightful shroud around her. She wasn't certain if what she was feeling was temporary or not. Was this simply a part of the healing process due to Luna's spell? She needed to know.

Kailey opened her eyes but the bruises and swelling hadn't lessened. Her vision was narrow, hardly a sliver, but she could see Luna seated before her with arms stretched upwards and her eyes closed. Luna's face looked veiled by peace, radiance. Magic flowed around her. Kailey felt it. Chills rushed through her.

Although she had witnessed some of Raven's rituals, she had never experienced a soothing ecstasy of comfort. Often it was quite the opposite. Raven's lust was a thirst for control and possession, and during those times, Kailey had never suspected Raven was using her magic for selfish reasons.

With a tearstained heart, Kailey understood the unseen dangers but only far too late. Even if Raven hadn't been turned into a vampire, she'd have never been content knowing Kailey had rejected her and found another. Most likely, Raven would have placed a curse upon Kailey, perhaps she already had, instead of inflicting the direct brutal assault.

The loftiness that had buoyed her into her tranquil state of mind deflated, much like releasing an untied balloon expelled its air and shrank. She sank quickly inside, filled with sudden sorrow. She sobbed, her body quaking.

Luna opened her eyes and without any hesitation she wrapped her arms around Kailey, hugging her.

"It's okay," Luna whispered. "What's wrong?"

"Everything," Kailey replied softly. Although her physical pain had numbed and was unnoticeable, her heart ached. Her mind hurt, wanting Brady and wanting to know he was safe and still alive.

Luna kissed Kailey's cheek, slowly brushed her lips to the side of Kailey's ear and gently shushed. "I'm here, Kailey. You're safe."

Luna cradled Kailey in her arms and eased her back on the bed, lying beside her. Kailey turned her back toward Luna and hugged a pillow. Her hot tears soaked into the pillowcase. Luna slid up against Kailey, spooning her. She combed Kailey's hair with her fingers while kissing the back of Kailey's neck.

"Go to sleep, Kailey," Luna said softly. She kissed from the curve of her neck along the edge of Kailey's shoulder. "I'll watch over you while you sleep. The spell is in place. Now, you must sleep to allow the healing to begin."

Luna pressed her hot lips against the center of Kailey's back. Then kissed a couple of inches lower, and even lower.

Kailey stiffened and took a deep breath. "What … are you doing?"

"Trying to make you feel better," she replied.

Kailey scooted away from Luna and rolled over to face her. "In *what* way?"

Luna's eyes widened, suddenly understanding what Kailey's insinuation meant. "Not like *that*. I was trying to comfort you. Honest."

"The magic I appreciate," Kailey said. "Your concern for my wellbeing touches me. Truly, it does. I'm more than flattered. But, you're with Blaze and I'm with Brady—"

"Kailey, no. Really, I wasn't trying to become romantic or arouse you. Goodness, certainly not in the shape you're in. I would never take advantage of anyone, especially not you. While I do *love* you, it's more a sisterly kind of love." Tears formed at the edges of Luna's eyes. "My heart breaks inside because of what Raven did to you. She's the most deplorable person I've ever encountered. I've never said that I hate anyone, and to remain pure in heart, it's something I cannot say or do, but she brings me to the edge of hatred."

Kailey stared at Luna for several long seconds. This young witch did indeed possess a heart of gold. The hurt expression and the pain in her eyes indicated Kailey had mistook her affection, but under the circumstances, Kailey also needed to admit that she was on the edge of mistrust, staring down into the bottomless pit caused by Raven's betrayal. Combined with all the losses in her life, Kailey took every action of friendliness as suspect. She had even done the same with Brady, too. *Am I really this broken?*

Kailey reached up and placed her hand against Luna's cheek. "I'm sorry, Luna. I overreacted. I love you like a sister, too. Thank you for doing what you've done."

Luna offered a tired smile but uncertainty lingered in her gaze. "If you want me to leave, I understand."

Kailey shook her head. "No. Please stay. I really would feel safer if you slept beside me tonight. I'm too tired to keep my eyes open. The doctor … he … had told Brady to keep a close eye on me whenever I fell asleep."

Luna took Kailey's hand and squeezed. "He's okay. I sense that in my spirit."

"I wish I could. I wish I could feel something … anything … other than loss, heartache, and pain."

"You know what I wish?" Luna said, looking into Kailey's eyes.

"What?"

"I wish you could believe the world isn't out to get you, that life isn't set against you. I know it's hard when tragedy has struck repeatedly in your life."

"Faith that things will ever truly get better doesn't exist for me right now. I don't know that I can ever expect better things to come my direction, Luna. More bad has occurred than good in my life. I fight—" She pointed at her face. "Not just physically, but I fight mentally to get through each passing day."

"You're alive because you're strong," Luna said.

"Let's face it," Kailey replied. "Had Brady not come into my life when he did, I might be in the cemetery plot beside my brother. He rescued me without knowing it. I ache at the loss of my brother, but fate has a strange way of working at times. I'd have never met you, Blaze, and the others had I not arrived at Seattle when I did."

"I know you better than that. You'd never have killed yourself."

"No, I wouldn't have. I didn't mean to imply I would. But Cassie would have done it. It's because of Brady and everyone else that we were able to save Cassie, which essentially saved me. And now—"

"Raven."

Kailey nodded. "Not to mention Flora. When does it ever end?"

"When they are turned to ash," Luna replied. "Please, lie down and get some sleep. Maybe by morning Brady will have returned."

"I hope so."

CHAPTER 33

Inside the hidden room, Brady breathed hard, trying to control his anger. He had interrogated people before, but never someone who had shot him. Such opportunities weren't allowed in normal police proceedings. But there wasn't anything *normal* about this interrogation or the situations surrounding it. The rules that governed law enforcement officers had been locked outside and ignored.

Andreas sat in a metal foldout chair with his hands cuffed behind his back. He kept his posture stiff. His firm jaw tightened as his eyes studied his surroundings. His pale face and death-blue lips were almost translucent in the dimly lit room. Thin blue veins spider-webbed across his hairless scalp. Under most circumstances, Brady would have believed his prisoner to be a vampire or a zombie instead of a human servant, but no zombie looked this good and any vampire would have already used his strength to break free and attack or escape.

The magical doorway they had entered from the alley was invisible once again. Eva stood in one corner of the room with her arms crossed. She remained silent, watching Brady pace back and forth. His hands formed into tight fists.

Brady turned and approached Andreas, staring fiercely into the vampire servant's eyes. The hunger of Brady's inner wolf wished to break through Brady's human façade and rip the vampire servant to shreds. It took every ounce of his strength to restrain himself.

The smugness Andreas had exhibited in the alley had vanished. Perhaps he understood the danger that stood before him. Whoever had entered the alley to rescue him couldn't find him. Even if his hands weren't cuffed behind his back, he'd have no more advantage.

"Why did they send you to kill Kailey?" Brady asked through gritted teeth. His harsh voice almost sounded a growl. Around his eyes shimmered the glow of the wolf wishing to break free.

Despite his obvious fear, Andreas didn't break eye contact. He swallowed hard. Long streaks of sweat trickled down his brow, his cheeks, and he shivered slightly.

Brady lurched closer. His teeth altered with more pointiness. "Tell me. Now!"

Andreas jerked back and gasped. Terror seized him. For a few seconds he uselessly struggled to break the cuffs. He spoke with a thick Slavic accent. "They didn't send me to kill your girlfriend."

Brady leaned back slightly and frowned. "Then who?"

"You," Andreas replied in a soft voice. He closed his eyes momentarily and when he reopened them, he stared down at Brady's feet and brooded.

"But you used regular bullets. You know what I am. Hell, the founding vampires know what I am."

Andreas nodded, panting. Brady couldn't believe it, but the man seemed to have paled even more. Andreas turned and spat on the floor. "Yeah. I know. They assured me that silver bullets were in the gun."

Eva glanced at Brady in surprise. "They set him up."

"What?" Brady asked.

"They want him dead," she replied.

Brady turned his attention back to Andreas.

"It's true," Andreas said. "It's why those people entered the alley. They returned to kill me, not retrieve me. I know it."

"You believe that?" Brady asked, taking a step back from Andreas.

Andreas nodded. "I realize that was their purpose now, but I … I never expected them to betray me. Once you were dead, I was to call them. Since I didn't, they knew I had failed. They came to make certain I was dead."

"Why would they want him dead?" Brady asked Eva.

She smiled. "They know he's the only link we have to trace them. By sacrificing him, they could remain in Seattle wherever they are hiding without any fear of ever being found."

"But he's their servant," Brady said.

Eva shrugged.

"I have been theirs to control for the past fifty years. They brought me from home country when I was only a boy. *Never* have I let them down, I've always followed their requests, and this is how they treat me. My reward—" Andreas looked disgusted and slightly remorseful. "Is death. But still ... I have no regrets."

"Why didn't they ever turn you?" Brady asked.

"It was not part of their plan. Vampires need servants to do their bidding during the daylight hours when they are unable to venture out. People like me ... we're chosen to protect the vampires while they sleep. Sadly, especially in Seattle, we're easily replaced. Hundreds of people would gladly offer their lives to be a vampire's servant."

"None of Flora's family has ever offered to make you one of them?" Brady asked.

Andreas took a deep breath and then he sighed. He let his head fall forward, resting his chin upon his chest. "Had I killed you, they promised they would turn me as a reward for serving them all these years. I am old. My remaining years are probably few. That's the only reason I sought becoming one of them. Of course, I'd have to train someone to replace me."

"Have they already chosen someone?" Eva asked.

Andreas shook his head. "No."

Brady frowned at him. "With all the loyalty you gave them, even to the point of murder, and they betrayed you. They're willing to simply put a bullet in your head and kill you. Tell me where they are."

"No," he adamantly shook his head. "I cannot."

"Why not? It doesn't bother you that to them everything you've done has meant absolutely *nothing*? They've used you for half a century."

Andreas laughed softly in an annoying manner. His eyes darkened. "So? At least I'm not cursed with being a wolf like you. But no matter, the longer you keep me alive, the quicker they will find you."

Eva shook her head. "That's where you're wrong. Inside this room, no one can see you. Not Flora or her brothers or sisters. You are hidden. It doesn't matter how long you decide to withhold information. Everyone has a breaking point."

"You misunderstand," Andreas said in a low voice. "Look on the back of my shoulder."

Brady stepped closer and peeled back the collar of Andreas' shirt. A tattoo of the Nocturnal Trinity symbol glowed orange-red like embers aroused by wind. Eva rose on tiptoe to view it from where she stood. She became uneasy. Brady released the shirt and stepped around Andreas.

Andreas smiled. "The vampires are no longer your concern. It is the demons who will find me, and ultimately, they will destroy all of you."

Brady flexed his right hand. Jagged claws sprouted around his fingertips. He raised his hand back, preparing to strike. "Don't be so sure."

Andreas stared at the claws with eagerness and smiled. "Go ahead and cut me open. The demons will smell my blood and come for you. No concealment spell will hide the scent. You see, wolf, I didn't need silver bullets to kill you. I only needed to provoke your rage."

Brady frowned and tilted his head to the side. His eyes had already changed. Fur was covering his face, arms, and hands. His wolf was rising to the surface, soon to break free of its human prison.

Andreas grinned. "You have no idea what these demons plan do to your little girlfriend, and what pleasures they will seek to partake with her before they finally sacrifice her."

Brady snarled and his face contorted. He growled and drew his hand back farther.

"Brady, no!" Eva said, rushing across the room.

But she wasn't fast enough to stop him. He raked his razored claws through the vampire servant's neck. Blood gushed out. In spite of the deep lacerations, Andreas laughed for the last few seconds of his life.

Brady turned to face Eva. Blood dripped from his claws. He reared his head back and howled in triumph. Where the pool of blood widened beneath Andreas' seated body, the floor suddenly vibrated. Andreas hadn't lied. Something was under the floor. Something large with immense power. The floor shook as it advanced and soon it would find its way to the surface. The only thing it could be was a demon, but this one seemed monstrous.

"Brady, I don't know if you can understand me, but we need to get out of here. Now!" She turned toward the door, yanked it open, and ran into her small apartment and toward the door that led to the outer hallway.

Brady stared at her retreat, then back at the bloody floor. The floor-boards were changing. A dark circle was forming. He snarled, but instead of staying longer to see what was coming, Brady used what little control he still maintained over his wolf and forced it to follow Eva.

All Hell was about to break loose.

CHAPTER 34

A half hour before sunrise, Forrest met with Jaclyn, Gillian, and Raine outside the hidden door. The rain hadn't dissipated overnight, but it hadn't grown any heavier either. The fog, however, was much thicker.

Ian and Gunner moved the debris that helped conceal the door. Then they slid the heavy rusty door aside.

After the brothers stepped aside, Jaclyn peered through the door with Gillian and Raine slightly behind her.

"You're right, Forrest," Jaclyn said. "Magic has been used here. The spell remains quite strong."

"You think something has been hidden?" Forrest asked.

"Possibly, but we cannot know for certain until we pinpoint the exact spot where the magic is the strongest," she replied. "Where's your new friend?"

"Lydia?"

Jaclyn nodded.

"She said that she needed to meet with her associates."

"Be leery of yielding your trust to her," Gillian said softly.

"Why's that?" Ian asked, crossing his arms and frowning.

"She's not easy to read, but she's cloaked by death. Wherever she goes, Death follows. A lot of blood is on her hands. She is Death's right hand," Raine said.

Forrest chuckled. "No more than me."

Jaclyn turned with her eyebrows raised. "Actually, yes, she's much worse. You kill only the undead. It's your calling. She has no conscience or discretion when it comes to terminating her enemies. Just don't cross the wrong line with her."

Ian lowered his arms. "You think she'd kill us?"

"If you get in her way, yes," Jaclyn replied. She reached into the pocket of her robe and retrieved a flashlight. She flicked the switch and a beam of harsh bright light shot through the doorway, revealing the swaying fragments of dusty spider webs. "If you gentlemen wish to accompany us, please do so in silence. We must hone ourselves into the same mindset to search for the center of the magic's aura."

Jaclyn entered through the doorway and took the first step down with Gillian close behind her. Raine waited several moments before she could set foot upon the old stairs heading downward. Jaclyn seemed to be in no hurry to descend.

Forrest liked that Jaclyn was not acting in haste. During his youth he had entered places filled with witch and sorcerer traps. Had a young witch not accompanied him to spring the traps, he might have suffered great injuries, so he understood why Jaclyn took her time. It showed her wisdom. Even if this was an old spell, or one that was used by an ancient witch, dangerous traps could be triggered.

Ian and Gunner had scoured the place unharmed, which relieved Forrest because he had not even considered the possibilities of magical snares. He shook his head at his own reckless foolishness. It should have registered in his mind of such dangers, but then, he hadn't had to deal with a lot of real sorcery for decades. Most of those who professed to be witches nowadays weren't. Like the wannabe vampires standing outside Nocturnal Trinity, the majority of *today's* witches were following makeshift fantasy spells and rituals that were no more effective than eating candy to cure a deadly disease. True magic worked through human conduits that were capable of wielding the power. Some were born to do so. A few stumbled onto their ability accidentally.

The downfall was intent. From what Forrest had learned over the years, most witches and sorcerers began their journeys with absolute innocence to use magic for the betterment of mankind and not for selfish gain. Over time, unless one kept him or herself in check, many tarnished their gifts and abilities by wreaking havoc or seeking revenge toward those who had slighted them in the past. Magic held no prejudice, but often the repercussions for misuse effectively took its toll upon an evil sorcerer. Eventually the deeds one sent into the world, whether good or evil, returned in kind; however, one often reaped far more than he planted.

Many religions used gardening as a metaphor, and he understood why. An old Gypsy had once read his fortune and explained Karma like this: *If you take a single grain of corn, plant it, and properly tend to it, you reap nearly a thousand times more seed from the one planted. The deeds you perform in life are the same, so be careful what kind of seeds you plant as you will harvest the fruit of what you planted bountifully.*

After the glow of the flashlight vanished from view, Ian looked at Forrest. "Should we follow after them?"

Forrest shrugged.

Gunner shook his head. "I think we shouldn't."

"Why not?" Ian asked. "Don't tell me you're afraid to go down there after we spent all of yesterday scouring it without seeing anything or getting attacked."

"That was before we had … *witches* involved."

"And what difference does *that* make?" Ian asked.

"They might unleash something bad."

Ian placed his hands on his waist. "Unleash something? Are you serious?"

Gunner nodded shyly and slightly embarrassed.

Ian glared at him and then glanced toward Forrest, pointing at his brother. "Do you believe this?"

Forrest said, "He makes a logical point."

"Logical?" Ian shook his head. "How?"

"Some traps might simply be physical, like hidden sharp projectiles that are fired when disturbed. But, when we're dealing with concealed objects, who's to say a witch hasn't trapped a zombie or ghoul to attack another witch that reveals what has been veiled. Perhaps even a demon."

"A witch could do that?"

Forrest nodded. "Of course, depending upon the witch's power."

Ian stared at the door with a bit of apprehension. "I didn't know."

"Gunner," Forrest said, "you can stay behind if you wish. I'd like to watch just to see what they might discover."

Forrest stepped past Ian and onto the first step. He glanced back for a moment to discover Gunner a few inches behind him. "I take it you're going?"

"Only if you are," he replied.

Ian scowled. "You don't think I can protect you?"

"You're better at criticizing than offering protection," Gunner replied.

"I'd die before I'd let someone hurt you," Ian said.

"I hope you're never faced with that decision, brother. I don't know that you can overcome the conflict in your brain to—"

"Boys!" Forrest said, glaring at them. "If you choose to argue, stay outside. Remember what Jaclyn insisted about us remaining quiet. If you're coming down, do so in silence. Otherwise, take it outside."

The brothers stared sheepishly at the ground, not saying another word, but followed Forrest quietly down the steps. Seeing their immediate reaction to his scolding almost made him laugh. It was hard not to grin. The brothers were nearly fifteen years older than Forrest, but even after the many decades of traveling together, the two still resorted to childish sibling rivalry. He doubted they'd ever mature past this stage, at least between the two of them. He attributed a lot of the problem to their inability to interact with the rest of society because they were shapeshifters and because of their deformities. He hoped they might decide to stay in Seattle with Micah and his pack, provided Micah ever came to his senses, and the brothers could learn how to fellowship with a family-like group.

The glow of Jaclyn's flashlight pierced the darkness ahead of them. Forrest stopped and observed as the three witches joined hands. They stood at the edge of the abandoned rails but didn't walk any farther. Jaclyn used the light to cut through the shadows; he guessed to see what items had *not* been hidden. She set the flashlight down and the three witches formed a circle, joining hands.

They chanted in low voices for a couple of minutes. When they stopped, the old oil lanterns hanging upon the old wooden posts beamed brightly. The tunnel wasn't fully lighted but visibility became enough not to need the flashlight or any other light sources.

Jaclyn stooped and picked up her flashlight, turned it off, and slid it into the pocket of her robe. The three stared down the long tracks.

"This tunnel is filled with anguish," Jaclyn said.

Gillian nodded. "A great conflict occurred in this place. A lot of blood was shed. A lot of humans died."

"Not as many as in the other part of Seattle," Jaclyn said.

Raine lifted her free hand toward the tracks and tilted her head backwards. "Maybe not, but the residues of magic linger. Something remains." She pointed. "There."

Jaclyn focused her attention on the spot.

"I sense it, too," Gillian said. "Don't you, Jaclyn?"

"I only sense … death. A corpse perhaps."

"No magical pull?" Raine asked.

"Definitely so, but not from the spot you're indicating. The greater source of the magic that I feel is on down the tracks."

"Then, let's go there," Gillian said.

"Not yet," Jaclyn said softly, shaking her head.

"Why not?" Raine asked.

"I believe we might find some answers here," she replied.

"How?" Gillian asked. "Do you wish to summon the spirit or raise what's left of the corpse?"

Jaclyn stepped across the tracks and squatted near the pile of rocks. She placed her left hand on the top of the rocky mound and took her wand from the sleeve of her robe. She waved the wand over the grave and closed her eyes. Her body jerked and then she stiffened. For several moments she sat transfixed before she stood up again.

"What is it?" Gillian asked.

"We should go find the stronger source of magic," she replied.

Forrest cleared his throat. "Sorry to interrupt, but what happened?"

Jaclyn shook her head and turned.

"No, Jaclyn," Forrest said. "I need to know. Is that where Penelope's buried?"

"Honestly, I don't know."

"Then call up the spirit and ask," Forrest said in a harsh tone. His brow tightened and his eyes narrowed.

"It's not that easy and the time isn't right for me to perform such a ritual. I also don't have the proper supplies on hand."

"Then when is the proper time?"

"Forrest—" Jaclyn said.

"No, I need an answer."

"That's why we came, Forrest," Jaclyn said. "I'm not attempting to ignore your request. But for such a ritual I need time to prepare, and I need the proper tools and supplies for raising a body or summoning the spirit. Besides, I've never conjured a spirit during the daylight. While there's no written rule, our tradition deems it unconventional to me. Black magic used to raise the dead should be used in the dead of night."

Forrest cocked a brow.

"I know. That was riddled with puns, but it's the common procedure. It's part of the balance."

"What balance?" Ian asked.

"Day and night. Black and white. Light and darkness. Northern and southern hemisphere. East, West, North, South. That's balance."

He nodded and looked toward Forrest. "She makes perfect sense to me."

"I'm not interested in how something makes sense. I need to know what happened to her."

Jaclyn forced a smile but her eyes were saddened. "I promise if I … we can find the answer for you, we will. I'll return with what's necessary to perform the ritual, and if I need to repeat it a dozen times to get the answer, I will. You have my word."

Forrest growled with frustration. "I've waited over one hundred and twenty years!"

Gunner patted Forrest's back.

"A half day won't make that much more difference, will it?" Jaclyn asked.

Forrest closed his eyes, trying to calm himself. He huffed a heavy sigh. "You're right, it won't. It's just … I'm so close to discovering the truth. I'm sorry for allowing my impatience to get the best of me."

Jaclyn smiled. "No apology is necessary. I know how you feel and your frustration is more than understandable."

Forrest held the night-vision goggles in his hand. He sighed, plopping down on the bench. "She was the only woman that I've ever considered who could have been my soul mate."

"Then let us return to what we came for. The three of us agree that something of great importance has been sealed in this tunnel, so your hunch was on target. Perhaps we can find the answers you've been seeking for so long, but we cannot guarantee she is what we sense."

Forrest gave a simple nod and then he leaned forward, resting his elbows on his knees while examining the night goggles in his hands.

Gunner sat down on the bench beside Forrest. "Mustn't give up hope. Don't lose your faith."

Ian glanced at his brother and then sat down on the other side of Forrest. "Gunner's right, Forrest."

Forrest regarded Ian with a side-glance. "Coming from you, that means a lot."

Ian smiled. "I've always been too cynical. It's time I learned to have some faith, too. The worst is waiting another dozen hours before they can do the ritual to summon whoever is buried there."

"Did you not see the grave during your investigations?" Forrest asked.

"No," Ian replied. "If someone is buried there, they're most likely too decomposed for a body to remain. The pile of rocks is all I noticed. I never suspected anyone to be buried in that spot."

"Nor did I," Gunner whispered.

"I appreciate the two of you for all you've done to aid me all these years," Forrest said. "You're the only family I have, even though we're not blood related."

Ian's eyes moistened with tears. "I feel the same way."

"Me, too," Gunner said. "But family really doesn't have to be by blood, does it?"

Forrest smiled. "I suppose not. I've seen some blood-related individuals willing to cut the throats of family members for personal gain. Flora is a good example of that. She sacrificed her own brother."

Forrest held the goggles in his hands and ran his thumbs along the brass frames. A flash of blue light illuminated down the old tracks where the trio of witches stood. He stood and looked in their direction.

"What was that?" Gunner asked.

"I don't know," Ian replied.

"Let's go find out," Forrest said, placing the goggles into his pocket and hurrying along the rails until he reached them.

Jaclyn turned and extended a hand toward him. "Stay back."

"Is it a trap?" he asked.

"Not sure at this point," Gillian said. "But it's definitely a magical barrier warning us to turn back."

"Why didn't this occur when Ian and Gunner were exploring the tunnels?" Forrest asked.

"They are not witches," Jaclyn replied firmly.

"So?" Ian said, half insulted.

"Since they're not magic practitioners, they are no threat to unlocking the concealment spell," Raine replied. "But whatever protective measures placed here readily identifies our power."

"Can you reveal what has been hidden?" Forrest asked.

"Patience," Jaclyn said. "Give us a few moments to discern what we're dealing with. For your safety, I advise all of you to give us some space. Even we have no idea what traps might have been placed."

Forrest turned. Ian and Gunner were already twenty feet down the tracks. He chuckled and shook his head. After he walked neared them, the blue light flashed again with blinding radiance. He glanced over his shoulder to see the three witches covering their eyes.

"We cannot unveil what is hidden here," Jaclyn said.

"You're certain?"

The trio nodded.

"Why not?"

"Only the witch who originated the spell can undo it," she replied.

Forrest grunted, closed his eyes, and shook his head.

"The good news is that I know the witch who originated the spell," Jaclyn said.

"I'm guessing there's also some bad news?" Forrest asked.

"Unfortunately yes."

"And what is that? The witch is long dead?"

"No. She's alive. I just have no idea how to find her."

"Why's that?"

"My mother is the one who hung the spell. Since I banished her, I have no idea where she has gone."

"Eva?"

Jaclyn nodded.

"Then we must find her," Forrest said. "Can you cast a location spell?"

"We can try," Jaclyn replied. "The only problem is if she has chosen to conceal herself where I cannot trace her whereabouts."

"You think she'd do that?"

"She was quite bitter about the outcomes after Micah's invasion. She's even more bitter that I have her Grimoire. I can only assume she's become my enemy. It's doubtful I can get her to reverse the spell or talk to me at all."

"You find where she is," Forrest said, "and I'll speak to her on your behalf."

CHAPTER 35

Kailey awakened in the warm embrace of Luna. For several seconds, she allowed her eyes to adjust to the dim lighting of the bedroom. Luna's arm wrapped around Kailey's abs, just beneath her breasts. The young witch was actually snoring with her face pressed against Kailey's back.

The puffiness remained around Kailey's eyes, but amazingly, she had no pain from all the bruising and battering she'd suffered in the cage match against Raven.

She gently took hold of Luna's wrist and lifted, sliding her body to the edge of the bed before lowering the girl's arm on the mattress. She swung her feet over the side of the bed and looked around.

All of the ritual candles had been snuffed. Nothing seemed out of place from what she could remember from the night before. If Raven had been in the room, she couldn't tell it.

Her feet sunk into the thick carpet. She quietly made her way to the bathroom, wishing she had not forgotten her purse in Brady's squad car. She had no way to contact him, and her stomach became queasy from sudden worry about his well-being. After she dressed, she'd go find Jacob and ask if he'd heard anything during the night.

As much as Kailey loved the thought of being in a relationship, she also realized the aches and panic one faced when the other became absent and silent. That type of trauma she could do without.

The more she thought about Jacob's advice, the more she believed what he had said was true. She wasn't placing her trust and faith into Brady to remain safe, even though he had survived as an officer for years before they had ever met. She was being childish and needed to grow up or else she'd eventually lose him anyway. Men didn't like women being clingy. Of course, she didn't like anyone trying to cling to her, either. If only she could get past her losses in life like Luna had told her the night before.

She didn't want to believe the world was out to get her, but the situations in her life often seemed to indicate otherwise. *Adversity builds character* was a slogan she had remembered as a child. She had chiseled it into her mindset, but too much adversity could kill the spirit and defeat the mind. Where did it all end? With all she had suffered, she figured eventually she'd collapse beneath the weight.

Inside the bathroom door Kailey hesitated in turning on the light. The last thing she needed to behold was another message written in blood. She took a quick breath, held it, and placed her hand upon the light switch. She flipped it and after the lights brightened, she glanced at the mirror.

She released her breath in a sigh of relief. No message. No blood.

Kailey walked to the counter and stared at her reflection in the mirror.

Tears came without warning.

She didn't recognize herself. Somewhere beneath the multi-colored array of swollen bruises was her face. She was too horrified to touch them. She stood in disbelief.

So this is what happens when a spiteful witch believes she was scorned?

"Are you okay?"

Kailey jumped and turned toward the door.

"Sorry," Luna said. "I didn't mean to startle you."

Kailey responded with a relieved smile. "It's okay. I was lost in thought."

"How are you feeling?"

"Other than depressed over my unrequested makeover?"

Luna chewed on her lower lip while she searched for words.

"Pain-wise, Luna, I'm fine. Thanks. Whatever you did to heal me did take away the pain. But, as you can see, the bruises haven't faded. They've gotten worse."

"I'm glad the pain is gone. Thanks be to our Goddess. As for the bruises, let them be a reminder for you not to let your guard down with Raven ever again. Let them stoke your need to seek vengeance."

"Vengeance? Coming from a witch?"

"Not my vengeance, but if you wish to survive, you have no other choice but to stake that vampire bitch. She's not human, and therefore, even I can help you destroy her."

Kailey wanted to smile, but she was too stunned by Luna's unnatural boldness. Luna had always seemed timid but now she held a fierceness that forewarned of her ability to leave a painful bite. "I appreciate your offer to help but—"

Luna crossed her arms. "Yes, I'm a witch. I'll never deny what I am. But being what I am and knowing what evil the vampires possess, it is part of my existence to lessen their hold over other humans, to prevent an increase in their numbers. The less there are of them, the better our world becomes. I don't think there's any witch statutes or mantras that dictate otherwise. You have this witch in your corner."

Kailey smiled and leaned toward Luna, hugging her tightly. Whenever one needed to face enemies it was nice having people stand beside you. Luna's offer was touching, but the young witch didn't have any true realization of what kind of power Raven actually possessed. There was no denying Luna was growing stronger. Her magical abilities had increased but was she strong enough to defend herself against Raven?

Kailey pulled back from the embrace and stared into Luna's eyes. "Thank you for the healing ritual."

Luna smiled. "So you have no pain in spite of the bruises?"

"I don't, and for that I'm greatly relieved. Now, you might want to wake Blaze up. I need to shower and then find Jacob. I want to know whether he's heard anything from Brady yet."

"Okay," Luna said, nodding. "I'm glad I was able to help you."

"Me, too."

Luna beamed a huge smile and exited the bathroom, almost skipping.

Kailey waited until the bedroom door opened and closed before she turned on the shower. She was thankful the pain was gone, but she really wished the swelling around her eyes had vanished overnight as well.

You can't have everything.

She sighed and replied to herself, "I know."

Kailey glanced at her bruised face again, stepped into the shower, and pulled the curtain shut. Her need for feeling pitiful and sorry for herself like she had the night before had faded. Now, she sought revenge.

Although her concerns for Brady continued to try to overshadow her fighting spirit, she couldn't let worry cripple her any longer. The act of worrying only slowed her down and offered no answers or solutions. Besides, whatever had transpired the night before couldn't be undone. She had to accept the outcome regardless. So, until she received the news, she forced it from her mind. Her focus turned toward Flora and Raven and how best to protect herself.

Kailey couldn't deny that their paths were going to cross again. It was inevitable. What she needed to do was to mentally zone in on her targets without surrendering to doubt and fear. She had been trained long enough to prepare for the cage bouts that she understood her greatest enemies weren't her fight opponents. They were: doubt, fear, and herself. Once she reined them under her control, everything else was easy.

Against two vampires? A master and a witch? Okay, maybe 'easy' is an under-statement, but I'm ready for this battle.

CHAPTER 36

Brady and Eva sat behind the wide altar in a cathedral.

"Andreas set us up," she said.

"So it seems." Brady readjusted his ripped shirt. The dark spots of blood on his shirt had dried where he had been shot. "You didn't know he was marked by the vampires *and* the demons?"

Eva sighed. "No."

"How could you not?"

"He stayed in the vampire VIP room whenever he was at Nocturnal Trinity, mainly when Flora was in attendance."

"Was Andreas her servant more so than the others?"

"I believe so."

"But you and Debra and Rose … none of you knew?"

"About his mark? No."

Brady stood and peered across the pews. "Seems Forrest has been right all along about the Circle of Unity and how unbalanced it was."

"It wasn't a secret to us witches," Eva said. "Right before Kailey came into Nocturnal Trinity, the circle was almost split then. What some might consider pranks were actually mean-spirited attacks, trying to provoke each faction to turn on the next. But we were careful in our revenge. We knew if we went too aggressively, we'd experience the wrath of the demons."

"So is that why we're holed up in this church?"

"Even the behemoths possess fear," she replied.

217

"Of the church?"

Eva rose and stepped beside him. "The priests in this church have conse-crated the sanctuary with prayer, holy water, and blessed salt along the perimeter."

"So the priests know about these demons?" Brady asked.

"Father Charles does, and he knows about the vampires, too. According to others, his heart is pure and his faith is strong. His name isn't unknown to the demons and the vampires that visit Nocturnal Trinity."

"You've met him?"

Eva chuckled softly and shook her head. "I hope to. We need all the allies we can get."

"I agree. So how long must we hide here?"

"Since the sun has risen, I believe it's safe for us to exit, but I cannot guarantee that."

"I can't stay in here forever," Brady said. "Besides I need to contact Micah and Jacob and let them know what has happened."

"Why not call them?"

"I lost my phone, either in the alley when I had pursued Andreas or when we fled from your apartment."

"Then, by all means, use mine."

Brady and Eva turned quickly. A silver-haired man stood near the back of the choir loft with a kind smile on his face. He extended his right hand palm up, showing his cellphone.

"Father Charles?" Eva asked.

The priest nodded, walked down to the pulpit, and set the cellphone upon the banister of the altar rail. "Yes. I believe you have the advantage over me. I don't recall seeing either of you at any of my services."

Brady extended his hand. "I'm Officer Brady. This is Eva."

Father Charles shook their hands. "A pleasure."

The priest was thin and about six feet tall. He wore a long white robe, wire-rimmed glasses, and had rosary beads wrapped around his right wrist. His complexion was pale, but Brady couldn't recall ever seeing a man with a more peaceful smile. His graciousness overflowed, and he seemed the type of person who could bring sunlight to brighten someone's darkest day. His charisma beamed volumes without him uttering a single word. Although Brady thought it wrong to consider, this man could have made a fortune in sales or as a therapist had he chosen an alternate path in life.

"How long have you been standing there?" Brady asked.

"I've checked on you periodically throughout the night. I don't tend to have many visitors in the early morning hours though. Of course, God never sleeps." He outstretched his arms and held his hands toward the lofty ceiling.

"Apparently neither do you," Brady replied.

Father Charles laughed softly, nodding. "The weight of the world is heavy these days. Turmoil runs rampant. Those who are shielded by faith are scarce. Prayer is more rewarding than sleep, oftentimes."

"Why didn't you introduce yourself to us last night?" Brady asked.

"One learns more by listening than speaking."

"Eavesdropping, you mean?"

The priest grinned. "I suppose some might call it that, but you must understand I do listen to confessionals because I am a messenger to God and one of his vessels. Of course, fewer people attend services these days. There has been a great 'falling away.' But, there are probably few things I've not heard."

"Likewise. As an officer, I'm sure I've seen and heard just about anything," Brady replied.

"I have no doubts. A noble policeman struggles to protect and serve the cities and communities, even when people consider him an enemy. The respect for the law and its officers has greatly diminished. I'm not one to spread doom, but trials and tribulations are upon us. The 'End Days' prophesied by ministers and priests for decades have finally arrived."

"In Seattle?" Brady asked.

"Throughout the world," he replied. "I'm certain you're aware."

"I am."

"Seattle has been burdened by its own apocalypse and needs to be cleansed of its pestilence. But you're aware of that, too, from what I've gathered during your predawn conversations."

"The situation in Seattle is much worse than you might imagine," Eva said.

"How's that?" Father Charles asked, gently folding his hands together at his waist.

"A behemoth demon was summoned last night."

Concern shadowed the priest's face. He cocked a brow. "A behemoth?"

She nodded.

"You're certain?"

Brady cleared his throat. "Let's just say that it's a strong assumption at this point."

"*Brady!*" Eva frowned. "It's more than—"

Brady shook his head and glanced toward Father Charles. "Neither of us actually saw the demon. However, we were warned that was what was coming. We didn't stick around to find out."

"Wise decision," Father Charles said, pondering for several moments. "Who summoned this monstrous demon?"

Brady looked at Eva, hoping she might have a better answer than he.

With an even smile, she said, "A man sacrificed his life to usher the demon to the blood circle."

"I see. A human sacrifice? Such an offering could attract its attention. So I take it, the demon is why you sought refuge in my cathedral?"

"Yes," Brady replied.

Eva nodded.

"I find that odd." Father Charles pressed his palms together in a prayer-like manner, and rested them against his lips.

"Why is that?" Brady asked.

"Certainly you know this cathedral is nothing more than a building; a house where worshippers can reside and seek communion with God and his children. The building alone can do nothing. It is the faith of the believer that has the ability to move mountains."

"I didn't come here for a sermon," Brady said with a slight grin.

"But you do seek the truth, do you not?"

"Of course."

The priest studied Brady for several moments. "Demons don't often hesitate because their victims have chosen to enter a church or cathedral. In fact, many possessed people have passed through these cathedral doors in order to have their demons excised. A behemoth, if that were truly what sought to find you, wouldn't stop outside the doors. One of them would rip off the doors and stomp his way to this altar to destroy you."

"Not *this* cathedral," Eva said with a devious smile.

"And how is this cathedral different than any other?" he asked, regarding her suspiciously.

"You have it fortified with a circle of protection."

A confused frown furrowed his brow. "What are you implying?"

"It might be invisible to everyone else, but I can see where you've poured the blessed salt along the edges of the walls. You have more bowls of holy water than any other church I've ever gone inside. Under each stained glass window you have banishing mantras written in Latin. They are hardly noticeable, but I can see them and feel their power. I also detect other wards. But that's not all of your defenses. You have sharpened stakes tucked neatly away under tables, pews, and various seats, just in case a vampire is bold enough to enter the church."

"You're most observant. Are you a witch?" he asked.

"It takes one to know one," she replied.

"I am no such thing," Father Charles said sharply. "But, I take it that you are? Only a witch could detect these things."

"I am, and before you start using your scripture to attack me, saying that God has commanded no witch to live, my religion was upon this Earth far longer than yours." Eva's brow grew fierce. Her facial wrinkles deepened.

"I assure you that I wasn't going to say that," he replied in a modest tone. "It was a witch who painted those phrases into the wallpaper pattern at my direct request."

"Why?"

"We war against demons, and have done so for centuries. Have you been inside this cathedral before?" he asked.

"Never."

"Then how did you know you'd find true refuge here?"

"Your name is known to those inside Nocturnal Trinity," she replied.

"Is that so?"

Eva nodded.

"That blasphemous establishment is what has brought so much evil into Seattle. It is why I have taken the precautions I have to protect my members. Don't tell me you partake in the unholy gatherings at Nocturnal Trinity?" Father Charles said.

"Not anymore."

"You did?" His eyes studied her closely.

"I was a member of the Circle of Unity at one time. I was one of the founders. I know about you and this cathedral because of them."

Father Charles shook his head. "So you knew about the vampires and the demons?"

She nodded.

"How could you associate with them? The undead are vile and evil. And the demons … apparently you understand. Otherwise you wouldn't have come to this church."

"Yes. I know all that and much more. Things I wish I had never discovered or partaken in, but the past is just that … the past. I am no longer one of the circle and have been banished from ever entering again."

"Not exactly heartbreaking, is it?"

Eva looked torn in how to reply, but said, "No, it's not."

The priest turned toward Brady. "And what about you?"

"I'm none of those things," he replied.

"Perhaps not, but I sense something *different* about you. Your shirt is torn to shreds. There is blood from the two holes in the material, so I can safely assume that you were shot twice, but why is it that you're still alive? How have you managed to heal so quickly?"

"It's complicated."

"I see. So what is your purpose for associating with *her*?" Father Charles asked.

"We both seek to have Nocturnal Trinity shut down."

As if it weren't possible, the priest's face brightened even more. "That's perhaps the best news I've heard in quite some time. And how exactly do you intend to do that?"

"We're still working on the details."

Father Charles returned his attention to Eva. "How is it that I'm known to those inside Nocturnal Trinity?"

"Young vampires and visiting demons are warned about your slayings."

"I see."

Brady smiled. "Priest by day, slayer at night?"

The priest stood expressionless for a few moments. "Not exactly."

"That would explain why you were up all night," Brady said.

"I never left the cathedral," he replied.

Brady smiled. "But I'd wager if I walk over to the door where you were eavesdropping in the choir loft, I'll find weapons and tools to slay vampires and banish demons."

Eva said, "Weapons against vampires, but with all these protective wards, it's highly doubtful a demon will enter."

Father Charles sighed. "Let's discuss Nocturnal Trinity some more. You're trying to shut it down. Surely you have some sort of plan."

"There is only one way," Brady said.

"And what is that?"

"Slay the founding vampires and banish the behemoths."

"That's not as easily done as it sounds."

"I'm not implying that it is. But one of the founding vampires has already been slain."

Father Charles' eyes widened with interest. "By whom?"

"A Vampire Hunter. He doesn't intend to leave Seattle until he has slain all of the founding vampires."

"And what is the name of this Hunter?" the priest asked.

"Forrest Wollinsky."

Father Charles' eyes flashed momentarily from recognition and then he grinned. "I'd be quite interested in meeting him."

"I'll pass the information along to him when I see him," Brady said. "He's hard to find at times."

"You can use my phone," he replied.

"Forrest doesn't use one."

The priest shrugged. "Still, you mentioned you needed to call someone. You may borrow it. But again I'd be quite interested in meeting Forrest. I believe he'd be the perfect asset for us."

Brady smiled. "He already has been."

CHAPTER 37

orrest stared through the doorway that led down to the tracks for several more moments. He held the heavy metal door and almost hated to hide the opening. He wondered if Penelope was somehow concealed by the spell and with him shutting the door, he wondered if she'd think he had given up his pursuit of finding her.

"You okay?" Ian asked.

"Shh," Gunner shushed. "Let him be."

Without a reply, Forrest set the heavy door in place and turned to walk away. Gunner and Ian began placing odd and end junk items against the door as well as large dead tree limbs and broken pallets.

Forrest placed the goggles into his pocket. He looked at the gray overcast sky but he didn't see the clouds. His mind focused on everything else. The witches had discovered what he had believed to be true. Okay, so they hadn't determined exactly *what* was hidden, but they all agreed something had been shrouded from public view. If it had taken magic to conceal it, whatever was there had to hold some significance.

He closed his eyes for a moment. The swirling mists coated his face and clung to his beard. In the tunnel he had finally admitted something that he had never told anyone except his father. He believed Penelope might have been his true soul mate, but he had never said it aloud even though his heart ached for her. But had she really been … *the one*? Was it conceivable that since he had lost communication with her and blamed himself for her possible demise that his mind had somehow placed her upon a pedestal, making all other women he had met unable to measure up? Had he pushed all other women away simply because it had been convenient? Perhaps his guilt had prevented him from moving on, which seemed most likely because why else would he continue lingering in Seattle? Instead of simply slaying Flora and her siblings, he had sought information about Penelope and that had brought him to the underground tracks. If, by some miracle, she were still alive, he'd be overjoyed. But he had accepted that she most likely was not living. Once he knew for certain, the inevitable confrontation would occur. He was going after all of Flora's immediate family *and* the five true demon founders, but not Jinn unless he got in the way.

Forrest understood that he might not survive, but he was confident he'd take out a few of them before he breathed his last.

"Forrest?" Gunner said softly.

Forrest opened his eyes. "Yeah, Gunner?"

"Are you okay?"

"Just thinking," he replied.

"About her?"

Ian frowned at Gunner. "Need you ask?"

Gunner looked down. "Sorry."

"It's okay. At least I should have an answer before tomorrow morning."

"Provided we can find Eva," Ian said.

Gunner gave Ian a mean glance.

Ian shook his head. "I'm not being negative, brother. I intend to look everywhere possible."

"She was banished," Gunner said. "*Where* do you plan to look? The world is *huge*."

"Perhaps we should catch up with the witches?" Forrest said.

Ian and Gunner glanced down the sidewalk and nodded.

Forrest walked at a rapid pace. Because of his long legs, it was difficult for the brothers to keep up without partially jogging. Within a few minutes, Forrest was walking behind the witch trio. "Jaclyn?"

She paused and looked over her shoulder. "Yes?"

"Wait for me. You still have the Grimoire?"

Jaclyn stopped walking as did her two companions. "Of course."

"How thoroughly have you studied it?" he asked.

"I've read through it several times," she replied.

"That wasn't what I asked. How extensively have you studied it?"

Jaclyn frowned. "Enough to know the history of Nocturnal Trinity and what things my mother had participated in. Why?"

"Was there anything written in it about what was hidden in the tunnel back there?"

She shook her head. "No."

"But a bloodbath occurred in the tunnel, right?" Forrest asked. "That's what you sensed?"

The witches nodded.

"Yes," Gillian replied. "We told you."

"So why wouldn't she have recorded that in her journal? That had to hold some importance."

"Perhaps," Jaclyn said. "But it's also possible that she had not begun using this particular Grimoire yet."

"Would she have written it elsewhere?"

Jaclyn shrugged. "It's possible. She was an avid note taker."

"What are the chances you can find your mother?"

She sighed. "It's difficult to say, Forrest. But we will work to locate her."

"Today?"

"We're returning to Nocturnal Trinity to talk to Micah and then we can work on a location spell in our VIP quarters," Jaclyn said. "What are your plans?"

She and the other two witches returned to walking alongside one another. Forrest and the brothers followed them. The mist danced with the variable flow of the wind.

"We can accompany you to the nightclub, too."

"But not for the incantation."

Forrest shook his head. "No, not at all. I have some things I need to discuss with Micah, too."

Jaclyn smiled. "The best part of being at the nightclub this early in the day is the quiet."

"I agree."

"The downside of Seattle is all the rain. The overcast skies never bother me, but the constant drenching … that gets old after a while."

"I've been in worse places," Forrest said. "Rain, fog, and cold mists are the least of my troubles."

"So your new friend, Lydia, will she be at the club?" Raine asked.

Forrest shrugged. "We have different agendas."

"Different auras, too," Gillian said.

"I don't doubt that," he replied.

Jaclyn smiled. "You're difficult to read, but she's obscured. That's why she makes me uneasy. There's no way to guess or predict what she might do."

"And how is that any different than Flora and Raven?"

"It's not, but—"

"I may not know Lydia that well, but what I do know is she's here to repay a debt to me, even though I had never asked for anything in return. She's on our side. The determination set in her eyes when she vowed to help is the same as mine. If I give someone my word that I will do something, I don't look for excuses to back out. Several times, my devotion has almost cost me my life, and on a few occasions, I've lost those precious to me. So let's worry less about Lydia and more about finding Eva."

Bitterness oozed on her words. "Do you actually think finding my mother is more important than pursuing Flora and Raven first?" Jaclyn asked with a glare.

"You need to set aside your contempt for your mother. While I'd rather find Flora and Raven first, I believe we need whatever is in that tunnel in order to defeat the demons. My gut tells me that these behemoths aren't going to allow another one of the founding vampires to die."

Jaclyn cocked a brow. "Your gut again?"

"Yeah," Forrest said with a stern frown. "It didn't fail me last time, did it?"

"No."

"Then let's quit arguing over minor details. It only delays the inevitable confrontation with the council members. We need to attack them before they've prepared a strategy of their own."

"And what makes you believe they haven't?" Raine asked.

Forrest grinned. "Because they're still in hiding."

CHAPTER 38

*A*fter Kailey had showered and arrived in the dining room, Luna and Blaze were finishing their breakfast.

"There's more on the stove," Luna said.

"What do we have?"

"Bacon, eggs, toast."

Even though she should be famished, the food didn't sound appealing at all. The thought of eating actually nauseated her. "How about coffee?"

"Fresh pot," Blaze said, raising his mug toward her with a broad smile.

"Perfect! Thanks," Kailey said, walking around the bar into the kitchen. "Where's Jacob and Barry?"

"Making rounds would be my guess," Blaze replied.

"Has he heard anything from Brady?" She grabbed a mug from the cupboard and glanced over her shoulder toward them.

"Told you," Blaze said to Luna.

"Behave," Luna said, with a giggle and smacking his arm.

Kailey frowned. "Told her what?"

"That you'd ask about Brady before you even took one bite of food."

Kailey poured coffee into the mug, set the pot back into place, and poured powdered coffee creamer into her coffee. "So I'm still worried a bit. Is that a bad thing? If Luna vanished, don't tell me you wouldn't try to find her or that you wouldn't be worried and concerned about her."

"Sorry," Blaze said. He glanced at Luna and smiled. "You're right. I'd be out of my mind, too."

"Well?" Kailey asked, sitting down at the table.

Blaze turned toward her. "Oh, sorry. As far as we know Brady hasn't gotten in touch with Jacob or Barry."

Kailey stirred her coffee and blew at the steam.

Outside the boat motor revved. She started to get up, but the patio door opened. Jacob walked rapidly across the room with a cellphone pressed against his ear.

"Yeah, hold on," Jacob said. He handed the phone to Kailey. "It's Brady. He wants to talk to you."

Kailey glanced toward the phone and emotions gushed through her. Before she took the phone, tears blurred her vision and leaked down her cheeks. A heavy weight lifted off her chest, making breathing much easier. Greatly relieved, she felt calmer inside and was amazed that for once she had been spared suffering more loss.

"He's okay," Jacob said, still holding the phone. "Barry's heading across the bay to pick him up. Take the phone."

She took it and pressed it to her ear. Swallowing hard, she whispered, "Brady?"

"How are you holding up?" he asked.

"Much better now," she said, wiping tears from her eyes. "How about you?"

"Nothing a werewolf can't heal from."

"I was afraid you'd been shot with silver bullets."

"That was the first thought that came to my mind, too. But, as you can hear, I'm alive so they weren't silver. I didn't mean to keep you worrying, but I lost my phone last night."

"Mine's in your squad car."

"I have your stuff. As soon as Barry picks me up, I'll bring them to you. But, I need to make another call. See you soon."

Before she could say good-bye or that she loved him, the phone disconnected. She stood and grinned.

"So everything's okay?" Luna asked.

Kailey nodded and headed toward the kitchen. "Definitely. The bacon and eggs sounds better now. I think I fix a plate after all."

$\sim$

B rady sat in the backseat of Father Charles' four-door Lincoln Town Car. The priest insisted on driving them to the docks since it was too dangerous to let them walk should the demon still be looking for them.

Frustrated, Brady frowned at the phone and shook his head. "That's the third time I've been sent to Micah's voice mail."

"That's unusual?" Eva asked.

"It's highly uncommon," he replied.

"Why's that?" Father Charles asked. "Maybe he's not answering since he doesn't recognize my phone number."

"I suppose that could be true, but the way everything else has been unraveling with the Circle of Unity in the nightclub, I suspect something worse might have happened."

Father Charles turned in the driver's seat so he could see Brady. "Let me ask the two of you something."

"Sure," Brady said.

"Where was this behemoth demon summoned?"

"A couple of blocks from here."

"Can you take me there?"

Brady shook his head. "Now is not a good time."

"Okay, then point me in the right direction."

"Father," Brady said. "Don't tell me that you plan to attack this demon by yourself?"

He shook his head. "No, but it's good to know the exact location where one emerges so I can keep track of it."

"You know of any other behemoths being summoned?" Brady asked.

"Not for a long time."

"My assumption is it's one of the founding demons."

Father Charles nodded. "That's probably the case, but I'd still like to check out the area where you saw the portal opening. It might not even be a behemoth."

"Can you tell the difference by the portal?"

"I can possibly tell more from what it did to the sacrificed body," he replied.

"If you can wait until another time, perhaps later in the day, I'd be happy to go with you," Brady said.

"Very well, but promise me this."

Brady said, "What?"

Father Charles took a business card from the console. "You can reach me at the number on this card. When the time comes for you to fight this demon, and don't deny that you will, I want to assist you in destroying it. Is that acceptable to you?"

Brady and Eva exchanged worried glances.

"Trust me, I can be a great asset to all of you. I've slain quite a few demons over the years."

Brady nodded. "Sure. I will contact you."

The priest smiled. "Now, don't you be lying to a priest. That's almost like lying to God."

Brady laughed and opened the door. "Father, I assure you that we're going to need all the help we can get. My biggest fear is not fighting one of the behemoths, but the possibility of having to fight all of them at the same time."

CHAPTER 39

Forrest remained outside with Titus after the trio of witches entered Nocturnal Trinity. Gunner and Ian had also gone inside.

"I see you're still alive," Forrest said with a grin.

Titus frowned. "For now, yeah. But for how long? You've provided me no guarantees, and the last I heard, Flora is still very much alive. Care to elaborate on the reasons *why*?"

"Have you seen her?"

He crossed his huge muscular arms and shook his head. "Nah. I ain't seen her or any of them, but that's beside the point."

Forrest smiled. "See? You're safe and sound."

Titus glanced at the Hunter box in Forrest's hand. "I don't have a kit of weapons for my protection like you, so pardon me if I don't feel all that safe."

Forrest slid his hand into his coat pocket and pulled out a sharpened stake. "Here. Feel better now?"

Titus shook his head and slapped Forrest's hand and the stake away. "What? You *trying* to get me killed. I can't take that from you. If they see me with that ... Man, don't you get it? They *own* this place. They might be leery of you right now, but they're not going to stay gone forever."

"When's the last time you've seen any of them?"

"Same as before. Weeks now. But they'll be back. And when they are, it won't be pretty what they do to me."

"Have you ever known them to be absent from the nightclub for this long?" Forrest asked.

"No. Usually, at least one of them makes an appearance each night, but like I said, it's been weeks since I've seen any of them."

"Even Raven?"

Frustration creased Titus' brow. "Look, man, I don't even work for you. Why you hassling me about who's been here when and where? Huh?"

"Because friends of mine have been threatened by them. I intend to prevent it."

"Yeah, I know, that's what you told me yesterday. Well, I'm not a friend of yours, and their threat on me is *very* real. They won't hesitate to carry it out."

Forrest placed his huge hand on Titus' thick shoulder and squeezed. "I intend to prevent that as well and maybe afterwards, you'll consider me your friend."

"It's a promise I hope you're able to keep. Because if you don't, ah Hell, what it's going to matter then, right?" Titus reached and pulled the door handle open. "Go ahead and get yourself inside. I've enough to worry about as it is."

Forrest laughed as he walked through the door.

"Sure, laugh it up at my expense," Titus said, peering through the doorway. "At least you have the luxury. I find nothing funny about the situation at all."

"Perhaps you should have a little faith that I'm on your side."

"Whatever, man," Titus said, letting the door close.

Forrest glanced toward the open dance floor. At least more lights were on than the day before, but it was still too early for most of the staff to arrive. No workers were in sight, and he didn't hear Ian or Gunner arguing, so he assumed they had followed the three witches to Micah's office. As much as he'd like to head over to one of the bars to get a couple shots of whisky, he figured talking to Micah was more important.

Midway across the dance floor, he was met by Jinn. Jinn grabbed Forrest by the elbow. "What the Hell did you do?"

Forrest turned and frowned down at the demon. "What are you talking about?"

"I told you to give me a couple of days, and I'd talk to one of the behemoths and set you up a meeting."

Forrest shrugged. "I know. I've done nothing."

Jinn's yellow eyes blazed, darkening to orange-red, and then heated to a smoldering blood red. "You must have done something."

"Why do you say that?"

"Because they are highly agitated."

"You have spoken to them?"

Jinn shook his head. His permed ponytail slightly swayed back and forth. "No."

"They came here?"

"No. Look—"

Forrest leveled a stern glare. "If you haven't seen nor heard from them, then how do you know they're agitated?"

"It's difficult to explain."

"Then try."

"The mood inside the demon VIP room changed. Last night several of my demon friends were up there, and the next thing I know, they all scrambled out. All of them. For demons to become uncomfortable in our lounge, it has to be bad." Jinn lowered his voice and looked around. "Honestly I expected at least one of the behemoths to appear. None did, but the tension is thick and still active, like one might materialize at any moment. I keep feeling like eyes are watching my every move."

"You're still not making any sense."

"Maybe I can explain it better like this. You ever been outside during the summer right before a storm?"

Forrest nodded. "Sure."

"I mean, it could be a picture perfect day, and within minutes you sense a change in the atmosphere. A harsh hot breeze cuts through the air. Birds suddenly burst into flight and dart into the forest for shelter. Then it grows calm for a bit and in the distance you see the black clouds covering the horizon. There's no denying the coming storm."

"I've experienced that many times."

"Well, it's the same with my superiors. The behemoths. The other lesser demons and myself, we felt the heat of their wrath last night. Anger that sent chills down my back, okay? The hairs on my neck and arms stiffened. Yeah, they *are* the storm. Someone or something has disturbed them. They're coming."

Forrest sighed. "I've not done anything. I've not even searched for them. I'm *not* a Demon-hunter. Like I told you before, all I want to know is what happened to the Demon-hunter who was my friend over a hundred years ago."

"So maybe it isn't you." He wiped sweat from his brow and glanced uneasily around the dark dance floor. "But, someone has caught their attention and not in a good way. I doubt any of the other demons will come to the club tonight with the oppression and wrath that's overshadowing our section of Nocturnal Trinity. I'm sorry, but right now, I cannot set up an appointment for you. I don't want to be anywhere near them. If one makes its presence known, I'm running for the door."

"I'll find another way," Forrest said, walking across the dance floor with his Hunter box in hand.

"I don't advise that you try to find them anytime soon."

Forrest smiled. "I have the feeling they will come looking for me."

A tinge of fear widened Jinn's eyes as he walked at a rapid pace alongside Forrest. His voice rose to a high-pitch tone. "And you're okay with that? Aren't you the least bit frightened?"

"What does fear have to do with it?" Forrest asked with a fierce stare. "I have to deal with whatever confrontations present themselves as they come. Instinct has kept me alive. Fear and worry are distractions, so I ignore them."

"Nerves of steel, huh?"

Forrest shrugged. "Forged in Hell."

"Un—likely. This isn't a joke. Okay? Well, just remember this. They *came* from the pit of Hell where it's hot enough to *melt* steel, okay? They're dangerous in ways you cannot imagine. Hell, I shouldn't even be warning you, but you know, I like your style. I like your determination and between you and me—" He lowered his voice to a harsh whisper. His eyes changed various fiery colors. "I'd like to see you drive a stake through Flora's cold shriveled heart. A lot of the workers in the club probably feel the same."

"Lack of loyalty?"

"To her?"

"Yeah."

"She has always been the instigator, causing the constant tension between the factions. She's the spoiled child in their regal family. I played along because I didn't want to be her next victim. Hell, all the witches, the *former* witches that is, they did as well. It was never a good thing to get on her bad side."

"Why is that?"

"Ask Nicodemus. Oh, right, you *can't* since she handed him over to you to be slain. See what I mean? If she's willing to sacrifice her own flesh and blood, how much worse could it be for the rest of us who aren't even related to her?"

"You make a valid point."

"Ya think?"

Forrest ran a hand through his beard. "Flora's only gotten worse over the decades, which is why one can never confide in a vampire. She'll sacrifice anyone if she believes it will advance her authority. You ever think the behemoths might be coming to rid themselves of her?"

"No. If that was their purpose, they know where she is. They'd simply appear where she was and kill her. Whatever's brewing is going to be severe."

Forrest adjusted his hat. "What about her other siblings? Were they playing these mind-torturing games?"

"No. They're always business-minded whenever they come into the club. Sure, they might hook up with some of the wannabes in the VIP lounge, but when it came to the antics like Flora and Nicodemus have participated in, they had no part in it. They are always reserved. Like nobility."

Forrest smiled. "That's because they were born nobles in their home country."

"Apparently they've never forgotten it. Honestly, they are well behaved and dignified. They frown on those wannabes who view vampirism in the Hollywood fashion. They won't tolerate cheap interpretations of what they consider an eternal blessing. Unlike Flora, they don't seek to draw attention to themselves."

Forrest shrugged. "It doesn't make them any less undead."

"Have you ever considered these demons might be getting ready to take out your cousin for intruding in the nightclub?"

"You think that's a possibility?"

"Don't you?"

Forrest remained silent as he mulled over the thought. "Look, I'd love to stick around and talk, but I need to see Micah about some matters."

"About this?"

"I'm sure it will come up."

"So another meeting?"

"Something like that."

"It must be. That's where the witches went with your two odd friends."

"I know. I need to catch up to them."

"Mind if I attend this meeting or is it closed to the demon faction?" Jinn asked.

"Being as you have an overwhelming fear of the behemoths, the less you know will probably keep you safer."

"I see." Jinn studied Forrest for several long seconds. "So you're trying to keep an eye out for me? That's progress. It makes me feel more comfortable being around you."

"Like I told you before, I don't view you as an enemy unless you get in my way."

"And just like that, we're back to arms length. Wow."

Forrest chuckled. "Are you planning to go behind my back?"

"No, not at all. It just makes me second-guess every decision I make as to whether it's something that crosses an undefined line between us. I'd be more comfortable if I knew we were on the same page. That we're friends."

"There are few people I allow inside my circle of friends. My trust in others is limited. Besides, there's an expression I've heard over and over during my long life."

Jinn frowned. "And what's that?"

"Never trust a demon." Forrest walked past him.

"Oh, now! That's cold, even for you, Hunter. You can't judge us all like that."

"Then prove it to me otherwise."

"I thought that's what I *was* doing."

"It's a start."

CHAPTER 40

Forrest climbed the stairs that led to the werewolf VIP lounge. The door was closed, so he knocked.

Cassie opened the door in her succubus form and smiled when their eyes met. She gave a side-nod for him to step inside. After he crossed the threshold, the flat end of her tail pushed the door closed.

He frowned with curiosity when he noticed the nervous expression on Micah's face. "What's going on?"

Ashley stooped behind Micah's chair with one arm draped over his chest and her head resting upon his shoulder.

"Cassie informed me of a disturbance in the demon lounge last night," Micah replied.

"Jinn gave me the same information," Forrest said, setting his Hunter box on the floor. He tipped his hat back and scratched his forehead. "But according to him, the oppressiveness hasn't faded."

Cassie bit her lower lip, crossed her arms, and stood, slightly swaying her hips back and forth. Her apprehension was as noticeable as Jinn's had been. "They're delaying their arrival, which means they're increasing their power before emerging."

"How?" Forrest asked.

"Drawing upon the negative energy and hostility in the city, which is never in short supply," she said.

"Have you heard from the others in your pack?" Forrest asked, flicking his gaze toward Micah.

He shook his head. "None of us can make a call out on our cellphones or the landlines. Cassie insists the demons have blocked all communications into the nightclub. Even the Internet won't connect."

"Cousin, it's time for you to cut your losses and abandon your fantasy of uniting the factions of this nightclub."

"Fantasy? You mean to *retreat*?" Micah was clearly perturbed by the suggestion.

"Call it whatever you like, but it strengthens your chances for survival," Forrest said. "You have continued to ignore the warnings made by the members of your pack, and only one has chosen to stay here with you."

Ashley replied with a nervous stare.

Forrest continued, "But Jinn made a point a while ago that you should consider."

"What's that?"

"If they have managed to keep you from contacting others outside of Nocturnal Trinity, Jinn's right. These demons might be coming to kill you. I say we pack up and get out. Even if you had the entire pack gathered here, you have little chance to defeat one of these demons. They aren't coming to negotiate. Their goal is to kill you. Even you're smart enough to realize that. They didn't sign your agreement when you rewrote the nightclub's charter, and neither did the other vampires except Flora. She only did because it prevented me from staking her then. But understand something. If you're still on these premises when they arrive, you're dead." Forrest looked into Ashley's troubled eyes. "You will be, too."

Micah gritted his teeth. His voice grew hostile. "I suppose you have a better solution?"

"I have a proposal, but I don't know that it will work."

"And what is that? Your calling in life has been to eradicate vampires, not demons, so what is your solution?"

"The first step is to get out of Nocturnal Trinity before these demons arrive."

Micah's nose flared, and he crossed his arms. "You already made that point. What else?"

"We need to find Eva," Jaclyn said with a soured expression on her face, possibly realizing they weren't getting anywhere with Micah.

The statement jolted Micah and he turned his attention to her. "Your mother? You banished her."

"I know."

"Then why do you want to bring her back?"

Forrest cleared his throat. "Because she's the only one who can remove the concealment spell in an old abandoned rail line."

"Why? What's there?"

"The one thing we lack."

"What?"

"Hope."

~

Forrest stood at the bar and downed a shot of whisky. It had been his fifth and he still hadn't added to the surrounding conversation.

Cassie took his shot glass. "You want another?"

He shook his head. Due to his massive size, the shots hadn't even given him a slight buzz. He needed at least five more to feel any effect.

Jaclyn sat on the stool beside his. "Go ahead and spit it out."

"What?" he said in a gravelly low tone.

"Whatever's on your mind is trying to eat its way out to be heard. So, tell us what you're stewing over."

Forrest ground his teeth and his lips formed a stiff snarl. At the end of the bar Ian and Gunner shrank down in their seats, eyeing one another with concern.

"Well?" Jaclyn said.

Forrest cleared his throat and looked at his reflection in the mirror behind the bar. If looks killed, ten cats had just lost all nine lives. "I've always been a stubborn man. Bullheaded, my father had often told me. But I cannot understand how Micah still refuses to budge from his idea of uniting the shattered Circle of Unity. Even with all the facts, he remains steadfast in his stupidity."

"Maybe it's hereditary?" Raine asked with a teasing smile.

Forrest glared at her. His huge hands balled into fists.

She took a sharp breath and swallowed hard. Her eyes widened. "The stubbornness, not the stupidity, just to clarify. That didn't come out like I had meant. Sorry."

He grunted and turned his attention to Jaclyn. "What's worse is that Ashley wants to please him so badly that she's staying beside him, even though it is obvious she wants to leave," Forrest said.

"I got that impression, too," Gillian said.

"You could definitely see it in her eyes," Cassie said.

Forrest folded his hands together on the bar and leaned forward, resting upon his elbows. "Back when he called me to help slay Nicodemus, he was a different person. A devoted Shaman. That Micah would have left in an instant if he knew Ashley's life was in danger. Hell, he'd have done it for any one of us. He'd have never left his pack for this place."

"What are you suggesting?" Jaclyn asked.

"He's been bewitched."

Raine turned on her barstool. "You think someone has cast a spell on him?"

"I do."

"I find his behavior quite odd myself," Jaclyn said. "But none of us have cast a spell over him. In fact, if he were spellbound, we'd have sensed it."

"Can you be certain?" he asked.

Jaclyn nodded. "Definitely. In the same manner I sensed my mother's magic in the concealment spell, I'd have noticed if Micah was acting under the influence of a spell."

Raine and Gillian nodded.

"All three of us sensed the magic in the tunnel," Raine said. "Pinpointing its exact location took some time, but the enchantment holds a sensitive radius to detect any approaching magic. Eva's buffer was set into place to activate her magical traps if any trespassing witches sought to break her spell. I have to agree with Jaclyn. No spell controls Micah."

Forrest released a frustrated sigh. "Then it's something else. He's never been this irrational. He's always been modest and compassionate toward others."

"There might be another reason for his abrupt behavior," Cassie said.

Everyone looked at her.

She smiled. "Since it's not magic, he might be under the influence of a demon."

"Possessed?" Forrest asked, straightening in his seat.

"Not necessarily possessed, but greatly subdued and influenced by desire."

"Desire?" Forrest shook his head. "That's preposterous."

"Is it?" Cassie asked. "Think about how radical he's become to what he once pursued. Some demons are enticers. Their drive is to make humans act contrary to their true nature. It gives them power and control. You said that Micah was modest, and now he wants to hold a place of authority. He's the one who *insisted* a new treaty was made for Nocturnal Trinity's council. That's totally opposite of his nature, right?"

"She has a point," Jaclyn said.

Forrest nodded. "Now that you put it that way, yes. It was contrary to his original plan."

"With the presence of whatever force entered the demon VIP room last night, Micah might be mesmerized by it, thinking by staying he's being helpful, but the behemoth might actually be influencing him to stay long enough for them to kill him."

Forrest cocked a brow. "Hmm."

"And remember," Cassie said, "Nicodemus had bound three shadow demons to me. No matter how much I fought, I was forced to do their bidding. Each time I resisted, they became more aggressive, and they had even tried to make me kill Kailey. Under their influence I had done a lot of bad things. Most of it I don't even remember. They were able to control my actions and *I'm* a demon. Imagine what they're capable of doing to a human."

"He's a werewolf," Forrest said softly.

Cassie laughed. "That doesn't matter. They only need to seduce his human side."

Jaclyn said, "Is it possible that one of the shadow demons attached itself to Micah after they had been excised from you?"

"I suppose."

"Are you sure there were only three?" Raine asked.

Cassie thought for a few seconds. "No, not totally certain, but that's what I had been told."

"How do we detect if that's what has happened to Micah?" Forrest asked. "Can we break their hold over him?"

"There are discernment rituals, but I would need some help from other demons I trust," Cassie said.

Forrest frowned at her. "Can't you tell if Micah is bound to a demon since you're a demon?"

"That's what I was about to ask," Jaclyn said.

"Not always," Cassie said. "It depends upon the type of demon and its power. Remember that demons like the thought of being strong and having influential control over humans. But, for a demon to exert its will over another demon, their gratification increases even more. Darker demons shun exposure and are secretive, so they won't openly boast their control for other demons to see."

"Wouldn't that in itself add to their indulgence?" Gillian asked.

"For some demons it might," Cassie said. "But for demons like myself who view such acts as manipulative and unsavory, we let the victim know when he has a demon leech."

"This coming from a succubus, no less, who gains energy and glamour by becoming a leech herself," Jinn said, standing near the restroom door on the other side of the bar. His brow rose from his haughtiness and his tone was bitter.

"That's not true," she replied.

Jinn crossed his arms and walked to the edge of the bar, boring a narrow gaze into her eyes the entire time. "Isn't it? I'm an incubus. We feed on blood, too. It exhilarates us more than any drug ever could. You fed on Vincent."

Cassie gasped at his insolence. "Only *with* his permission. Besides, he was my husband, and he understood my need. He didn't want me to feed from other humans."

Jinn cocked one brow and grinned shrewdly. "Only him? Really, Cassie?"

"Except when the shadow demons were controlling me," Cassie said, correcting herself. "But I don't seduce humans into sex in exchange for blood. Not like you."

"Then how do you get your fix lately?" Jinn asked.

Tears crested in Cassie's eyes. Hurt, she glanced toward Forrest with a bit of shame.

Forrest stood and kicked his barstool back. He faced Jinn. "I don't know how long you were standing there or how much you heard, but you're veering our conversation off topic and starting to piss me off."

Jinn's eyes blazed. His demon teeth sprouted into jagged fangs. "I've waited a long time to have a go at you. Your smugness appalls me."

The three witches turned their attention on Jinn, too. Each held her right hand toward him. A slight bluish glow flickered at their fingertips.

"One wrong move," Jaclyn said.

Forrest placed his hand into his coat pocket and took a step toward Jinn. Ian and Gunner both left their seats, growling in low tones. Ian's claws had already protruded. Gunner's eyes turned green, ominous.

Jinn shook his head, returning to his less demon appearance. He raised his hands to calm them. "Whoa! Sorry. Did anyone else feel it?"

"What exactly?" Forrest asked. "All I know is I wanted to rip your head off your shoulders."

"Yeah, that," Jinn said. "Massive aggression and negative energy are flowing all around us. Can't you feel it?"

Raine said, "I suddenly became angry and was about to … use my magic in a hostile way."

"Me, too," Gillian whispered.

Jinn's hands trembled. "I just came back from the demon VIP. The growing oppression is spreading, causing hostility." He looked at Cassie with genuine sorrow in his eyes. "I'm sorry, Cassie. For what I said and for my rude accusations. You know I'm never like that."

Cassie nodded, wiped her eyes, and forced a smile. "I know."

"But a pattern is forming on the VIP floor. A demonic seal. Once it is complete, one or more of the behemoths can pass through the portal into the VIP room. Who knows what will happen after that." Jinn looked at Forrest. "I see your meeting is over? What are your plans now?"

"We're leaving Nocturnal Trinity. We tried to get Micah to come, but he's not budging," Forrest said.

Jaclyn pointed toward Rain and Gillian. "We're going to cast a location spell to find my mother."

"I see. I really suggest you find another place," Jinn said.

"Because of the portal?"

He nodded.

Jaclyn said, "Could you get us a picture of the growing portal?"

"Sure," Jinn said. "I had wanted to attend your meeting because I had some suggestions, but Forrest kind of opposed. Anyway, from what little I heard of your conversation, there is something that dawned upon me."

"What's that?" Forrest asked.

"Cassie mentioned a demon might be influencing Micah, and if so, I think I know why."

Cassie frowned. "Why?"

Jinn adjusted his ponytail and let it fall. "Since the werewolves led the charge into Nocturnal Trinity, the behemoths probably blame Micah for Nicodemus' death. As long as they have Micah under their control, the pack is divided and weaker. Since Micah won't leave with you, he's an easy kill once they emerge."

"That's kind of our theory already," Forrest said.

"So you agree with Forrest that they will kill Micah?" Jaclyn asked.

Jinn shrugged. "I'd say it ranks high on their agenda. But they might hold him hostage to draw the rest of the pack into the nightclub to kill all of the werewolves."

Forrest glanced at Jaclyn. "We have to find a way to convince Micah to leave before it's too late."

She nodded.

Jinn sighed and continued, "These demons have always allowed the vampires to make the major decisions and do the grunge work. But it looks as though the vampires have abandoned the nightclub altogether. One thing is for certain, if the behemoths choose to stay inside the nightclub, Micah's pack won't be able to stop them, even if they want to avenge Micah's death."

Forrest chuckled. "What makes you think that?"

"They know what werewolves are and the best way to kill them."

"From what you've implied, you don't think the vampires will return?" Forrest asked.

"With the growing portal upstairs, it's doubtful they will return until after the demons get rid of the werewolves. And you? You're their biggest threat."

"Apparently. Since they need to rely upon the demons to fight for them, it simply shows their cowardice," Forrest replied.

"Not cowardice, you foolish Hunter!" Flora shouted from the shadows of the neighboring dance floor. Her voice reverberated from the walls. "I wouldn't miss your death for anything!"

Flora's laughter echoed through the rafters.

Forrest grabbed a stake from his overcoat pocket and smiled. "Finally. The day might not end on a sour note after all."

CHAPTER 41

Kailey flung her arms around Brady's neck when he entered Micah's house. She squeezed tightly, but due to her swollen lips and face, she couldn't kiss him, even though she ached inside to do so. The scent of his sweat aroused urges that she desperately wished for him to fulfill.

After an overly long embrace, Brady loosened his hold around the small of her back, allowing her to step back slightly. He looked at her face and shook his head with sadness in his eyes. Gently, he cupped her cheeks in his hands.

She stared into his eyes for a moment and then looked away. "I'm hideous."

He shook his head and kissed her forehead. "Nonsense. You're my Kailey. These bruises prove you are a fighter who refuses to back down. That's the type of woman that turns me on. Not the prissy ones."

Kailey placed her hands around his, lowered them from her face, and held them while staring into his brown eyes. The warmth of his gaze excited her, and she never wanted to look away.

"I'm sorry," he said softly as he stared at her bruises. "I tried so hard to get to you before Raven hurt you."

"It's okay. Trust me, it looks far worse than it is. Thanks to Luna, the pain is gone. Of course, the swelling … I suppose that won't leave any time soon."

"That's great she lessened the pain."

Kailey shook her head. "No, whatever she did *removed* the pain."

Brady gently kissed her forehead again. "I was worried about you."

She looked down, squeezed his hands, and then she noticed the dried blood on his shredded shirt. "You were worried about *me*? I watched you get shot *twice*."

Brady shrugged. "It hurt a lot worse than it looked, but no scars."

Kailey punched his arm. He laughed and rubbed it. "Don't make light of the situation. The next time it might be silver bullets."

"It was supposed to have been this time."

She frowned with concern, studying his eyes. "What do you mean?"

"I'll explain later."

Outside the door, Barry laughed. A couple of seconds later, he pushed the door open and walked in with Eva.

Kailey gaped. "Eva? What's she doing here?"

"As soon as we get everyone in the dining room, I will explain," Brady said.

"If she's here, it can't be good."

Eva looked at Kailey and smiled. "Things are harsher than you can imagine."

"What's she talking about?" Kailey asked.

"Let's get everyone together so I don't have to explain the details several times."

Jacob came through the door.

"Could you round everyone up?" Brady asked.

"Sure." Jacob placed two fingers inside his mouth and whistled. The piercing sound caused Kailey and Eva to cover their ears. "Blaze and Luna! Get down here for a powwow!"

"I could have done that," Brady said.

"Then why didn't you?" He laughed and then clasped Brady's shoulder. "Glad you're all right."

"No more than I am."

"Whenever you get the time, have a heart to heart with your girl there. She got all frantic and weepy when we left the docks to protect her. Then she kept whining for me to call you. Explain to her what you told us about priorities."

"I wasn't that bad," Kailey said.

"She was worse," Barry said with a slight grin.

Kailey tilted her head back and almost rolled her eyes, but caught herself. Her face reddened, causing the bruises to darken. Brady's turned crimson in response to hers.

She leaned in closer to him. "So I got a little girly, okay? Is it a crime for me to worry about you, especially after you were shot?"

Brady shrugged. A sly smile crossed his lips. "I'll have to evaluate that after I cuff you and take you upstairs for further questioning. I might need to strip search you in the process, too."

Her eyebrows rose. "And what happens if I resist?"

"Things might get a little rough," Brady replied, placing his hands on his belt.

"I'll hold you to that," she said, crinkling her nose.

"Behave, you two," Jacob said. He glanced toward Eva and his face reddened. "Have some respect for your elders. You might embarrass someone."

"I'm not complaining one bit," Barry said, combing his white beard with his hand. He winked at Kailey. "In fact, I'm enjoying it."

"I wasn't talking about *you*," Jacob said in a near growl. "God."

Eva chuckled. "If you were referring to me, save your breath. I was young once, and after all their trauma, it's good they can exchange playful banter. It lessens the stress."

Barry loosened his shirt collar. "I think I need to go check the thermostat. It seems a little hot in here."

Blaze and Luna eased into the dining room and slid quietly into their chairs. Luna's hair was tussled and her makeup smudged. The buttons on her blouse were in the wrong holes. She blushed and refused to make eye contact with anyone.

"You too?" Jacob groaned and shook his head, walking toward the patio door. "I need to get a girlfriend."

Brady looked around the room. His brow furrowed. "Is this all of us?"

"Reckon so," Barry said.

"Where's the rest of our pack?"

Still looking outside the patio door window, Jacob sighed. "I've wondered the same. Since the walkout on Micah at Nocturnal Trinity, most everyone has gone off to do his or her own thing."

"Can you contact them?"

Jacob turned and shook his head. "I'm sure I could call them, but most of them assured me that until Micah left Nocturnal Trinity or we accepted a new pack leader, they weren't putting their lives on the line. Not that I could blame them."

"I know."

"That's why I told you we need a new leader," Jacob said.

Brady nodded. "It's not that simple. Choosing a new Alpha requires all pack members to assemble. Loyalty must be given by all or any disputes for leadership must be settled before the new Alpha can preside."

"Can you do that without Micah?" Kailey asked.

Barry slid a chair back from the table and sat down. "Micah's pretty much abandoned us."

"He's gone AWOL," Jacob said, crossing his muscled arms.

"But what if he changes his mind after you've chosen a new leader?" Kailey asked.

"He could make a challenge," Brady replied. "Most likely he would not."

"Why not?"

"It's damn near impossible to gain back loyalty once it's lost. If the majority of the pack is happy with the new leader, the old leader won't have much success convincing the members he's the best choice."

Barry pulled a pack of cigarettes from his pocket. "Situations like that can get nasty."

"You've been in those situations?" Blaze asked.

Barry flipped open his Zippo, lit his cigarette, and nodded. "Yeah, I've been in a few nasty brawls because of pack divisions. Never thought we'd be at this stage with Micah, though. There's no place for leadership passiveness in a group of werewolves. As I think about it, that's probably why he convinced us to confine our wolves with his spell for almost two years, so no one could challenge him."

Jacob gritted his teeth. His nose crinkled in a near snarl. He pointed a stiff finger in the air to make his argument. "I had openly stated that for the last six months he held our wolves hostage. I had nearly come to blows with him several times, but I knew if I allowed myself to attack, I'd kill him. With him dead we were stuck with our wolves trapped in limbo. He understood that, too. It was his leverage tool. The rage of my wolf was becoming more difficult to control."

"His spell caused a lot of resentment from others, too," Brady said. "Which is why none of us have supported his decision to join Nocturnal Trinity. We can call this meeting to order, but until we have everyone together, there's no sense discussing the choice of a new leader, although the more I've thought about it, the more I believe it's time to start afresh."

"If that's the type of meeting you'd like to have, I can start making the calls," Jacob said, pulling his cellphone from his back pocket.

Brady held his hand toward Jacob and shook his head. "Not yet. Let's all take a seat and discuss what's going on. Eva and I stumbled into a dangerous situation that concerns us all. It's a threat to all of us, and unless Micah renounces his union with the other factions in Nocturnal Trinity, he's as good as dead."

Kailey frowned. "What is this threat?"

"Andreas was the man who tried to kill me last night," Brady said. "I captured him with the help of Eva, but it turned out to be an unexpected trap."

Barry tapped the ash of his cigarette into an ashtray. He cocked his head slightly to one side, giving a curious stare. "What kind of trap?"

"From the information I obtained from Andreas, the founding vampires had told him to kill me. He was told the gun had silver bullets, which is why he shot me twice."

Kailey gasped.

"They had tricked him."

"For what purpose?" Jacob asked.

"I'm still trying to figure all of that out. But they had used him for a reason. They knew he'd provoke my anger enough to turn me and cause my wolf to kill him."

"Did you?" Kailey asked.

Brady's jaw tightened. He stared down at the table, partially angry with himself and partially from regret. "I did."

"Good. You killed their servant." Jacob shrugged. "That's a good thing. So how was that a trap?"

Eva leaned forward on the table. "Because Andreas had been marked by the founding demons of Nocturnal Trinity. Once Andreas' blood spilled, these demons were summoned into action."

"Which indicates they've been planning this for quite some time," Brady said. "Perhaps that explains why the vampires have been absent."

"I agree," Eva said.

"But why the need to kill Andreas?" Kailey asked. "Couldn't these demons simply materialize and do whatever it is they want? I've always been under the impression that they could teleport or project themselves to wherever they wished to be."

Eva sighed. "That would have been my thought, too. The behemoths are not bound or imprisoned. They are part of the Circle of Unity, sort of like silent partners, but they're not being silent anymore. The only reason for them to mark Andreas—that *I* can think of—was to force us to kill him."

"Why would they want that?" Jacob asked.

"So they could use his death like a grievance to vindicate their reason for the coming slaughter. For one to kill a member of another faction, even if it's a personal servant, the murder nullifies any pact agreements between the werewolves and the rest of the Unity, justifying the act of war."

"That's a great explanation," Brady said. "I was still trying to piece together their reasons for sacrificing Andreas."

Eva laughed softly. "I've been on their council for far longer than any of you have been alive. I know how they think and act. But, until Debra and Rose had been killed when Nicodemus was, no one had taken such extreme actions. That's another reason Micah shouldn't have decided to mend the Circle of Unity. It's not possible. The war had already begun."

"Doesn't that mean Micah's life is in jeopardy?" Kailey asked.

Barry glanced toward her. "His life was in jeopardy the moment he decided *not* to crush the Circle of Unity. Our onslaught has put targets on our backs, but had we stuck to the original plan, there'd be no threat aimed toward us."

"Which is probably why the other members in our pack have scattered," Jacob said.

Barry nodded. "I agree with you on that."

"Has anyone been able to contact Micah?" Brady asked.

Blaze, Jacob, and Barry all shook their heads.

"I haven't been able to, either," Brady said.

"Perhaps we can make a trip to the nightclub and see what's happening?" Jacob asked.

"Not yet. There are other issues."

"Like what?" Barry asked while taking another drag on his cigarette.

"We have a new ally," Brady said.

Jacob's eyes narrowed with suspicion. "Who?"

"A priest."

Barry pressed his cigarette into the ashtray, snubbing it out. His sudden laugh was deep, raspy, and hearty. "What the hell for?"

Eva leveled a harsh stare at him. "Because he knows how to deal with demons."

"Black Jack or Gin?" Barry said, unable to suppress his grin and laughter. He slapped the knee through his torn blue jeans before elbowing Jacob in the ribs.

Jacob grinned.

Eva rose to her feet. She pointed her crooked aged finger. "You dare to laugh when you're about to face evil monstrosities capable of ripping your bodies in half? When you followed Micah into Nocturnal Trinity, you didn't fight against any demons. None. Some of your pack nearly died. Magnify what you faced before by a thousand or more. Short of a miracle, we're up against creatures that are nearly indestructible and you want to laugh at having a priest as an ally?"

Barry's grin faded. He cleared his throat. "Sorry, ma'am. But how can a priest help us?"

Eva eased back down in her chair. "For one thing, the cathedral where he resides is fortified to prevent a demon from even entering. If he's capable of doing that, he knows how to handle demons."

"He even told us that he's destroyed some of them before, too," Brady said.

Barry maintained an apologetic expression as he glanced toward Eva. "Not trying to be offensive or belittle this priest, but how do you know he's on the up and up? I realize that church leaders are supposed to be righteous examples for the believers and nonbelievers, but the priests and pastors have lost so much credibility with society because of how corrupt some of them have been. How can we know that he's trustworthy?"

"I understand your skepticism," Brady said. "After meeting him, I'm not fully convinced of what he can do, but his sincerity was genuine. He wanted to know where the demon had appeared even after I told him we didn't have time to take him there."

"He was going to go alone?" Kailey asked.

Brady nodded. "How many people do you think would check it out without someone with them?"

"Nowadays?" Barry asked. "Hell, these younger punks have no sense at all. Nothing frightens them and their stupidity gets their asses into trouble all the time."

"I'm not talking about the younger people. I'm talking about ministers and priests."

Barry sighed. "You have a point, Brady. I'd say it would be difficult to get one to go without asking for a donation or charging a fee."

"What?" Eva asked with a look of disbelief.

"You've seen the Internet ads or those in the community newspapers, haven't you? So-called priests wanting to perform demon excising for people or houses. They won't do it without a few hundred dollars upfront."

"I doubt they're priests or that they've ever dealt with a real demon," Eva replied.

Barry shrugged. "I know. That's why I'm wondering about your priest."

"He's not *my* priest." Eva frowned.

"You hold him in high regard for some reason," Barry said.

"Because he's not prejudice. He actually hired a witch to write protective mantras on the walls and to secure the perimeters of the cathedral with a protective circle. Most priests and ministers frown upon witchcraft altogether, insisting witches are Satan worshippers, when we're not."

Barry flicked his attention toward Brady. "I'll be honest. I don't know whether or not it's a good decision. I'll leave that to you."

Brady looked at Jacob. "What about you?"

Jacob's deep frown of thought faded and a grin crossed his face. "We could put him to the test."

"How?" Brady asked.

Jacob smiled. "Since he said that he wanted to know where the demon was, we could take him to the spot where the demon emerged and see what his reaction is. If he wants to charge a fee, that automatically disqualifies him. Besides, I'm curious to see the spot where this demon appeared."

"That's a good idea," Barry said.

"I agree," Brady said, taking the priest's business card from his pocket. "I'll call him. Jacob, you and Barry get the boat ready. Everyone else, if you're coming be outside in ten minutes."

CHAPTER 42

Forrest set his Hunter box on the bar, unlatched it, and flung the top over, revealing some of his vampire hunting gear. He grabbed several bottles of holy water, two globe-shaped bottles of pure garlic juice, and shoved them into his pockets.

Ian and Gunner grabbed stakes out of the box as fur slowly covered their hands, even though with their jagged claws they didn't need the weapons. But during the blur of aggressive melee, extra weapons came in handy.

Forrest glared at Jinn. "I thought you said that she wasn't here."

"I'm being straight up with you. I didn't know that she was. If I had seen her, I would have told you. She must have come in through the Founders' door. *Recently.*"

"Never trust a demon," Forrest grumbled.

"Hey!" Cassie said with a glare.

"You're the exception," Forrest said.

"And I'm not?" Jinn's voice indicated his hurt for not gaining Forrest's trust.

Forrest grinned, handing two stakes to Jinn. "Like I said earlier, prove yourself."

Jinn held the two stakes and smiled. "If that vamp bitch shows herself, I'll ram a stake through her heart. I might just miss by a few inches on purpose the first time to make her suffer."

"No," Forrest said. "Don't give her any chance to escape."

"I owe her payback from the last prank."

"Trust me. Turning her to ash is punishment enough." Forrest eyed Jaclyn. "Take the other two witches through the front door. Check on Titus. Make sure he's okay. Afterwards, get the Hell out of here. Perhaps you could go to Micah's magic shop to perform the ritual to locate your mother. I'm going after Flora."

Jaclyn nodded. She placed her hand upon Forrest's right wrist. "Be careful. It might be a trap."

Forrest waited until the three witches had crossed the dance floor and made it out the door. He looked at the others. "Let's find her."

Ian and Gunner lowered to all fours and moments later, they completely altered into their shifter forms.

Cassie walked along the edge of the wall. Somehow, she had veiled herself in shadow and had almost become invisible in the areas where the darkness prevailed.

Forrest peered around the empty dance floor, hoping to catch a glimpse of Flora. He needed to find her. He couldn't allow her to escape. If she had heard their conversation, they had lost their advantage and every opportunity to catch the demons off guard. "Ian, go tell Micah and Ashley that Flora's here."

Ian huffed and scampered across the floor toward the stairs, obviously angered to not be pursuing Flora. He enjoyed vampire slaying better than most actual Hunters.

"Hunter! Do you like games?" Flora asked, her voice echoing.

"Show yourself and let's get this over with, Flora."

"No reprieve?

"Your pardon has ended."

"Well, since you're the Hunter, that means I'm the prey. Let's see how good your hunting skills are then," Flora said in a haunting whisper.

"I should have killed you ages ago," Forrest said, firming gripping a sharp stake.

"And yet, you didn't." The whispered words came near his ear. The iciness of her breath pricked his skin.

Forrest turned and slashed the stake through the air, hoping to strike her before she moved outside his radius, but he wasn't fast enough.

Flora's laughter drifted higher, echoing in a pleasant tone. "Close, Hunter! But not on target. Are you getting old?"

Forrest growled at her mockery.

"I take it you're fond of me," Flora said.

"Don't flatter yourself."

Her laughter billowed. *Ah, now Hunter, you've known for over a century where I have resided, but you have allowed me to live. Surely that's affection at its purest, is it not? If I truly were your enemy, you'd have sought me long ago and driven a stake through my heart before my strength magnified even more with age.*

Forrest held a stake in each hand, slowly turning in a circle, listening and looking, trying to get a glimpse of her.

You can't kill me because you still desire me. A part of you still wonders how it could have been between us, how surrendering yourself to me and fulfilling your lusts might have changed your life forever. I remember. I wanted it, too.

"Old age has made you delusional," Forrest said through gritted teeth.

Is that so?

"Definitely. You do realize I was only nine years old when we first met?"

Silence.

Forrest chuckled. "I realize that you didn't know."

You lie.

Forrest shook his head. "No, it was part of my being *chosen* as a Vampire Hunter. My body might have been that of an adult, but my mind was still maturing, trying to catch up. So stop flattering yourself. What you remember is far different than my memories."

Flora's laugh was soft and filled with flirty charm. *You can deny your desires with these fantasized excuses, Forrest, but I saw the longing in your eyes when you held up the stake and made it appear to the others that you were going to stake me. There was that flicker of warmth and compassion, making you remember what you had felt long ago. The eyes reveal the soul, Forrest. And I saw the instant relief in your eyes when Kailey begged you to spare me and you pretended to acquiesce. I know you. No amount of pleading could persuade you not to kill a vampire when you had the undeniable opportunity to do so. Your passion for me is still there, although it's buried deeply.*

"You're a fool."

Tsk. Tsk. I allowed you to slay Nicodemus because he had been the one who prevented us from being together a century ago. He only disapproved of our union because you had killed our father, but you can have me now. He's no longer an obstacle.

Forrest laughed. "Your glamour and compulsion have no grip on me, so you can quit trying."

I have no need of either with you. Your heart cannot hide its ache for me.

Forrest took a sharp breath and swallowed hard. Sweat cropped his brow. His frustration increased. "If you truly believe that, appear before me. I'll show you how little I desire you and how much you repulse me."

Not here. Not now. You're not being honest with yourself about me, us.

"There is no *us*."

Forrest, yield to your desires. Allow the old memories you've buried to resurface. Do so, and Kailey will be spared. I'll call Raven off and make her never harm Kailey again.

"Blackmail? You're the one who has deceived yourself for more than a century. As I recall you were scorned because you were unable to compel me into having sex with you. I rejected your every attempt to seduce me. Like you're trying to do now, but it didn't work then and it certainly won't work now. You want to know why?"

There was a long pause before she replied. *Why?*

"You're not only cold because you're undead; you're cold because you don't have the capability to express love. It's not something you've ever known, nor have you ever given it. It fleets from your presence like light dispels the darkness. I could never stomach the thought of being with you because there's no way I'd ever give myself to a heartless bloodsucking corpse."

How dare you!

"Is that enough proof for you?" Forrest shouted, looking toward the rafters. "Show yourself and I'll end your delusional misery!"

We shall meet soon enough, but only after I've destroyed everything else that's precious in your life. I will fill your life with sorrow unlike you've ever known. Another time, Forrest!

She shrieked at such a high decibel that several of the overhead lights burst and showered down bits of glass.

Forrest stared at the floor. Her threat, for the most part, was meaningless. He didn't believe his sorrow could ever be greater than the losses he had already suffered during the early years of his life. Of course, she was threating to kill his current friends, but she'd never succeed if he figured out where she was hiding.

As the last of the raining glass fragments settled, Micah and Ashley descended the stairs from the werewolf VIP. A disgruntled Ian followed behind them.

"Flora did this?" Micah asked, looking at the lights and then to the floor.

Forrest nodded. He turned toward Cassie and Jinn. "Let's go! She's gone!"

Micah stared at Forrest. "You're sure she's gone?"

"I am. She's up to her usual taunting, cousin. And since you're my family, I can only ask you once more to reconsider what we discussed earlier. I cannot protect you if you remain inside Nocturnal Trinity. The situation is getting grimmer. You won't be spared. Sadly the same fate will befall Ashley. Are you willing to sacrifice her for your stubbornness?"

Forrest didn't wait for Micah to reply. He turned and walked to the bar to gather up his box and slaying tools.

Cassie stepped up beside him. "She's really gone?"

Forrest nodded, latched the lid on the box, and slid the box off the bar.

"How do you know?"

Forrest smiled. "She told me she was leaving, but with her chaotic plans, she won't be gone long. The shattering lights indicated her theatrical exit, which is something she enjoys. We need to find Eva and return to the tunnel to discover what's there. After that we locate Flora and slay her."

Cassie responded with a curious frown. "Did she speak to you like she has Kailey in the past?"

"Yes."

"What did she say?"

"I'd rather not talk about it. But we cannot waste any more time here."

CHAPTER 43

Kailey stood beside Brady in the parking lot at the docks with the rest of his group. The sky was gray, thickly overcast, and the breeze off the choppy bay was quite cool, but at least the rain had stopped. In many ways she was beginning to love Seattle for its constant dusk atmosphere.

Father Charles pulled into the parking lot and appeared nervous seeing the unexpected group of people standing with Brady. For a few seconds, Kailey thought the priest was going to turn the car around and leave, but he didn't.

He pulled into a parking spot, got out, and clicked the lock mechanism on his car key. The lights on the Lincoln blinked twice. He wasn't wearing a robe but instead, he wore dark jeans and a long-sleeved flannel shirt. He looked more like a lumberjack than a priest. His eyes did a quick survey of each person before finally resting upon Brady.

"Father," Brady said, extending his hand and shaking with the priest. "Allow me to introduce everyone."

After the introductions were completed, Father Charles looked somewhat relieved. "While I know that you realize the danger this demon presents, I didn't think you'd bring a small army along with you."

Brady offered a slight smile. "We work together so much that we consider one another family."

"I see," he replied. "You have your *own* congregation."

"Don't know that I'd describe it quite like that," Brady said, glancing at his entourage.

Father Charles smiled for a moment and looked at Kailey's face once again. His expression revealed his obvious concern. "Young lady, what happened to you?"

Embarrassed, she cleared her throat. "Fight. With a vampire."

"A vampire?"

She nodded.

"Vampires generally *bite*. They don't pummel one black and blue and various shades of purple."

"This particular one wanted to punish me."

The priest studied her face for a few more seconds. "I do hope you got even."

"Not yet."

"Normally I object to revenge, but when you're dealing with undead creatures and demons, make them suffer before you slay them, but don't allow yourself to become careless. They are still supernatural creatures and take advantage of human weaknesses."

Brady nodded. "That's another reason why we're all here. We don't want to leave her alone."

"Not questioning your strategy or motives at all," Father Charles replied. "To be honest, I don't expect this demon to have remained where you and Eva had witnessed its surfacing. In this line of work, it never hurts to have extra help."

Brady pointed toward the narrow alley that began on the other side of the overpass. "It's not too far down that alleyway. If I may be candid, I wouldn't have even considered returning to the place without someone who knows how to banish a demon."

The priest walked around to the trunk of his car, unlocked it, and popped the lid open. Inside the trunk, he had a vast array of ancient weapons Brady had never seen before.

Brady's brow rose. "Perhaps you've missed your true calling?"

Father Charles laughed. "Not at all. Each part of what I do strengthens my other duty. Slaying demons strengthens my devotion, and my pursuit to make the world more peaceful causes me to hunt these evil demons." He pulled a double-sided ax from the trunk. It wasn't the type of ax one found at a hardware store and was possibly missing from a museum somewhere in the world. The weapon looked to be a few centuries old. Strange symbols had been welded into the metal handle. With the priest's choice of rugged outdoorsy clothes, the weapon actually suited his attire.

"What's that for?" Kailey asked.

Father Charles winked. "Just in case."

Jacob offered a shrewd grin to Brady. "And all this time I thought priests sought to practice peace and civility."

"Do you oppose ridding the world of its demons?" the priest asked with a stern but polite stare.

"Not at all," Jacob replied.

"Less demons means more peace."

Kailey suddenly felt nervous and sick at her stomach, thinking about Cassie.

Father Charles recognized her apprehension. "Is there a problem?"

"Do you consider all demons evil?" she asked.

"You think they're not?" He hefted the heavy ax and rested it upon his shoulder as he began walking across the wet parking lot in the direction Brady had pointed.

"No worse than humans," Kailey replied.

The priest stared at her with curiosity. His long silence made her uneasy.

She wondered if she had said something wrong or given too much information away. What would the priest think if he discovered she was friends with a demon? She crossed her arms as she walked. "The world has its share of evil men and women. Right? Is it fair to automatically lump all demons into the *evil* category?"

Father Charles looked amused.

"Do you think my speculation is wrong?" Kailey asked.

"No, I don't believe God deliberately created any species to be born evil. Anyone with freewill can become susceptible to temptations and thus take the wrong path in life. A lot of what a person becomes is because of the direction he or she has chosen. As a priest, I see two opposing forces: God and Lucifer. As a man or woman could be persuaded to turn from the path of righteousness and hope, is it impossible for a demon to turn toward the Light?"

"I would hope such a choice was *not* impossible," Kailey replied.

"As would I," Father Charles said.

"So you don't scour the city, hoping to kill all of the demons?" Eva asked.

"Not at all," the priest replied. He shrugged. "Who has the time? I seek to annihilate those who deliver pestilence, oppression, and cause turmoil for society. While it is true that some criminals and ruthless people have been influenced by demons, vile humans who have no outside influence also defile our world. A vast majority of children aren't being taught morals and integrity. It's easy for others to blame the demons, but in truth a majority of the demons have gotten tired of being faulted for behavior even they find appalling. Those aren't the demons I seek to destroy. The lesser demons often are mischievous but the greater demons are the ones who are blood-thirsty and cause carnage throughout the world. They are the most deadly but fortunately, the least encountered."

"So these demons were fallen angels?" Kailey asked.

The priest chuckled and shook his head. "That's a common misconception, and yes, the church has a lot to do with the rumor. The demons were here before the great battle in Heaven between God and Lucifer. Ancient Greek texts record them as do a lot of Egyptian hieroglyphics. They were creatures that lived underground on Earth. Once Lucifer had rebelled and was cast out, he sought these creatures of darkness, which were hideous and feared by mankind, to build his earthly army. But, not all demons chose to follow him. A large percentage shunned him. The majority of them still do. They prefer living deep beneath the Earth's crust."

"Interesting," Brady said. "Why?"

Father Charles shrugged. "To follow Lucifer is to commit to constant war against what is considered holy. The reward is slim. Why obligate oneself to constant strife and tribulation when it's not necessary?"

"Why isn't this taught?" Kailey asked.

The priest laughed softly. "Erasure of hundreds of years of tradition is more difficult than having Lucifer confess the error of his way. But in his mind, he has made no errors."

"Trying to eradicate all other religions that existed before the church is as great a sin, is it not?" Eva asked with a shrewd cold stare.

Father Charles nodded. "Sadly, early church leaders overzealously sought to rule the world. They usually purged the religious leaders first, in the hope the rest of the civilizations could be spared, but seldom did that happened, which caused needless carnage and genocide to occur. However, it has not stopped. One only has to look to the Middle East to witness the bitterness and wrath that has continued to fester for centuries. Clergy and explorers employed by the Vatican created enemies who haven't forgotten. These enemies seek bloody vengeance. The church now seeks a passive mission, but those they persecuted have no desire to relent. Their goal is to eradicate all other religions to reign."

"Like the Vatican?" Eva asked.

"Yes, the old church and its greedy leaders. But that's all a debate for another time. Right now, we need to see what we're dealing with."

"I agree," Brady said, hurrying his pace.

Kailey assumed Brady disliked where the conversation was heading, and since they were walking with a priest, he didn't want to be pulled into the discussion. The information the priest had given about the history of warring religions brought her full circle again as to why she found it difficult to choose a deity. Although Father Charles hadn't touched on the subject, Kailey knew that Eva's comment was about the persecution of witches more so than other religions coerced to convert by the church. Hailed as the oldest religion in the world, the pagans had almost been exterminated, but instead of their beliefs vanishing forever, the traditions had been secretly handed down through the generations.

To learn that the demons had been a species all its own before the church ascribed them as fallen angels, Kailey wondered what else had been hidden from the world. Was all the speculation about aliens and subterranean reptilian creatures not really myths?

Midway down the alley, Brady stopped between the two dumpsters. The rest of the group stood beside him, waiting for Eva to catch up to them.

Father Charles gave a curious frown. "Why are we stopping here?"

Kailey had wondered the same thing.

"You'll see," Brady replied.

Eva smiled, stepping between Brady and the priest. "Give me some room."

Everyone backed away.

Kailey glanced around the alley and up to the windows of apartments, but no one was looking out or loitering.

Eva raised her frail hands and muttered a chant that was almost inaudible. The words weren't words Kailey was familiar with, but spoken at such a low tone, it was hard to determine if it were another language or not. After she had finished, the doorway slowly materialized.

"Amazing," Father Charles said, shaking his head.

Eva stepped aside and extended her hand toward the door handle. "Who'd like to do the honors?"

Kailey, Brady, and Jacob glanced at the priest with insistent nods.

"I guess it's unanimous," Eva said with a grin.

Father Charles nodded. "I suppose so."

CHAPTER 44

Forrest exited Nocturnal Trinity with Ian and Gunner. Titus stood with his back to the wall beside the door. His thick arms were crossed. Other than giving Forrest an irritated side-glance, he appeared unharmed. "See? I told you that Flora was not going to hurt you.

Titus' frown deepened. "What are you talking about?"

"When Flora came inside earlier?"

"I haven't seen Flora's out here," Titus replied.

"She was inside somewhere. She spoke to me," Forrest said.

Titus pushed off the wall and walked to the steps, placing his hands on the rail. He glanced toward the street and then across to the parking garage. "There's still too much daylight for her to have arrived after I took my post. If she's inside the nightclub, she's been in there before daybreak."

"So she never exited?"

"Not through these doors or the Founder doors."

Forrest frowned and rubbed his bearded chin. "Is there any other way out?"

"Not on this level," Titus replied, shaking his head. "Now Jaclyn and her party did pass through. They asked if I were okay, but they never mentioned anything about Flora. I simply thought they were asking about how my day was going."

"Thanks," Forrest said. He turned toward Ian. "Do you and Gunner mind reentering the nightclub and checking the underground tunnel?"

Ian groaned and rolled his eyes.

"I don't mean for you to follow the tunnel all the way out. Just go and see if you can get her scent."

Ian glanced at Gunner and shook his head. "We're dogs now, brother. Hounds tracking a scent."

"No," Forrest said.

"I'll go," Gunner said with a slight shrug. "I like the tunnels better than these streets anyway. Besides, I remember her odd smell from the last time. Like something dead sprayed with expensive perfume. It's not something I could easily forget."

"Oh, all right," Ian said, "I'll go, too."

The door opened and Cassie stepped outside. She wore a snug jogging suit that was barely more than a bodysuit beneath a thin cotton jacket that hung an inch below her butt. Her hair was pulled into a ponytail and she wore a red headband. Before the door closed after her, Ian hurried inside with Gunner right behind him.

Forrest walked down the steps with Cassie walking alongside him. They walked to the damp sidewalk, stepping over shallow puddles.

"What's wrong with Ian?" she asked.

Forrest chuckled. "Ian's being Ian."

"I see," Cassie said.

"Jinn's not coming?" Forrest asked.

"No," she replied.

"Do you trust him?"

A narrow smile crossed her lips. "As much as I trust any other demon. Why?"

"He swore that Flora wasn't in the nightclub when I had asked him earlier. Titus said that she had to have been inside before daylight because she didn't come through the door after he arrived."

Cassie pursed her lips. "You think he's working with her?"

"Honestly, I don't know. I thought since you worked with him—"

"I wish I could help you, but even though we work together, he has always kept me at a distance."

"Any reason why?" Forrest asked.

"Because I'm a demon."

Forrest frowned.

She laughed and shrugged her narrow shoulders. "His preference is hot female humans. It's his fetish, but as you know, I chose a human for a mate, so it's not anything out of the ordinary for a demon. But since he held no interest in becoming intimate with me, he didn't waste his time trying to get to know me. I don't think he'd deliberately deceive you about Flora, though. He wasn't overly fond of her."

"I sort of had that impression, too, but then she showed up." Forrest sighed. "I'm skeptical of people, but more so when it comes to supernatural creatures."

"Gee, thanks," Cassie said with a teasing smile.

"After all you and I've been through since I arrived in Seattle, I know I can trust you, which is why I was asking about Jinn."

"Thanks," she said. "I think he's on the level."

"Let's hope so, for his sake," Forrest said in an icy tone.

Cassie took a quick breath as she offered a nervous side-glance.

"A problem?" he asked.

"Not really," she replied.

"You've heard the expression, 'Actions speak louder than words,' I'm certain."

"I've just never met anyone like you."

Forrest laughed softly but kept walking without looking in her direction. "I've been unique since I was a child."

"Every mother tells her child that."

He roared with hearty laughter. "Trust me, it wasn't my mother or father who called it to my attention."

"It's just you only seem to have two modes."

Forrest frowned. "What do you mean?"

"You seek to kill all vampires, but if someone you *tolerate* crosses you, you immediately write them off. Your approach toward Jinn … I can't tell if you intend to kill him if he's sided with Flora or if you're going to pound an apology out of him."

Forrest replied with a quick smile and said, "I guess we'll see when I know for certain."

"Really?"

He nodded.

"How long have Ian and Gunner been your friends?"

"Over a hundred and twenty years, why?"

She gave an incredulous stare.

Forrest sighed. "It's a long story."

"How have they stayed with you that long?"

He laughed.

"I'm serious. With your approach to life and not having any friends in general, you've managed to spend your life with them."

"I consider them family, so that's different."

"Are they related to you?" Cassie asked.

"Not by blood. But in truth, Gunner saved my life."

"Gunner?" She stared in disbelief.

Forrest understood her skepticism. "Yes. He pulled me from a river. Had he not, I would have drown. My back was broken. He was insistent upon saving me while Ian scolded him for doing so. At the time, Ian would have been fine with me dying. It was the first time, I believe, that Gunner had stood up to his brother."

"And you get along fine with Ian even though his initial approach was for you to die?"

"Oh, Ian and I have differences almost every day. But we're all we have as family. In so many ways they rely upon me, and I know I probably wouldn't have kept my sanity without them. I don't care who you are, you need others to confide in and we have a bond that cannot be broken, regardless of our skirmishes. Should any one of us die, it would devastate the other two. We are united as one and continuously watch one another's back."

Cassie nodded. "I feel that way about Kailey. Somehow she got past what had happened when I had tried to kill her."

"She knows that wasn't you, but those shadow demons controlling you."

"I know, but still. Humans hold grudges, deep grudges at times, and even when someone has faulted another unintentionally, the recipient of the misdeed tends not to forget. She could have written me off, and she had every right to do so, but she didn't."

"Kailey isn't the typical human," he replied with a sly grin.

"She isn't."

Forrest turned and stepped to the edge of the sidewalk, hailing the approaching taxi.

"Where are you going?" she asked.

"To Micah's magic shop. You're welcome to come along."

"Is that where Jaclyn went?"

"Yes."

"I don't want to get in the way," she replied.

"You won't be."

The cab slowed and stopped. Forrest opened the door and allowed her to get inside first. As he started to get in, a woman said, "You have room for one more?"

He glanced over his shoulder.

Lydia.

She stood with her hands tucked into her front jeans pockets. She didn't smile. Her cold eyes indicated only one thing. She was an assassin to the core and more ruthless than Forrest was when he slayed vampires.

Forrest took a step back and extended his hand toward the open door. "After you."

"Thanks," she said in a low frozen tone.

After she climbed into the cab, Forrest sat down beside her and closed the door. He told the cab driver the address. The driver gave a quick nod and turned on the meter.

With Flora's continued taunting, Forrest was glad to see Lydia, but he worried that perhaps she still didn't understand the full dangers of the situation she had volunteered to participate in. However, he understood that people like Lydia never weighed the risks. Often they sought the thrill of the hunt, which spiked their adrenaline rush to levels otherwise unknown. People without consciences reacted from instinct. Their minds calculated risks during the moment of battle. Because they held no fears, they ran straight into the conflict, seldom ever retreating.

Since Forrest didn't know the exact power of the force or forces they were about to encounter. It might well be that he'd need an army to succeed, and turning away a volunteer was foolish.

CHAPTER 45

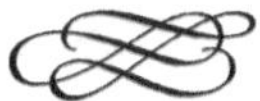

Kailey stood at the rear of the group and watched Father Charles enter through the door. Andreas' body was pressed against the wall, somehow affixed about two feet off the floor, but a closer examination offered no clues as to why his corpse had not fallen to the floor. He appeared to be held in place by some unseen force. Demonic symbols painted with Andreas' blood were on the walls and floor.

Brady glanced around the room before finally making eye contact with Eva.

Eva was nervous.

Luna was pale and placed a hand over her mouth. She was seconds from rushing back out the door and hurling beside one of the dumpsters. Blaze wrapped his arm around her shoulder. She turned slightly and pressed her face against his chest, closing her terrified eyes. Although he was trying to remain brave, he wasn't able to hide his uneasiness.

"You okay, kid?" Barry asked.

Luna nodded without pulling her face from Blaze's chest.

"What do you make of this?" Brady asked Eva.

"It's not good at all."

The priest shook his head. "You're right. This is bad. Even worse than I imagined."

"In what way?" Kailey asked.

"The symbols are ancient, and the proper interpretation details the true dangers we are in," Father Charles said. "The burnt tattoo-like symbol on his shoulder definitely indicates that he was marked. They were keeping tabs on his whereabouts at all times. Better than modern day GPS, too."

"So what does all of this mean?" Brady asked.

Father Charles walked around the room, going from symbol to symbol. He kept his hand over his mouth as he studied them. "We're running out of time basically. This sacrifice of blood and the symbols represent a great summoning."

"Of the other four behemoth demons?" Eva asked.

He shrugged. "No, those demons are already in Seattle. These symbols are to usher forth more demons from underneath the city, which possibly live in deep underground crevices. These are demons that spread disease and cause major epidemics, like the Black Plague or tuberculosis or possible diseases we've yet discovered. Devastating outbreaks that can take out seventy-five percent or more of the population. They have been summoned, and most likely, they will arrive soon."

"Is there any way to stop this?" Kailey hugged herself, suddenly cold.

"There's a way, but accomplishing it will be almost impossible," Father Charles replied.

"What is it we need to do?" Jacob asked.

"We need to scrub the blood symbols off the wall with holy water, and then we must kill the demon that was channeled into this room," he replied.

"Scrub off the blood?" Luna asked. She heaved a little, covered her mouth, and managed not to throw up. "I'm sorry, but I can't do this."

"Luna," Father Charles said softly. "It's not an easy task for any of us, but if this isn't done in a timely manner, think about the number of deaths that might occur. This ordeal doesn't simply involve us. We're talking about the lives of thousands of people."

Luna took several deep gulps of air, but the greenish tint on her pale face didn't lessen. She closed her eyes and puffed air through her mouth. "I can try."

"At this point, I'm willing to accept that," Father Charles said. "Try not to think of it as blood, but the room must be scoured before we hunt the demon."

"And what about the other four demons?" Brady asked.

"They don't matter, yet, but to stop the summoned demons from invading, we need to purify and consecrate this room and kill the demon within the next twenty-four hours. It's the only way we can deter the situation."

Eva looked at Father Charles. "I suppose you brought the holy water?"

He smiled. "Fortunately, as a priest, I'm never in short supply. However, I don't have enough on my person to go around. Certainly not enough holy water to clean the walls. I need someone to get the canteen from the trunk of my car and there should be a bag of clean rags, too." He held up his key ring.

Luna stepped away from Blaze. "I can go."

Brady shook his head. "We need someone fast." He nodded toward Jacob. Jacob took the keys from the priest and sprinted out the door into the alley. As runners went, Jacob was the fastest person in the room.

"You don't think I'd return?" Luna asked.

"It really is about the speed, Luna," Brady said with a reassuring smile.

"A canteen?" Eva asked.

Father Charles shrugged. "Why go small when I can bless gallons at a time?"

"I suppose so," she replied.

"I'm certain you do similar when you're mixing your concoctions?"

"Sometimes, but the potency isn't as strong whenever I make large batches."

He grinned. "I would have thought you'd maintain the same consistency throughout your potions because your magical abilities should have increased in power after all these years."

"Yes," Eva said with a soft chuckle. "But old age weakens one's connection as well. My mind isn't as sharp, and the required amount of time to concentrate takes much longer than it once did."

Kailey leaned closer to Brady and whispered, "I'd have never imagined seeing a witch and a priest discussing spells and prayers."

Father Charles had his back to her and was standing across the room. "Kailey, in order for us to defeat the coming enemies of destruction, we must set aside our differences and fight together using whatever blessings or powers we have. When a city's under the threat of total annihilation, you seek allies if you wish to survive."

Kailey looked surprised. "How he'd even hear me?"

Brady shook his head and shrugged slightly.

Father Charles turned and gazed into her eyes. His eyes were a strange blue color, like a cloudless sky on an autumn afternoon. "When you pray, you learn to listen for the softest of answers, often quieter than a whisper. It's a honing skill that I've perfected after years of service. But don't be alarmed. I was listening for the slightest noise, which might indicate the presence of these demons' approaching hoofbeats. Because my concentration was so focused, I *happened* to hear what you were saying."

"What happens if we scour this room of the blood symbols but fail to kill the demon?" Kailey asked.

"Removing the symbols delays their summoning, but it won't stop them if the demon isn't destroyed. They will still arrive, as the demon is still linked to this summoning room. No matter how much holy water we use in this room, we're not going to totally remove the blood. There will still be a faint trace of the blood left behind, keeping the symbols partially intact. But, you'll see something else once we wash away the blood."

"What's that?" Brady asked.

"Shallow grooves in the wall that also form the symbols. These were carved with the demon's claw as he was drawing."

"So there's no way to removed the summon, is there?" Kailey asked.

"No, but our actions will delay them because of how faint the calling marks are. It will take them longer to pinpoint where this room is. That's why it's necessary for us to kill the demon to break his binding hold."

"I'm guessing that won't be easy?" Brady said.

"No, that's the worst part we face," Father Charles replied.

Jacob sprinted through the door with the canteen in one hand and a plastic bag filled with unused garage clothes in the other. He wasn't panting and hadn't even broken a sweat.

Luna shook her head and looked at Blaze. "Brady was right. I could never have gotten back that quickly."

Blaze rubbed her back.

Father Charles smiled. "Thanks. Now, let's hurry and wash the blood off every symbol in this room. Be thorough but quick. If ever you knew how important a day's time was worth, today is that day."

Chills pricked up Kailey's back. Lightning flashed over the alley outside, and a cold breeze rushed into the room. She nervously glanced toward the door, wondering what might enter with the wind. But she suddenly realized it wasn't the doorway she needed to be wary of. It was the dried circle of blood beneath the chair where Andreas had been killed and the behemoth had appeared. She grabbed a cloth, soaked it with holy water, and immediately began scrubbing the symbol closest to her like her life depended upon it, which it did.

CHAPTER 46

orrest unlocked the side door of Micah's Magic Shop and allowed Cassie to enter first.

A strong blend of various incense and perfumed oils overwhelmed him. The only light in the rear room of the shop was the glow of five slender candles spaced to form a pentagram on the floor.

Forrest leaned forward, grabbed Cassie by the crook of her elbow, and gently pulled her toward him. She turned and opened her mouth to speak, but Forrest placed his thick finger against her lips and shook his head.

The witch trio began chanting. The flickering candlelight revealed enough to show their nude outlines. After they repeated the chant for the third time, Jaclyn offered her thanks to the Goddess, as did Raine and Gillian. Then they broke the circle.

"Forrest?" Jaclyn asked softly.

"Yes," he replied. "Cassie's with me, too."

"Ah, welcome. I'm certain you know that Titus is okay, then?"

"Yes. I spoke with him."

Raine snuffed the candles. For at least a minute the room was still. The only noise was soft, almost silent movements. Finally someone flipped a switch and the overhead fluorescent lights brightened the room. The three women were dressed in robes.

"Any good news?" Forrest asked.

"I believe so. We were repeating the ritual for the second time when you entered the shop. I was certain we had misinterpreted the first premonition I had received."

"What do you mean?" Cassie asked.

"My mother is still in Seattle," Jaclyn replied. The flare in her nostrils and her narrowing brow indicted she was quite miffed at her discovery.

Forrest chuckled. "In spite of *you* banishing her?"

"What do you think?" she said.

"Sounds like you have a rebellious parent on your hands," Forrest said.

Jaclyn offered a shrewd grin. "I suppose I had it coming from all the stress I've caused her over the years."

"At least we don't have to travel far to find her."

"You're right. She's only a few blocks from here."

"Then let's get her," Forrest said.

"No."

Forrest's mouth dropped for a moment. His jaw tightened from his sudden anger. Rage and desperation was steadily rising inside him.

"Easy, Forrest," Jaclyn said. "Don't resort to hostility. I've sent a messenger to request her assistance."

"And if she refuses to answer or come?"

"She won't."

"How do you know?"

Jaclyn sighed. "I promised to give her back the Grimoire."

The news astounded Forrest. "Really? I never thought you'd part with it."

"There are sacrifices we all must endure. I'm sure you've done so over the years."

Forrest nodded. "There has to be more than simply that."

"You're right."

Cassie crossed her arms. "You sensed something more, didn't you?"

Jaclyn glanced toward Raine with nervousness. "Yes, all three of us did. That's why the Grimoire is of little importance to me right now. I can't use it if we're all dead."

"Dead?" Forrest frowned. "Because of the vampires?"

Jaclyn shook her head. "The vampires are the least of our troubles now."

"Then what did you discover?"

Jaclyn walked to a small table in the corner of the room and sat down. "When we located my mother, we found that she was surrounded by dark oppressive energy. The same energy that has emerged inside Nocturnal Trinity in the demon VIP lounge."

"You think she's involved in it?" Forrest asked.

"For a moment I wondered to what extent she might have gone to gain back her power, but that's not the case. No, she's attempting to orchestrate a counterattack, but she's not doing alone. So whatever you led us to in the abandoned rail tunnel is of great significance."

Forrest offered a grim smile. "I'm glad you agree with me about that, but what changed your mind?"

"All the connections point to the tunnel, Forrest," Jaclyn replied. "For whatever reason, my mother is the key to unraveling our dilemma. She has hidden something there, and the last thing I ever expected to learn was that she is still in Seattle. Something evil is coming, a gateway has been opened, and she's the only one who can help us stop it. Everything has fallen into place, but we only have one real chance to defeat whatever is headed our direction."

"Nocturnal Trinity?" Forrest asked with narrowed eyes.

"It originated there, Forrest, but it's far greater than the Circle of Unity. In fact, like you've continually pointed out, that circle is fractured beyond repair."

Cassie nervously glanced toward Jaclyn. "So what you're saying is that the demons have decided to take over everything?"

"I think it's far worse than that," Jaclyn said.

"What exactly then?" Forrest asked.

"The demons plan to wreak havoc by committing massive carnage. They might even go so far as to turn most of the city to ash again. Worse than the Great Fire. But whatever it is they plan to do, it will be devastating."

"We need to warn Micah," Forrest said.

"Do you even think he'll listen?" Cassie asked.

Forrest said, "I can only hope. He's not been rational at all lately. Can you call him?"

"He said that the phones weren't in service," Jaclyn said.

Forrest flicked his gaze from Jaclyn to Cassie. "At least try. If the phones are operational, I might need to return to the nightclub and talk to Micah in person."

Cassie nodded and walked to the counter where the cash register set. She picked up the phone and dialed. After a couple of seconds, her face paled.

Jaclyn rose from her seat. "What's the matter?"

Cassie took a slow deep breath, and exhaled through her mouth. She pushed the intercom button on the phone. "Listen for yourself."

The deep voice that spoke gurgled. "Thank you for calling Nocturnal

Trinity. If it's Micah or Ashley you seek, they are mine. I will give them your condolences before they are sacrificed, but know their blood was necessary to fulfill our needs."

The message repeated itself again, apparently recorded to loop constantly. It almost seemed like a twisted prank, but the horror was all too real, enough to terrify a succubus and draw worried looks from three powerful witches.

Cassie disconnected the call and placed the phone into its cradle. She shivered and hugged herself. "It's been a long time since I've heard such an evil voice."

Forrest turned and headed to the door.

"Stop, Forrest!" Jaclyn said.

Forrest placed his hand on the doorknob and glanced over his shoulder.

"You can't go there."

"Why not? Someone has to rescue him and Ashley."

"It's what they expect you to do," Jaclyn said. "They probably need more people to sacrifice for whatever ritual they are planning to perform. You cannot beat this demon alone."

"I can try."

Jaclyn shook her head. "The only way to defeat this behemoth is by using whatever is hidden in the tunnel. It will take a concentrated effort from all of us."

"But we don't know that for certain."

"Where is your faith now?" Jaclyn asked. "You were insistent that we help you, and now, you're willing to disregard your own convictions about what's down there?"

"He's my family."

"I understand that. But … you cannot defeat this demon alone."

"And if Micah dies?" Forrest asked.

"Not to sound cold and heartless, but he knew the risks by staying. You've warned him ample times," Jaclyn said. "Besides that, we have all become a part of the dilemma because of him. None of us would even be in this situation had he done what he originally set out to do."

Forrest released the doorknob and stared down at the floor.

"She's right," Cassie said. "You've done everything possible to get him out, and he's stubbornly resisted."

"I've done everything except drag him out by his feet," Forrest said.

"I know you want to protect him, but he's a grown man. He made his decision. Regardless, you cannot exert your will over his. He'd just find another way to go back," Jaclyn said.

"Sadly, you're right. I can't. But, I still believe he's spellbound or controlled by a demon," Forrest said.

"That might be," Jaclyn replied. "And if so, the best thing we can do is work together to destroy this behemoth. If our luck is right, maybe it's the one that had mesmerized his mind."

CHAPTER 47

ailey took the towel soaked with holy water and scrubbed the odd blood-painted symbol on the wall. Behind her Eva gasped. Kailey turned to see Eva standing transfixed, staring straight ahead at nothing in particular. The elderly witch looked temporarily frozen, like a human mannequin. Whatever Eva was staring at, it was something Kailey could not see. "Are you okay, Eva?"

Eva didn't reply, nor did she blink. With all the bizarre occurrences Kailey had witnessed since moving to Seattle, she worried that perhaps Eva had been bewitched by a more powerful witch, or worse, the demon responsible for the symbols had somehow taken possession of Eva.

"Eva?" Kailey frowned.

Eva's lips suddenly trembled and a few seconds later, she whispered, "I understand."

Kailey placed a gentle hand on Eva's shoulder, fearing Eva might be having a stroke due to the overwhelming stress of the situation. "What's wrong?"

Eva shook her head, snapping out of the trance, and then she looked at Kailey. "I need to go."

"What? *You're leaving?* To where?" Kailey asked.

"Micah's shop."

Father Charles walked to her. "Is something wrong?"

Eva sighed. "It's difficult to explain, but I am needed elsewhere."

"If it will quicken things, I can drive you," the priest said.

She shook her head and motioned a shaky hand toward the demon symbols on the wall. "No, I cannot take you away from your work to make this demon gateway fade. As important as what I need to do, what all of you are doing in this room is far more essential, and I truly regret that I need to leave. Besides, the magic shop is only a few blocks away. Walking a couple of blocks doesn't take me long, even at my age. Provided the task doesn't take too long, I will return."

Father Charles stared at her for a moment, smiled, and pulled a small card and a ballpoint pen from the front pocket of his flannel shirt. He wrote something on the back of the card. "My cell number. Call me if you need assistance in any way or if you happen upon more information concerning this." He pointed to the demonic symbols.

Eva graciously accepted the card and nodded. "Thank you. I will. I'm sorry I have to go."

"We all have our missions in life," he replied. "Don't let me keep you any longer."

Luna stood with her soaked cloth in her hand. She still had not found the courage to clean the drying blood off the wall. "If you need someone to walk with you—"

"No, dear," Eva said softly. "Come here though."

Luna stepped closer. Eva placed her thumb to Luna's forehead, closed her eyes, and mumbled some words.

"You're much braver than you think," Eva said after she finished. She smiled. "Never forget that. I see great things in your future."

Luna smiled, took a deep breath, and then offered a gracious nod. "Thank you."

"Now, I really must leave." Eva waved to everyone and hurried out the door. Once she was on the other side of the doorway, she turned and spoke a few words, concealing the door from any potential passersby in the alley.

Kailey returned to the symbol she had been scrubbing and used both hands to scour away more blood off the wall. She tried not to think about this being blood, but it wasn't easy. She also didn't like knowing Andreas was dead because of Brady. But it had been his wolf that killed Andreas. Was that still murder? Where did she draw the line? Where did Brady do so?

She wondered what had been the trigger point for Brady to slash his claws through the victim.

Me?

She hoped not. But the demon had used the victim's blood to enhance the markings on the wall. It was necessary, she supposed, to attract the attention of other demons. Suddenly, she wondered about something she had never considered before. The blood-written threat on the mirror left by Raven … could a demon have written it and not Raven?

"Brady?" she asked.

Brady turned from the symbol he was trying to wash away. "Yes?"

She explained her sudden theory to him.

Brady glanced toward Father Charles. "What do you think, Father?"

"That is quite possible," he replied. "I've never heard of such occurring before, but it seems plausible."

"But it doesn't excuse Raven, does it?" Kailey asked.

"No," Father Charles replied. "The demon was using her influence to mimic Raven."

"It definitely explains how the message got there," Brady said. "Since she would have needed permission to enter our apartment. She has never received that from either of us. In fact, it's been quite the opposite. Our disdain toward her is not a secret. The vampires have completely joined forces with the demons."

"Which means anyone at Nocturnal Trinity is at risk," Kailey said.

Brady nodded. "Let's pick up the pace on washing this blood off the walls. We need to warn Micah, but the last time any of us tried to contact him, no one answered."

"I can go check on him," Jacob said.

"No," Brady replied. "We concentrate our efforts on removing the blood symbols first. Micah is resourceful. I'm certain if the dangers increase where he's at, he'll leave."

Kailey scrubbed harder. Everything was beginning to make a lot more sense. The demons had been in league with the vampires, and for some unexplained reason, they wanted her dead, too. But why?

Then it dawned upon her. Her brother, Vincent, had married a demon, actually had fallen in love with her, even after knowing exactly *what* Cassie was. From her guestimate, the founding demons must have disapproved and resented Vincent *and* Cassie.

So it's okay for demons to intimately date humans, but marriage is out of the question?

That seemed to be the case, but she really didn't know. What she did know—her investigative instinct kicking in—was the way the vampires and demons had tricked Cassie into becoming a part of their scheme to kill Vincent, which was something she'd have never done for ever how long a succubus could live. She had truly loved him. Once Vincent had been killed, and Circle of Unity finished using the shadow demons' control of Cassie, they had planned to kill Cassie and none would have been the wiser. But there had been only one thing they had never counted on, nor had they even anticipated.

Me.

Kailey's eyes widened. She scrubbed the bloodstained wall harder as a bit of the rekindled anger rose inside her as she remembered her brother's murder. None of the council had expected Vincent's sister to arrive and stick her investigative nose into places they believed it didn't belong. But she loved her brother, and she had been determined to get to the real reason for his death. In the end, it had cost two witches on the council their lives and the death of one founding vampire—Nicodemus. A justified vendetta, at least in her eyes.

Apparently though, demons and vampires don't believe in "An Eye for an Eye."

She paused in her cleaning actions and glanced toward Andreas' partially levitating corpse. Her heart jumped. The dried dark blood around his throat had made them overlook something else she had not noticed before. She walked slowly toward the body, her eyes transfixed on the area beneath Brady's slashed marks, and noticed for the first time, two sets of bite marks, almost invisible beneath the darkening blood.

"Brady," she said without realizing she had spoken.

"Yes?" he asked, turning.

Kailey glanced over her shoulder. "We have a problem."

"Currently we have a *lot* of problems. You care to narrow that down?"

"Come here," she said.

Brady set down his rag and hurried across the room. "What's wrong?"

Kailey pointed at the bite marks. "Did you bring a stake?"

He reached to his back pocket and then shook his head. "No, why?"

"It's too early to tell, but I think they might have prepared Andreas so he'd turn into a vampire."

"What?" He glanced down at her for a moment. "Prepared him?"

She nodded. "He was their servant. Did he ever mention that they were going to turn him?"

"He said that their original plan had been to do so, but—"

"They set you up. They set *all* of us up."

"What are you talking about?"

"There," she pointed to the bite marks again. "He was bitten *twice*. My guess is that Raven and Flora fed off of him *after* you killed him."

"That would mean when the demon arrived, the vampires came here, too?" Jacob asked.

"I don't know if all of the founding vampires showed up," Kailey said. "Flora and Raven have been the ones who have caused us the most problems. I believe, though, it was them and not Flora's other siblings, simply because they would have fed, too. If this were a part of a group ritual, there would be more than two bites. There aren't."

Brady scratched the back of his head. "I still don't see why they'd need to go to this much trouble."

"Since Andreas was their servant, they probably ordered him to partake of their blood, so that after you killed him, he'd turn into a vampire. They intended for him to anger you enough to kill him, which was why he didn't have *silver* bullets. It's all making more sense now."

"In what way? Because you now have me confused," Jacob said.

Kailey sighed. "Basically, it was blackmail. If he wanted to receive eternal life as an undead, he needed to do one last task. The Circle of Unity had marked him, but they needed a sacrifice to summon the other demons from their lair, so they sent Andreas. He served the purpose of being the blood sacrifice, and afterwards, since he had already ingested their blood, probably right before he got out of the limo, he was destined to become one of them. So, he served his greatest purpose to the Circle of Unity, but he was never going to die. He was going to become one of the undead."

"A sacrifice without actually losing him."

Father Charles walked to them, examined the bite marks, and a grim expression crossed his face. "She's right, but even if he's been prepared, he won't turn for a few more hours. I'm certain we can find something to use to stake him."

Kailey looked at Brady. "While we can safely assume that a demon was the one that entered the apartment on Raven's behalf, the more frightening part, at least to me, is that a blood pact has been made between the demons and vampires. They are enhancing one another's strengths, which makes them more dangerous than ever before. I'm fairly certain they had never wanted Nicodemus' death, but I'd almost wager they weren't too disappointed by the death of the two witches."

"You believe they wanted to be the only two factions in Nocturnal Trinity?" Brady asked.

She shrugged. "It is quite evident that they hold the most power. The witches weren't necessarily essential to their foundation. Even if they needed the use of magic later, the vampires could compel a witch to do their biddings. They didn't need witches as a part of their Circle."

"So they had planned to downsize the Order?" Brady said, thinking aloud.

"Exactly, but then we attacked the nightclub, and Micah did something even they had not expected. Rather than disband the Circle altogether, he added another faction to the foundation, further pissing them off, which is why neither the vampires nor the demons have returned to Nocturnal Trinity."

Brady's jaw tightened. His eyes widened with a moment of uneasiness. "So they're going to kill Micah and Ashley."

"Then we need to get to the nightclub immediately," Jacob said.

Brady shook his head. "No, we need to scrub down this room as quickly as possible first."

"Look," Jacob said, his eyes darkening. "I'm not fond of Micah at all. That's no secret, but I'll be damned if I let him die at the hands of these demons and vampires. If anyone gets a shot at him, it's me. *Not* them." He offered a slight smile with the last statement.

Kailey shook her head and groaned. *Don't start the comedy circuit if that's the best you have.*

"One obstacle at a time," Brady said. "If Father Charles is correct, we can slow the summoning of these other demons by scrubbing away the marks. Let's double our efforts and focus on doing that. We should be finished within a half hour. Then we turn our attention toward getting Micah out of Nocturnal Trinity."

Jacob snarled, released a partial growl, but gave a slight nod of agreement. "Fine, but no one better be slacking."

"Before you return to scrubbing, Jacob. Give a call to one of the pack members and tell them what's going on. Have that person call everyone else. With what's about to occur, it's going to take all of us together to succeed."

Jacob nodded and smiled, pulling his cellphone from his back pocket.

"Wait," Father Charles said with sudden realization. "What exactly do you mean by *pack*? Werewolves?"

Brady shot Kailey a nervous glance before he smiled at the priest. "Let's scrub the bloodstains, and I'll explain."

CHAPTER 48

After Eva had left through the hidden door and entered the alley, she walked toward the docks since the alley was a dead end. She needed to go down one block and then head north for two more blocks to get to Micah's shop.

Lightning flickered over the bay occasionally. Although no rain was falling from the deceptively dark overcast sky, something more sinister than an impending storm awaited her. She sensed the darkness of its spirit the moment she had left her apartment. For a few moments, she had considered going back inside where she could be better protected by the werewolves and the priest. But necessity had ushered her to leave her haven. She couldn't prolong the inevitable.

Two shadows slinked into a narrow alleyway at the side of the street. Immediately, she flung a protective spell over her that she had hung and prepared the day before. She had cast a similar one when the werewolves had invaded Nocturnal Trinity, which was probably what had spared her life. Unfortunately, it had not been strong enough to protect Rose and Debra. She was being watched and once she passed the alley, she was certain to be followed.

Veiled by the gray skies and her want to become invisible, Eva could use her magic to lessen and partially mask her visage to passersby. Such was something she had often sought any time she was out in public. She'd rather take in the sights unnoticed and unbothered by others. Whether this spell worked against whatever was farther down the street, she didn't know, but she anticipated that, within a few minutes, she'd discover the power of her spell or their ability to discern her presence. The strength of her concealment spells had been invested in keeping herself undetected by her daughter, Jaclyn, and somehow her daughter had still managed to find her. But Jaclyn might have only located her because of the number of people in her apartment, which greatly weakened the veil since the spell had only been for Eva.

Although the messenger Jaclyn had sent to present her missive had been vague, the only reason Eva was willing to meet with her daughter was due to the promise that she'd retrieve her Grimoire. The Grimoire was more than a book that detailed the history of her spells. It was a deeper part of her mind and soul. While Jaclyn might have believed attaining the book granted her more power, she had been wrong. The Grimoire wasn't simple scrolled out spells, concoctions, and memories. No other witch could see what else was on those pages.

Eva chuckled.

Each spell on each page had been cleverly crafted with codes that enfolded like the chambers inside a person's mind. She had blessed the book to become a hidden file cabinet, a vault known and fully accessible only to her, and while great components of key spells were written out, a lot of the necessary knowledge needed to carry out the spells was hidden. Only Eva could see them unfold inside her mind. To anyone else, even to her own daughter, the essential words were concealed.

Even with all the written words and fragments of spells in the book, the pages were useless to Jaclyn. Eva could imagine the levels of frustration welling inside her daughter. The aggravation was another reason Eva knew to be wary. This meeting might be nothing more than a sinister trap to coerce Eva into revealing everything veiled inside the tome, but even torture couldn't make Eva divulge the intricate elements of the hidden spells. Eva understood that she didn't have long to live since she had been removed from the Circle of Unity. So any threats from Jaclyn were empty. Torture or even death held no leverage to a person that knew Death was knocking at the door.

Noise clattered along the side alley. She was less than half a block from where she could take a causal glance down the alley to see what had crept into it.

As a witch, Eva had learned never to be engulfed by fear; also she had never been fully exempt from moments of terror like these she currently found herself. She understood Jaclyn's distrust, but Eva now realized more than ever before how little she should have placed her trust in the vampires and demons. She had experienced several deep, long and agonizing nightmares about what had happened beneath Nocturnal Trinity on the day Nicodemus had died. These dreams tapped at her again, now. How she had failed to see the dangers of remaining in the Circle of Unity was alarming. Could Flora have somehow compelled her into not seeing the truth?

Yes, possibly. She and Flora had been at one another's throats for several months when Kailey had arrived in Seattle. There had seemed no remedy to soothe the building tension between them, so Flora attempted to do what naturally came best to the vampire—kill her opponents. She had partially succeeded when Debra and Rose had died, but Eva had somehow survived. Then Jaclyn had intervened and sent Eva packing.

A half smile curled on Eva's lips. Thinking about how those events had unfolded, she realized her daughter had actually done her a great favor in making her leave Nocturnal Trinity. Since Jaclyn practiced much darker magic, Flora had also fled the nightclub, as had her siblings. A part of Eva's bitterness faded toward her daughter, and she felt a sense of pride at what her daughter had accomplished, even though it might not have been intentional.

The most recent dreams had revealed to her the real truth, but only because she was no longer a part of the Circle of Unity. She was supposed to have died on the night when Rose and Debra had. It was all part of the plan contrived by the demons and vampires. They had wanted to totally eliminate the witches, and had nearly succeeded.

Eva edged her way slowly along the sidewalk as she neared the alleyway entrance. She turned her head slightly to glance down the alley but didn't pause in her slow footsteps. A glance was more than enough. Her heart thudded harder. Standing near the dumpster were two shadowed figures. At first she thought they were demons, but then she realized they were enchanted living souls, somehow bound to roam the Earth between the living and dead. Not ghosts, but trapped souls forced to linger.

She had only encountered one of these souls once before, which she had originally taken as a premonition, but later she discovered they appeared whenever a portal between the realms of the living and dead opened or whenever a demon portal became fractured. They came with the hope of leaving the in-between. The souls weren't necessarily evil, but from what she recalled and from her research and conversations with other witches that had seen them, these wandering souls' desperation to pass from this realm into another caused them to become aggressive. They sought diviners of magic, and true witches were the only ones who could actually see their physical appearance.

Those naïve individuals who foolishly used Ouija boards at parties for fun could unintentionally lure these sorrowful souls or demons into performing mischief because the boards allowed them to communicate with humans. One was perhaps safer if a lingering soul used the planchette than when a demon grasped it and spelled out its threat. The boards acted like portals, too, but not to seek another dimension. This access allowed them to *haunt* the people who had interacted with them.

Often the souls reacted out of frustration and anger, lashing out at the ones trying to communicate with the departed spirits. A lingering soul whose thoughts were weaved into the board found partial relief in *finally* reaching a human that had picked up their thoughts. But when the souls realized they didn't have any chance of getting help to pass through to the other side, they had lost the last thing they valued the most: hope. Without hope, they resorted to punishing the Ouija board users for what the souls believed to be the ultimate deceit. Even though the souls weren't able to pass through into a different afterlife, they had been given the ability to perform physical acts to torment others into believing a place was haunted.

These two hovering souls at the edge of the alley weren't here for her; they had come for when the demon portal opened, which meant Father Charles was right. Something horrible was coming. Eva hated abandoning the cleaning of the bloodstained symbols, but she couldn't risk the possibility that she might get back her Grimoire. With the turmoil brewing, she needed to mend whatever differences she and her daughter had not resolved.

She picked up her pace, and causally glanced back over her shoulder. The two hapless souls lingered, apparently uninterested in following her, which was perfectly fine by her. But then, she noticed something else. Behind those two drifted several more. Near the hidden doorway of her apartment a half dozen more searched along the wall. They couldn't find the door, but they seemed to know it was close.

In spite of her aching knees, Eva found herself nearing a jog. She wasn't certain what exactly was happening, but she wanted to get away from the half-opened portal. While these souls might not physically cause harm to Brady and Kailey and the rest working inside her apartment, she feared something worse might happen along.

Sharp pains that pricked like needles jabbed the front and sides of her knees. She wasn't moving that fast, but her breathing became labored. As much as her body protested her sudden zeal to move faster than she normally walked, she refused to slow down.

"It's only two blocks," Eva told herself, but never had two blocks seemed so long.

Ahead of her came more of these souls. Her approach didn't deter them, and a couple of them bumped into her before spinning slightly to get around her. Unlike spirits, they were unable to pass through her. If she were unable to see them, she'd have never noticed their feathery touch. They were being drawn toward her apartment, seemingly uninterested in her, despite her being a witch. Their desperation was getting to the apartment. But why?

Eva thought about the symbol on Andreas' shoulder. The mark that had tied him to the demons and the vampires suddenly made more sense. Why hadn't she noticed it before? Magic enhanced his mark.

The demons and vampires might have been in cahoots to take over Nocturnal Trinity, but they weren't able to fully perform their tasks without the aid of witches. That was the reason for the Circle of Unity in the first place, and why Micah was a fool to think he could change it by intrusively including werewolves into the circle. Werewolves held no importance by the other three factions, and even though Jaclyn had vowed the witches to be his ally, the vampires and demons never would be.

And if Andreas' mark was touched by magic, it only meant one thing: A witch had placed it there.

Would Jaclyn have done such a thing? No. Eva highly doubted Jaclyn would side with the vampires or the demons. But what about either of the other two witches Jaclyn had chosen to replace Debra and Rose? That was something she needed to talk to her daughter about.

Eva took a brief moment to look down the street once more before heading down the narrow alleyway that led to Micah's shop. A mob of gray souls formed a shallow moving wall as they drifted and hovered searching along the walls on both sides of the alley. A part of her wanted to turn back to help Father Charles, but from the looks of things, she needed to join forces with her daughter and the other two witches, which might be like shaking hands with the devil, placing her own life into jeopardy or selling her soul for a modest price for a request in return. It all depended upon the stakes Jaclyn initiated.

CHAPTER 49

Kailey grabbed an unused rag, soaked it in holy water, and scrubbed at the symbol on the wall. Everyone was focused upon the task of removing the blood, even Luna. She had gotten past her reluctance and managed a stronger resolve to help clean. Kailey didn't like the idea of what they were doing, but it needed to be done.

"Werewolves, eh?" Father Charles asked Brady without looking away from his scrubbing. A note of partial surprise and humor rang within his verbal observation.

"Yes. Me, Brady, Micah, and Jacob."

"I see."

"I suppose you view what we are as much a curse as the vampires?" Brady asked.

"That has been the church's view for many centuries, but no, I'm not narrow-minded in that sense at all."

"So the fact that werewolves exists doesn't surprise you then?"

"Not at all."

Brady half-grinned. "That's good to know."

"Here's the thing. A good person can have something horrendous happen to him, but inside, if he's truly a kind, compassionate individual, he maintains that and finds a way to cope with what has been dealt to him. I believe a good person who happened to get bitten or scratched and became a monster like a werewolf can somehow rein some control over the beast inside him. On the other hand, if the person was already vile inside, he can use his inner beast to unleash his wrath and destruction to kill or maim as many people as possible. What do you think?"

Brady paused scrubbing for a moment and sighed. "I wish I could accept your logic."

"But you can't?"

Brady shook his head.

"Why not?"

"There is a point where my mind ends and the wolf inside me takes full control, blocking from my memory of what it does. I've done some bad things. Well, my wolf has. There's a brief but fleeting moment, like right before dawn breaks the night, where I am both a wolf and a man. During those few seconds, we are fully aware of one another but never really have time to communicate."

"These bad things you've done," Father Charles asked. "How bad are they?"

"Andreas is dead because of me."

"I know. But weren't you forced to kill him?"

"To protect Kailey, yes."

"Do you ever fear your wolf will harm her?" Father Charles asked.

"Actually, no."

"And why is that?"

"The wolf is loyal to those I love. For whatever reason, he's capable of recognizing them. He's also capable of knowing who my enemies are. He doesn't hesitate to kill them when I'm under attack."

"In a sense, you're backing what I had said earlier."

"Murder is still murder," Brady said.

"True, but I believe your wolf sensed something sinister about Andreas, probably not concerning the fact Andreas was set to be turned into a vampire once he died, but it might have detected the vampires' scent of blood on him."

"I suppose that's possible."

Father Charles shrugged. "And Andreas had shot you, had he not?"

"Yes."

"So, the wolf part of you would have held some resentment for you having been shot. It would have sought revenge. You cannot fault yourself because of what an animal's instinct knows and how it reacts."

Brady chuckled and shook his head. "I'm an animal?"

"I'm beginning to think most humans are," the priest replied. "Though they don't have an *inner* beast. They're just mentally depraved or warped."

Kailey continued listening to them and glanced toward Andreas' body while she fought to remove the blood from the deep grooves carved into the sheetrock. His complexion held an eerie glow. His skin had an odd paleness on the first night she had seen him in the vampire VIP lounge. He had looked like a walking corpse then. She kept a wary eye in his direction because she was certain he'd awaken as a vampire at any moment.

Father Charles assured them that Andreas' transformation was still hours away, but she wondered if there was actually a time period before someone became undead. She understood it couldn't happen instantly, but Andreas had been a human servant of the founding vampires for most of his life. She held no doubt at how much they must have treasured his assistance and devotion throughout the years. It only stood to reason that they would have taken some insurance to make certain no one killed him. She wouldn't have put it past Flora to make him drink her blood on a weekly basis. She imagined Flora had probably been insistent that Andreas do so any time that he left Nocturnal Trinity unattended by her or one of her siblings.

"Father," Blaze said, from inside the adjoining room.

Father Charles turned and looked toward the door. "Yes?"

Blaze stepped into the smaller room with a wooden stake in his hand. "I found this, if you'd like to use it on Andreas."

The priest's brow creased. "Where did you find that?"

"On Eva's altar," he replied.

Brady and Jacob came closer, exchanging glances.

Luna pointed to rune symbols carved on the stake. "She's blessed this stake."

Brady took the stake from Blaze and walked toward Andreas' hanging corpse.

"What are you doing?" Father Charles asked.

"Sending a message," he replied, pressing the tip of the stake against Andreas' chest."

"To whom, exactly?"

"Flora and Raven." Brady placed both hands around the stake and shoved his bodyweight against it, driving it through the man's chest and into his heart. Andreas' eyes opened for a brief second before his body incinerated into a pile of ash on the floor.

"Do you think they will really know that you staked him?" Father Charles asked.

Brady nodded. "Since he bore their mark, the vampires and the demons will sense his loss and know that he's no longer theirs."

Father Charles returned to scrubbing the symbol. "Then I suggest everyone double their efforts to erase the blood symbols as best we can. You've just set things into motion quicker."

"Is that necessarily a bad thing?" Jacob asked.

"Maybe not for us, but for Micah or anyone else you care about at Nocturnal Trinity, it might get nasty for them." The priest glanced from symbol to symbol. "If we work hard, it shouldn't take us another ten to fifteen minutes. Then we load up in my car and head to the place Eva has gone."

"Why?" Kailey asked.

"It's best if we all stick together. To defeat what is coming, we must rely upon one another's strengths."

CHAPTER 50

Forrest turned when Eva opened the side door of the magic shop and walked inside. She looked haggard and somewhat shaken.

Cassie smiled at her for a moment. "Jaclyn? Your mother is here."

With her long robe touching the floor and hiding her feet, Jaclyn appeared to glide from the adjoining room and across the floor in her swift approach toward Eva. Eva took a step back and cringed. Her nervous eyes revealed she wasn't certain what she should expect from her daughter.

"Is that any way to greet your own daughter?" Jaclyn asked, opening her arms wide and embracing Eva.

Eva reluctantly patted Jaclyn's back with little enthusiasm, offering no hug in return. "Based upon how we last parted? I'd say I'm justified in my skepticism at what might transpire here."

Jaclyn leaned back, looked into her mother's eyes, and smiled. "Fair enough. Things have changed and I realize I was a bit too impulsive in making my abrupt decision to banish you from Nocturnal Trinity and Seattle. I'm seeking a truce between us, if you're willing."

"Cut the bullshit, Jackie," Eva said with an angered scowl, brushing the front of her robe with her hands in disgust as though she could cleanse herself of Jaclyn's touch. "You need my assistance or else I'd have never received this invitation to meet with you."

Jaclyn attempted a feigned hurt expression but realized her mother saw through the feeble attempt and wasn't buying it.

"Your spoiled childlike tactics don't work on me," Eva said. "So cut to the quick or I'm leaving."

"If I may," Forrest said.

Eva eyed him sternly. "Forrest, this is between she and I and doesn't concern you. Either she gets to the point or I leave."

Forrest took a deep agitated breath and crossed his huge arms. Cassie looked like she wanted to add to the conversation, but Eva shook her head in warning.

"Oh, very well." Jaclyn turned to the bookshelf and grabbed an old worn leather-covered book. She handed it to Eva and dramatically waved one hand in her frustration. "Here, Mother. *Your* Grimoire. It's yours and should be with you. I had no right taking it from you in the first place."

Eva laughed, taking the book and hugging it against her chest.

"You have it back, no strings attached, so what's so funny?"

"It was useless to you anyway, wasn't it? I imagine it didn't take you too long to realize that."

Jaclyn pursed her lips, planted her hands on her hips, and then forced a condescending smile. "Clever how you masked the pages, Mother, keeping the pertinent information from being read by me or anyone else."

"In time you'll learn to do the same. Trust is something earned, not freely given, even to family."

Jaclyn sighed. Her shoulders drooped. The coldness that once dominated her gaze faded. She spoke softly. "Once again, you're right. You've proven—"

"Jackie, it's not about being right. Wisdom comes with age. So what is it that you need from me you presumptuous ungrateful child?"

In an instant, Jaclyn shot her mother a fiery glare. Her face hardened and her delicate fingers slowly curled into tight fists. Her inner rage unleashed.

Eva laughed softly with a slight side grin. "Ah, now *there's* the daughter I remember. She's never buried deeply beneath the surface. You shift back and forth so quickly. It shows a lack of restraint on your part. It's why you wanted to rein control over me because you have no control for your own inner turmoil."

"Not entirely true, mother," Jaclyn hissed through gritted teeth. "If you'll recall, you banished me long ago."

"Because you had no self-control and brought too much attention to yourself by flaunting your power."

"Still it wasn't a reason to cast me out of the Circle."

"So this was all about revenge. Now, we are getting to the depth of the truth."

"The truth isn't something you'd—" Frustrated, Jaclyn took a deep breath and slowly released it through her mouth. "Why is it that you can easily bring out the worst in me?"

Eva studied her daughter for a moment. Her anger receded and her frown eased. She shook her head. "Some mother/daughter relationships are always contentious. Ours, I suppose, is just one of those. Blame it on our astrological signs, if need be, but I doubt we'd be any closer a hundred years from now, if we lived that long, regardless of how hard we tried."

Jaclyn's eyes moistened with tears. She nodded. "You're probably right, although I hope that isn't the case. I have been presumptuous though, and for that I apologize. My behavior and my banishing you from Seattle was uncalled for. Revenge was a great part of my motive, but I really am offering a chance for us to bear no malice."

Forrest cleared his throat. "Ladies, look, I hate to break up this warm family reunion, but the reason for asking you here, Eva, is because of the urgency of the situation."

"Sarcasm noted," Eva said. "What is this urgency?"

After Forrest explained the tunnel and what he hoped to find, Eva glanced toward Jaclyn. "You want me to remove the concealment spell?"

Jaclyn nodded. "We cannot remove it without you."

Eva shook her head. "It's been ages since I was there, and to be honest, my memory of the tunnel had escaped me until now. Yes, we hid something there, but I cannot be certain whether it was something good or evil. But, nonetheless, now that you have nudged my curiosity, we should go right away."

"The time isn't right yet," Jaclyn replied.

Eva frowned. "And when exactly will the right time be?"

"We perceive that many people have been buried there. I plan to use a reanimation spell to awaken any old bodies to glean information—"

"Forgive me if I'm wrong," Eva said, "but don't you have to have a body to resurrect? These would have died over a hundred years ago."

"Normally, I'd say that's true, but in this case, since you concealed what lies in the tunnel, I'm hoping their corpses have been frozen in time. Even if they are, it must be the dead of night before I can cast it."

"Nonsense," Eva said with a grin.

"Mother, you indeed have great magical abilities, but you're *not* a necromancer."

"No, I'm not. But, you have three witches who can accompany you. With our powers combined, the time of the day for you to perform your spell isn't a necessity."

"I've never done it any other way," Jaclyn said.

"Now is the time for you to experiment then."

"No, I cannot risk the consequences."

"I'm afraid a delay in performing the ritual will usher greater consequences. We cannot afford to wait."

Cassie and Forrest frowned.

"What do you mean?" Cassie asked.

"A portal is opening soon." She explained the number of wandering souls and Andreas' sacrifice. "What's coming won't be waiting for the dead of night. They will, however, take the opportunity to issue destruction the moment they surface."

Cassie nodded. "Eva's right. Just like the phone message we received from Nocturnal Trinity."

"Yes," Forrest said, "Micah and Ashley's lives are in grave danger."

Eva looked at them with confusion. "What's happened there?"

"Micah and Ashley are being held by at least one of the behemoths. They will possibly be killed," Cassie replied.

"I see." Eva flicked her gaze back to Jaclyn. "Where are the other two witches?"

"I've sent them out for supplies that are necessary for the ritual," she replied.

"Do you fully trust them?" Eva asked.

"Of course. That's why I chose them to join the Circle of Unity. Why do you ask?"

"How well do you know them?"

"Raine I've known for over ten years. Gillian, only three. Why?"

"Andreas' mark was enchanted by a witch," Eva replied.

"And you think one of them did that?"

Eva offered a slight shrug. "It would have to be done by someone both the vampires and demons know. That's why I was asking you how well do you know and trust Raine and Gillian?"

"Until a few moments ago, I trusted them far more than I did you," Jaclyn said with a wry smile. "But, honestly, I don't think either of them even want to be unified with the vampires or demons. They wouldn't aid them at all."

"Okay," Eva said softly. "As long as you can place your total confidence in them, I'll say no more about the subject."

Jaclyn sighed. "Now you have me wondering."

Eva glanced around the magic shop shelves. "With all the supplies you have here, what more could you possibly need for the ritual that would have you send them elsewhere?"

"To raise the dead requires fresh blood sacrifices. They've gone to buy a few chickens and two goats."

Eva looked surprised. "That's a lot of blood."

Jaclyn nodded. "It's a complicated ritual, but it doesn't require that much blood. In this case, however, I want extra animals should something unexpected occur."

Eva smiled. "At least you're planning ahead. That's a good thing."

"Thanks. More than dead bodies might be there."

"Like what?" Cassie asked.

"Demons," Jaclyn replied. "After all, Forrest hopes to find his Demonhunter friend. If she's somehow locked away in there, she might not be alone. She might have demons guarding her."

Cassie looked at Eva. "You really don't remember what you concealed in the tunnel?"

"I don't, but maybe going there will jar my memory."

The bell attached near the top of the door rattled. Everyone glanced as the door opened wider. Forrest looked confused seeing the priest walk inside, but was a bit more at ease when Brady, Kailey, and the others walked in behind him.

Father Charles grinned at Eva and set two gallons of water on the floor. "I guess we're in the right place."

CHAPTER 51

$\mathcal{K}$ailey stood inside Micah's shop. A part of her was in total awe. Once this was all over, provided she survived, she planned to return to writing her preternatural blog. What she was witnessing was surreal and far beyond what her imagination could have ever thought possible.

The last thing she had ever expected to see was a priest working with werewolves and witches in order to destroy demons. And Father Charles did so without prejudice or any hint of judgmentalism, which was refreshing considering how many religious people she had met in college that had spent more time pointing their fingers of condemnation than they did expressing the love their God supposedly held and exhibited for the world's population. This priest was far different in his approach to the abnormal misfits the rest of the religious world would have carted off to Hell or into the abyss or whatever else form of eternal torment they chose to justify.

The humorous thing about writing this out for her subscribers was that most of her devoted readers probably couldn't fathom the reported events to be true. Kailey kept her sources totally confidential, as she did her true identity, and many might construe that these accounts were farfetched because she didn't reveal pertinent facts and details where others could investigate for themselves. She understood the possible scrutiny and skepticism her blog might encounter from the droves of Internet trolls who would attempt to bash her report or verbally assault her. Others would probably express their utter disbelief, which, all things considered, would be her first response, too, if she happened upon any article that lacked properly detailed credentials. But revealing her sources, the exact locations, and the spells used could place all their lives in danger once more. She refused to risk that, even if it meant a lack of credibility. Half the time, people believed what they wanted to believe regardless of obvious facts. They clung more to legends than vivid truth.

Raine and Gillian entered the shop from the rear side door. There was no hiding their surprise when they noticed Father Charles. Although he was wearing regular work clothes, he had placed his collar around the neck of his flannel shirt during the drive from the bay to the magic shop. After giving him a quick once-over glance, they noticed Eva and then they gave uncomfortable, curious stares at Jaclyn.

Jaclyn smiled reassuringly, offering quick introductions, but Raine and Gillian didn't appear any more at ease. They were well aware of the contention between the mother and daughter.

"Any luck?" Jaclyn asked.

Raine nodded and cleared her throat. She bit her lower lip and seemed reluctant to speak, glancing toward the priest. Finally, she said, "The animals are in the back of the pickup."

"Good."

Father Charles suddenly looked uncomfortable. "Animals?"

Jaclyn gave a slight nod. "Yes, for what is necessary, I will do what I must."

"To use for a sacrifice?" the priest asked.

"To expose the truth, sometimes one must go to unthinkable lengths."

Father Charles was frighteningly silent for several long seconds. "You must also beware of what else you might summon."

"We are careful and exact with our spells," Jaclyn said evenly.

"Perhaps," he replied. "But to whom do your incantations go?"

"Certainly not to a god whose followers treat him like Santa Claus with their inane lists of requests. We draw our power from the Earth and our Goddess and return our tribute to her in kind, taking nothing for granted and bestowing everything to Her."

"The Goddess?" he asked.

Jaclyn offered a smile that held no kindness at all. "I sense a rebuke by you is soon to follow."

Father Charles shook his head. "Not at all."

She cocked one brow. Her skepticism was near scorn. "No? Most any male-chauvinistic religion frowns on the idea of a Goddess and suppresses the role of its women. Yet, I hear a lot of church people talk about Mother Earth. Isn't that hypocrisy in itself? We worship the Goddess and offer adoration because She is the mother to all of us. She was our womb and births all that is to come. We seek no malice or ill content towards others, in spite of how we've been treated throughout the centuries. Ours has been a way of peace unless we were provoked and had no other choice but to react in self-defense."

Father Charles sighed. "I'm not here to chastise or offer any judgment. The whole reason I offer my aid is that our enemy needs to be defeated and doing so requires all of us working together, regardless of our beliefs or differences. Each of us has access to different powers. If we can unite as one force, we can succeed. But, I am not here to judge or condemn. Ask Eva."

Jaclyn glanced toward her mother.

Eva nodded.

"Very well," Jaclyn said. "It's just that I have dealt with enough hostility over the years—"

"I am aware," Father Charles said softly. "So I do understand your defensiveness. But, trust me, I am not like those who wish to oppress and condemn others who don't worship as I do."

"Then you are a rare priest," she replied.

He shrugged. "With that aside, how can I assist you?"

Jaclyn took a deep breath, held it, and then slowly sighed. "We have need of my mother to remove a concealment spell in an old abandoned rail tunnel."

"What are you looking for?" Father Charles asked.

"We don't exactly know, and my mother doesn't remember."

"Splendid. I suppose we're in for a surprise then?"

Jaclyn grinned slightly. "The surprise might be nothing at all."

Forrest shook his head. "No. Something's there. It might not be what I'm hoping to find, but something is hidden there."

"Why are you so certain?" Father Charles asked.

Jaclyn offered a wry grin. "Because his gut *tells* him so. One should be so lucky. Half the time my gut fails to remind me when I need to eat."

Forrest frowned. "I won't criticize you for what you deem yourself connected to, or how you raise the dead, but being as to what I've been chosen to do, I will always trust my instinct as a Hunter. The only times it has ever failed me was when I chose to ignore it."

"Point taken, Forrest," Jaclyn said. She glanced around at everyone. "Since we have everything we need, it's time that we get to the tunnel and find out what's there."

Brady nodded. "We're racing the clock as it is."

"We're all aware," Jaclyn said.

Forrest's eyes narrowed. "Maybe, but you're not sensing the true urgency of the situation."

"Oh, I do," she replied. "But one thing I've learned over the years is that haste leads to mistakes. Yielding to pressure conflicts the mind and prevents one from having clarity. The last thing any of us needs to suffer is the inability to think clearly and rationally. Remain calm. Panicking aids no one except our enemies."

"Well spoken," Father Charles said. "Spot on truth."

"Agreed," Brady said.

"Let's brag on one another as we make our way there, if you don't mind," Forrest said, walking past them and toward the side door. "My cousin's life is at risk."

Brady and Jacob nodded, their faces grimmer.

Father Charles picked up the two gallons of water. Eva and Jaclyn and the other witches took leather packs filled with unknown items, perhaps for whatever spells they needed to use. Brady grabbed a small cardboard box of sharpened stakes from behind the counter and followed.

Nervousness crept up inside Kailey as she watched the others head outside. She wondered how many of them would still be alive twenty-four hours from now.

CHAPTER 52

The underground tunnel was dark and musty, so Forrest pulled the night vision goggles over his eyes, partly to enhance his vision and partly to hide the heated tears brimming at the corner of his eyes. He couldn't fight the tears of his building emotions. This was the first time in over a century that he might actually discover the truth of what had actually happened to Penelope.

He looked around the tunnel. To his surprise Ian and Gunner were both seated on the bench near the rusted rails. The brothers smiled when they noticed him. Gunner waved eagerly. A sense of relief reflected in Gunner's eyes.

Forrest was relieved to see them and understood the importance they had added to his otherwise dismal life. He lived for one thing: to kill the undead. The task was the sole purpose of his life. He knew no other skill or trade. His lifelong career had also almost killed everything else important to him, including his remaining sliver of hope. He was weighted beneath the agony of ridding the world of vampires, and he feared that what Eva uncovered in the tunnel might destroy the last fragments of his sanity, making his mind plummet and abandon his compassion toward humanity. Once he lost the last tiny splinter of hope he possessed, Forrest's rage loomed inside, waiting to consume him with an undying fury.

The whole reason Forrest had avoided Seattle for so long was because he didn't want to uncover the truth. As long as Forrest didn't know what her fate had actually been, she remained alive in his memory. No finality existed. Even though the greater part of his mind likened to Ian's pessimistic attitude that she was no longer alive, he fought to hope and believe she might have somehow survived. But he knew better. She couldn't possibly be alive. Otherwise, she'd have searched for him. In a century's worth of time, their paths should have crossed.

With the information Jinn had given him about the behemoths and how Penelope had killed one of them, Forrest didn't believe the last moments of her life had been pleasant. The time had arrived for him to face the truth. He couldn't turn back now. He had to know. He *needed* to know.

For the first time in his life, Forrest wanted to pray. At this point, though, it no longer mattered. Even having a priest in their midst didn't ease his apprehension. The inside rims of his goggles captured his leaking tears and caused the lenses to fog, making it impossible to see through them. He wondered if having the priest with them would help them or not.

Brady turned on his police-issued flashlight, which forced Forrest to look away and remove the goggles due to its blinding brightness. He wiped away the tears. Then Jacob turned on another flashlight, which brightened the tunnel enough to see the tracks and both curved walls of the carved out tunnel.

Forrest wrapped his hand around the goggles, remembering when Penelope had given them to him right before she boarded the ship to sail around the world to reach Seattle. For a moment, he closed his eyes and pictured her cute dimpled smile while pressing the goggles over his heart. A few seconds later, he slipped them into his right jacket pocket.

Jaclyn and Raine tethered two goats to the bench where Ian and Gunner sat. Gillian placed a crate with several hens beside the bench.

Eva followed Jaclyn and the other two witches a few yards down the tracks to where they had sensed the wall of the concealment spell.

"Mother?" Jaclyn said. "Any recollection of what happened here?"

Eva was quiet. She stepped to the edge of the magical barrier and visibly shivered. A bright sparking blue light flickered like miniature lightning. Her mouth dropped open and trembled.

"Mother?"

Eva raised both hands, palms upward toward the flickering light. A strong breeze whistled through the tunnel, which shouldn't have been possible, as it had been sealed off, but the wind stirred up dirt and dusty old spider webs.

Jaclyn looked at Raine and Gillian with great uneasiness. Their uncertain glances revealed their sudden anxiety.

"Stand closer, sisters," Eva said. "Set your focus to aid me with your strength to reinforce my magic."

The wind sweeping through the tunnel rose to a roar.

"So do you remember what happened?" Jaclyn said, raising her voice.

"I do, dear, and trust me, it wasn't good then." Her jaw trembled. "And it's about to get a lot worse."

Father Charles glanced toward Forrest. "Are you sure she needs to do this?"

Eva didn't give Forrest a chance to reply. "It's too late to stop what's coming. The veil is splitting. There was a reason I didn't remember. It had been blocked from my mind."

"Why?" Jaclyn asked.

"Because if ever I returned here, the invisible gate would crumble. It was in the original incantation to do so. Nothing I do now can prevent it from collapsing. But I have no idea what was sealed inside. So, everyone stay behind us so we can attempt to form a magical barrier of protection. But prepare yourselves! Once our protective shield drops, you must defend yourselves."

Father Charles slid silver crosses from his back pocket and handed them to Kailey, Blaze, and Luna. With a moment of uncertainty in her gaze, Kailey took one. Blaze and Luna each grabbed one. Father Charles took another cross and held it between himself and the opening vortex.

Jacob and Brady stood slightly hunched forward. Neither seemed to be transforming, but they were defensively preparing themselves to fight whatever might rush forward.

Cassie cast-off her human appearance and became full succubus. Her fiery gaze focused on the shifting shadows on the other side of Eva.

The wind intensified, knocking Eva back. Jaclyn and the other two witches pressed their palms against Eva to hold her upright and steady. The fierce blowing breeze roared unbearably louder, but everyone stepped closer.

Ian and Gunner stood on each side of Forrest. Forrest held a sharpened stake in one hand and a bottle of holy water in the other. The brothers were halfway transformed into their Were forms.

Forrest glanced toward Kailey. The areas around her bruises were bright red. She was worried and shouting at Brady. Even though they stood side by side, Brady shook his head and pointed toward his ear, indicating that he couldn't hear her. The howling wind was loud, but she kept shouting.

He glanced around, wondering what had disturbed her. He saw nothing but took a step toward them. Kailey placed the cross in her left hand and took a stake from the box on the ground. A second later the flashlights went dark. When Brady and Jacob turned the lights back on, Kailey was gone. Her cross and stake lay on the ground where she had been standing.

~

The roaring wind overcame any other sounds. Kailey held the cross firmly inside her fist, wondering why the priest had given her one. She didn't know what might emerge from the opening vortex, but a vampire wasn't one of the first things she expected to encounter. Most likely, she figured, demons might emerge.

In spite of the boisterous wind, she was startled to hear whispering near her ear. Since she stood between Brady and Jacob, she half expected the words to have come from one of them but their focus was on the opening barrier that slowly began to materialize. Whoever had spoken, it wasn't one of them. Somehow the projected whisper magnified. Instantly, she recognized the speaker.

Flora?

'Why yes, my dear!' Flora replied.

Kailey looked around and then quickly behind her, but she didn't see anyone other than the group she had entered with.

'We're not finished with you yet.'

Show yourself, so we can finish you.

Flora's high-pitched laughter pierced Kailey's ear, even though the furious wind should have subdued the sound.

'Remember how I told you that you cannot rely on others to fight your battles for you?'

Then show yourself. I'll stake you with this cross.

"You couldn't survive against me," Raven said in Kailey's other ear. "And you *think* you can stake Flora? All this time I thought you were so much smarter than I. I guess I was wrong. It's just you and me, sweetie. If you can stake me, Flora has promised to spare you. But, you won't die if I defeat you. I promise you that. I want you to know what I feel since you abandoned me. I want you to live forever craving blood."

I never abandoned you!

"This happened to me because I had loved you."

No, you became a vampire because of your obsession for me. There's a difference.

"We can argue about the details later. We have an eternity to sort it all out."

Kailey grabbed a stake from the box Brady had brought into the tunnel. *Not if I can help it!*

Before Kailey could take a defensive stance, the cross and stake were snatched from her tightened fists. She was yanked into the bluish opening, but on the other side of the threshold, she didn't see Flora or Raven.

What the hell is happening?

CHAPTER 53

Forrest rushed toward the opening veil with a stake in both hands. "Kailey!"

Brady apparently noticed his approach from the corner of his eye and turned toward Forrest with a half startled expression.

Eva swayed as the power loomed like flickering blue static around her. Jaclyn, Raine, and Gillian continued holding their hands against Eva's back to support her. All were chanting, and none of the witches had noticed Kailey being dragged past them into whatever gateway was opening because their energy and magic focused upon the shimmering fissure.

The wind died in an instant. All the quieter sounds were suddenly magnified.

"What is it, Forrest?" Brady asked.

"Kailey," Forrest replied in his deep voice. His facial muscles tightened from his anger as he peered into the narrow opening.

Brady glanced around and looked at the cross and stake on the ground. "Dammit! Where'd she go?"

"Through there. Something snatched her and yanked her through," Forrest replied, running toward the narrow opening.

"No, Forrest!" Eva said without opening her eyes. "Not yet!"

"But Kailey's in there," Brady said.

Eva's eyes popped open, and she glanced toward them. "How?"

The other three witches opened their eyes and straightened slightly.

Gillian and Raine stepped aside, forcing Jaclyn to catch Eva's limp body before she collapsed on the rails. Almost fainting, Eva placed a feeble hand against her brow.

Brady glanced at Forrest. "What took her? What'd it look like?"

Forrest shrugged. "I didn't actually *see* anything."

Jacob stood beside Brady. "Let's go get her."

Cassie pushed past them, her long tail swaying behind her. "No. Allow me."

"Why you?" Forrest asked.

She pointed with a nod of her head. "Because there are other demons in there. Eva has awakened them. I'm guessing they are the ones that took Kailey."

"But I didn't see anything."

"They have resources at their disposal. Some can make themselves invisible."

"What else is in there?" he asked.

Cassie shook her head. "I can't know for certain until after I get inside."

"You're not going in without me," Forrest said. He glanced at the portal. It was strange. The rest of the area around the gate looked the same as it had when he, Ian, and Gunner had searched the place. The opening was a narrow rectangle without an actual door or frame, just a threshold where one could walk through. He squinted, trying to make out some shapes or figures, anything to let him know what was inside.

"It's best if you don't enter yet," Cassie said.

"Why not?"

She smiled. "It's a demon stomping ground."

Forrest scratched his bearded chin and grinned.

"What?" Cassie asked.

"Then it's the exact place I need to invade."

She gave him a curious stare. "Why's that?"

"Penelope has to be in there."

"And if not?"

"It's something I need to know, one way or the others."

Before Forrest stepped across the threshold, dozens of sprawled dead bodies were covered in blood and appeared along the rails. Their tattered clothes were from over a century earlier during the time when he had been the boy who had met Penelope. Their bloody wounds and lacerations leaked fresh blood like they had been killed only moments earlier.

"What the hell?" Brady said, stepping off a lifeless body.

Eva looked in Jaclyn's direction. "You best get ready, child."

"What do you mean?"

"An army lies on the ground before you. You're going to need their help."

Jaclyn frowned. "Resurrect them?"

Eva grinned. "You boast of your power as a necromancer. The opportunity to prove yourself is at your feet."

Strange sounds shrieked on the other side of the narrow gateway.

"But you must hurry. That's what killed these men as they tried to flee," Eva said.

"Just now?" Jaclyn asked.

Eva shook her head. "No. Well over a hundred years ago."

"But their injuries are fresh," Brady said. "How is that possible?"

"When we sealed this area beneath the veil of our magic, everything was preserved to remain the same as their time period," Eva replied. "Almost like they were frozen in time, without ice, of course."

"Penelope? So ... there's the chance she's still alive?" Forrest rushed toward the open portal door.

"Possible? Yes, but not likely," Eva said. "Forrest, it's not safe for you to enter yet."

"I'm going with him," Cassie replied.

"Very well," Eva said. Her furrowed brow and weak voice indicated that she didn't want to waste energy arguing. She flicked her tired gaze to Jaclyn. "You don't have much time. By ourselves we're no match for what's coming toward us."

Jaclyn turned toward Raine and pointed. "My bag. Bring it to me. Gillian, bring one of the goats. Hurry!"

Raine hurried to where they had set down their packs of magical supplies. Gillian ran to fetch the goat.

Eva's weary eyes searched Jaclyn's. "You think you can raise that many bodies at once?"

"Apparently I don't have much choice, do I, Mother?"

"I'm afraid I'm too spent to offer any assistance."

Jaclyn took her pack from Raine and flipped it over. "The three of us should be able to handle this, provided everyone else keeps the demons at bay until we compete the ritual."

Gillian brought the goat to Jaclyn. Jaclyn tied the goat to an old block.

"Get the blessed salt," Jaclyn said to Raine. "Make the circle around us. Gillian set the candles and light them."

Both witches did as she instructed without question. Raine stood facing north and poured salt, forming a large circle to enclose all of them and the goat as she walked clockwise. When she had finished the circle, Gillian set the candles at equal distances to form a pentagram. Eva instructed Brady and all the others to move back away from the rails. No one protested, but each seemed genuinely interested in what the witches were doing.

Jaclyn took a bell from her pack, her athame, and her boline she tucked behind the cord tied around her waist. All three witches faced north while Jaclyn chanted, motioning her athame in delicate gestures forming symbols. Raine and Gillian faced Jaclyn and placed their hands on her shoulders, softly speaking words different than those Jaclyn recited.

Sweat beaded across Jaclyn's brow. She tucked her athame behind her cord and drew the boline, still chanting quietly. Her body shook for a moment, her lips trembled, and then her body grew rigid. Her eyes opened, showing nothing but white. The air in the tunnel plummeted. Clouds puffed from their mouths as they spoke. She leaned to the goat, and in one swift movement, she slit its throat with the boline. Blood spilled.

A breeze whistled from down the corridor. The dead bodies twitched for a few moments but then became lifeless once more.

"It's not working, dear," Eva said.

"Shush, Mother!"

"Child, you haven't much time."

"I know," Jaclyn said. "They're trying to come to us."

"True, but that's not what I'm talking about."

"Then what?"

"Those souls I mentioned earlier?"

"Yes?"

"Apparently, this portal has caught their attention. They're coming down the stairs. If you don't make these bodies rise from the dead, the souls can enter them and bring them to life."

"Isn't that a good thing?" Brady asked.

"No. The last thing we need is for those souls to enter the bodies."

"Why is that?" Jacob asked.

"Undead beings make a better army. Jaclyn, hurry. Those souls I mentioned before are coming down the stairs."

Jacob turned his flashlight toward the stairs. "I don't see anything."

"You cannot see them," Eva replied. "Only a true witch can."

"How can these undead be better soldiers?" Jacob asked.

Eva sighed. "Undead zombies are much more difficult for the demons to take down."

"Can you guarantee none of us will get infected by them?" Jacob asked.

Jaclyn cocked a brow and glanced at him in sheer disbelief. "You've watched too many television shows. Besides, the zombies I raise are under my guidance and obey what I command. They will do as I say. Now, *please*, if you'll all let me focus—"

Raine and Gillian stood to each side of Jaclyn. Jaclyn took her boline and sliced her palm with its razor-edge. Blood filled the laceration. She formed a fist and squeezed, allowing a stream of her own blood to trickled into the goat's blood. Gillian and Raine took their bolines and did the same to their hands.

Jaclyn continued her chant. Seconds later, the dead bodies writhed on the ground. In spite of their fatal injuries, they came slowly to life. Their chests rose and fell, gulping in air to their reanimated lungs. Dead eyes opened, blindly searching their surroundings.

"Brady!" Kailey shouted from inside the open gate.

Forrest figured that was the best time to rush through the portal doorway to rescue Kailey, if nothing else. As he did, Cassie was right behind him.

CHAPTER 54

*H*asty decisions had been far more common to Forrest than calculated attacks. Sometimes, a well-prepared strategy worked, but when one dealt with the undead and the unknown, the luxury to plan ahead often wasn't even an option. Most undead creatures were unpredictable, especially in areas shrouded with darkness. This was one of those occasions.

Oddly, thrusting himself through the portal had placed him into an environment unlike anything he'd ever seen before. The doorway seemed to be a line that divided the past from the present, or at least 1889 had been suspended on this side of the threshold.

Cassie stood beside him. A moment later, Gunner and Ian emerged behind them in their morphed otter forms. Their long sharp claws extended several inches from the tips of their fingers. They opened their mouths and snarls curled their upper lips, revealing the points of their teeth.

All four of them stood inside the tunnel, but the once shiny rails were coated with specks of blood from dozens of dead broken bodies like those that had appeared on the outside of the doorway.

A standing wall of smoke that reeked of sulfur limited their visibility to only a few feet. Roars and odd growls echoed behind the smoky veil. Sharp, panicked shrieks of pain abruptly ended. The sounds and pungent smell of brimstone indicated that Penelope had been correct when she had seen the demons in the picture of Seattle's Great Fire in 1889. Forrest had not seen them in the picture, but she was a Demon-hunter and he was not, so she was more capable of detecting them than he.

Forrest held the two stakes firmly. "Should we spread out to look for Kailey?"

Cassie glanced at him with nervous eyes and shook her head. "No. We're safer together."

Ian and Gunner vanished into the smoke.

Cassie gave Forrest a strange side-glance, questioning their sudden departure.

He shrugged. "At least I asked."

"What the hell are they doing?"

"They're scouts and predators. They'll be fine."

"You know little about demons," Cassie replied.

"Brady!" Kailey yelled.

Cassie grabbed Forrest's right wrist. "Come on."

She pulled him into the denser, nauseating smoke where the flames flickered and bodies burned.

As best he could tell, no one was alive except for them and Kailey. He didn't know how she could still be alive or how much longer, he, Cassie, and his friends would live. All the dead bodies were a good indication that humans weren't welcome here, and those who chose to enter didn't live long.

Even though the creatures howled crazed animalistic cries, nothing charged from the smoke toward them. At least nothing had yet.

"Someone help me," Kailey said in a tearful voice. She sounded weaker and was coughing. A few seconds later, she wheezed, fighting to get her breath.

Cassie tugged Forrest. "Over there."

"You see her?"

Cassie nodded.

"How?" The smoke stung his eyes, bringing tears and further handicapping his vision.

"How can you possibly forget *where* I came from, Forrest?"

Forrest chuckled. "From this?"

"A place very similar but much darker with flames hot enough to scorch a demon."

"I can see why you don't want to return."

"Yeah, it's no picnic," she said.

"Maybe not, but it seems like a good place to smoke fish and hams."

Cassie's eyes narrowed a moment before she looked away, but she didn't reply.

Forrest shook his head at his own stupid remark.

Coughing and sobbing caught his attention, which made Cassie jerk his arm harder and then she knelt.

"Kailey, we're here," Cassie said.

Forrest placed his stakes into his coat pockets. For the moment it didn't seem that he needed them, but with all the impenetrable smoke, he didn't know that with absolute certainty. Instinct and Hunter intuition let him know they were being watched. Perhaps, *studied* was more accurate.

Kailey lay in a fetal position beside the rail. He knelt in front of her.

"Are you okay?" he asked.

Her frightened eyes met his. She nodded. "I think so."

"What took you?" he asked.

"I have no idea," she whispered. "I never saw anything. I only felt its scaly skin."

Forrest scooped her up into his massive arms. "It's okay. We're going to get you out of here."

"Before I was snatched and brought to wherever this is," Kailey said, "Flora and Raven were whispering in my ears."

Forrest held her and glanced around. "Are they here?"

"I don't know," she replied.

Cassie peered into the dark smoke. Burning planks crackled and bubbling flesh popped and sizzled. "I don't think any vampires have slipped through the gateway."

Forrest looked at Kailey. "And you don't have a clue as to what dragged you in here?"

"No."

Forrest sighed. "Cassie, where are the demons? Why haven't they shown themselves? I'm under the impression that they know we've come through the gateway."

"For some reason, they're staying hidden."

"That's too odd for my comfort," Forrest said. "They're probably sizing us up."

"You're probably right about that."

"There doesn't seem to be any other reason." Forrest adjusted Kailey in his arms. With the shifting wall of hazy smoke, he wasn't able to see the doorway. "Can you lead us out?"

"This way," Cassie said almost in a whisper.

"What's wrong?"

She flicked her gaze to Forrest but kept her silence.

"You sense them, too?" he asked.

"Yes. They are all around us," she replied. "Following us. Each step we take, they take one, too."

Kailey coughed and cleared her throat. "What kind of demons are you talking about? Like those at Nocturnal Trinity?"

Cassie shook her head. Her voice lowered to a soft whisper. "No. Apparently the ones Eva trapped in time are the foot soldier demons that first burst through the portal when the Great Fire occurred. They are the most vile and ruthless lesser demons and follow whatever orders the behemoths command. Should they escape, the evil in Seattle will escalate. We really need to get outside and hope the witches can reseal the gateway."

"No," Forrest replied. "I need to find Penelope."

"Forrest, she might not even be here."

"She is. I just need to find her."

"We cannot risk it."

Forrest's jaw tightened. He handed Kailey to Cassie. "I understand the dangers. Take Kailey to safety. I'll scout around. I couldn't live with myself if I didn't search for her. Besides, I'm not leaving Gunner and Ian behind."

"Forrest—" Kailey said with pleading eyes. "Don't stay."

Cassie took Kailey and ran, vanishing into the smoke.

CHAPTER 55

Forrest took the handkerchief from his pocket, folded it into a triangle, and tied it to cover his nose and mouth. The brimstone was bad enough, but the smell of smoldering flesh sickened him.

Although the area where he stood was identical to the neglected track and tunnel on the outside of the time portal, it was like being in a foreign land. Nothing looked the same, but he wasn't able to examine anything from a distance. The thick smoke prevented him from seeing any object farther than ten inches away. Occasionally, heavy snorts, which sounded like angered bulls puffed too close to allow him to lower his guard. He guessed these were demons trying to get his scent, but they made certain never to come into view. Sometimes *not* seeing a foe was more frightening than actually seeing it.

Forrest shoved his hands into his pockets and grabbed his stakes. Although he couldn't stake a demon like a vampire and vaporize them, he could drive one through its skull and kill it, should the need arise. He wondered how many of these demons were hiding in the smoke and what kind of hellish creatures lurked with them.

The last thing he had expected to discover was that he might soon face the foot soldier demons Penelope had encountered long ago. Even though he knew ranks existed for demons, just like vampires and other supernatural creatures, he had never considered how vast an army Penelope had chosen to face without him. And even worse, she had stood against them … alone.

Regret pierced his soul. He had wanted to go with her. He had even told her so, but she couldn't wait a few more days. And stubborn in his own fashion, he couldn't abandon his mission at that time, either. He had made an oath, a costly oath that he now regretted. He had lost Penelope in the process, and his father, too. Why couldn't he have postponed his pledge and gone with her?

Forrest took a step over the arm of a dead man. The fingers curled and twitched. He paused and studied the man for several moments, but no further movement was detected. Was the smoke creating strange illusions or playing with his eyes? With all the bizarre creatures and strange encounters he had faced during his lifetime as a Vampire Hunter, out of the ordinary situations were more common occurrences than not.

He kept moving. He hoped Gunner and Ian were okay. They had been silent since they had left him and Cassie. That should have been a good sign. They had not wailed in pain or called out to one another at all, so most likely they were alive and unharmed, but still searching.

The air suddenly became thicker and more difficult to breathe. He placed his hand against the strange textured wall and growls uttered in low threatening tones. He pressed again and slid his hand partway into the cold goo. He looked up and shook, but not from the cold. His eyes widened.

Penelope?

She stood like a frozen statue at the center of this strange substance inside a bell-like dome. Penelope's open eyes detailed her final emotion before she had been confined to this odd prison, somehow trapped like an insect in hardened amber. The determined firmness of her brow indicated her focus was on an enemy. Her right hand remained tightened around the grip of her bow. Her left hand was raised as if reaching for an arrow in the quiver on her back. The expression on her face showed no fear, even with the dead bodies scattered around her position. She had not died violently, as he had feared, but she had been imprisoned inside this strange tomb.

How?

Why?

The jelly-like substance solidified around Forrest's forearm. The cold bit painfully to the bone. The viscous gel resisted his advance, even though he had shoved his weight and strength behind his right arm, trying to get into the enclosure to get closer to Penelope. He attempted to move his fingers and found he could not.

He gazed into her frozen eyes, remembering the warmth they once showed him long ago. She still looked the same as he had remembered her before she had become trapped for more than a century. Her suspended image was the same teenage Demon-hunter except she appeared much younger than his memory served him. But, at the time when they had parted ways, she had been older than he, which might have made her look older in his eyes when he had been a boy.

Eva had preserved and concealed the area, but why had the surviving demons that were trapped inside with Penelope not killed her? Could they even get to her through this barrier? He certainly was having one hell of a time penetrating the cold wall.

Forrest attempted to pull his arm out, but the substance held fast, gripping firmly, and refused to release its hold. Afraid to thrust his other arm into it for fear it would become trapped as well, he gripped his right elbow and tugged. Nothing. Not an inch.

Chattering echoed within the dark smoky veil. A tone of eagerness flowed with their strange cries. He wondered if their bloodlust was aimed toward him, or if were they hopeful he'd somehow release her. He had no way to tell, but he was quite certain he wasn't going to get anywhere near enough to reach her, much less free her. His arm was ensnared.

A bloodcurdling shriek echoed beyond the deep smoke. He recognized the growl that followed to be Gunner's. His growl had not come from injury but was Gunner's signature triumphant roar.

"Gunner!" Forrest shouted. "I need your help."

"What is it?" Ian asked behind him.

Forrest glanced over his shoulder. Ian stood in his otter form. Blood dripped from his razor-sharp claws. Demon's blood. Ian didn't seem to have any injuries at all, and the brothers' bold search through the smoke might have been another reason the demons had yet emerged to attack Forrest.

He had never thought demons to be cowardly, but he supposed that was possible since it had required an army of them to have enough courage to bring carnage to Seattle. These demons seemed apprehensive to attack. Perhaps it was due to their curiosity since no one had set foot into this hidden pocket of time until now.

"My arm is stuck," Forrest said.

"I see that."

"You mind helping?"

"What exactly do you wish me to do?" Ian studied the gelatin wall that enclosed Forrest's arm up to his elbow. He leaned closer, sniffed the gooey substance, and placed his altered hands against the wall.

"No," Forrest said, "it will trap you, too."

Ian grunted, lowering his bloody hands. He stepped behind Forrest, wrapped his arms around Forrest's waist, and tugged with all his strength.

"Ian! Stop!"

"It's not working?"

"No. Not unless your goal is to rip my arm off."

Ian released his hold on Forrest and stepped back. His whiskers twitched and his shiny black eyes studied the strange gel wall. He rubbed his furry chin and shook his head. "No give at all?"

"Nope."

Ian scrunched his black snout in an odd grimace.

"Look what I got," Gunner said, emerging from the smoke and walking toward them. In one hand he held a silver short sword with strange symbols welded into its hilt. In the other hand was the head of a gnarled-faced demon. Its eyes were widened by the sudden shock of its decapitation. Blood dripped from the demon's head.

"What is that?" Ian asked.

"It's a demon head," Gunner said with a prideful gnarled smile.

"No, the blade, you twit." Ian narrowed his eyes. "Where'd you find that?"

"It belonged to the demon," he replied. Gunner looked at Forrest and noticed Forrest's arm stuck inside the gel. He peered closer. "What happened?"

"What does it look like happened?" Ian snapped.

"Ian," Forrest said, shaking his head.

Ian huffed. "Well, it couldn't be any more obvious, could it?"

"Maybe not, but considering that we're surrounded by demons and whatever else was trapped in here from the past, now isn't exactly the time to berate Gunner."

"Why the hell did you thrust your hand into that mess anyway?" Ian asked.

"You don't see her?" Forrest asked with a fierce glare.

"Who?" Ian asked, turning his attention to the gel enclosure.

Ian and Gunner both stared into the thick wall for several moments until their eyes widened. Perhaps due to the texture's odd bluish-green tint, they had not noticed her at first glance either.

"Is that … Penelope?" Gunner asked.

"That's her," Forrest replied.

Gunner smiled. His eyes widened. In a near whisper, he said, "She's beautiful."

"I've always thought so," Forrest said.

Ian frowned. "Is she alive?"

"I honestly don't know," Forrest said. "She's been somehow frozen in time, but I cannot get any closer and as you know, I cannot pull my arm out either."

Gunner dropped the demon head and offered the short sword to Ian. "Perhaps you could use this to slice through the barrier?"

Ian took the sword, studied the blade for several long moments, and then glanced questionably at Forrest.

Forrest shrugged. "It's worth a try."

"It might get wedged tightly like your arm," Ian said.

"If so, it won't fall into the hands of another demon."

"That's true." Ian took the hilt in both hands and placed the tip of the blade against the gooey wall near Forrest's arm. He shoved the blade. The wall offered no resistance, nor did it seek to grasp the sword like it had Forrest's arm. Ian carved out a small wedge of the wall. The squishy substance plopped to the ground with a sticky smacking. Ian moved the blade closer to Forrest's trapped forearm and trimmed away another long strip. After Ian lowered the blade, Forrest pushed down on his arm and dislodged it.

Forrest's arm fell limp to his side. The cold substance that had trapped his forearm had completely numbed it.

"I think I can cut a path to her," Ian said.

Guttural growls and hisses formed a tighter circle around their position.

Forrest gave a quick glance toward the smoky wall. "Do so, but hurry. I'm afraid our releasing her is what they have waited a long time to occur. They are going to attack soon."

Gunner glanced around. The smoky veil was too thick for any of them to see through, but the chattering and hungry squeals of what was hiding pressed even closer. Several deep snorts and chuffs gruffly expelled from what must have been larger demons or unknown creatures. These didn't seem to be trying to get the scent of Forrest, Gunner, and Ian because they were already aware of their intrusion into this concealed chamber of the past. The impatient sounds of these unseen demons indicated what Forrest had already predicted. They were preparing to charge.

Ian fileted his way through the cold gelatin-like wall, carving a narrow path toward Penelope. Even though the blade flayed through Penelope's domed prison, the task wasn't a quick process because whatever layers he sliced through needed to be removed before he could advance any further. The good thing, at least from Forrest's observation, was that the dissected walls weren't congealing back together. At least not yet.

Forrest rubbed his numbed right arm, trying to get some of the feeling to return. After a few minutes of squeezing and massaging his forearm, the fingers on his right hand tingled. Heat pricked like sharp stinging needles from his hand to his elbow as the circulation slowly returned.

The strange cold goo retreated from Ian's blade as he had carved a path to Penelope, but she was still encased. He stopped short of her and glanced toward Forrest with a curious stare.

Forrest took a long sharp hunting knife from its sheath on his belt and tried to cut through the wall's surface. Unlike the short sword Ian used, Forrest's blade proved ineffective. The blade penetrated through the wall but wasn't able to cut away portions of it like Ian had done with the sword. Wherever Forrest inserted the knife, the goo congealed around it. Any movements he made with the knife was not any more effective than stirring water in a pot with a large spoon.

"Forrest," Ian said. "I'm afraid to cut much closer to her."

"Why's that?"

"I don't want to accidentally cut *her.*"

"I'd help, but the path you've cut is too narrow for me to walk through."

Ian turned and with several harsh overhead and downward swings, he sliced wider swaths on each side of the path as he walked to Forrest. "Is that better?"

The slices of the loosened gel slid and sloshed onto the narrow floored path, oozing out from the once protective dome like a sluggish stream. Oddly, whatever part of the gel this blade touched, it liquefied whatever properties that had kept the walls upright.

Forrest looked at Gunner. "You got this blade from one of the demons?"

Gunner nodded.

"Odd," Forrest replied.

"Why?" Ian asked.

"I'm just curious as to why they've never used the blade to get to her?"

"Perhaps they are the ones who had imprisoned her?" Ian asked.

"I don't think so, although I don't rightly know," Forrest replied. "To me it appears she was sealed inside this jelly dome to protect her *from* the demons. Since she killed one of the behemoths, it's doubtful they'd allow her to live."

Gunner frowned. "That's not exactly living."

"I know, but leaving her like this would be a constant taunt to the other demons trapped inside this portal with her. Don't you think?"

Ian frowned and nodded. "I see your point."

The guttural growls grew angrier, pressing closer.

"They don't seem happy about us trying to get to her, so it might be possible that they did enclose her," Ian said.

"Either way, we need to get her out," Forrest said. "Gunner, stand at the opening of the path while Ian and I free her the rest of the way. Once we release her, they are probably going to charge."

Gunner bore his sharp gnarled teeth and growled, looking toward the closing smoke. The jagged claws on his hands lengthened.

Forrest followed Ian down the path that stopped only inches from Penelope. He gazed into her still eyes and a lump rose in his throat that was almost impossible to swallow. He didn't know if releasing her would be a rescue or not. She might already be dead and had been placed into the gel dome to preserve their victory by having killed one of the Demon-hunters. Pulling her out of the adhesive goo might be in vain. She might be nothing more than a corpse.

Ian shook his head and offered the blade to Forrest. "I don't want to cut her."

Forrest smiled. "Look, just carve slowly around the base of her feet and up to her hand holding the bow. Once I get a grip on her arm, cut as close as you can. The blade seems to be dissolving whatever this substance is. But, with my help, I might be able to pull her free. I need to catch her, if that happens."

Ian took a deep breath. Steadily, he ran the tip of the blade around her boots and slowly brought the blade up, slicing an outline up the side of her leg to her belt. The viscous gel peeled away, cascading like thick sludgy water. He continued until he reached her extended left arm where her hand clutched the bow. Once her arm was released from the gel, Forrest grabbed it with both hands.

"Keep carving around her. It's working. You don't have to be too close. It appears she's was encapsulated by a spell, and if so, I don't understand why they never used the sword. Hurry."

Ian made his way around Penelope, slicing thin layers of the dome away from her. Within a few minutes, the entire center of the dome dissolved and Forrest scooped her limp body against him, preventing her from falling. Her face touched his. It was colder than marble. Like death. He wrapped his arms around her, hoping his warmth dispelled the coldness that claimed her. Tears burned his eyes.

"Penelope," he whispered in her ear. She didn't respond, nor was she breathing. He held her tighter, afraid to lose his final hope, but worried that it didn't matter.

"Forrest," Gunner said. "Here they come!"

The smoke vanished and a small horde of horned demons with black evil eyes rushed toward them. Their hideous faces resembled nothing he had ever seen before. Their deep wrinkles outlined the constant fury of their anger and hatred. They held absolute revulsion toward mankind. Cassie had been right. These demons were nothing like those he had seen at Nocturnal Trinity. These vile creatures thrived by bringing destruction. They were the front line that carved through flesh and bone to make a path for the greater demons.

No rationality reflected in their gazes, only madness and their lust to shed blood.

Forrest realized his new dilemma. He couldn't set Penelope down without one of these demons killing or taking her, and he couldn't fight effectively at all while holding her. Now that she was in his arms, he simply couldn't release her because he didn't want to lose her again.

He doubted Ian and Gunner would be capable of fighting all of them without his help. And if she was already dead, it didn't matter. He had no need to protect her. *No, you mustn't think that way.*

The dead bodies on the ground shifted suddenly. Hands flexed as he had seen before, which he had thought were only his eyes playing tricks on him. But, it was very real. Their bodies squirmed, slowly pushing themselves upward and trying to stand. They outnumbered the demons more than five to one from his observation, but that was only in the area nearest him.

The undead men turned toward Forrest and the were-otter brothers, alongside the approaching demons. Forrest clung to Penelope. He didn't want to lower to the ground. He had waited far too long in hopes of ever being reunited with her again.

The demons shrieked, extending their long claws, and bearing their sharp pointed teeth. None of them held swords or weapons. They didn't need them. He was curious as to why the one had the sword that allowed Ian to cut through Penelope's prison.

These demons kept their attention on Forrest, Ian, and Gunner. The dead men didn't interest them. The demons had killed them once before, so the demons were bent on killing everything else that wasn't a demon. But each one looked to have only one goal in mind. Taking Penelope.

CHAPTER 56

Forrest cradled Penelope in his arms, holding her upright as they demons scrambled over and around the rising bodies. He firmly wrapped his left arm around her, holding her tightly to his side, and took a stake in his right hand. He might be able to fend off a few demons, but once they swarmed, he had little else he could do with one free arm.

Gunner and Ian growled and used their sharp hardened claws to impel the demons closest to them. Ian shoved his extended claws into the gut of a snarling demon. Its eyes widened. Black blood leaked out its mouth and nose. Its body stiffened and the glow of its reddish eyes dimmed.

Gunner raked a harsh swipe across the throat of a demon, cutting deeply and ripping to the spine. The demon clutched its throat and staggered backwards against three more demons. Its comrades watched with bewilderment as the demon dropped lifeless at their feet.

Perhaps the demons didn't actually realize what Ian and Gunner were. But once the demons noticed their fallen comrades had been eviscerated, their charging onslaught abruptly slowed. They exchanged nervous side-glances with one another, hesitant to proceed.

"Kill them!" The low voice rattled like thunder and echoed from farther down the tunnel.

The tone of the voice sent chills down Forrest's back. The demons trembled at the roar of its command, but still they hesitated.

The momentary pause in the demons' attack had allowed enough time for the undead men to turn and maul the demons. It was then Forrest understood they must have risen, not because of something the demons had done, but because Jaclyn's ritual had been successful. She had brought them back from the dead and they were under her control.

Demons shrieked and pushed at the clawing dead men to no avail. The zombies didn't react to injury. They had no pain.

One zombie grabbed the arm of a demon, twisted, and violently ripped the arm from its shoulder socket. The demon wailed with a horrendous cry. More of the undead men clambered to the demon and pulled it apart.

The demons chattered in a strange hissing gargle with words unidentified by Forrest, and he guessed, any other human. It was a unique language.

"Kill the witch outside the portal door, you fools," the voice said. "Before she seals the summoning circle.

Several demons avoided the undead mobs and rushed for the portal door. Since they were swifter than the zombies, a half dozen demons reached the opening unscathed.

Fierce snarls rose from the other side of the doorway. Seconds later Brady and Jacob came through the door. Brady swung his hand toward one demon, extending his long claws with a harsh raking motion, slicing through a demon's throat and decapitating it.

Jacob grabbed another demon, placed it into a headlock, and yanked its head off its shoulders with little effort. They advanced toward Forrest's position, killing more demons as they approached. Even though their efforts were successful, they couldn't prevent some of the demons slipping past them and rushing out the doorway.

"They're going after Jaclyn," Forrest said, pointing.

Brady glanced toward the door where the demons exited. "All we can hope is that the witches can fend them off."

Forrest shook his head. "You don't understand. If she is killed, we're all as good as dead."

~

After Brady and Jacob rushed through the portal, Kailey watched in horror as six demons exited a few minutes later. These hideous creatures were unlike anything she'd ever imagined. She understood why Nocturnal Trinity would shun these demons from ever being seen in the public eye. They were frightening to the core, despicable, and as she read in their eyes, the purest of evil. She also understood why Cassie and Jinn, and other demons like them, were the representatives for the demon faction at the nightclub. They displayed enticing charisma and were pleasing to the eye, even in their demon forms. Ill intent seldom manifested on one's outer appearance and could be buried deeply that others didn't notice, only to emerge when soon-to-be victims least expected. But one glance at these demons sent chills throughout Kailey's body, registering a deeper fear than she had ever known before, and worse than Raven and Flora's threat on her life. Everything about these unleashed demons flaunted the vileness of what a world without conscience and compassion offered. Such was a dark world she hoped never manifested itself.

I never thought Hell existed. It must, in order to house demons like these. The truth was, she hadn't given much thought to such an eternal place of torment, not until after her brother had been killed and she had met Cassie and other demons. Even then, though, she teetered on the threshold of doubt.

Kailey held a stake in her hand, crouched low, and eased her way back into the shadows. Her sudden cowardice overwhelmed her. She wondered if they could be killed, and she questioned whether she could even defend herself during an attack.

One of the dark demons glanced her direction and noticed her. His eyes narrowed with lustful interest and eagerness. She not only read the intent on his face, but it somehow radiated from him and projected his thoughts into her mind. Not pleasing thoughts, either. Far from it. Such tortures could make heartless murderers squeamish.

Drool dripped from the sides of the demon's mouth. His long black tongue slid across jagged teeth. He marched with slow sure steps toward her, never taking his eyes off hers.

Cold fear shot through Kailey. She shook involuntarily. Her teeth chattered. She wanted to run but couldn't. She couldn't feel her legs enough to attempt to stand. She was locked in a moment where she wished herself invisible or at best, she could awaken from what was the most intense nightmare she'd ever endured. But it wasn't a nightmare, and sadly, the situation was about to get worse.

"Have you had enough, dear?" Flora asked with a haughty laugh.

Kailey found herself paralyzed by fear.

"I believe she has, Raven," Flora said softly. Her words flowed and spiraled into Kailey's mind.

Everything seemed to close in around Kailey, growing smaller and smaller, darkening. She trembled. Breathing was jagged gasps. Her heart hammered in her chest.

"Like a frightened rabbit. You're so fragile, Kailey," Flora whispered.

"And she thought she could be an MMA competitor? Sheesh," Raven said with a sneering tone.

"Shall we rescue her?" Flora asked.

"Let's," Raven replied in her throaty voice. Vibrant eagerness rose as she said, "It shall be so fun being roommates again."

Kailey's eyes darted like a frightened trapped animal. She watched the approaching demon, then she flicked her gaze to Cassie. Cassie read her concern and launched herself toward the demon.

Kailey wanted to shout a warning that Flora and Raven were close by, but the words wouldn't form. Her mouth was exceedingly dry and if she didn't somehow get control of her breathing, she'd hyperventilate. Her elevated heartbeat had already made her dizzy and faint.

In desperation, she looked around the shadowed corridor, trying to locate the vampires but unable to do so.

Are you really here?

"We are," Flora replied. "Yield yourself to us, and we'll protect you."

Raven made a wet smacking sound with her lips. "We can be blood sisters forever."

The thought sickened Kailey. She shook her head with an uncontrolled bobble, trying to protest, wanting to deny her need for their help because she understood the subtly of what cost came with accepting their rescue—a price she did not wish to sacrifice: her soul.

The demon sauntered toward Kailey, but Cassie rushed like a blur to intercept. Cassie's long tail wrapped around the demon's throat, lifting it into the air with a startled muffled squeal. It turned to view its captor and violently hissed its disdain. It flexed its arms, forcing its thick black claws to lengthen. A crazed look creased its feral face. It widened its mouth and reared back its head to bite her. The sharp tip of her tail swung downward like a spike through its brain. Its entire body fell limp.

Cassie uncoiled her tail, dropping the lifeless imp to the ground. She gave a quick wink to Kailey and rushed for the next closest demon.

Jaclyn, Raine, and Gillian stood helpless in their trances as they worked to keep the undead troops under control. Blaze and Luna stood with their backs to the witches' circle with stakes in what looked like a last effort to protect the witches should the demons attack.

Eva pushed herself up to her feet, extended a weak hand in their direction, and mumbled a short chant.

From out of nowhere one of the demons rushed between Blaze and Luna, ramming into Jaclyn, knocking her hard to the ground. Her head struck a broken block, rendering her unconscious, and breaking the magical circle.

"No!" Eva shouted, her face tightened with desperation and dread.

Father Charles stood at the portal entrance, trying to prevent more demons from escaping the time chamber where Forrest and the others were. His left hand clutched the narrow neck of a demon. He pressed his silver cross against its forehead, which blistered its skin. The bubbling flesh sizzled. A second later, the priest drove the cross between its eyes as he banished the demon from the Earth, commanding it to return to the pits of Hell. As he did so, two demons leapt from the portal and clambered up his body, their stocky weight driving him to the ground. Three more stood around him while he struggled to break free of their hold. Sinister sneers widened their strange mouths.

Cassie brought her tail around sharp and fast, decapitating another demon before it got anywhere near Kailey. She turned toward Kailey and walked in her direction, extending her hand to help Kailey to her feet.

All the sounds of the tunnel blurred together indistinguishably. Kailey reached her hand toward Cassie, and a moment later, everything fled from her vision. She moved lightly through the air at such a rapid speed that the high shrill of Cassie screaming her name lessened to a whisper in less than a second, almost like the fading cry of someone falling off a high cliff into a pool of water below. It was then she realized Flora and Raven had snatched her. She wondered which fate would have been worse, the demons or what Raven intended to do to her.

CHAPTER 57

orrest had thought the resurrected undead men would turn the battle in their favor against the raving demons, and for several minutes, it had.

Although the demons had inflicted some damage to the walking cadavers, no pain or fear thwarted the undead's attacks. Several demons lay on the ground with appendages torn from their sockets. Like humans, the damage and loss of blood was draining their lives. They had suffered lethal injuries. They were not resistant to death.

Jacob and Brady were using their viscous claws to sever the throats of the demons, too. The demon horde was diminishing in number at a rapid pace.

But then something happened.

The undead stiffened for a moment, and they no longer kept their focus on killing the demons. Instead they turned and reached for Brady and Jacob. It was like a reset button had been pressed.

Ian and Gunner stopped fighting the scattering demons and shredded into the undead men hobbling toward them.

Forrest's attention was caught by the harsh growl of a man being mobbed by demons. He recognized the victim to be Father Charles.

"Gunner! Ian!" Forrest shouted.

When they glanced toward him, Forrest pointed toward the portal door. They nodded and abandoned the undead mob to help the priest.

Forrest lowered himself to the ground and cradled Penelope's lifeless body in his arms. The demons weren't the biggest concern for him now. Most had been killed, and those few that had survived had fled deeper into the corridor, their bravery snuffed.

Dozens of the undead slowly walked in Forrest's direction. A huge circle of zombies slowly shambled in an ever-tightening circle toward him. He held Penelope closer, pressing his cheek against hers, whispering in her ear, hoping to awaken her. Nothing else weighed upon his mind except his flickering hope that she'd open her eyes.

Penelope wasn't responding. She remained motionless.

The best he could hope for was to set her down and resort to his melee tactics he had used for over a century, but he was too tired. He had endured so much throughout his dismal lifetime, and now, with his final hope lying dead in his arms, he wanted nothing else except to join her. Death was peace. No more slaying vampires. No more bloodshed and watching acquaintances grow old and die, leaving him to press onward, cursed with longevity he had never requested. He had suffered more than the vampires he had slain because he was still alive in a world filled with cruelness and despair. Dying eliminated all of that. If an afterlife existed, he'd roam it until he found her.

Forrest took a deep breath and sighed. He was comfortable with this being his fate. At least he had gotten to see Penelope one last time. Not in the way that he had hoped, but he now knew her demise had not been a violent death. That gave him some comfort.

Forrest held her tightly, rocking her back and forth. The undead mob moved closer. Their eyes never shifted. They were frozen, lifeless, never blinking. An unnatural force controlled them, drawing them toward him.

"Forrest!" Gunner shouted.

Forrest turned his head. Gunner stood over three decapitated demons. Black blood dripped from his claws. Ian was strangling another demon while Father Charles held the last demon by the wrists. The demon squealed and frothed at the mouth. A strange fiery golden glow shone around the priest's hands. The light caused severe pain for the desperate demon.

Gunner's facial expression was crossed between sadness and utter disbelief. His black eyes shifted to the mass of undead men encircling Forrest. Even if Gunner ran, he'd never reach Forrest before the undead did. Gunner's shoulders drooped in defeat.

Ian grabbed the last demon by the back of the neck and flung it off

Father Charles. The demon struck the smooth edge of the tunnel wall with the golden light incinerating its hands and slowly moving up its arms. The demon's eyes widened and it squalled until the light consumed it.

The priest rose to his feet and dusted himself off. White light radiated on his palms. For a moment, his eyes held a strange luminous glow before returning to normal.

Gunner patted the priest's arm and pointed toward Forrest.

Father Charles came inside the portal and stared at Forrest. "You're giving up? A Hunter never gives up."

A broad smile widened on the priest's face. The gleam in his eye caught Forrest by surprise. Suddenly, whatever guise the priest had been using faded. Forrest recognized the man from another place and another time. Hell, decades earlier, when death had tried to claim Forrest during his youth.

"No," Forrest said. "It can't be ... *you.*"

Father Charles nodded. The priest outstretched his arms. Bright light radiated from his fingers with the brightness of the sun, forcing Forrest and everyone else except the undead to shield their eyes. A blast of warmth permeated across Forrest in a pleasant wave of peace.

When the warmth faded, Forrest opened his eyes. All of the undead lay on the ground, nothing more than smoldering ashes, incinerated by the light. The few surviving demons staggered aimlessly. Their eyes were completely burned from their sockets.

Father Charles knelt with his head facing down. Large feathered wings stretched from his back. A pale light shone around him, illuminating his outline. When he rose to his feet, he was no longer a man. He towered eight feet in height and the wings weren't an illusion. They were a part of his anatomy. He was an angel.

"After all you've witnessed and all I had shown you years ago, you still deny God exists?"

"It's not that I don't believe in Him, Sauriel," Forrest said. "I just don't believe He'd be interested in keeping tabs on me."

"Believe it, my friend," Sauriel replied. "Why else would I be here?"

"That's information only you would know. But the priesthood is a bit beneath your level."

The angel chuckled. "Indeed. But what better disguise that still allows me to do my Creator's service."

Forrest held Penelope closer, hugging her. "I suppose that's true."

"She's why you'd die?"

"I've spent my life clinging to the hope of finding her, only to find that she's dead."

"Any yet, you've offered not a single prayer?"

Tears burned Forrest's eyes. "At this point, I don't see how praying makes any difference. I understand the balance between good and evil, but my heart has grown so cold with my duties of slaying vampires that I've become indifferent. So, why are you here, other than to add to my misery by letting me continue to live?"

"To offer you one last gift."

"And that would be?"

"I can revive her," Sauriel said. His eyes glowed with holy fire. A purity that burned from deep within. "Not like the witches did these undead men. But with permission from on high, her soul can be returned to her. She can live again."

Hot tears streamed down Forrest's face. "At what cost to me?"

"None."

Forrest frowned and eyed Sauriel with suspicion. "There has to be a reason."

"There is. The time for explanations comes later. But, like you, she was given a mission. She was Chosen to rid the world of the vile demons like the ones trapped here. So, are you ready for her to return?"

Forrest sobbed. His body shook. He ached inside that the opportunity to finally reunite with Penelope was at hand, but he feared losing her in other ways. "In so many ways, yes. In others … I'm not the person she knew. Back then, I was full of innocence, almost untainted, still with the mind of a child, and what I've become after a century of slaying vampires is most likely something she cannot stand the sight of."

Ian placed a hand on Forrest's shoulder. "She'd be most proud to be with you. Anyone would be. You're the best family Gunner and I could have ever hoped to have. Besides, nearly all the demons here are dead. Brady and Jacob are killing those still staggering around."

"This isn't over by any means," Sauriel said. "The summoned behemoth is still coming. Understand, once I revive her, I cease to have my powers for some time to come. I can no longer aid you in battle against the demon forces."

Ian frowned. "Then why don't you kill the behemoth?"

Sauriel shook his head. "The permission is not granted for me to do so.

Only a Demon-hunter like Penelope or other humans can. Angels are not permitted to kill the greater demons."

"But you're enemies, are you not?" Gunner asked.

"Yes. We are. But murder isn't something we can perform without tarnishing ourselves. Vampires and zombies have no souls. Destroying those aberrations has always been permitted and encouraged. But demons are different. Angels have the power to banish demons to the abyss at times, but sending a behemoth back is far more dangerous than having a Demon-hunter eradicate it."

"Why?"

"They rally together even in the abyss. Lesser demons fear the behemoths more than they do me. Sending a behemoth back allows it to grow in strength while commanding lesser demons to kill the enemies that sent it back. They never forget the names of their enemies. Believe me, for a Demon-hunter to kill a behemoth is far better than killing a thousand lessers."

Forrest stared at Sauriel with tears in his eyes. "If you can revive her, why hadn't you already done so?"

"I could not find her."

"You're an angel," Ian said. "Why couldn't you find her?"

"The magical veil hid it from me."

"You're not stronger than magic?"

Sauriel laughed softly. "Mysteries abound that confound angels, too. We're not omniscient. Otherwise, we'd be gods in our own right. We are servants."

"Brady!" Cassie said, rushing through the portal door. Blaze ran in behind her.

Brady turned. His wolf ears perked at the alarm in her voice. His eyes met hers.

"Kailey's gone! Someone took her!"

Brady snarled and his eyes narrowed.

"Luna, too," Blaze said. "She's been taken."

"What?" Forrest asked.

Cassie nodded. She panted hard, trying to control her apprehension and growing rage. Her wild eyes turned crimson, narrowed. "I was trying to reach her, and she was snatched away."

"To where?" Sauriel asked.

"I don't know. I suspect Flora has taken her."

Jacob and Brady released low growls, walking toward the portal.

"Wait!" Sauriel said firmly. "Don't run off. That's what they want you to do. Let me resurrect Penelope before we make any further plans. She will be an even greater asset to you than I."

CHAPTER 58

"I envy you," the young woman said as Kailey awoke and opened her eyes.

At first, Kailey couldn't see the woman clearly. She blinked hard, hoping to make the blurriness go away. Her vision was almost equated to opening her eyes underwater in a swimming pool. After several more blinks, the thick viscous film leaked from the sides of her eyes and allowed her vision to clear somewhat.

The young woman cocked her head to the side while she examined Kailey. Her long black braided pigtails hung downward. An odd frightening grin creased her face. Her crazed eyes widened with glee and caused Kailey to take a sharp uneasy breath. Her stomach tensed. She had only seen such bold lunatics in the movies and the fate of those fictional victims or hostages that had encountered these unbalanced psychos never ended well. She had a deep uneasy feeling that things weren't going to end any better for her, either.

The girl leaned her face forward, her nose stopping just an inch or so from Kailey's. Kailey tried to squirm and move away but discovered her wrists were cuffed to the heavy metal chair where she sat. She yanked against the metal restraints without any success. Someone obviously knew her strength and had decided to use metal instead of rope to confine her.

"Where am I?" Kailey asked, avoiding eye contact and turning her head to the side. The last thing she remembered was being yanked away from

Cassie's reaching hand. The exact details as to how she had become unconscious and bound in this chair, she didn't know.

"You're so lucky," the girl said with a sigh, ignoring the question. She puckered her lips in sadness and backed away slowly. Her lofty voice reminded Kailey of Luna, but Luna's voice was far more tolerable.

"Lucky?" Kailey frowned. She tugged at the cuffs. "How can you call *this* lucky?"

"No, sweetie," she said. "Not the restraints ... well, ... if properly used, yes, that could be considered pleasurable luck, too, depending upon your partner. But your gift is greater."

"What gift?"

"Immortality, silly."

"Who are you?" Kailey asked.

"Tiffany. Why?" She played with the ends of the tied scarf around her neck.

Figures. Kailey rolled her eyes. "Why are you here?"

"I'm part of the ritual."

"What ritual?"

"For you to become a vampire," Tiffany replied.

So Flora did take me. Kailey frowned. "Where's Flora?"

"She'll be here soon, I imagine."

"And what part do you play in this ... ritual?"

Tiffany's face lit up. "I've been chosen for you to feed from after they kill you and you come back as a vampire."

Kailey's eyes narrowed. "You're happy about that?"

Tiffany smiled and blushed. Her overly sweet pitch worsened into a near fakeness that grated on one's nerves. "I'm eager to appease Flora. I'd do absolutely anything to make her happy. Oh, how I wish it were I she was turning. I've begged and pleaded for her to give me eternal youth, but to no avail. Apparently she doesn't think me worthy of the gift. I suppose she does know best, but I'd still do anything she requested, even give you every drop of my blood so you could be blessed by her with life eternal."

"Come off it, Tiffany! Your charade isn't fooling me. Deep down, you're one sick twisted bitch, aren't you?" Kailey said in an even tone.

Tiffany's eyes widened. She placed her hand against her chest and gasped.

Daft. Kailey rolled her eyes at the feigning gesture and wished she wasn't cuffed so she could smack some sense into the mesmerized young woman.

She half expected Tiffany to hand her some sort of proselyte tract for Nocturnal Trinity.

Tiffany rubbed her nose with the back of her hand. She was actually sniffling. "What? You don't think the offer of eternal youth is a great thing?"

"Take a good look at the bruises on my face. Raven did this to me and Flora was elated about it, so no, forgive me if I don't see becoming the likes of either of them as something wonderful."

"Raven did this to you?"

Kailey nodded.

"Why?"

"Because that's how deeply her jealousy is rooted."

Tiffany came closer and placed a gentle hand against Kailey's cheek. Kailey flinched and jerked her head back. "It's okay. I won't hurt you. Doing so would totally jeopardize any hope I have that Flora might change her mind and let me become part of their communion rather than the sacrificial meal. But, don't think I'm complaining. I'm not. I volunteered."

"You *volunteered* for me drink your blood?"

Tiffany nodded.

Kailey stared at Tiffany for several long moments. Over the past six months she had seen some bizarre things, but this ditzy girl ... she was a new kind of creepy. She wondered what was happening to society and why anyone would willingly sacrifice her life for something that offered no benefit at all, except death. The girl didn't seem suicidal, but was overly eager to let Kailey drain her blood and take her life.

"Flora's compelled you," Kailey said in a near whisper.

"Compelled? What ever do you mean?"

"She's taken control of your mind to make you offer yourself to me."

Tiffany shook her head. "No-o-o. I'm a willing soul. I have been since the long agonizing weeks when every evening I waited in line at Nocturnal Trinity until finally Flora *chose* me. I never felt more honored than the night she took my hand and led me away from my desperation. She made me a member."

Kailey cringed and shook her head, trying to stop the painful pitch of the girl's voice. *I'd rather hear a swarm of gnats whining in my ears ...*

Tears trickled down Tiffany's cheeks in spite of her broad smile. This poor girl viewed Nocturnal Trinity as some sort of church and being accepted as a member was salvation, or at least the path that led to eternal youth.

Acolytes are often the most naïve fools.

Kailey flexed her arms and pulled against the cuffs, even though she knew she didn't have the strength to break them. "I'll have you know the membership isn't worth the hype."

"You're a member?"

"Lifetime."

Tiffany laughed.

Kailey gave an incredulous stare. "What's funny about that?"

"You meant *eternal* membership, didn't you?"

"Actually, no. I revoked my membership."

Fury set in Tiffany's eyes. "Why would you do something so foolish?"

"It's not—"

"To be given such an honor only to trample it under your feet!" Spittle formed at the sides of Tiffany's mouth. She pointed a stern finger at Kailey. "Hundreds of people have hoped to one day have such a blessing to be recognized by the Founders. They crave it more than their next breath. How could you toss it aside as though it meant nothing?"

"Perhaps because I have better goals in life?"

Tiffany rushed toward Kailey and slapped her face hard.

Kailey winced in pain, her teeth rattling. She jerked forward, trying to break free. Fury shot through her. If she could get free ...

Tiffany took a step back, her mouth dropped open, and she placed both hands over her mouth as she gasped. Fear widened her eyes. She looked around the dark room and then back to Kailey. "I'm soooo sorry. I ... I, oh God, I'm sorry. Truly. I lost control."

Heat rose on the handprint welt on Kailey's left cheek. She tasted blood. Warmth trickled from her upper lip. Blood.

Tiffany dropped to her knees in front of Kailey, placed her hands on Kailey's knees, and looked into her eyes. Her fear wasn't of Kailey, but the coming repercussions for striking her. "Please forgive me? I didn't mean to—"

"Don't worry about it," Kailey said through gritted teeth. Although she shouldn't, Kailey actually felt sorry for the young lady. Apparently Tiffany had a lot of insecurities and emptiness in her life. That would explain why she had plunged every fiber of her being into seeking Flora's approval.

Tiffany rested her head on Kailey's lap and wrapped her arms around Kailey's waist. "I screwed things up."

"What do you mean?"

"Striking you. There's no way Flora will ever consider turning me now. I just don't understand it."

"What's to understand?"

"Why she'd force you to become like them but not turn me. I've done everything willingly from the very beginning. Everything they have ever requested, I've done without argument or a single complaint."

Kailey stared at the top of Tiffany's head and cringed. She didn't want to know the exact details of this girl's devotion.

Tiffany slid her hands from around Kailey, placed them upon Kailey's knees, and pushed back so she could look into Kailey's eyes. "Do you know why I've not gained Flora's favor?"

Because she's a heartless selfish bitch? Kailey bit her tongue to hold back the words. The girl was unhinged and Kailey didn't want struck again for saying something the girl would immediately cause Tiffany to take offense, especially since she wasn't able to defend herself.

Tiffany's eyes pleaded for an answer.

Kailey sighed. "Some people like to pursue those that play hard to get. Only I'm not playing. I don't want to be like them, nor do I want to associate with them. And since they know that, it has become their obsession to obtain me. Since you've never resisted and always complied, they have no need to hunt you. They consider you their own, albeit it *not* in a respectful way. They'd rather look for someone that presents a challenge. It's a cat and mouse type of game. Only I'm not timid and running anymore."

She scoffed at her own statement. *At the moment, I can't run anywhere!*

Tears crested in Tiffany's eyes. She sobbed and swallowed hard. Leaning back, she began unwrapping the scarf around her neck. "All I ever wanted was to be considered special by them. I thought I had proven that. See?"

Kailey sickened after Tiffany removed the scarf. The girl's neck was dark purple with several calloused bite marks where vampires had fed. Some of the bites had been severe and were more shredded tears than simple bites. How she'd not bled to death from those gashes was beyond Kailey's comprehension. There had to have been pain, which worried her because the girl must be a masochistic. The girl had never been compelled. She was certain of that now. How deep did her desperation for acceptance go?

Kailey bit her lip and tucked her chin to her chest to dissuade her gag reflex.

"See? I've been a good servant. Why won't you look at me? Is it the scars?"

Kailey offered a slight nod, but still refused to look toward her.

"Don't think me second rate because you won't be the first to drink from me. Look."

Kailey dared a glance.

Tiffany turned her head and exposed the other side of her throat. "See? No bites. If the other side bothers you, you can partake on the fresh side."

Kailey looked away. "I'd rather not take from any part."

Tiffany huffed and stamped one foot. "You'll change your mind. They all do. I just thought I'd receive the honor of what they're offering you."

"There's no offer to me. This is against my will. Forcing someone into submission isn't an honor for the unwilling party. Can't you see that?"

Tiffany stood and stared in pity at Kailey. "Afterwards, you'll see it differently. You'll understand why we envy you and why we long to become one of them. But I will consider my sacrifice an honor in its own right."

"Why? They don't care about you. Don't you understand that? They are self-serving. All the things you've done have meant nothing."

Tiffany looked hurt. Her haunted eyes studied Kailey.

"That's where you're wrong," Flora said in a cold voice, standing at the dark doorway. "She's proven her usefulness and tonight, she'll perform the greatest sacrifice ever."

A smaller form stepped around Flora and said, "But there'll be a lot of pain before you finally submit to the pleasure."

Raven.

$\mathcal{E}$va watched in horror as her daughter was knocked to the ground by the demon. She pushed herself partway up, but didn't have the strength to stand. Jaclyn wasn't moving. It was hard to discern if she was alive or dead, but she was no longer able to hold control over the zombies she had created.

Raine and Gillian turned from their trance-like states, apparently due to the loss of connection with Jaclyn. The zombies that had risen on this side of the portal were hobbling toward them. Raine and Gillian exchanged worried glances, uncertain of how to fend off the approaching undead.

Defending oneself with magic ahead of a battle or confrontation was preferred. Unexpected attacks prevented witches from rapidly dispelling an enemy, especially *undead* enemies. Since the zombies' new objective was attacking the living and not the demons, Jaclyn must not have incorporated a kill spell to override the resurrection spell in case she lost control. Had she done so, the zombies would have simply fallen to the ground as unmoving corpses again. Only pure arrogance in one's magical strength and abilities made a witch disregard her need for a nullification spell. Sadly, Jaclyn was *that* arrogant.

Eva usually worked her spells days ahead of time. Jaclyn did the same and Eva could only speculate the other two witches followed the same agenda since the look of terror in their eyes meant they had no magical defense to call upon.

Eva sighed and shook her head. *The naivety of our youth.*

Being too weak to stand, she flung her hand toward the zombies in hope to at least draw their attention away from Gillian and Raine, and that was when the wave of bright light flashed from the portal door and washed across the tunnel in one harsh moment. The burst of light numbed her entire body, disorienting her. Afterwards, she couldn't see anything for several long minutes. It was the most helpless she had ever felt in her life, and she feared she had been blinded for the remainder of her life.

After her blindness subsided, she had expected to find the witches dead. Instead, the zombies lay on the ground as smoldering ashes. Jaclyn was still sprawled on the ground while Gillian and Raine sat huddled together with their arms wrapped around one another.

Eva weakly crawled to Jaclyn and lay face-to-face with her. Jaclyn was breathing, so she was alive. A large bruise had grown on her temple. Eva pressed a hand to her daughter's cheek.

Where did we go wrong? Why are we so equally stubborn?

Jaclyn blinked. Her eyelashes fluttered. Recognition fixed in her gaze, and Jaclyn hurriedly pushed herself into a seated position. "Mother, what happened?"

"You were knocked unconscious by a demon," Eva replied.

Jaclyn quickly peered around. "And after that?"

"I'm not certain what took place, other than a bright burst of light flashed."

Jaclyn stood, slightly wobbled, and once she had steadied herself, she extended her hand to Eva. "Where are Kailey and the others?"

"I don't know. I was too concerned about you to notice."

Jaclyn looked into her mother's eyes. For the first time in years Jaclyn's eyes softened with compassion at her mother. The rigid coldness and resentment Jaclyn had clung to faded. Her daughter embraced her fiercely.

Gillian and Raine joined them.

"Now what?" Raine asked.

Eva glanced toward the portal door. "Perhaps we should investigate what lies on the other side of the threshold? Maybe that's where everyone else has gone."

"What about those demons?" Gillian asked.

Three of the demons walked around aimlessly; their eyes melted inside their eye sockets.

"For the moment, they're harmless," Eva replied. "I'm sure one of the others will tend to them soon."

"Provided everyone is still alive," Jaclyn said, eyeing the door.

CHAPTER 60

Flora extended her arms and looked at Tiffany. "Come to me, my pet."

Tiffany smiled, hurrying into Flora's arms. Flora hugged her tightly.

"Pathetic," Kailey said.

"What?" Flora replied. "You think I've compelled her?"

Kailey shook her head. "No, I'm certain she's not. Just overly needy."

"I've found no other more devoted than she," Flora said, gently rubbing Tiffany's back.

"It's frightening to think she's so blindly devoted and foolish enough to offer her life for your ritual."

Tiffany sobbed against Flora's chest. "She doesn't appreciate my offer. She's repulsed by me."

"There, there," Flora said, shushing in her ear. Flora's eyes narrowed as she stared at Kailey. "She's about to learn her place, dear. If only all servants were as devoted as you."

"Yes," Kailey said. "Self-sacrificial could wipe out your population rather quickly."

"She's not a vampire."

Kailey nodded. "Because you don't find her worthy enough?"

Tiffany glanced toward Kailey with hurt in her eyes and then peered up to Flora.

"Don't listen to her, child," Flora said in a soothing tone. "She knows *nothing* of your worth."

Tiffany rested her head against Flora's chest, but the look in her eyes indicated that Kailey had planted enough seeds of doubt to cause the young lady to question everything about Flora and her need for Tiffany in the ritual.

"So, lover," Raven said, crossing her arms and staring intently into Kailey's eyes. "We've got some catching up to do."

"We've never been lovers."

"No, you saw to that and you missed out. But now, we can be. You know I can make you. I can make you *beg* for me."

"Compulsion? Really? You'd resort to that? I guess you understand just how much I detest you that you'd have to mind-rape me into having a relationship with you because there's no other way you'd ever win my affection. That indicates that you cannot find a lover apart from using your vampire knack."

Raven's face darkened. Her eyes glistened like wet obsidian. "Careful, your succubus bitch isn't here to rescue you this time."

Kailey laughed softly because even though the statement was true, a slight edge of fear brought a small level of uncertainty to Raven. Her eyes nervously glanced around the darker corners of the room. That was the good thing about having a friend that was a demon. She could pop up at any moment and Raven realized it. The only downside was that Cassie didn't know where Kailey had been taken.

Even though Kailey trembled inside, she tried to maintain a hardened exterior, which was why she responded with her own taunting words and challenged them. Besides, she was restrained to the chair. She had no way to run, and she wasn't going to give Raven and Flora the satisfaction of seeing her cower.

Hell, if I'm going to die, I might as well go out looking like I'm brave, right?

After several moments of quietly scanning the room, Raven's condescending smile returned.

Kailey frowned and wanted to wipe the smirk off Raven's face. She tightened her fists and flexed her arms. Her anger sought to find a way to break free, but not to flee. In spite of how badly Raven had beaten Kailey in the ring, nearly killing her, Kailey wanted revenge. She wanted another shot. She understood that Raven was more powerful, but Kailey simply didn't care. She had gotten some good hits on Raven before Raven's rage took over. Kailey believed she had inflicted enough damage to cause Raven to become a little more leery. But she needed Raven to remove the restraints. To do that it really wouldn't take too much prodding to succeed. As deeply as Raven's hostility festered, Raven wanted to hurt Kailey.

"Waiting for your succubus to rescue you?" Raven asked.

"Sure, you have the upper hand since I'm cuffed to this chair. Did it pleasure you to cuff me while I was helpless and unconscious? You must really fear me since you've gone to this much trouble to keep me from fighting back. It's real brave of you to make your snide comments when you know I cannot get up."

"Oh, I can release you—"

Flora left Tiffany at the door, glided past Raven and held up her hand to silence Raven. "Girls! Enough with the lashing out at one another. You've shown enough pettiness between yourselves. You need to resolve your differences now. You cannot possibly coexist with immortality as you are right now."

Raven pouted her thick lips.

Kailey stared at her former best friend and roommate. She found absolutely nothing appealing about Raven. *Nothing.* A year ago she'd have never thought being in the same room with Raven would disgust her. But she was sickened to her stomach by looking at her.

"Can you two make amends?" Flora asked.

"I don't want any part of your offer for immortality or to ever coexist with *her*," Kailey said. "She hates me as much as I hate her. My fading bruises should indicate how much she detests me. So why are you forcing us to be together and insistent on having me turned?"

"It is what Raven has requested," Flora said.

Raven beamed a bright patronizing smile.

Kailey frowned. "Well, Raven can go screw herself!"

Contempt flashed in Raven's eyes. In a moment she had crossed the room, nothing more than a blur, clutched a hand around Kailey's throat, and squeezed. Raven's long hard nails pressed into the softness of Kailey's skin. Raven's glance flicked from Kailey's eyes and focused on her lips. She leaned down without loosening her tight grip and licked the blood off Kailey's lips before stealing a short kiss. "I can rip your throat out right now."

Kailey's heartbeat hammered in her ears. Breathing was almost impossible. Her cheeks flushed red. She glared and spit at Raven. "Then do it, you damned bitch!"

The murderous look in Raven's eyes was darker than any time before. Kailey took a sharp breath, realizing her boldness had far overreached its boundaries. Raven was going to kill her. There was no mistaking her intent. Before Raven could act upon her exploding rage, she was hurled across the room and smacked the wall hard with enough force that any mere human would have died. Flora glared down at Kailey and thrust a stiff finger in her face. Kailey flinched and wished she hadn't.

"Enough!" Flora glanced toward Raven and gave a simple nod. Raven brushed herself off and hurried out the door like a scolded child.

Flora had saved Kailey's life, but Kailey knew it was only to prolong her agony until they sacrificed her. No amount of thanks would be accepted by Flora as gratitude, and Kailey couldn't mouth the words anyway, even if she wanted. Her distaste toward the elder vampiress remained bitter and always would. No love lost. Kailey would rather be dead than feel indebted to any vampire.

"Flora, I want no part of your ritual. Let me go."

"I cannot."

"And why not? There's more to this than simply Raven wanting me turned. So spit it out!"

"Aren't you the petulant little brat? Trying to give me orders?" Flora's eyes turned a frigid icy-blue. "You forget who's in charge here."

"Don't forget that you're alive because I begged Forrest to spare you."

"I imagine you regret that decision now, don't you?"

"More than you'll ever know."

Flora shrugged. "Hindsight always magnifies our obvious mistakes. But we wouldn't even be in this situation had you left well enough alone."

"Is that what this is all about? Still? You want to turn me into a vampire because I avenged my brother's murder? Seems you drew first blood and are pissed that it bit you in the ass."

"You destroyed *everything*!" Flora hissed. Her nostrils flared. Her delicate hands turned into tight fists. For a moment her countenance was broken, revealing the evil aged monster beneath her veil of youth and beauty.

Kailey tried not to flinch at Flora's true hideousness. "How did I ruin everything?"

"Our sanctuary, Nocturnal Trinity, is gone forever. What we treasured is gone. You destroyed it by dragging the filth of those werewolf mongrels across our threshold and forcing our allegiance to them. So, yes, turning you into a vampire *is* my punishment for you. It is my payback. It's to prove how much more powerful I am than you and your werewolf friends are. Even Cassie cannot help you now and I dare her to try." Flora gave a nervous side-glance as she spoke the last challenge. It seemed both she and

Raven expected Cassie to appear and both were worried what might happen if she did.

Oh, God ... Goddess, if you're here Cassie, now's a good time to intervene.

A smirk formed on Kailey's face. "You forget one thing."

"What's that?"

"Forrest will never stop until he kills you."

Flora smiled. "After this evening, Forrest will never slay another vampire. It's well past time that he paid his dues. He's been a thorn in my family's side for generations."

Kailey felt uneasy about Flora's response. If they did kill Forrest, his death was on her. She had pleaded for Forrest to spare Flora, not realizing at the time exactly how heartless vampires really were. "How do you plan to stop him?"

Flora reared her head back and released a long fit of laughter. Pure elation. When her laughter finally ceased, she said, "The witches might have sided with the werewolves, but don't forget the demons are on our side. We have called upon one of the behemoths to aid us in assassinating Forrest. He has agreed but in return we owe him. We have to open a summoning portal to unite him with his small army of demons."

Kailey grinned and shook her head. "We know all about that. We've scrubbed away Andreas' blood to stop the summoning."

A haughty grin spread on Flora's lips. "Did you forget that we have our own summoning circle right here beneath Nocturnal Trinity? You have seen it as I recall and it has since been repaired."

Her eyes widened. *I'm in the cellar of the nightclub?*

Flora tapped into her thoughts and grinned. "You are."

She had wondered where they had taken her. "From what I recall, it takes the aid of the witches to activate the portal. They're busy elsewhere."

"That's one way," Flora replied. "However, there is another alternative. One I favor over the other."

"Like what?"

"Blood sacrifices, dear." The gleam in Flora's eyes was most disturbing. "We simply need to sacrifice a few people to activate the portal and summon the behemoth's army. We have brought some people to sacrifice for that very purpose. Once we have done that, Forrest and everyone else you hold dear will cease to live. The behemoth will kill them all."

Kailey swallowed hard.

"Raven!" Flora craned her neck, looking over her shoulder.

Raven shoved a terrified Luna through the door. Her mouth was gagged and her hands tied behind her back. Black streaks of running mascara lined Luna's cheeks from her tears. Her ragged breaths blew strands of mucus out her nose. She looked like she had been crying for a long time.

Flora smiled. "We need to sacrifice the blood of a witch and we've chosen a couple more to offer as well."

Raven shoved Micah and Ashley through the door. Raven forced them to kneel. The chains that bound their wrists were made from some type of black metal.

How had she managed to restrain both of them? Werewolves had the strength to break any metal restraint except silver, and silver would be blistering their flesh. Why were they bound and unable to escape?

"They've all been waiting for your arrival. Like I said, there's a price to pay for the coercive unification to our Order. While you had a hand in it, Micah's far guiltier than you. It was his master plan, however, pitting himself against a true master like myself and my siblings was his most foolish scheme ever. His head shall be a trophy on my wall. Perhaps displayed above the bar as a warning to any other filthy mongrels that enter Nocturnal Trinity. Of course his head will have to be taken while he's still in his beast form, otherwise the police would never leave us alone, even those officers who have devoted themselves to our cause. You can't put a normal man's head on the wall."

Kailey glanced at Micah. He didn't seem to notice her and looked hypnotized. *What did they do to you?*

Raven took a silver knife and pressed it against Luna's throat. "You know how much I dislike this witch, don't you?"

Luna swallowed hard and stared at Kailey in pure terror.

"She's never done anything to you!" Kailey gritted her teeth and yanked at the restraints.

"She was annoyance enough," Raven replied. "And when the time is right, I'm going to enjoy slitting her throat and spilling her blood."

"Raven, you can't," Kailey said, leaning forward in the chair and pulling against the cuffs.

"Watch me," Raven said. She eased the tip of the blade across Luna's neck just shallow enough to cause a narrow line of blood to leak through her skin. Raven ran her tongue across the laceration. Luna winced. Raven scrunched her nose and turned to spit. "Yuck! Reeks of garlic and airheadedness."

Flora turned toward Raven. "Enough with the taunting games. We have a ritual to prepare for."

CHAPTER 61

Forrest stood and held Penelope in his arms.

Sauriel placed a hand upon her head and lifted the other upward. The rest of the onlookers stood in silence, waiting to see what the angel planned to do.

Sauriel swept a quick glance at each person's face before finally resting his gaze upon Forrest. "It's essential for all of you to know that once I've brought her back, my angelic powers and strength will cease for a while. I will become too weak to assist you."

"How long will you lose your power?" Cassie asked.

"Days? Weeks?" Sauriel said softly. "There's no accurate way to predict the length of time."

Brady said, "Look, I don't mean to rush things, but they took Kailey and Luna. They have Micah and Ashley already. Jacob and I can head to Nocturnal Trinity now and wait for Forrest and the rest of you—"

"You cannot enter Nocturnal Trinity," Sauriel said to Brady. "They will be expecting you, so they will be armed with silver bullets."

"I can go instead," Cassie said.

"Cassie, you cannot face them alone. The urgency of the situation is great, but it will take more than you to rescue them," Sauriel said.

Blaze ran a hand through his hair. "If Raven has Luna, she'll torture her to death. She hates Luna."

"She hates Kailey, too," Cassie said.

"Let's remain calm and rational and take this one step at a time," Sauriel said. "It's not been that long since they've taken them. If they wanted to kill them immediately, they would have done so. They wouldn't have taken them."

Blaze frowned. "Yeah, thus the torture part."

Sauriel stared at Blaze firmly. "Please? Everyone, give me a few minutes of silence."

"Listen to him," Forrest said. "Believe me, Penelope can help us rescue them, and it will be us who tortures Flora and Raven."

Blaze, Jacob, and Brady shoved their hands into their pockets and walked away. The others exchanged silent glances. Forrest didn't like having them wait. He understood their impatience, and their aggravation was justified.

Sauriel closed his eyes, placed both hands upon Penelope's head, and sang in a language that few humans had ever heard. The purity of his resonance brought tears to everyone's eyes. They sobbed, falling to their knees without resistance. Even Jacob, Brady, and Blaze were not immune. Cassie curled on the ground, hugging her knees.

Forrest trembled, holding Penelope in his arms. A pure white light glowed around Sauriel's hands. Warmth cascaded from the angel. Forrest was unable to look away. He watched the glowing light on Kailey's forehead. Her eyelids fluttered, and she began to blink. Hot tears leaked from Forrest's eyes. A few seconds later, the light faded, and Penelope's brow furrowed as she examined her surroundings.

Then she looked into Forrest's eyes and a slight smile came to her lips. "Forrest?"

Sauriel's wings withered and faded. He returned to his human appearance of Father Charles. Drained of his strength, he staggered. Jacob and Brady caught him and supported his weight until they were able to help him to an old bench.

"Forrest," Penelope said. "Is it really you?"

He nodded. "It's me."

She frowned, placing a hand to his cheek. "You look so different."

"It's been a while."

"No more than a few months," she said, frowning. "A year at most?"

"Try over one hundred years."

Forrest lowered her so she could stand. She held fast to his arm to steady herself.

"Impossible," Penelope replied.

"I'm afraid he's telling you the truth," Cassie said, wiping tears from her eyes and slowly rising to her feet. She was still in her succubus form.

Penelope yanked a dagger from its sheath on her belt. She attempted to rush at Cassie, but Forrest wrapped his arms around her waist. "What are you doing, Forrest? She's a demon!"

"She's also a friend."

Penelope's head turned sharply. She glared at Forrest. "What? You've befriended this … this demon?"

"I know this is a bit premature, Forrest," Cassie said. "But based upon my first impression, I'm not too fond of your girlfriend."

"She is on our side, Penelope," Forrest said. "She's fighting with us."

Hurt and betrayal reflected in Penelope's eyes and her facial expressions. She tucked the knife into its sheath. She simply shook her head, thinking. After a minute or so, she spoke in her thick accent and said, "I simply cannot believe this, Forrest. How would you take the news had I befriended a vampire? Would you be offended?"

"It's a different thing altogether."

"Perhaps in your view."

Ian and Gunner stood nearby, still in their Were-otter forms. Gunner smiled but his gnarled teeth didn't look like a smile at all. Only those who knew Gunner understood it to be his smile. One could readily mistake it for a snarl. Gunner realized the misinterpretation, so he offered an overly enthusiastic wave.

"And what is that bizarre creature?" Penelope asked.

"These are all friends," Forrest said, waving his hand toward everyone else in the room.

"You sure pick a homely lot to associate with."

"In my line of work, you cannot get too choosy," he replied. "Look, you've been kept inside this time portal for more than a century. What is the last thing you recall?"

One of the few remaining blinded demons staggered along the curved wall of the rail tunnel. She grabbed her bow off the ground and pulled an arrow from the quiver, lined it up, and then hesitated. "That's not a friend of yours, too, is it?"

Forrest grinned. "No."

She released the bowstring. The arrow zipped through the air, pierced through its skull, and dropped the demon. "How is it even possible that I've been kept here over a hundred years and don't remember it?"

"Magic sealed you inside some sort of barrier that somehow prevented demons like the one you just shot from reaching you. You don't remember being frozen inside the chamber?"

She shook her head. "No. I don't."

"What's the last thing you do remember?"

"Killing a behemoth," she replied. She pointed to the dead demons along the ground. "Those were his soldiers."

Cassie edged closer, leery of Penelope. "May I ask how you managed to kill the behemoth?"

Penelope looked up and down the succubus' seductive physique. Her mouth hung open for several seconds before she flicked her gaze to Forrest. "What sort of … *friendship* do you have with this demon, Forrest?"

Forrest was appalled. "Nothing like that!"

"Oh, God no!" Cassie said. "Strictly platonic."

"Have things changed so drastically over the century that humans are befriending demons now?" Penelope asked, ignoring the question.

"Demons are like humans," Forrest said. "Some are evil and some are good."

"And you're going with that theory?" she asked. Her eyebrows rose as she awaited his answer.

"It's true," he replied.

"I'm certain that's what they'd like for humans to believe. I suppose the guise is quite popular for you to be carrying on with the likes of her."

"Hey!" Cassie said, glaring at Penelope with crimson fiery eyes. She pointed a firm finger at Forrest. "You might explain to her that I risked my life to help you save her! First impressions—" She turned and stormed off.

"Hostility's every bit a demon's," Penelope said.

"You offended her," Forrest said. "What do you expect?"

"I expected …" She sighed. "The Forrest I knew was far different. He'd have never befriended a demon."

"The Forrest you knew was a child. I was only nine years old when we met. I looked like a man but I was still a child."

She stared incredulously at him. "Is that true?"

"Why would I lie to you?"

"You never revealed it to me then."

"Would it have mattered?"

Penelope shrugged. "Perhaps not. But I can tell by looking in your eyes that you've hardened over the years. You're colder. The warmth I recall is no longer there."

Forrest sighed and looked down. "I know. But with what I've done during my lifetime, it was destined. The more undead one kills, the heavier it weighs upon the soul."

"Forrest," Brady said with a pleading look. "We don't have time."

Forrest nodded. "Penelope, some vampires have taken our friends, even one of my family members, and a behemoth is behind it. What Cassie asked you is important. How did you kill the behemoth?"

Penelope patted her belt and then she looked around. "I used a blade. A short sword."

"Gunner!" Forrest said, waving him over.

"What the hell is that thing?"

"A dear friend who saved my life not long after you left for Seattle, right after my father was killed."

"I see." Sadness filled her eyes. "Your father was killed after we parted ways?"

"Just a few days after." Forrest nodded and then quickly looked away. "That's a discussion for another time."

"Sure."

Gunner offered a goofy toothy smile as he walked to them.

"Show her the blade," Forrest said.

Gunner untucked it from his belt and presented it with both hands.

Penelope nodded. "That's it. The Wrath-bone."

Forrest frowned. "You named it?"

"It was given to me by another Demon-hunter when I first reached Seattle, just moments before his death. It's what I used to kill the behemoth. Nothing else I had tried even scratched it. But this blade cut through its tough skin and pierced deeply. When I yanked the blade out, black blood gushed out in a spraying stream. Apparently the behemoth was unable to heal from the injury and bled to death. The last thing I recall after that was the other five behemoths shrieking fierce commands and charging at me with all of their soldiers. I should have died." She looked slightly confused and a bit sad as her mind retraced her memories. "I shouldn't even be here. How did you bring me back?"

Forrest wrapped his huge arms around her and hugged her tightly. "Those details we'll save for later. Right now, we need to rescue some people and kill some demons and slay some vampires."

CHAPTER 62

Forrest picked up his Hunter box he had left near the stairs of the underground rail station. Penelope walked beside him. The others weren't far behind as Forrest led the way up the stairs. At the top, Lydia stood there with three men. Their gazes were almost as cold as hers.

None of them bothered to step aside. They simply stood blocking the exit. Penelope placed her hand on Forrest's forearm.

Forrest eyed Lydia. "I thought maybe you had left Seattle."

"And miss all the fun?" she replied.

"How'd you know I was here?"

Lydia took out her cellphone and grinned. A map of Seattle covered the screen. A red dot blinked where they stood. "I placed a tracker inside your coat pocket."

"Oh? Why's that?" he asked, frowning.

"Since you don't have a cellphone, I had to have some way to find you. You might reconsider joining the technological age before we enter something even more advanced."

"I assume these men are part of your—"

"Group," Lydia said quickly. "Yes, they are. So have you decided when you're going after the vampires?"

"Right now," he replied.

Lydia noticed Penelope clinging to Forrest's arm and gave him a questioning glance. "Still finding new recruits?"

"This is Penelope."

"The young lady you last saw before the Great Fire?"

He nodded.

"What's the holdup?" Brady asked in an agitated voice.

"Lydia, we are pressed for time," Forrest said. "The vampires have Kailey and Luna, the werewolf pack leader and his alpha female. We're fairly certain the vampires plan to kill them."

Lydia gave an even smile. "Why didn't you say so? We're more than eager to join you."

She turned and her three companions backed out of the entrance to let her and the others pass.

"Brady and Jacob cannot go in with us," Forrest said. "Silver bullets or daggers can kill them."

"While that might be," Brady said with anger in his voice, "we cannot abandon Micah and Ashley. They are part of our pack. They are our family."

Jacob nodded.

Forrest spoke through gritted teeth. "He *is* my family. Since we now have the weapon that can kill the behemoth, it's essential that I go."

"Forrest, you need our help to succeed," Brady said.

Forrest sighed. "If you get shot with silver bullets, you'll die. Then you'll be no use to us at all. You know they will be prepared to take all of you out."

Brady nodded. Jacob bore his teeth and his eyes darkened.

Lydia looked at Brady. "Their bullets can kill any of you, but they won't us." She uncrossed her arms and placed her hands on two holstered 9mm pistols. The three men with her showed their weapons. On the surface these men appeared as normal as any other man. They certainly didn't look to be fighters. Of course, most werewolves fell into that description, too.

A slight smile broke Lydia's stony face.

"Your guns won't hurt that demon," Penelope said.

Lydia flicked her cold gaze to the Demon-hunter. "The guns are for any others who get in our way."

Penelope looked uneasy and glanced toward Forrest with questioning eyes.

Forrest nodded. "Things are about to get bloody."

"She's talking about killing innocent people," Penelope said.

"If I'm forced to shoot anyone," Lydia said, "the person won't be innocent."

Penelope's brow furrowed.

Forrest regarded her with disappointment. "I hate to tell you this, but society today has a lot more corrupt evil people than when you and I knew each other years ago."

"The world is that bad?" she asked with tears forming in her eyes.

"I'm afraid it is."

"Then I wish you had left me sealed in whatever had confined me. I'd hate to believe the world has fallen to such a state of depravity."

"Believe it, sister," Lydia and Cassie said simultaneously before grinning slyly at one another.

"What has made the world such an evil place? Is it because other Demon-hunters like myself have been imprisoned?" Penelope asked.

"Don't even start to blame demons," Cassie said. Her eyes blazed.

"What else am I supposed to accuse?"

"Evil exists because of the vile spirits that influence both human and demons," Sauriel said. "Every creature with a conscious makes the decision on whether to follow evil or follow righteous behavior."

"But I thought—"

"Things are not what we had believed for so long," Forrest said.

Sauriel unlocked his car and opened the driver's door. "Brady and Jacob, you two know the risks of going to the nightclub."

"We do," Brady said. "But getting to Kailey, Micah, and Ashley is going to require all of us working together."

"I wish you'd reconsider," Sauriel said.

"Brady, you might want to take his warning to heart," Forrest said. "Your pack is getting smaller as it is."

Lydia opened the back hatch of a red Jeep Cherokee. "I have something that will help you two."

"What?" Brady asked, looking her direction.

She held up two Kevlar vests and smiled.

Brady took them and smiled broadly.

"It won't make you invincible though," Lydia said.

"That brings a whole new slant to being *armored to the teeth*," Brady said.

"Like she said, Brady, it doesn't totally protect you," Forrest said.

"I know, but our wolf senses will aid us, too."

Sauriel placed a gentle hand upon Forrest's shoulder. "Since I'm unable to offer any further assistance, I will wait at the cathedral where I will be steadfast in prayer."

A smile parted Forrest's beard. "I'm forever indebted to you for bringing Penelope back to me."

"Your debt is God, not me," Sauriel said with a slight grin. "Do not forget that."

"Then while you're praying, let Him know of my thanks."

"You can do that yourself."

"After all of this is over, I will."

Kailey sat handcuffed to the heavy metal chair. Rather than release her and move her to the portal room, they had carried her on the chair. If her life was not in grave danger, she might have taken the time to gloat because she had been correct. Raven feared any possibility of retaliation from Kailey even by letting her free for only a few moments, and apparently, Flora held some reservations about such a risk, too, which seemed odd since Flora was an ancient vampire. Perhaps they both still worried that Cassie was hidden in the shadows.

Several lit torches flickered on each wall. The large symbol on the floor beneath her was identical to the one that hung over the front entrance of the nightclub and in every dance hall and bar as well. She couldn't find any traces of where the werewolves had previously invaded on the night that Nicodemus died and Raven had become a vampire. This was where Skye had sacrificed herself to keep Raven from dissolving into dust after Nicodemus was slain. Even Skye's love for Raven had been misguided, as had Kailey's.

Micah and Ashley had been outstretched and tied to wooden X crosses. She wasn't certain, but they must have been drugged with something quite powerful as neither acknowledged her presence or the fact that they were being restrained and about to be sacrificed. She didn't understand how Micah had allowed the vampires to overpower him and Ashley. In retrospect, however, Micah had not made the keenest observations or decisions and had ignored all warnings from Brady, Forrest, and the others about abandoning his quest to incorporate the werewolves into the Circle of Unity, which was far too divided to ever unite.

Fear seized Kailey's heart. *Where's Luna?*

Tiffany's hands were bound together and tied above her head. The former eagerness she had held earlier about being Kailey's first meal had faded. She appeared fatigued and overly glum. Her nervousness widened her eyes, and her complexion was even paler. "You were right. They didn't care about me or what I had willingly contributed to their cause. None at all."

"I told you that vampires are heartless. Discovering the truth now is a bit late, don't you think?" Kailey asked.

"We're going to die, aren't we?"

Kailey frowned at her. "That's a pretty solid *given*. You already volunteered to die, so don't bitch about it now. As I recall you considered it an honor."

"It would have been grand, if Flora would have recognized my loving gift to further her cause, but—"

"I warned you."

Tiffany tilted her head backwards, staring up at the cobwebs on the ceiling. She wept. Her body shook from the heavy sobs.

Kailey rolled her eyes and shook her head. If the girl wanted sympathy from her, she didn't have any to offer. Sometimes stupidity far exceeded one's rationality. Tiffany was a poster child for dumb, but pointing it out was useless. No doubt she'd give Kailey a blank stare because an explanation wouldn't register. It also didn't matter if Kailey offered sympathy and tried to coax Tiffany into believing everything was going to be all right. At this moment, Kailey couldn't even convince herself of that lingering hope.

Tiffany sobbed and shook while standing on tiptoes. Slowly she lowered her head, but the tears had been faked. The crying was a ruse. Her eyes held coldness similar to Flora's, and for a moment Kailey believed Flora was watching her through Tiffany's eyes. Her eyes suddenly narrowed like an enraged animal. "You don't deserve what they're offering you. You certainly aren't worthy to drink my blood. You should be standing here waiting for me to suck you dry. They should be turning me into a vampire. *Not* you!"

Laughter came from the girl's mouth. Her frightening lunacy was not an act. The poor girl was twisted inside, unhinged, and had probably been so long before she had become one of Flora's deranged pets. Her mental fragileness was most likely the reason why Flora refused to turn the girl. Feral vampires were difficult enough to control when they first awakened as an undead. She couldn't imagine how Tiffany's bent mind would magnify once she turned into a vampire and Flora sought to rein her back in. Flora was old enough and wise enough to be choosy in whom she picked to become vampires. She apparently sensed how deranged this girl was and flatly refused to ever let Tiffany join the vampire coven. But that was the closest Kailey could ever come to giving Flora any sort of valid compliment.

Tiffany's laughter ceased. She tilted her head to the side and peered blankly at Kailey, becoming deathly still; like she had gone into deep slumber with her eyes wide open.

Kailey looked away. She feared looking into the girl's eyes for too long. Even though insanity wasn't contagious, she didn't want to risk the possibility that Flora might somehow still be able to compel Kailey through Tiffany's eyes.

But Flora wasn't controlling Tiffany. Kailey held no doubts about that. Flora was able to read Kailey's thoughts whenever she chose to, so Flora must know how unbalanced Tiffany was. Kailey also believed Flora was glad Tiffany had volunteered to be the blood offering for Kailey, just to rid Nocturnal Trinity of the disturbed girl. After all, the nightclub had an image it wished to portray to the city of Seattle. Mental deficiencies were common amongst their guests, but it wasn't a quality they wanted shining like an obvious beacon to those more reserved. The vampires wanted their clientele to attract and appease a ritzy society where people might *act* crazy, but not actually *exhibit* crazy.

Kailey scooted to the edge of the chair, which was the limit of distance the cuffs allowed. She strained her neck while looking around the room for Luna. As best she could tell, Luna was not here. Her stomach ached from sudden sickness and worry. She knew Raven hated Luna, and Kailey feared what Raven might do to the young witch.

Kailey had no way to alert the others of where she had been taken and what was about to take place. They had helped Father Charles scrub the bloody symbols off the walls to slow the coming of the demons, but had that been in vain? From what she understood, this was the portal Flora and the behemoth actually intended to use. Where the symbol had been broken, she noticed its obvious repaired. The welded metal was different than the aged symbol. They seemed fairly certain the repair would work. And even if it didn't, the portal didn't need to work for Flora and Raven to bite Kailey and convert her to the life of a living undead vampire.

She couldn't picture such a life. She'd rather stake herself than drink human blood. The thought of biting Tiffany's throat and devouring the girl's blood sickened her. She didn't think the need for blood could override the repulsion she held toward the rite of passage new vampires took. And if she were wrong—she didn't want to become a vampire.

The scent of burning sulfur permeated the dank room. The pungent odor made her cough, and she wished she could cover her nose and mouth. The smell indicated one thing: the behemoth was nearby. Whether it was only the one or all five, she didn't know, nor did it matter. One behemoth was quite powerful in its own right, and she was defenseless, bound or otherwise.

The floor shook. Dust and debris broke loose from the ceiling and rained downward. She closed her eyes and tilted her head downward to prevent any of it from getting into her eyes. The floor rattled after another thunderous step, which indicated the demon was approaching.

"Are you ready for your initiation, Kailey?" Flora asked, suddenly standing beside her. "The night has approached swiftly. The time for our ceremony to welcome you to our fold is about to begin."

Kailey dared to open her eyes. While looking down to the floor, she noticed the royal blue hem of Flora's elegant dress. Slowly she craned her head upward with the harshest glare she could offer.

Flora laughed softly. "Oh, dear, you can thank me later. You don't need to reply now. Believe me, the look on your face is already thanks enough. Raven has a special surprise for you."

Kailey glanced away from Flora and toward two shadowy figures moving toward the portal. Her anger drained and was replaced by horror.

Raven stood with a dagger pressed to Luna's throat. Luna showed no fear, no resistance. Her mesmerized eyes signified she had been compelled. By Raven or Flora? It really didn't matter. Three of Kailey's friends were here, but none of them could speak or offer any assistance to attempt an escape. And she was as vulnerable and helpless as they.

The situation was far uglier than Kailey had ever imagined. The ground shook again. Through the doorway the massive thickness of the behemoth's leg came into view. She had yet to see its face and already she trembled. Things were about to get bad. Really bad.

CHAPTER 63

Forrest rode in the passenger seat of Brady's squad car. Penelope rode in the backseat. The lights flashed but the siren was off as they sped to Nocturnal Trinity. No need to alert others with the harsh wailing siren.

Traffic was nil, at least along this side street, and the need for the flashing lights wasn't even necessary. Forrest wondered if Brady was using them strictly out of habit or if the lights were somehow encouragement of his sworn duty to protect and serve.

Lydia and her team followed behind the squad car in her Jeep. Father Charles, or rather Sauriel, was driving the others to the nightclub in his car.

Forrest frowned as Brady drove, but not from anger. Though he wasn't pleased about the hostages Flora had taken, his mind drifted more to his surprise of seeing the angel after more than a century. He had almost allowed their first meeting to fade completely from his memories, when he should not have.

While it was true that Sauriel had offered his assistance long ago and prevented Forrest from a premature death, Forrest still refused to yield himself to any deity in spite of obvious miracles. Even now, after Penelope's release and their reunion, Forrest remained bitter about the loss of his mother and his father while he was only a young boy. Who else could he blame, other than God? It wasn't that Forrest denied God existed. He denied that he'd ever kneel because he viewed his entire life of vampire hunting as a curse. The loss of those he had treasured dearest prevented him from forgiving the One supposedly in charge of people's destinies.

Their untimely deaths had livened his rage to kill the undead. Oftentimes, he deliberately placed himself into situations where he hoped his death would find him. When the dreariest times shadowed him and he could see no possible way to survive, he had been spared. Not always victoriously, but for an angel to intervene meant that a higher power had proven that Forrest wasn't totally in charge. He didn't necessarily wish to believe that God had exerted His divine control over Forrest, but Forrest often despised the fact that he was still alive. He was being kept alive strictly to serve the purpose of slaying the undead, which was why he part of why he refused to live because he hoped by not doing so, he'd meet his fate. But as of now, death was still outside of his grasp. Constant misery was the unkind blanket nestled around him.

He wondered whether a person could step so far outside of God's reach that no hope for redemption existed?

Penelope had mentioned that he wasn't the same person she had known, which had been a great fear of his if ever their paths crossed again. He couldn't deny the truth, and he wholeheartedly agreed with her assumption. She was only the same because she had been frozen in the past and unable to move forward. No doubt she would have been forced to make decisions that might have cost innocent people their lives. He had.

Did he have regrets? Of course, but he buried them deep inside and kept traveling the world seeking to slay the undead they feasted in the night.

A couple of times Forrest glanced into the rearview mirror to look at Penelope. She was still as beautiful as he remembered. More so, it seemed, because an aging mind ceased to recall vivid details over time. Images dulled or blurred, giving only a trace of the countenance the heart held dear.

Penelope maintained the innocence from the past where he had first encountered her while they traveled through the snowy mountain passes. Although the majority of her purity was intact, her eyes studied her new surroundings with awe and questions. Things had definitely changed since she had been entombed in the strange cold goo.

Being inside the moving patrol car frightened her. She watched uneasily as the buildings and trees passed by in a blur. Unlike Forrest, she had not witnessed the growing age of technology and the slow evolution from horse-drawn carriages to the first gas engine vehicle. She had not seen airplanes. Everything was foreign to her, and well it should be. The streetlights and the brilliantly colored skylights of buildings captured her attention.

She held to her bow tightly; her knuckles white. Her eyes darted, taking in her surroundings. Her boldness that he recalled seemed greatly overwhelmed by her intense curiosity. Time had propelled forward. She had not. He wanted to help bring her up to speed, but he couldn't. Her mind needed to absorb and sort everything in its own timeframe, if she possibly could.

Penelope's brow creased, and she flicked her gaze from the window and met Forrest's eyes in the mirror. Her haunted eyes troubled him.

"Are you okay?" he asked.

She shrugged. "Too much has changed. This city when I had first arrived was so … different."

Forrest offered a gentle smile, hoping to ease her apprehension. "You've missed a lot."

"I miss the old world," she said with a whisper.

Brady kept speeding. "Forrest, we're getting close. About a block away. Is she capable of fighting this demon?"

Penelope gritted her teeth. Determination set in her eyes. "That is a task I'm more than qualified to accomplish, no matter how confusing everything else is."

"Good," Brady said, glancing into the mirror. "As long as that remains your focus, you're going to be okay. Just remember something when the melee begins."

"What's that?" she asked.

"Werewolves, the Were-otters, and Cassie are the good guys. The other demons and vampires we seek to destroy." Brady nudged Forrest's arm. Forrest looked at him. "You might want to tell her about *what* you are."

Forrest chuckled and nodded. He glanced over his shoulder. "Right. Um, should you happen to see a grizzly, don't be alarmed. It's only me."

"What?" Her stunned face contorted with the question.

Forrest sighed. "It's a long story. One I will definitely tell you after this is all over."

Penelope still looked confused. "I look forward to it."

He grinned. "To be honest, I don't look forward to telling it."

"Why not?"

"Because you might never view me the same again," he replied softly.

"Nothing can be so severe to make me think less of you."

"That's something only you can judge and easier said before you learn the truth, but nonetheless, judge me you will."

CHAPTER 64

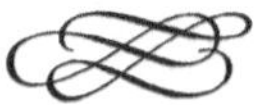

A half block from Nocturnal Trinity, Forrest took a stake from his right coat pocket. Brady turned off the flashing lights.

The area outside the nightclub where the lines of desperate people usually waited was barren. Parked across the street was the silver limo.

Brady and Forrest exchanged confused stares.

"This isn't a good sign," Brady said.

Forrest shook his head. "No, it isn't. You and Jacob wait out here. If Flora's siblings are inside, they've come to enact vengeance, which means they will not allow any werewolves to survive."

"You don't know that," Brady said.

A bullet struck the windshield of the squad car with a sharp *thwack*, giving it a spider-web outline in the glass. The bullet embedded into the hard console.

"Dammit!" Brady said, fumbling for his 9mm.

"Don't question my wisdom," Forrest said with a sly grin. "Get down!"

Brady pulled his gun and grabbed his intercom. "We're taking fire, Lydia."

Lydia drove the Jeep past the patrol car and parked on the other side of the road near a large moving truck. Sauriel drove his Lincoln to the other side of the truck.

"Stay down," Forrest said. "The bullets are silver."

"How can you tell that?"

Forrest wiped his finger across the console where the bullet had hit. Bits of silver dust and fragments came off on his finger. "Need any more evidence?"

Brady put the car into drive and sped forward several parking spots, stopping beside a tree with thick branches.

"Gunman on the roof," Lydia said over the radio.

Forrest opened his door and exited, squatting behind the car to use it as a shield. He eased to the backdoor and motioned Penelope to open the door. She did as he instructed and after he pulled the door partway open, she squeezed out.

Brady crawled across the seat and scrambled out onto the pavement, shutting the door closed.

One of Lydia's companions lifted a gun with a silencer and fired three rapid shots toward the nightclub's roof.

"Gunman down!" Lydia shouted, crossing the street in a sprint, gripping the butt of her 9mm with both hands and aiming toward the roof.

"Gunman's back up!" her companion replied, running to catch her.

"Psi-Vamp!" Blaze exclaimed from the rear of the moving truck.

Forrest placed a gentle hand on Penelope's back. "Heart-shot with an arrow, Penelope, if you can see him."

She pressed her back against the car door and peered over the roof of the car. "I see him."

"Can you get a clear shot?"

"I think so." She loaded the bow with an arrow and pulled the bowstring back, hesitating only a moment before she released the arrow.

"You got him," Jacob said.

Forrest glanced across the street. "Any others up there?"

Blaze shook his head and followed Lydia's other companion across the street. Cassie appeared behind Brady.

Ian and Gunner made a few sign gestures with their hands and darted toward the alleyway beside the nightclub. They were going to enter via the underground passage.

"Come on," Forrest said.

They jogged down the sidewalk until they reached the main entrance of Nocturnal Trinity. Lydia and her two companions each held 9mms as did Brady and Jacob.

Titus noticed their approach and his eyes widened. He shook his head. "Ah, hell no, guys! What are you doing? The damn place is closed tonight. I don't need this shit. Forrest, you keep causing me problems."

"This place never closes," Brady replied.

"Trust me, man," Titus said. "It's closed tonight. Strict orders from the Founders to turn away everyone."

"Even the police?" Brady asked.

"You got a warrant?" Titus replied, crossing his thick muscled arms while delivering his rehearsed intimidating bouncer frown.

Five 9mms leveled at Titus' head. Eyes widened, he held his hands in surrender and backed away from the door. "Shit, man. Look, it's not worth my life. The door's not locked. Go on inside."

"Who all is in there?" Brady asked.

"Hell, I have no idea."

"Don't give me that," Brady said. "You're the bouncer. You're here most every night."

"Yes, but I didn't arrive until a half hour ago. Honest. I was told not to come until then."

"So no one was waiting out here when you arrived?" Cassie asked.

Titus shook his head.

Cassie crossed her arms. "That's just too odd for me to believe. There's always a crowd."

"I agree," Titus said. "But it's the truth. From what I gathered on the phone was that the club was closed tonight and a massive robo-call sent messages out to all of the members. The wannabe people must have seen it on the evening news or heard it on the radio. I honestly don't know if only the Founders are inside or if there are dozens of other people in there, okay?"

"Then why are you here?" Lydia asked, stepping closer with her gun aimed at his chest. She didn't blink and her gaze was hard and cold.

Titus flinched, placed his hands behind his head, but never took his eyes off the gun. "I suppose they want me to inform any stragglers that didn't know we were closed that no one is allowed inside tonight."

"Their silver limo is parked across the street," Brady said. "Does that mean all of the vampire founders are inside?"

"Honestly, *I don't know* who is inside. Why are all of you packing heat anyway? Did something happen?" Titus swallowed hard, apparently still afraid to lower his hands.

"Flora has taken Kailey, Micah, and Ashley hostage," Brady said.

"And Luna," Blaze said, seething.

Brady nodded. "Yes, and Luna. We believe their lives are in danger."

Titus was dumbfounded. "You really think she'd hurt them?"

Cassie's eyes flashed crimson. "The Founders of this nightclub are not reputable people. They never have been."

"I can attest to that," Forrest said.

"They are highly dangerous murderers," Cassie said.

Titus' shoulders drooped. He lowered his arms to his sides and shook his head. "Man, I had no idea. I seldom ever talked to them since they hired me."

"Even if you had learned about how ruthless they really are," Cassie said, "they could have erased it from your memories."

"Really?"

She nodded. "You knew Andreas?"

"Yeah. Why?" Titus asked.

"They marked him and used him as a sacrifice for worse things to come."

"Really? Like what?"

Cassie sighed. "At this point it doesn't matter. We don't have time to discuss it anyway."

Forrest stepped past Titus. "Come on."

"Forrest, wait," Cassie said.

"What?"

"I'm going in first," she said. "Just in case."

"In case of what?" Titus asked.

"It's a mystery even I don't know yet. But like you said, Titus, it could only be the Founders who are inside or dozens of others waiting to attack us."

Forrest shrugged and extended his hand toward the door. "After you, Cassie."

CHAPTER 65

Forrest allowed Cassie to enter first and then he took Penelope by the hand and led her to the side of the door while the others entered. Lydia motioned to her two companions to head to the outer perimeter. If they were capable of turning into werewolves, they showed no obvious signs of changing like Jacob and Brady were. These men with Lydia looked more comfortable using guns than relying upon transformation. Their eyes had not altered but both Jacob and Brady no longer peered into the darkness with human eyes. Their eyes glowed like wolves'.

A few emergency lights were on, allowing just enough light to see the floor but not enough to easily find someone hiding in the shadows.

"Demon," Penelope said softly.

"Where?" Forrest asked.

"You don't smell it?" she asked.

Forrest took a deep breath. "A bit of sulfur is in the air."

"She's right," Cassie said. "It has to be one of the behemoths or a foul demon. Lesser demons like myself favor more pleasant aromas to attract and lure the attention of humans."

Lydia took slow calculated steps, careful to set each foot down silently. Gunfire erupted from the left side of the dark room. One of Lydia's companions groaned and dropped to the floor. Lydia rushed toward Brady and Jacob, knocking them to the ground while another series of gunshots came in their direction. She was hit several times in the back before she landed atop them. She showed no sign of pain, in spite of the bleeding gunshot wounds.

Cassie hurried across the room and flipped several switches to turn on the overhead lights. Two men dressed in vampire garb held guns but quickly shielded their eyes when the glare of the lights blared.

Forrest crossed the room and drove a stake through the one's heart. He dissolved to ash in less than a second. The other turned and attempted to dart but an arrow pierced through his back, striking him in the heart.

Brady and Jacob eased Lydia off of them. She lay facedown. Blood trickled from four bullet holes.

"Damn," Jacob said, shaking his head. "You should have given her a vest, Brady."

Brady ran a hand through his hair and shook his head.

Forrest knelt beside Lydia. "You okay?"

"You need to asked," she said, giving him a side-glance.

Jacob and Brady watched alongside Forrest as the shiny silver bullets slowly expelled themselves from her back and the wounds began knitting shut.

"What the hell?" Brady asked.

Angered, Lydia pushed herself to her feet. She glared at Forrest. "Any idea where the rest of them are?"

Cassie smiled. "If they're anywhere in the nightclub, they will be at the portal in the basement."

Lydia seethed. "Lead the way."

Jacob gave a side-glance toward Brady. "That had to hurt like hell."

Lydia glanced over her shoulder. "I wouldn't know. I don't have any pain receptors so I don't experience pain."

"Must be nice," Jacob said.

"It has its benefits."

Her two companions hurried to catch up to Lydia.

Penelope placed an arrow into her bow and followed Forrest. The Wrathbone blade hung on the side of her belt.

A demon rose from behind the bar with a gun. Before he fired a shot, she released the arrow, striking between its eyes. The gun fell from its hand and it slumped across the bar.

"Down the stairs," Forrest said, watching the others descend before them.

She nodded but remained silent.

"Wait, Forrest."

Forrest turned around. Jinn emerged from the shadows with a worried expression on his face.

Penelope aimed her bow at him.

He raised his hands and shook his head. "I'm not armed."

"No, but you're a demon," she said.

"Penelope, no," Forrest said.

"Another demon friend?" she asked.

"I wouldn't go that far with my description, but he's not proven himself to be an enemy, yet."

Jinn rolled his eyes. "Thanks, I suppose. I'm here to relay a message."

"I don't have time to waste, Jinn."

"Forrest, I understand that. All I can tell you is that I tried to stop Flora and Raven after they brought Kailey to Nocturnal Trinity. Needless to say it didn't work. Flora stopped me before I could sneak into the room to help Kailey. And as you should know, Flora never lets a grudge die. I'll have to watch my back from now on."

"We're aware that they have her and Luna," Forrest said.

"Micah and Ashley, too," Jinn said. "I just cannot believe how thick-headed Micah is."

Forrest nodded. "It's been obvious for quite some time."

"One of the behemoths arrived less than an hour ago." Jinn suddenly frowned and glanced at Penelope. "Is she the—"

Forrest placed a firm finger against his lips and nodded. "Yes."

"Good, then. Because I have the feeling that without her, we're all doomed."

Forrest pulled an extra stake from his pocket. "You can help us out."

Jinn nervously took the stake. "I don't know, Forrest. I hate to tell you this, but even with the numbers you've brought with you, we're outmanned."

"I've been in worse situations. But, you can help reduce their numbers by putting that stake to good use."

"Flora moves faster than my eyes can track when she's angry. She could snap my arm and stake me with it before I even saw her move."

"Let's hope it doesn't come to that," Forrest replied.

"Oh, I'm already *hoping*. Let your girl here do her magic."

Penelope frowned at Jinn. "I do not know magic."

Jinn laughed. "I guess her vocabulary hasn't caught up to ours yet, has it?"

Forrest shook his head. "No, not yet."

"Speaking of magic, where are the witches?" Jinn asked, looking around.

Forrest sighed. "Eva's too exhausted to offer any help. Jaclyn took a nasty hit from one of the dead behemoth's foot soldiers. Gillian and Raine are still with them. So we're without any magical assistance."

"No magic? That's not good," Jinn said. "The summoning circle is really unbalanced."

"It has been that way for quite some time. It isn't unity we've come to invade. This is war."

"No magic though," Jinn said, shaking his head. "That's rough."

Forrest shrugged. "We'll have to make due."

"Without magic, it won't be easy."

"Perhaps not, but this will be the last time Flora and I face one another."

"I'd worry more about the behemoth," Jinn replied.

Penelope frowned. "Leave it to me."

Jinn regarded her with a brief moment of nervousness. He glanced toward Forrest, almost questioning her boldness.

Forrest offered a solid nod to reaffirm Jinn's obvious doubt that Penelope was ready to battle.

"This way," Jinn said, walking past the stairwell.

"Where are you taking us?"

"There's another entrance. With everyone else headed down the stairs, we really need to enter from the other side to give a moment of surprise should Flora's attention be focused on the stairs."

Jinn led the way down the dark narrow corridor.

Penelope grabbed Forrest's hand and tugged.

Forrest turned and Penelope shook her head. "What's wrong?"

"I don't trust him," she whispered.

"Because he's a demon, right?"

She shook her head. "Not just that. Why is he separating us from the others?"

"For one, we cannot all go through the one entrance together."

"So you believe him?"

"Not wholeheartedly, but—"

The floor beneath them shook. Forrest grabbed Penelope to keep her from falling. A deep bellowing growl echoed from the floor below. Penelope's eyes narrowed with sudden determination.

"If we don't stop the demon now, it's going to kill a lot of people," she said.

"**Kill her!**" The voice was deeper than thunder.

Jinn turned toward Forrest. He had seen Jinn nervous before, but the fright that seized the incubus was greater than any fear Forrest had witnessed on anyone's face.

"Now do you understand why I didn't want to set up that meeting for you? I've *never* liked the thought of dealing with them. I certainly don't want to right now. Especially not *him*."

"Who?" Penelope asked.

"Diaboch," Jinn whispered, fearful of speaking the demon's name.

Penelope frowned. "I remember the name."

"If we don't hurry, someone's going to die," Forrest said.

"I'd prefer it wasn't me," Jinn said.

"Get us there, or *I'll* kill you," Penelope said, pulling back the bowstring.

"Forrest, you really pick some strange women to hang around. You know that?"

"Jinn, I'd simply do what she requests. They do have three female friends as hostages."

"Come on," Jinn said.

CHAPTER 66

"Flora, don't let Raven kill Luna," Kailey said. "Please?"

Raven held the knife to Luna's throat. There was no hint of taunting in Raven's expressions. She wanted to kill Luna and would take great pleasure in doing so. Her hatred for Kailey and Luna was that powerful. She'd kill Luna without any hesitation or remorse.

"Blood must be shed for the ceremony to begin," Flora replied. "Since we can't spill yours and well, Tiffany's already pledged hers for you, Luna's really the only other choice we have. We cannot use Micah or Ashley. We cannot possibly taint and defile our portal with werewolf blood, now can we? Soon those mongrels will learn true loyalty."

"Let Luna go!" Kailey said, tugging the restraints.

Raven glared at Kailey. "If only you could have shown a fraction of that affection toward me that you are for this dimwitted witch—"

Kailey ignored her and kept her focus on Flora. "Look, you let her go your wretched vampire bit—"

Flora crossed the room in a split second and clutched her hand tightly around Kailey's throat, pressing her back in the chair until her neck ached and caused Kailey to gag and choke. "Behave or I'll scar your pretty little face before you're turned. Then you'll have to see it throughout your immortality. Such a reminder will never allow you to forget who is in charge."

"Let her go," Kailey gasped, barely able to speak. "I'll let you turn me without any further problems. I won't resist. You have my word."

"It's too late for that," Flora said. "We're going to turn you regardless, so you need to learn your place with me. You should never dictate orders to your master."

"You're not my master."

Flora cackled and loosened her hold on Kailey. "Defiant until the end?"

Kailey narrowed her gaze. "I might as well be since the two of you are too afraid to release me."

"You're about to learn the true meaning of fear, child," Flora said softly.

The floor shook. She flicked her gaze toward the ten-foot tall demon that snorted and gnashed its teeth as it looked at her. A hiss escaped its mouth. Drool dripped from between its teeth in long strands. When the viscous saliva touched the floor, streams of smoke rose from where the acid burned holes into the stones. The behemoth took a crushing step forward; his long thick tail twisted like a snake as he walked and it was wider than an alligator's. Sharp bone spikes protruded along the tail. Large black wings unfolded from its back. Evil dominated its face, so much so that Flora shook and took a step away from Kailey.

The behemoth was the most hideous creature she had ever seen. She couldn't understand how it had managed to squeeze through the doorway.

Raven lowered the knife from Luna's throat. She seemed to shrink and her complexion became even paler, but she looked too scared to run.

Flora swallowed hard. "Diaboch? You're ... early."

"My eagerness could not be repressed any longer. My excitement equals that of emaciated man set before a banquet. The euphoria rejuvenates me."

"But we're still preparing for the ritual," Flora replied, nervously glancing toward Kailey.

The demon regarded Flora for several moments. His sharp teeth looked less menacing than his double set of black tusks. His glowing yellow eyes resembled the cold stare of a serpent. "Ye-e-e-s-s. I see you've chosen a defiant spirited one to foster this time. One worthy of becoming a warrior. Are you certain you're comfortable with such a choice?"

Flora couldn't hide her nervousness. "And why shouldn't I be *comfortable* with her as my newest progeny?"

His gravelly voice raked like rough stones being rubbed together. "Because she's smarter and more rebellious than you ever could be, Flora. She stands to take your place and could quite possibly outdo anything you've ever done. I detect her untamable spirit. She's lively and an opportunist. She cannot be suppressed nor will you be capable of controlling her like you do her former girlfriend. Kailey fully hates you. Turning her into a vampire will not change that. You cannot compel affection when her heart truly despises you. Seldom does a servant outrank one's master, but she does. She will. You're a fool if you think she'll ever bow her knee to you like her former dimwit counterpart over there."

"How dare you!" Flora seethed. Anger creased her face with sheer fury.

Raven's mouth dropped open, but she didn't respond in an outburst of anger like she'd normally do.

A loss for words, Raven? For a moment Kailey fought to suppress the grin on her face but found herself unable to contain her sudden glee.

The behemoth examined the room. "This is it? I've warned you that others might interfere with our ceremony this evening. We cannot afford to have our concentration disrupted. Have you not sentries to prevent outside disturbances or possible attacks?"

Flora huffed. "They are well hidden, awaiting to attack any trespassers. I don't appreciate your condescending natural, Diaboch. How dare you insult me openly."

Diaboch exhaled heavily. His hot breath reeked of brimstone and decay. He took another bold fearless step toward Flora. "You've always allowed your emotions and selfishness to rule your actions, albeit normally your impulsive behavior causes you to disregard the strict rationality necessary for a vampire to survive more than a century. I imagine had it not been for me and my brethren, you would have received a stake through the heart well before now."

Flora formed tight fists. Froth formed at the sides of her mouth, but she didn't dare rush toward the behemoth. She seemed to know her place, and her fear ushered great hesitation and respect. She didn't dare make a physical challenge.

"You despise the truth like always, Flora," Diaboch said. It placed its huge hand atop Tiffany's head like an NBA player palmed a basketball. He peered down into Tiffany's frightened eyes. "This one, though simpler minded than I like, has willingly offered to give herself to you and become your child without argument or opposition. I doubt a human could find a dog more obedient than she, and yet, you mandate that she become the blood sacrifice for Kailey? You might be centuries old, Flora, but you're nothing more a spoiled brat. A fool. Why are you so blinded by your own recklessness? Why Kailey and not Tiffany?"

Flora's eyes grew dark and black like wet obsidian. Her true inner self emerged. A wicked monster. "Kailey's smarter. Stronger."

"Yes," Diaboch said with an eager grin. "I agree. Too smart and too strong for *you* to control. And this one—" He twisted his huge hand sharply, snapping Tiffany's neck with little effort, killing her instantly. "She has lost her purpose for yielding to you."

"Why?" Flora asked, rushing to Tiffany. Sadness actually resonated in the coldhearted bitch's voice. "*Why* did you do that?"

"Because once you turn Kailey, she shall drink *my* blood to forge her spirit and will to mine. She will become *my* servant, not yours. She will eventually become stronger than you. It's time Nocturnal Trinity has new blood and new vision. It's time to make our Foundation stronger."

Flora held Tiffany's head upright and pressed her cheek against her former wannabe's cheek. Kailey never thought the vampire could show regret or the pain of loss, but these emotions showed on Flora's face. She wrapped her arms around Tiffany's limp body and for several seconds seemed to be trying to console the girl by whispering in her ear, even though Tiffany was already dead. She turned with tears glistening in her eyes. "You didn't have to kill her! And now, you want me to hand Kailey over to you?"

"No. Kailey's already mine. You will simply turn her and we'll begin rebuilding the Circle of Unity."

"And should I refuse?"

Diaboch snorted and then defiantly laughed. His eyes flamed like molten steel. "You have no choice."

"After what you did to Tiffany?" Flora shook her head defiantly. "No. I won't give Kailey to you. She's mine and Raven has requested her as her future sister."

Raven glanced nervously at Flora.

Diaboch smiled evenly, revealing rows of jagged teeth. "Tiffany was a lost cause. Your wisdom about her was correct. She wasn't worthy of becoming immortal, but she's not a worthy blood sacrifice for Kailey either."

"Just like that? You think I'll—"

Gunfire erupted in the corridor on the opposite side of the chamber, breaking the contention and causing everyone's attention to turn.

Flora glared at Raven and nodded. "Stop them!"

Raven darted toward the door that led to the corridor and was struck in the chest by three bullets. She shrieked, clutched her chest, and stepped against the side of the doorway where the intruders couldn't shoot her.

"They're only bullets!" Flora shouted. "They can't kill you!"

"No," Raven said with tears in her eyes. "But they *hurt.*"

Kailey wanted to laugh and probably would have had the situation not been so severe. The behemoth looked as though he had rolled his eyes at Raven's statement. Raven had lost her courage. Flora's seemed to be fleeting. Micah had been right about the severe disunion within Nocturnal Trinity. So much had fallen apart. Each faction was at the others' throats. But it seemed more than that. Flora and Raven seemed weaker. Was the demon capable of absorbing their rage and hostility to fuel his strength?

"Raven is showing her true weaknesses, her cowardice. You see, Flora," Diaboch said, "either your old age has waivered your ability to distinguish worthy humans to mentor or—"

Flora fumed. She pointed at Diaboch and glared harshly. "I *never* chose her. Nicodemus did! It's not my fault that kids today have no resourcefulness. Raven would have proven to be a worse choice than Tiffany!"

Raven's mouth dropped open. Her lower lip trembled. The hurtful statement had struck deep inside her. Tears trickled down her cheeks. "What?"

Flora waved her off. "She's as mindless as they come with all her petty needs to seek revenge. See how she cowers in the corner?"

"You should have had her for a roommate," Kailey said.

"Silence!" Flora said, snapping her head around and pointing a stern finger. "If I want any comments from you, I'll smack them out of you."

"Raven uses people," Kailey said. "But she never offers anything in return."

Flora turned back toward Raven. "Stop them! Don't let them into this chamber. If you cannot prove yourself worthy to me, you'll be nothing more than a heap of dust!"

Raven looked like she was going to burst into tears. Instead, she took a deep breath, her eyes darkened, and she growled in rage as she ran into the doorway. Three more shots struck her but this time she didn't flinch. She didn't retreat. She shrieked and disappeared into the tunnel.

Suddenly, out of their daze, Micah and Ashley shook their heads, looking around, freshly awakened.

The gunfire ceased inside the tunnel. A few seconds later, Raven staggered back into the chamber, riddled with bullet holes, and leaned against the wall. Blood seeped from the wounds, but the wounds were knitting together. The bullets weren't going to kill her but she wasn't able to hide her pain.

Diaboch shook his head. "I don't know why I bothered to send a vampire to fight in my stead. You've been pacified for too long. How Nocturnal Trinity has lasted this long is puzzling."

Flora scoffed but held her silence.

The demon flexed his muscles and balls of fire engulfed his fists. He stomped toward the door, roaring. The echo rattled the walls. Bits of dust and chips of stone danced upon the vibrations.

Micah yanked against the metal cuffs holding his wrists. The bands snapped like thin plastic. Ashley broke free of her cuffs, too.

Flora and Raven kept their attention on the doorway while the demon walked toward it. Gunfire started again, but the bullets flicked off the demon's thick skin, hardly gaining his attention but not arousing his anger. He acted amused.

Micah quietly hurried to Kailey and snapped the handcuffs that had held her to the chair. Micah stared into her eyes with kindness. Ashley crouched beside him.

"What happened to you two?" she whispered.

"We were drugged and Raven must have placed us under a control spell," Micah replied.

All the turmoil and Raven's pain must have broken the concentration necessary to keep them under her control or she no longer cared to help Flora. If the latter were true, Kailey didn't blame Raven for rebelling, but it didn't gain Raven any points. Kailey could never trust Raven again.

"Ashley will get you to safety," Micah said.

"What about Luna?" Kailey asked.

"If the demon and Flora remain distracted, I can get Luna to safety," he replied.

Ashley took Kailey's hand, but movement from the ceiling caught Kailey's attention. Shadows moved near a circular opening that she had remembered from the time she had been in this area of the nightclub before. At that time, the hole had been covered with decorative stain-glass. It connected to the room above, which had been occupied by Nicodemus before he was slain.

Jinn poked his head down and glanced around the room.

For a moment, Kailey believed she and the others might survive what seemed to be their final confrontation, but she had already learned the hard way to never allow her hopes to grow.

CHAPTER 67

Forrest stood beside Jinn and Penelope in the chambers that Nicodemus had once used for his bedroom. Jinn slid a piece of sheathing board aside, revealing the hole where the stained glass once covered.

Jinn lowered onto his hands and knees and stuck his head down to see what was going on.

"Well?" Forrest asked as Jinn peered back up.

"It's not good. Diaboch is here. He's the worst of the five behemoths. We'd best drop down if you want to save them." Jinn didn't wait for a reply. He plummeted through the hole to the floor below.

Forrest grunted and shook his head. "Hold my hand and I'll help you."

"Forrest, I may have been inactive for over a century, but I'm not helpless. Thanks, but no." Penelope took an arrow from the quiver, dropped into the hole and disappeared.

Forrest waited until after she had landed and stepped aside, then he lowered into the hole and dropped down as well. He regretted allowing her to go first since he had finally been reunited with her and that he didn't trust Jinn completely. Not to mention, Penelope might have landed near Flora or Raven, both of which were more dangerous than Jinn.

Since Forrest was a massive man, his feet hit the floor so hard that sharp pains ran from his soles halfway up his calves. He winced momentarily, jerked a stake from his pocket, and searched the room for Flora.

Cassie zipped from the corridor and flung herself toward the behemoth, but the monstrous demon gripped her throat with its huge right hand. The anger in Cassie's eyes drained and filled with sudden fear.

"Fool!" the behemoth said, flinging her across the room. "You dare attack one of your own?"

Forrest reached out and grabbed her succubus tail, preventing her from slamming into the wall. Catching her spun him around and he faced Cassie. She turned and offered a slight grin.

"Thanks," she said.

Penelope cocked a brow toward the demon. Cassie wasn't flirting, but a succubus smile always looked that way.

"Don't mention it," Forrest said, turning to find Flora or Raven. Both needed to be slain. He didn't really care which one he killed first.

Diaboch turned toward Flora. "Do you not have other vampires here to aid us?"

She shook her head.

"No?" he asked, angered and yet surprised.

Flora placed a hand upon one hip and waved one hand toward him. With a haughty tone, she said, "Since you requested for us to summon your demon soldiers I wasn't about to place our vampires at risk. Your demons kill unnecessarily as I last recall. You have about as much control over them as what you predict I'll have over Kailey."

Diaboch gritted his teeth and growled. "Touché. No matter."

Micah motioned Luna to run toward Kailey and Ashley toward the opposite corridor. After she was a good distance away from Diaboch, Micah reared back his head and howled. In full werewolf form, he rushed the behemoth and slashed at the demon's hard skin with his sharp claws but caused no damage. Diaboch uttered a deep bellowing laugh and back-handed Micah. Micah yelped and lost his footing, pivoting into the air and soaring across the room, landing with a hard thud. He rolled over onto his stomach, dazed, but was trying to push himself up again.

Brady and Jacob lowered to all fours and charged toward the behemoth. Diaboch swung his tail around, snapping like a thick whip of bone, muscle, and scales. The sharp spikes stabbed into the two werewolves, ripping flesh and tearing fur from their chests and stomachs. They cried in pain and rolled across the floor. Lying on their sides, they panted. Blood, lots of blood, poured from their wounds.

Ashley rushed to Micah as he struggled to stand.

"Brady!" Kailey yelled, running toward him.

"Kailey, no!" Cassie yelled.

Flora turned toward Kailey. "And how, pray tell, did *you* escape?"

Forrest gripped the stake tightly and jogged toward Flora. Her eyes widened slightly.

"I warned you that the next time we met," Forrest said, "that I'd slay you."

Diaboch stomped the floor, jarring Forrest slightly off balance, and his tail slashed around, knocking Forrest's legs out from under him. The pain was instant.

Anger rushed through Forrest. The stake lay on the floor but outside of his reach. He stretched and reached for it anyway. His hands swelled. Thick brown fur sprouted over the back of his hands. Black claws lengthened at the ends of his fingers. His transformation was beginning.

Not now. Not yet.

Jinn hurried toward Diaboch.

Diaboch stared down at him. "Whose side are you on?"

"Yours," he replied. "I brought you this."

"The Wrathbone?" Diaboch asked. "Where did you get this?"

Forrest glanced back toward Penelope. She reached and patted her belt. In horror she looked toward Jinn and then toward Forrest. Neither of them had ever seen him take it.

"Traitor!" she spewed, placing an arrow into the bow's groove. She fired the arrow, but it bounced off the behemoth's thick skin.

Diaboch smiled, staring down at the blade. "You've done well. I see we chose someone worthy of being a member of the Circle of Unity and a replacement for our former Founder."

"Thanks," Jinn said with a broad prideful smile. "Yeah ... about that ..."

Without any further hesitation, Jinn rammed the blade through the behemoth's gut until the hilt was flush with his thick skin. Jinn twisted the blade and jerked harshly across its abdomen. Bullets had ricocheted off the demon's skin, as had the arrow, but this blade sliced easily through. Black blood streamed.

Diaboch clutched his wound, roared, and tried to prevent his entrails from spilling to the floor. His eyes widened in horror at the betrayal. He snarled, looking at Jinn. The behemoth was too stunned to attack him, even at the close distance.

Jinn yanked out the blade, brought it back, and in a swift upward arc, he cut through the behemoth's throat.

Diaboch dropped to his knees. Blood streamed from his throat and gut. His glowing eyes dimmed. Choking on his blood, he attempted to speak, but no words came. He reached for his throat and his entrails splattered on the floor. A pungent odor permeated the air.

Outraged, Flora glanced toward Jinn. "What have you done?"

Before Jinn replied, Flora crossed the room in a flash, struck Jinn dead center in the chest with her palm and sent him reeling. The blade dropped from Jinn's hand and he hit the wall hard.

Penelope aimed an arrow at Flora, but Flora zipped from sight. A second later Flora appeared behind Penelope and clutched her throat tightly. The bow and arrow fell from Penelope's hands.

Flora smiled. Her fangs became more prominent as her eyes stared at the pulsing vein in Penelope's neck.

Cassie crouched like she was readying herself to charge.

Flora snarled at the succubus. "She'll be dead before you reach me, so don't."

CHAPTER 68

Forrest growled. His inner rage was too much to contain. *No. Not Penelope.*

His hands widened. Bear claws emerged. His bones and joints popped, causing him to roar in agony.

"If you change into a grizzly, Forrest," Flora said, "I snap her neck. It won't require but the slightest twitch, and she's dead."

Forrest's skull widened. No matter how hard he tried to prevent his change, at this point, there wasn't anything he could do to stop it.

"I'm warning you, Forrest," Flora said. "And you know I don't offer those readily. As for the rest of you, yield or she dies and then Kailey and Luna and everyone else."

Thick brown fur sprouted over Forrest's face, his hands, and his arms and legs. His muscles swelled and thickened.

All this time I've wanted to see you, Penelope, to find you, and now that I have, I will undoubtedly cause your death.

"Your stubbornness betrays you, Hunter," Flora said. "Perhaps the threat isn't enough? How about I make her one of my own?"

"He has gone too far. He cannot stop his transformation," Micah said, steadying himself against Ashley.

Raven rushed across the room and grabbed Kailey. She yanked Kailey's hair and pulled her head back, running her tongue across the exposed softness of Kailey's throat. "You're going nowhere."

Brady clutched his side with one hand and attempted to push himself up, but couldn't. Blaze grabbed Luna's hand, and they ran for the corridor at the other end of the room.

Forrest stretched and arched his back. A deep growl rumbled inside him.

"I have a clear shot," Lydia said, aiming at Flora's head.

Flora laughed. "You're a fool if you think that gun can stop me."

Micah shook his head. "No, Lydia, don't."

"Between the eyes might not kill her," Lydia said, "but from what I understand, that kind of damage takes some time to heal."

A smirk curled on Flora's lips. "Try it. I dare you. I'm faster than any bullet. You pull the trigger, and I can assure you, it will be Penelope's head you hit. Not mine."

"Lydia," Brady gasped. "Please, put the gun down."

"What? I do, and we're all at her mercy. She's going to as she wants anyway."

"Where are your men?" Brady asked.

Lydia shrugged. "They're still in the hallway, probably dead. Raven ripped their throats out. They can't heal like I do."

A triumphant look claimed Raven's face. She held up to bloody patches of fur-covered flesh and tossed them to the ground.

"Why must you reign with defiance, Flora?" Micah asked. "I've only tried to maintain the Unity within Nocturnal Trinity, as it was unraveling at an alarming rate. Not only that, I have continuous tried to offer and reestablish peace."

Flora laughed. "Maintain unity? Peace? You're a fool! You invaded us, and there's no way I'd ever seek peace with a group of mongrel werewolves. You're less than us, touched by a darkness we loathe. It is because of you … and Kailey … that we've *lost* what we once had. And Diaboch is now dead because of your intrusions. None of this had to be if you'd left well enough alone."

"Seems you were at great odds with Diaboch as it were. Jinn did you a favor."

"Did he now?" Flora glared. Her fangs lengthened. "Now, we must face the wrath of the other four behemoths. Such a meeting … I dread to even imagine what will occur then. But, if nothing else, killing you and your pack members, as well as the dreadful thorn of a Hunter in our sides, should appease them enough to prevent more disarray."

Forrest's vision blurred. His ears popped. His subconscious understood what was going on, but his primal bear nature was slowly gripping control. A hand grasped his shoulder.

"Erreichen tief, finden sie ihre ruhe," Gunner whispered softly.

Forrest stiffened slightly at the words, took a deep breath, and slowly released it. Gunner repeated the words.

"Sorry, we are late," said a slender gorgeous blonde as she traipsed from the corridor into the room. She wore a crimson gown that flowed to the floor hiding her feet. A necklace with large rubies hung around her neck. Her pale complexion left no doubt that she was a vampire.

"Niki?" Flora said, beaming a sudden smile. "What brings you back to Nocturnal Trinity this evening?"

"Sister," Nikolina replied. Her eyes darted toward Tiffany's corpse. She tsked and shook her head. "We received word of tonight's ceremonial ritual. Sadly, the news did not come from you."

"Yes," a dark-haired man said, suddenly appearing beside Nikolina. His facial features were perfection, movie star quality, and his eyes peered with regal confidence. "Why is that, dear sister?"

"Orsova? Brother," Flora said. "I—I thought all of you had ventured to Vancouver and planned to stay awhile?"

A thin muscular blonde male appeared beside Diaboch's corpse, just outside of the black pool of blood. "Seems tonight's events … didn't quite go as planned?"

Flora shook her head and laughed. "No, Alec, they did not."

A hand gripped Flora's shoulder. A woman with long curls of red hair stood beside Flora. The woman's eyes dazzled a deep blue that could make sapphires envious. "Must we always clean up your messes?"

"Irina?" Flora released her hold on Penelope. Penelope rushed over beside Forrest and Gunner.

In a blur, Orsova moved across the room and grabbed Raven by the throat, lifting her into the air, and then he darted with her back to where he had been standing. "Behave, you petulant brat."

Raven's eyes widened. Her hands unsuccessfully tried to loosen his grip. Orsova didn't lessen his grip and held Raven effortlessly several inches off the floor.

Forrest's body had aborted its transformation, which was something he'd never experienced before.

"So Vancouver wasn't—"

"Dear sister," Irina said, escorting Flora closer to Orsova. "We've pondered why you'd hold such festivities without our presence?"

Brady and Jacob slowly rose to their feet. Their wounds had knitted shut and their bleeding stopped. Brady gave a look of question to Micah. Micah shrugged.

Flora sighed. "I thought you held no interest in such activities. Normally, you decline when I offer, but if you wish to partake, I will gladly bestow such honor. Look around, there's plenty of blood to be shed. Just spare Kailey, as I have a keen interest in keeping her for my own purposes."

"That won't be necessary," Orsova said in his thick accent. "We've not come for them, but for you."

"Me?" Flora's eyes widened, and she placed a hand across her heart. "Whatever for?"

"After much debate and discussion," Irina said, "we've come to accept that you're more a liability than an asset. It's time we take action."

Flora frowned for a moment and then laughed nervously. "Action? Like what exactly? Are you inferring that you wish me slain?"

Alec ran a hand through his blonde hair. "It's the only ideal solution in order for us to make amends to those you have harmed."

"But I'm family. Your sister—"

Orsova frowned. His eyes darkened with rage and pure evil. "Nicodemus was our brother. You convinced him to play your petty little games. Do you not remember his fate? It is because of you that he was slain. You and no one else. Your meddling set all of this into motion, severing what we treasured and held dear in this humble nightclub. Nocturnal Trinity can never recover from such losses. And you killed Andreas, who was our most loyal servant."

"So you're going to slay me?" Flora said with wide eyes. She searched their gazes in desperation and spoke in a pathetic pleading voice. "Your own sister. Imagine how horrified our father would be—"

"Enough!" Irina said with an icy glare. "Father died because of *your* games. Or have you conveniently forgotten that?"

Irina slipped behind Flora and gripped her elbows tightly, restraining her.

"So which one of you will strike the blow?" Flora asked, tears forming in her eyes.

Orsova flicked his gaze toward Forrest. "Hunter, this is a delicate subject for us and one that took days of deliberation, but not one of us can put her to rest. Doing so jeopardizes our trust in one another. Together we came to a united decision. We beseech you to slay her on our behalf."

Forrest took a stake from his pocket. His eyes narrowed as he peered into Flora's nervous gaze. "My pleasure."

Alec lifted a finger toward Forrest. "Hear out our conditions first."

"Conditions?"

"We offer a truce, but other conditions must be met," Irina said.

"Like what?"

Orsova smiled. "The werewolves must leave the Unity immediately, and they shall be spared."

"Done," Brady said.

"Seconded," Jacob said with a firm nod.

Micah frowned but offered no argument.

"And we ask that you, Hunter, pardon us from your hunt. We had no part of what happened over a century ago. That was Flora and father's doing. Not ours," Orsova said. "And unfortunately, you've spent over a hundred years seeking your revenge. That in itself weighs heavily upon one's … cough … soul, and now you can lay that to rest with her so we can get about to our business."

"You wish to keep Nocturnal Trinity open?" Forrest asked.

"We do. We wish to have no contention between ourselves and you, Forrest. We want to put all of this behind us. With those as our conditions, what say ye?" Irina asked in an aristocratic tone. "But before you answer, note that we can detect if you're lying."

Alec nodded. "We know your hatred for us has never faded, even after all these years, but the contention was never our doing."

Forrest thought for several long moments. He had never offered immunity to any vampire before. It went against his morals and beliefs to allow these undead predators to escape. But even he understood he couldn't possibly kill all five master vampires by himself. Everyone else in the room would be killed too.

He glanced at the others. The werewolves held angered stares, but more at Flora and Raven than anyone else. Kailey offered an almost pleading stare for him to agree so that Flora would never threaten her again. He nodded. "I accept the conditions."

Irina gripped Flora's arms tighter. Alec stepped behind Irina, reached around Irina, and grabbed Flora's shoulders tightly.

"Is there no way I can change your minds?" Flora asked, turning her head slightly toward Irina.

"No." Irina's short reply matched the coldness of her brilliant eyes.

Forrest stepped toe-to-toe with Flora, gripping the stake tightly. He brought it up and pressed the sharpened tip against her left breast, indenting the skin.

Flora swallowed hard. Her pleading eyes detailed more than her begging words could ever express, but she didn't beg. Instead, she said, "I suppose this brings you long awaited satisfaction?"

Forrest narrowed his eyes. "It is not the challenge I had hoped for, but it will do."

Flora closed her eyes. Tears of blood etched from the sides of her eyes and trickled down her cheeks. A moment later, Forrest shoved the stake through her heart. Her body became ash and crumbled to the floor. Irina and Alec moved like a blur to place distance between them and Forrest since he still held the stake.

Orsova clutched Raven by the throat. "And now, Forrest, this one. She is the last to remind us of our brother's untimely death."

Forrest smiled, but instead of walking toward Raven, he extended the stake in his hand toward Kailey. "Kailey, you deserve this honor."

CHAPTER 69

Kailey stared at the stake in Forrest's extended hand. With Flora being nothing more than a pile of ash on the floor, Kailey felt a partial weight of oppression lift. She wanted to cry but not from sadness.

You'll never bully me again, Flora. I warned you that Forrest would kill you.

Indeed she had, but she would have never thought in a thousand years that Flora's brothers and sisters would have turned against her. She supposed a vampire had to be repulsively evil for her own vampire siblings to plot her death.

Apprehensively, Kailey took the stake from Forrest. Her stomach tensed with nervousness. Her heart hammered in her chest. This was the opportunity she had been hoping for, waiting for, and now that it had been offered to her, she discovered her reluctance in executing Raven. Not because she didn't believe Raven needed to be slain, Kailey understood Raven's mind was too warped to allow her to remain on Earth as a vampire. When someone who had once been your best friend was capable of pounding your face until it was too bruised to recognize, imagine what she'd do to strangers?

Anger pulsed through Kailey as she recalled seeing the swollen, massive bruises on her face in the mirror.

With every eye in the room watching Kailey approach Raven, Kailey's hand tightened around the stake. She couldn't look Raven dead in the eye, although she really wanted to, but the danger was too much. Raven was a vampire, a young vampire, but she was still capable of compelling Kailey.

Kailey didn't expect an apology from Raven. It was doubtful she'd hear such words from Raven. Flora hadn't offered an apology to any of them, including her siblings, so why should Kailey think for a moment that Raven would.

"You hate me, don't you?" Raven asked.

The question took Kailey by surprise and actually caused Kailey's anger to lessen.

"I can't say that I blame you," Raven said. "You should hate me for what I did to you and how I spied on you and Brady."

"How'd you get into our apartment without being invited?" Kailey asked.

"By combining my magic as a witch and compelling a demon, it wasn't too hard. The demon probably doesn't remember obeying my commands."

"So you were never in our apartment?"

Raven shook her head. "I simply wanted to show you how much power I have over you."

"You mean, 'had,' don't you?" Kailey's jaw tightened. Her eyes darkened with rekindled anger. "That's about to end."

"Say our last goodbyes, I suppose?" Raven asked, trying not to tear up. "I know you won't miss me. I want you to know that I still love you."

Kailey ground her teeth. Her nostrils flared. "Take a good look at my face. See the bruises?"

"I know, Kailey. I do. I allowed my jealousy to get the best of me."

"The sad thing is that I did once love you, Raven. I really did on a deeper level. The external factors and how you treated me doused the flame. And now, you could apologize for an eternity and it wouldn't make any damn difference to me. Nothing at all. Because I could never view you as anything less than my enemy. The hurt you have caused me is that deep. Words cannot amend that. A half hour ago you put a knife to Luna's throat, threatening to kill her. What did that accomplish?"

Raven smiled. "This is good."

"What is?"

"Releasing your anger. If you're going to kill me, keep that anger, that rage, and use your hatred to help mask the—"

Kailey lifted the stake. "I'm not slaying you out of anger or hatred or rage. I could see how some people might act on those emotions. None of those emotions have anything to do with why I'm going to plunge this dagger through your blackened heart. It's not even revenge. I'm going to slay you because it's the right thing to do. You're a threat to anyone you come into contact with. And you heard Flora … she even said that she'd have never chosen you to become a vampire. That should speak volumes."

Raven took a sharp breath and exhaled jaggedly. She trembled. She glanced around the room. Everyone was watching her and Kailey. "Then, by all means, finish this, okay? No reason to prolong my execution unless you simply wish to extend my punishment."

"One last thing," Kailey said.

Raven rolled her eyes, making Kailey want to call her out on it like Raven had done Kailey so many times before.

"What?" Raven said. She appeared genuinely interested in hearing what Kailey wanted to say. There was no malice or anger. For the first time in a long time, Raven looked reasonably calm. At ease.

Had she realized her evil nature and knew death prevented her from hurting others?

"I really tried to rescue you when Flora took you. I really did. And because of me, both Flora and you were permitted to live undead lives. But Skye—" Kailey choked on unexpected sobs. She fanned her face with her hand, but didn't wipe away forming tears. "Skye sacrificed what little bit of life she had in her to ensure that you didn't dissolve into ash after Nicodemus died. She … she loved you that much, Raven."

Raven tilted her head downward in shame. Tears dripped from her eyes and glistened on the dusty floor. She sobbed.

Kailey wiped away tears with the back of her hand. Raven was broken. Kailey looked at the stake in her hand and shook her head. Instead of staking Raven, Kailey just wanted to reach out and hug her. Kailey sighed and almost allowed the stake to slip from her hand.

Raven's head suddenly lifted. Her widened eyes were black and reflective like small obsidian mirrors. She wailed in laughter, crazy laughter, and tried to lunge at Kailey but Orsova was too strong for her to escape. She hissed and her voice deepened with venom. "Skye allowed me to remain like *this*? If she had survived, I'd have ripped her heart out, Kailey. She always held me back, saying it was out of love and compassion and that misuse of magic was deadly. But it wasn't that. She didn't want me to become more powerful than she! She saw in me what she wasn't able to achieve and I was on the correct path. You think I pity her death, her sacrifice? No, not one bit. Not a spit of remorse for her death moistens my mouth. You know I should weep over her? Huh? What do you think? Do you think I misused my magic?"

Kailey tightened her grip on the stake. "No, I think Skye misused hers."

"See? I knew you'd understand."

"No," Kailey said, "you *mis*understand. She misused her magic by allowing you to live. Forrest was the only one of us that had enough sense to see it, and my pleading persuaded him to spare you and Flora, which I regret, but do know something."

"What?"

"I don't regret *this*." Kailey plunged the stake through Raven's heart and took a quick step back. She expected Raven to plummet to the floor in a pile of ash, but she didn't.

An evil deep laugh escaped Raven's mouth. She smiled wickedly. "Is that the best you have, Kailey?"

Kailey gasped and placed a hand over her mouth. The stake had done nothing except stick in her chest. Blood oozed around the stake, but she wasn't disintegrating.

Orsova and Irina exchanged confused glances. Irina and Nikolina rushed toward Raven.

Kailey glanced toward Forrest. "How?"

Forrest shrugged, plucked a stake off the floor, and charged.

"Don't free her," Irina said. "And keep that stake lodged inside her chest."

Orsova squeezed Raven's throat. "How are you still alive?"

"Like I said, Skye tried to hold me back. I'm more than just a vampire. I'm a witch that was turned into a vampire and who fed off the blood of a behemoth. You're all going to die!"

Raven shoved Orsova hard enough to dislodge his grip on her throat, but Irina and Nikolina each grabbed one of Raven's arms and held fast. Even their combined strength didn't seem strong enough. Raven walked, dragging the sisters behind her.

Cassie rushed across the room and scooped up the Wrathbone by the hilt. "You've hurt too many people, Raven. That ends now."

Raven turned. "Bring it, you succubus bit—"

The Wrathbone blade sliced through Raven's neck in one swift swing. Raven's head dropped to the floor. Seconds later, she was nothing more than smoldering ashes.

Cassie looked at Kailey and shook her head. "You know I never liked her, right?"

Kailey's hands shook. Cassie wrapped her arms around Kailey and squeezed tightly. "Thanks. It's finally all over."

"You know I will always have your back," Cassie whispered in her ear. "Now, you have two less vampires to worry about."

After Kailey parted from Cassie's embrace, she made her way to Brady and fell into his arms. Brady hugged her fiercely. "I love you. Take me home."

"Not yet," Brady whispered.

"Why not?"

Brady nodded.

Kailey looked over her shoulder to see Forrest standing in the center of the room. The last four vampire Founders stood before him. A long silence passed as they intently stared at one another.

"Isn't this over?" Kailey whispered.

"I'm not sure yet."

CHAPTER 70

Forrest stood with his arms crossed as he faced the vampires. Ian and Gunner stood behind him.

Orsova motioned Brady, Micah, and Jacob over.

Lydia was nowhere to be found. Apparently she had left, surprisingly honoring the truce that Forrest had agreed to.

"I'm guessing that you want our assistance for something more?" Forrest asked.

Irina shook her head. "No, Forrest. You fulfilled what we regretfully needed."

Orsova glanced at Brady. "I'm giving the werewolves a half hour to get whatever possessions you have stored in the VIP lounge out of Nocturnal Trinity. After that, whatever you've left behind is forfeited."

Brady narrowed his eyes. "I'm a police officer. Are you saying that I cannot enter Nocturnal Trinity?"

Alec smirked. "Not at all. You can enter whenever a brawl occurs or we need someone arrested. Outside of that, what we're saying, is that we cannot guarantee any werewolf's safety. While we cannot exclude were-wolves, we must warn you of the dangers. It's advisable that you pass that information to the rest of your pack."

"What about the witches?" Forrest asked.

Irina sighed. "We're only going to be Nocturnal Trinity in name. The

Circle of Unity has proven to know longer have stability. Too many trusts have been broken."

Jinn limped over to stand near Cassie. "And what about demons?"

"You can remained employed by us as a bartender, if you so choose. But, you're no longer a member of the Circle of Unity," Orsova said.

"I'm guessing you've not run this by the remaining behemoths yet?" Jinn asked.

"No. That's not a meeting we look forward to."

Cassie held the Wrathbone up. "Then you might want to have this with you."

"Are you suggesting they kill the remaining behemoths?" Jinn asked.

Alec's jaw hardened. "They're not simply going to accept our terms."

"How exactly do you intend to run this nightclub now?" Jinn said.

"The outward appearance remains the same. The three dance halls will be the same. We'll have VIP rooms for witches, vampires, and demons like before. It's just that the council won't consist of three factions, only us. The nightclub was ours from the beginning, but we made pacts with the other two factions as needs arose. We no longer require the assistance of the others."

A grin parted Forrest's thick beard. "Then I suppose you will be battling those demons alone?"

The vampires nodded.

"It would be hypocritical for us to rally others to this cause," Nikolina said. She looked at Brady. "Thirty minutes. No more."

Brady shrugged. "Come on, Jacob and Micah. Let's clear out Micah's office."

"I'll help," Forrest said.

Before they reached the corridor, Orsova said, "Forrest, thank you for … giving Flora rest. You're always welcomed in Nocturnal Trinity, so long as you're not here to hunt."

Forrest didn't pause in step, nor did he reply. Silence was often the best reply. It kept others guessing.

～

At the office Micah had been constructing and organizing, Forrest heaved a metal filing cabinet and carried it to the door. He regarded Micah with a slight smile but offered no words.

Micah opened the desk drawers and began emptying the contents into a cardboard box. Brady pulled books off a shelf and tucked them into another box.

"What gave you the right to agree to their terms?" Micah asked, glaring at Brady.

"For the werewolves withdrawing their union?"

"Yeah."

"A lot of reasons. The first and foremost is that you forced your union with the Circle of Unity, and this was after you had never suggested doing so to us. That should be a pack decision."

"I'm the leader," Micah said.

Brady shook his head. "Do you actually believe that?"

"You question my authority?"

"Take a look around, Micah. Jacob and I are the only two pack members who bothered coming here to rescue your ass. None of the others came to assist. Is that not warning enough for your *lack* of authority?"

Micah dumped a drawer of pens, paperclips, and folders into the box. Then he slammed the drawer atop the desk. "Perhaps they didn't know."

"They knew," Jacob said. "I called all of them."

Hurt reflected in Micah's gaze. "I see."

"If so, it's the first time in a long while," Brady said softly.

"What?" Micah said. His jaw tightened.

"He's right, cousin," Forrest said. "You've been blinded to most obvious things for quite some time."

"We're not going through this again," Micah said.

"No, we're not," Brady said. "Jacob and I will help you get this outside, but then you have a decision to make."

"Like what?"

"You rescind your pack leadership and leave. Or should you choose to stay, you submit yourself to the new leader."

"Who?" Micah asked, his eyes shifting back and forth between Brady and Jacob.

"Brady has my vote," Jacob said. "And my guess is the rest of the pack will back him as well."

Micah rested his hands on his hips. Ashley slipped up behind him and wrapped her arms around his waist, pressing the side of her face against him. "Let me get this straight. You want me to abdicate my leadership without a fight?"

Brady shrugged. "That's a better alternative than bloodshed."

"You cannot defeat me," Micah said.

"You're already defeated," Brady replied. "Your decision to reside in this office indicated your lack of concern for the pack. They know it, too. Why else do you think they didn't bother to help you? They're not blind or stupid."

"Are you quitting the police force?" Micah asked.

"No."

"How do you intend to do both?"

"Even doing both, I'll be putting in more time with the pack than you have been," Brady replied.

"Can we not bring it to a vote?" Micah asked.

Jacob shook his head in disbelief. "*Now* he wants a vote."

"It's my right as the leader, is it not?"

"*Former* leader," Jacob said.

"Just like that? You think they're going to follow you? You have to earn their trust and respect."

Brady sighed. "Micah, it saddens me to inform you that you've lost both of those things with the members. Don't be blind to this like you were about—"

Micah grabbed the heavy cardboard box and slid it off the desk. Carrying it to the door, he said, "You'll have to fight me for the leadership."

"Micah," Forrest said, as Micah brushed past and exited with the box in his hands. "Don't be foolish."

Micah stamped heavily down the steps. He offered no verbal reply. Ashley hurried after him.

Brady shook his head. "Stubborn to say the least."

Forrest chuckled. "He was born like that. He was bullheaded and difficult for his parents to rear. I'll speak with him."

"We'd appreciate that," Jacob said. He glanced at his watch. "We'd best hurry. Time's running out."

Brady looked around the room. "I'm not sure what belongings he wishes to keep?"

"Don't worry about it," Forrest said. "Just grab what you can carry and let's get the hell out of here."

CHAPTER 71

Forrest took Penelope for a long walk, holding her tiny hand inside his massive one. Things weren't how he had remembered them, but he understood that he was no longer a child. He had matured, and he had also darkened with time. Whatever optimism he had known as a child had died.

But all it took to rekindle his love for Penelope was simply looking into her sparkling eyes. Her bashful smile brought a smile to his otherwise grumpy-looking face.

She continued to ask details of what had occurred during his life after they had parted ways, but he couldn't force himself to share the things that haunted him the most. Of course, none of those haunted him like his fear of never knowing what had happened to her. Now that he had found her, he didn't want spoil the newness of their friendship or hopeful relationship by miring her mind with hundreds of vampire kills.

He'd rather spend the time explaining the changes in technology, which for quite some time he had found necessary, especially when large jets passed overhead or loud sirens blared in the distance, or the cellphones people had pressed to their heads. She acted like an innocent child and in some ways she was, which was why he didn't want to rush things.

Finally, standing on the dock while watching the white-crested waves on the bay, he turned her toward him. Her sparkling eyes stared into his and she scrunched her nose in the cute way he remembered from long ago. For several moments he feared this was a dream, that he'd awaken to find her gone, and his heart ached. He leaned down and kissed her. At first he thought she'd turn away, but she didn't. She kissed him more passionately than he'd ever been kissed before.

When their kiss ended, he lifted her up and wrapped his massive arms around her in a fierce hug, whispering into her ear. "I love you. My world was so empty without you."

Penelope didn't reply. She simply kissed his cheek and wrapped her arms tightly around his neck.

People had a way of fading from one's life at times. He thought about Lydia and how she had come to help and vanished once the task was completed. He didn't know that he'd ever see her again. If he did, he wanted to offer his thanks, but he had a feeling that seeing her meant trouble was not far away. So perhaps, he'd be more pleased if he never got the chance to thank her.

❧

Kailey rode in the passenger seat of the patrol car while Brady drove. "That was all you had found? Micah had left a note on the box?"

Brady nodded. "Yep. Said he'd be seeing me sometime in the near future and to be ready."

"I never took him to be the violent type," Kailey said, staring out the window.

"He never really was. He was always too passive."

"Then what has changed?"

"Your guess is as good as mine. The best thing is that we no longer need to worry about Flora and Raven."

Kailey nodded. "Yes. I am thankful for that."

She looked out the window. For the first time in a few months she felt at ease. She didn't need to watch over her shoulder, wondering when the next attack might come.

After Kailey had staked Raven, she worried that she'd be burdened by remorse, but she had no regrets. She had already accepted that Raven had lost her soul. She wasn't the person she had lived with. A ruthless monster had replaced Raven and killing her was the best thing for society. She did occasionally recall Raven before she had been turned and some of the places they had visited while in Boston. The scariest part was not having known how Raven really was. But now she never had to worry about Raven. She was gone. Forever.

But she wondered what new monsters might emerge in Seattle, and what dangers she'd find herself in as she dug for facts to write about in her blog.

Regardless of whatever strange things she uncovered, she knew she had Brady to love her cares away.

Giving her heart to Brady placed her into a fragile situation, because most of the people she had treasured the most died. And with Micah's solemn threat that vengeance was coming, she had new problems to fear. She could hope for a peaceful resolution, but she knew that was impossible. Werewolf packs were almost as territorial as rival gangs.

Brady had crossed the line that made Micah his mortal enemy. So now, instead of looking over her shoulder for Raven and Flora, she and Brady were waiting for Micah's wrath to be unleashed. Until Micah or Brady was dead, this battle wasn't over. The situation was almost like hers with Raven —friends that had become enemies. Kailey thought it strange how those who did their best to not look for trouble tended to be the ones who found themselves buried up to their necks with misfortune.

When there were no floodgates, nothing prevented or stopped the coming destruction. Death was coming and the casualties would be many.

The End

AUTHOR'S NOTE

Thank you for purchasing this novel. If you enjoyed this book, please check out my website and join my mailing list at www.leonarddhilleyii.com to receive a free digital copy of Forrest Wollinsky: Vampire Hunter.

If you could also take a moment and leave a review, it is greatly appreciated!

Blessings to you and yours.

ACKNOWLEDGMENTS

A special thank you to KC Riley-Gyer for the extra set of eyes to catch my mistakes. Thanks for the edits and feedback!

ABOUT THE AUTHOR

Leonard D. Hilley II grew up a quiet, shy kid with an inquisitive mind. Learning to read at an early age, he fell in love with books. He read every book he could get his hands on and stacks of dark comics about ghosts, monsters, and creepy things that stalk the night.

Like a lot of boys, he caught beetles, wooly bears, butterflies, and had an ant farm. When he was ten, his interests in science increased even more after seeing a professor's insect collection. Soon he set out on his quest to build his own collection. He also learned to rear butterflies and moths to obtain perfect specimens. He learned botany, gardening, and set his goal to become an entomologist.

At eleven, he watched the original Star Wars on the big screen. His imagination soared. Soon after, he discovered Roger Zelazny's Chronicles of Amber. Six months later, he had written the first draft of a novel. A novel he later discarded, but the characters stuck with him. Years later, these characters came to life in Shawndirea, which Hilley intended to be a novella for Devils Den. The characters, however, refused to be ignored and took the opportunity to unveil Aetheaon in their first epic fantasy. Lady Squire: Dawn's Ascension was quick to follow.

Shawndirea was Hilley's farewell to butterfly collecting, and those who have read the novel understand why. He has taken Ray Bradbury's advice to heart: "Follow the characters." He does. He follows, listens, and take notes—often never knowing where they're going to take him, but he's never been disappointed in the results.

Hilley earned a B.S. in Biology and an MFA in Creative Writing to combine his love of science and writing.

Sci-fi Titles: Predators of Darkness: Aftermath, Beyond the Darkness, The Game of Pawns, Death's Valley, The Deimos Virus.

Epic Fantasy: Shawndirea (Aetheaon Chronicles: Book One), Lady Squire (Aetheaon Chronicles: Book Two), Frosthammer (Aetheaon Chronicles: Book Three), Shadowfae (Aetheaon Chronicles: Book Four), and Devils Den.

UF/PR: Succubus: Shadows of the Beast (Nocturnal Trinity Series: Book One), Raven (Nocturnal Trinity Series: Book Two), A Touch of the Familiar (Nocturnal Trinity Series: Book Three)

YA UF/Paranormal: Forrest Wollinsky Vampire Hunter; Forrest Wollinsky: Blood Mists of London; Forrest Wollinsky: Predestined Crossroads.